I0825372

BLOOD TRIAL

VAMPIRE TOWERS

KELLY ST. CLARE

Blood Trial
by Kelly St. Clare

Edited by Hot Tree Editing
Cover design by Covers by Christian

BLOOD TRIAL

ABOUT THE AUTHOR

When Kelly is not reading or writing, she is lost in her latest reverie. Books have always been magical and mysterious to her. One day she decided to unravel this mystery and began writing.

Her works include *The Tainted Accords, Pirates of Felicity, and The Darkest Drae.*

Kelly resides in New Zealand with her ginger-haired husband, a great group of friends, and whatever animals she can add to her horde.

Join her newsletter tribe for sneak peeks, release news, and disjointed musings at kellystclare.com/free-gifts/

For love
And hatred
For rocks
And hard places.

1

Groaning, I peeled my cheek off the damp ground in the alleyway. Being homeless was overrated. Most people who slept on the street probably didn't have a choice. Kind of like me.

Well, nearly.

There was another option left to me, but I hadn't wanted to explore Plan B without giving homelessness a try. For all I knew, it could have been the secret high life.

It wasn't.

Not at all.

A pain stabbed in my temple—a result of the flickering lamp post down the end of the alley. Which explained why this godforsaken, slimy sliver of space between two concrete buildings was empty of other upstanding homeless citizens.

I held my head and sat, and a pulpy chunk of miscellaneous garbage peeled off my cheek. The soggy pulp fell onto my lap and I ignored it to better keep up the illusion it was newspaper in a past life. I'd started sitting up against the wall, jumping at every echoing scuffle, but at some point, I must've slid into oblivion—and the pile of garbage beside me. To say my life had taken a sudden turn would be an understatement.

Heiress to the largest fortune in Bluff City—and the seventh largest in the world—to pauper. Overnight.

By choice.

Fists curling in my lap, I snapped my back into a straight line. I was a *self*-exiled heiress. I had my reasons for being here. Reasons that wouldn't be shaken by a night on the cold, hard ground—or by miscellaneous pulp.

I reached over to grab my plaid and leather *Elegance* backpack, throwing the skinny straps over my shoulders as I stood.

"Time to get your shit sorted, Basi," I said in a firm voice, dusting myself off.

Setting off for the end of the alley, I realised the massive hole in my plan.

Crap.

Where did Tommy live? She was my Plan B.

Ugliness churned in my stomach as I searched left and right down the empty shopping street. I *hated* when my snobbish ignorance showed. It only ever hammered in the lonely fact that I wasn't like everyone else. How the hell did normal people get around? Scrap that. I knew they got around with buses and trains and cars. The details of how those systems ran? No fucking clue.

My heart thumped and I swallowed down the hysteria creeping up my chest.

Think, Basi—you rich bitch.

I'd come here because the area was semi-familiar. Baroness Street, despite its misleading name, had only a few high-end boutique shops, but I'd visited them on occasion. There were far more run-down buildings and clothing chain stores around—so visiting here had always felt like a small rebellion. Which was also why I'd picked this place for my first night as a self-exiled heiress. Baroness Street felt somewhere between the life I'd left and the life I wanted.

A life that wasn't planned for me. A life where I didn't feel like part of a well-run, predetermined game that I had no control over.

The problem being that I didn't actually get here by myself. I'd asked my chauffeur to drop me off a couple of blocks away.

The ugliness churning in my gut intensified, but I had to remember that I wouldn't always be so ignorant of how *real* people lived.

I could only think of two options.

One, walk around aimlessly until I found a bus or train stop thing. I did have a small amount of pocket change on me.

Two, ask for help.

Considering the sun was just peeking over the tops of the concrete shops around me, finding a person to ask seemed unlikely. I rubbed my forehead, dislodging more miscellaneous pulp.

A tired smile graced my face.

Homeless people.

There had to be a few around.

Hoisting my *Elegance* pack higher on my back, I set off down Baroness Street, peering into the grey depths of the narrow gaps between buildings. I ignored the alleys with flickering lamp posts at the ends. Even I knew to avoid those.

I struck gold near the corner of Baroness and King Street. A man with a shaved head and black hoodie was there.

"Excuse me," I called, waving when he jumped and whirled.

Stepping into the shadowed alley, I approached the tall man.

He darted his eyes to my left cheek, and then to our surroundings. His eyes were wide and bloodshot. Bad sleep?

But why did he keep licking his lips?

I hoped sleeping on the streets was just thirsty work, but I kept ample distance between us in case he was a psychopath.

"Hey," I said brightly. "I don't suppose you could help me with directions?"

He peered over my shoulder. "You're alone?"

Scariness intensifying. "Sure am." I hoisted my pack again. "I'm trying to get to my friend's house."

The man had frozen midway through rolling what appeared to be a thin length of foam. He continued the task, licking his lips again.

I eyed the cuts on his shaved head and the layer of grime on his visible skin. Despite the warning vibes he gave me, my heart sank, and I renewed the energy behind my purpose in being here.

The system was faulted. It rewarded a select few and punished everyone else. Why was this man homeless? Why wasn't anyone helping him?

He rested the mat against the cracked cement of the closest building. "Where does your friend live?"

His question wrenched me to a halt. Shoot. Where *did* Tommy live? I'd been there countless times—though she tended to come to mine, with her father being the estate's stablemaster and all.

"Uh..." I glanced around.

My eyes caught on the grey roof of the shop on the other side of the street. Of course. I must be more tired than I thought.

"She lives in Orange," I declared proudly.

He licked his lips and cast me a doubtful look. "You're from Orange?"

Licky Lips judging my friend's lack of wealth seemed a tad hypocritical.

"Orange," I repeated, forcing my hands, already creeping up to rest on my hips, to remain by my sides. Hands on hips and foot-stomping were snobby habits I was trying to kick. Poor people didn't do that kind of thing.

He straightened, illustrating just *how* tall he was. And his eyes. The bloodshot part made sense. He'd just woken. But the wide part was *slightly* disconcerting. People were meant to blink a certain amount of times per minute, right?

And the licking lips thing...

"Seriously, dude. Collect rainwater or something." I joked, my grip on the bag straps tightening.

Licky Lips frowned. "What?"

"Uh, nothing," I mumbled, edging away. "That's okay if you don't know where Orange is. Just thought I'd ask. Thanks for your help."

"I haven't helped you yet."

Well... if he planned on doing so, there was no time like the present. I forced a smile. "I'd appreciate if you could point me in the right direction."

The man shoved his hands in his hoodie and hunched. He jerked his head to the right. "Walk that way."

I glanced at the wall. "I need to head right?"

A nod was my answer. "Yeah, then straight. That'll get you to Red."

A silent sigh escaped my lips. From Red, finding Orange would be easy enough. The suburbs of the city circled in a colour gradient, all except Grey—the central business district—which was smack bang in the middle.

"Thank you," I told him, allowing some of my genuine worry to seep into the words.

He peeked up. "You're not the first to ask for help. We get a lot of rebelling rich brats here."

Unnecessarily harsh. I tossed my hair. "Is that so?"

Licky Lips stood tall again. Whether he meant the gesture as a subtle reminder of who would win in a fight between us or not, I took it that way and my muscles coiled in readiness to run.

The man didn't advance, and I relaxed after a few seconds.

He'd labelled me as a *rich brat* with a single look, but I wasn't like the other runaways he came across.

Swinging my bag off, I flipped the top back and reached into a small zip pocket. Riffling through the notes, I drew out a one-hundred-dollar bill.

"Here. Have this. For your help." I smiled encouragingly at him.

The money was gone from my fingers in a flash.

Phew. Pretty quick when he wanted to be. Entering this alley wasn't my best idea.

He inspected the note as though I might have handed over Monopoly cash. "The last one gave me five hundred."

The last one!

My jaw dropped. "The last rich brat gave you money too?"

Licky Lips shrugged a shoulder. “They all do. Usually on an *I feel trapped* bender.”

... *I feel trapped bender.*

I swung my pack on again and pressed the heels of both palms into my eyes. This guy’s manners were atrocious. Then again, they weren’t. Even if the comments he offered weren’t particularly tactful.

I didn’t need his approval.

And I didn’t need the approval of my wealthy friends and their parents.

Even my grandmother’s approval came second to me living in the way I saw fit.

“Thanks,” I said shortly, backing away before spinning on my heel.

“Got any drugs?” the man asked.

I quickened my step, laughing nervously. “No, not my scene. Good luck with... that.”

The urge to look over my shoulder heightened and I shoved back the instinct. When I reached the corner and turned right, I only increased my pace and didn’t slow until several blocks away.

Note to self: Profuse lip licking may indicate usage of drugs.

Still, he’d given me directions, so that was a win.

I stretched out my legs into a comfortable stride that my grandmother would have called an unladylike stomp. Though she always made the comment and half blamed, half complimented the stomp on my *Amazonian* legs.

I wanted to get to Tommy’s as soon as possible.

Asking to be dropped off close to Tommy’s house might have been a better idea. And perhaps I should have worn shoes that didn’t tear up my feet.

By the time the bright roofs of Red appeared in the distance, my *Hatch* flats had caused two juicy blisters on the backs of my heels.

“Fuck my life,” I muttered.

Turning left, I noticed my lengthy Amazonian stride had turned into a hobbling jig that Rumpelstiltskin would’ve been proud of. When I reached the outskirts of Red, I clenched my jaw and finally stopped to remove the damn shoes. Normal people walked barefoot all the time. Right? Sure, maybe their feet weren't bleeding. But it was all about the *spirit* of being poor.

Crossing the median from Red to Orange boosted my morale enough to carry me until I recognised my whereabouts. Relief overwhelmed the pain from the raw patches on my feet, and it was only as I turned onto the street of orange-roofed houses where my best friend lived that I began to fear what I would tell Tommy.

Bleeding, filthy, stinking.

Tommy shared many of my views on the world—one that profited only a handful of people and turned a life for living into a life for working to make ends meet. Yet on my inheritance... hell, even on my allowance, I could have lived a full life. One where I catered to each of my whims and interests. My friend didn't have that luxury. She busted her ass six days a week to get by. How to tell someone, even my best friend since childhood, that I didn't want to be handed a life of riches and luxury on a silver platter?

I wanted a real life. I didn't want to play their rich fucking game.

My feet slowed and, facing Tommy's house, I traced the cracked paint of the cream cladding and the burnt orange of the house's roof tiles. I shifted my gaze to the orange door, and to the uneven path leading around the left wall of the abode.

Sneaking into her room via the window felt immature for my twenty-one years of age. However, Tommy was my Plan B for a reason. Her father worked for my family's estate and had for most of his life. I didn't know if my grandmother would have eyes on me or not. I *did* know that Mr Tetley would feel morally bound to inform my guardian of my safety and location if he answered the front door.

I moved to run a hand through my coiffed blonde tresses before glimpsing the grunge streaking my palm.

Nope. Call me a coward. Or a rich brat. I was going for the window.

Hobbling down the uneven path like the goblin I was, I rapped gently on her dusty windows.

"Tommy," I hissed.

I waited and knocked again. *Please be home.* She'd mentioned a hot guy named Dean when we last spoke. She usually made them jump a few hoops before any sleepovers occurred, but she'd seemed enamoured by this new specimen.

"*Tom.*"

The curtains were yanked apart. I choked on surprise and watched anger, shock, and relief flicker over my friend's oval face in quick succession.

So everyone knew I'd run...

I didn't have time to message her before storming out—and I'd stubbornly left all my electronics at the estate. Tommy must have heard through her father.

Leaning forward, I breathed on the window to fog it up and wrote, H E L P.

The corners of her brown eyes crinkled, and she propped open the window.

"You're okay?" she asked immediately. Her soft voice was a balm to my soul.

"I'm fine."

"Uh-huh." Tommy scanned me from head to toe. "You're fine in the same way the loser of a boxing match is fine."

I glanced down at my feet and winced. "Yeah... didn't pick great shoes."

"Oh, they're *great* shoes," she said, whistling low. "Just not practical shoes."

My shoulders sagged. "Can I come in?"

"Like you need to ask. Come to the front door."

I hesitated. "I don't want your dad to see me and tell my grandmother."

"I wasn't born yesterday, Basil." She cocked a brow. "The only people who come to my window are drunk you, lonely you, angry you, and idea you."

"Have all four versions of me ever shown up at the same time?" I asked, a grin spreading across my face.

"One time, I swear there were five. It was a real party." She surveyed me again and shook her head. "Front door, Basil. Now. You need a shower. Stat. Maybe three. Then I want to know what the hell is going on."

2

"Basilia Le Spyre, wake yo' ass up! There's work to do."

I jolted to life, bolting upright in a disorientated mess. "Where me?"

Tommy, used to my delirious waking moments, merely cracked a grin at my disjointed question. "You in my house."

I'd left the estate. Slept on the street. I was in Tommy's house in Orange.

Sagging, I focused on my breathing until my heartbeat stopped thundering in my ears. "How long did I sleep?"

"All day. If this is how you plan to be poor, you're doing a terrible job of it. We never get sleep."

I glared at her.

She bounded onto the bed and sat against the back wall where a bedhead would usually be. Tommy didn't have one, and I wasn't sure why that always disconcerted me so much. Was there even a point to bedheads?

"So you're sure about this?" she asked eventually. "I mean, you've hated the rich world for as long as I can remember, but if a fight with your grandmother is the only reason you left, then forgive me for saying that your grandmother and her friends are the best part of that bullshit parade you were born into."

"It wasn't. She's the only reason I stayed so long." I thought back to our heated conversation. "The argument was silly, really. She was on at me again to start attending functions as the up and coming face of the estate, and I just cracked. Not at her, at the... the constant feeling of being detached and outside of reality. The fight was just the tipping point. Tom, I want to *live.* I want to help people. Sure, I could mindlessly throw cash around. I could even try to research where that money would have the most effect. But without living this life, how can I ever truly understand what I need to do?" *And who I am.*

A heavy silence settled in the room.

Tommy broke it by shoving black and white pages onto my lap. I regarded them through bleary eyes. The word eventually came to me. "Newspaper."

"Well done, grasshopper."

I shot her another glare. "We get newspapers at the estate."

"Yeah, yeah. Your butler delivers it on a silver platter. I was looking at the job section for you."

That caught my attention. "Glasses."

My bag had toppled onto the brown carpet during my sleep-nap. She scrambled to collect it and I dug around, drawing out my glasses case.

I pushed the thick black-framed specks onto my face and stared at the open newspaper. Three red circles disrupted the page.

"Those are the suitable ones," Tommy murmured. "I rang my boss at the laundry service, but they aren't hiring. Probably not until the uni students go back to school in two months."

My heart sank. Working with Tom would have been the tits.

Let's see what we've got here.

My eyes landed on the first one. "Tomato factory worker." I turned accusing eyes on her.

"Beggars can't be choosers." She reminded me.

True story. "What else have we got?" I shifted my gaze to the next page. "A newspaper run! You're shitting me?"

She grimaced. "I was iffy on that one. I had a newspaper run when I was thirteen. Fucking sucked."

"What about the other ones?" There were tons of jobs on the two pages.

"They all require qualifications—that you don't have. I don't think business lessons from your grandmother count."

Dammit. "Someone may want me to manage their billions though."

Tommy snorted. "We both know you have no trouble with that, but can you manage just a few dollars? I have a feeling they're different things."

Maybe. Surely the same principles applied.

With no small amount of trepidation, I squinted at the last circled job. "Huh! Pet shop assistant. That one isn't so bad."

Could I be a pet shop assistant? Cuddling kittens and puppies all day? I mean, shovelling poop wasn't my idea of a good time, but there would be definite perks.

"I'll take it," I declared, jabbing at the page with my finger.

Tommy shooed me away. "Not that easy, Basi. You need to make a résumé first and there will be at least one interview."

I rolled my eyes, scanning the other listings. "I'm not completely ignorant of life outside the estate."

Her lips trembled. "You mean you've watched enough soap operas to piece us peasants together?"

"I watch *Truth Ranges* for the quality acting."

"And we read *Fernando's Eighth Ab* for the complex plot line."

Sniggering, I ran my eyes over the other listings. *Ugh*, she was right. I certainly didn't have a medical degree. Or an early childhood certificate.

A tiny listing shoved in the bottom left corner caught my attention, if only because the advert looked like it didn't want to be found. "Hey, what about this one?"

Tommy peered over my shoulder.

"Realty trainee," I read aloud. "It's an apprenticeship thing by the looks."

"Don't bother," she said dismissively. "Live Right Realty never hire outsiders. They must have a policy to advertise to the public, but they always promote and hire internally. I've gone for that job three times —and other people too. No one has ever been hired."

I adjusted my glasses to read the advert again. "Really? It sounds perfect." The pay cheque had to be larger than a pet shop assistant wage. At least a realty traineeship would have a better chance of promotion. Some of the neighbouring estates to Grandmother's built their empires from realty origins. Not that I wanted to build my own cage when I'd just escaped one, but money was security in this world and, for the first time, I only had a minuscule amount. I needed enough to eradicate corporation corruption from the world.

My nerves came back in full force.

"I need to make a résumé," I announced, glancing around the room for inspiration.

Tommy put the newspaper aside. "Tomorrow. We'll need to visit the public library to use their computers and printer, and it closes at 4:00 pm. Tonight, I'm taking you out to dinner."

"I can pay for it myself," I replied.

"Y S I S," Tommy quipped back, folding her arms.

I spluttered. "My snob is *not* showing."

At ten years old, we'd developed a mnemonic that served as a warning. When I was with her friends, she'd say Y S I S—your snob is showing—to warn me I'd done something weird. When amongst my rich friends, I'd say Y P I S—your peasant is showing—for the same.

In this situation, when I already felt so out of my depth, I didn't appreciate the jab. Unfortunately, my friend was immune to my scowl.

"If your snob isn't showing, you'll let me take you for dinner," Tommy said, folding her arms. "Especially because my father will be back soon."

My stomach chose that moment to remind me I hadn't eaten since last night. And I wanted to avoid her father.

"Food," I grumbled. "Then résumé."

She cut me off. "Then job. Then apartment. Then destroy all the baddies. Got it."

Someone was listening to me at last.

3

Dressed in my powder-blue silk blouse and black slacks, I slipped the newspaper into my pack and pulled out my freshly printed résumé.

I craned my neck to read the bright yellow sign. *Purrfect Pets*. A picture of a smiling dog and cat hugging each other completed the store's branding.

Jesus.

I was at the right place, alright—back in Grey. After helping with my résumé, Tommy had quickly coached me on how job enquiries went down.

It was time to act my ass off.

Taking a deep breath, I forced my legs to move me across the pedestrian-only street where I pushed open the electric-blue door into the pet store.

The smell of three-day-old roadkill fell over me like a woollen blanket on a summer's day. I shoved down the urge to gag.

"A woofing welcome to *Purr*fect Pets! I'm Jenny. How can I assist you right meow?"

Fuck me.

Would I have to say that?

Spinning to face a stout woman, I hastily schooled my features into a disarming smile—growing up rich had taught me some things. "Hi, yes. Thank you, Jenny. I'm Basi. I saw your job advert in the paper and would love to submit my résumé for consideration."

A pent-up breath quivered in my chest.

The woman's pleasant expression dropped, and I blinked at the change. She reached to tuck her frizzy hair behind her ears. The hair popped out again as she scanned me from head to toe. "You want to work *here*? At this pet shop?"

Too late to question my wardrobe choice. Thinking fast, I kept my smile at full wattage. "I do. I've just come from brunch with my aunties." That I didn't have.

The woman's eyes narrowed. Was she the owner? I really hoped not. The way she was circling had me wondering if she'd sniff my butt at any moment. Maybe she'd taken on some animal characteristics during her time here.

She held out a hand, and I stared before realising it was for my résumé.

"Here you go." I placed the two sheets in her hand. "I haven't had much job experience, but I assure you I'm a fast learner. And I love animals. This would truly be a dream job for me." I crossed my fingers behind my back.

Tommy said I should lie to get the job. I felt bad about it, but she'd assured me hardly anyone had jobs they liked so lying was expected.

Jenny lifted her eyes from my résumé, and I read the derision in them before she continued reading.

Had I laid on the charm too strong?

The urge to fidget itched in my limbs. Forcing them to remain still, I peered around, trying to keep my nose from wrinkling at the roadkill smell. Rows of stock filled the space around the cashier. Fenced areas occupied the middle space and I smiled at the fluffy rabbits I could glimpse between the slates. My ears picked up sounds of chickens, and I could see bird cages lined the far wall with fish tanks along the right wall.

If I worked here, more body wash was in order. I'd go through that shit by the litre.

"What's your favourite breed of dog?" Jenny shot at me, lowering the résumé.

"Easy," I quipped. "Frenchies."

Her mouth pulled down.

"Their heads are too large for natural birth," she snapped. "Over 90 percent of the mothers are forced to have C-sections."

Shit. Should have said Labrador. "That's terrible. I wasn't aware of that."

Jenny held out my résumé, eyes hard. "I'm looking for someone with more experience."

More experience, my butthole. "I really am eager to learn everything you can tell me about animals and the pet shop business."

I could salvage this. I could—

"Not what we're looking for." The woman shook the résumé my way and I backed away.

Dammit. In Tommy's coaching, the owners just took the damn résumé with a fake smile and a thank you.

I scrambled for a save. "Uh. That's a real shame, Jenny. I thank you for your time. Is it possible to leave you with my résumé anyway? Just in case you change your mind?"

She sighed. "Sure."

My résumé was going in the bin.

"Okay, thank you! Lovely to meet you."

I nearly tripped over my feet in my haste to escape the roadkill store. After closing the blue door behind me, I hurried away in a random direction, lest she followed to watch me.

Paranoid much?

Groaning, I threaded my hands through my silky butter-blonde curls. "That did not go well."

It was the only job out of the three that interested me in the slightest. Looked like I'd be dropping my sheets of paper off at the other two after all. In my tossing dreams last night, I was hired on the spot.

Reality was a bitch.

Maybe the other places were within walking distance. It was Monday, and Tommy was at her laundry job 12:00 p.m. until 7:00 p.m., six days a week. I didn't relish the thought of returning to her house alone to marinate in my failure.

I dodged between the people on the pavement and leaped for a free space on the steps of a bank that was owned by a family friend. I sent the building a withering look even though I genuinely liked Sir Olytheiu.

Shaking out the paper, I studied the addresses of the other two circled job listings. I'd caught the bus from Orange to Grey with Tommy, but I only knew where the stops for that route were. The tomato factory job was in the agricultural district. The suburbs of the city were bordered on one side by expansive fields where all the produce for our population was grown. It was a point of pride to most inhabitants of Bluff City that we were a self-sustaining economy. With such a small population, it shouldn't be possible. What *made* it possible were the huge estates—where I came from—that bordered the city on the other side.

I didn't know if a bus drove out in the direction of the tomato factory and was too scared to try by myself. I definitely couldn't walk there in my borrowed sandals that thankfully didn't press on any of my *Hatch* blisters.

Stuck again.

Pursing my lips, I read the address of the newspaper gig. *Level 26, Heraldson-Jamie High-Rise, Jonker Street.*

I had no idea where Jonker Street was, but all high-rises were in Grey, so the place was within walking distance. *Dang.* Part of me had hoped getting there wouldn't be possible. Was I really going to do a paper run? Or was I rushing into this? How often did the newspaper come out? If there were two pages of jobs each time, something better was bound to turn up in short duration.

... But what if nothing came up? I had barely any money with me. The longer I was stuck in limbo, the more afraid I'd get. I was determined to keep an open mind to the strangeness of my current lot.

As though drawn, my eyes trained on the tiny advert in the bottom left corner. The notice was still there despite its goal to remain unnoticed. Tommy had said not to bother with *Live Right Realty*. I wasn't sure I had that luxury.

I read the address. *Level 44, Kyros Sky, Marquis Street.*

Another high-rise. Okay, I had five copies of my résumé. Time to spread the mother-trucking news that Basi was in town.

Emboldened, I stepped into the throng of city-goers.

Oof!

The air squeezed from my lungs as a large body slammed into me. Forced back several steps, I sucked in a painful breath. Intense heat spread across my stomach. Yelping, I plucked the silk off my stomach.

My eyes dropped and a moan escaped my mouth at the brown stain covering me.

"You crashed into me," the man accused. He towered over me, and either side of me.

I clenched my teeth. "Not on purpose."

"You spilled my coffee too. I just got that."

Whoa, where was the freakin' apology? I was the one with boiling coffee on me. He'd halved the number of tops I had to wear. "I wore your coffee. There's a difference."

"Whatever. Watch where you're going."

I sidestepped him. "Ditto, douchebag."

He spun after me, and I dodged into the crowd, soon swept into the anonymous midst. *Ha!* Turned out this chaos had some perks.

My shirt was another story. I cursed the hulking man under my breath. I couldn't drop my résumé off looking like this—though Jenny might have liked me better for it. She could have pretended it was the remnants of dog vomit.

Spotting a fast-food chain, I adjusted course. *Montgomery's* had public bathrooms. Tommy told me about them in one of her drunken nightclub stories.

I sidled past queues of customers, wondering if they were aware they supported a corporation who had fingers in all sorts of pies—including what food laws were passed in government. When money was tight and junk food was cheaper than fruit and vegetables, of course the poor would eat it daily. And they had the health problems to prove it.

Shaking my head, I searched for a toilet and was rewarded by a sign in the far corner.

Success!

Smiling, I weaved between the chairs and tables and entered the female toilets. I scanned the toilet in no small degree of disgust. *Yuck.* There was water on the tiled floor. At least I hoped it was water. The place could do with a serious mop and a sea salt and saffron candle or three.

I pulled out handfuls of paper towel and dabbed at the stain on my shirt. He'd soaked the entire bottom half.

"Lucky silk dries fast," I muttered.

A day before, I wouldn't have given a thought to chucking the soiled shirt into my bathroom hamper that one or other of the half dozen maid staff emptied each day. Two days ago, I'd had a walk-in robe filled with clothing. *Today*, this shirt was one of the few things I had to my name.

I ended up removing the powder-blue garment to soak and wring the coffee out. I ignored the startled looks of the women going in and out of the toilet as I did my laundry in the sink of *Montgomery's.* If they knew I'd slept on the street, they'd think twice about making eye contact.

Most of me was just thanking Zeus's left nut that no one I knew came here, a sentiment which also pissed me off.

I swung the garment back on, buttoning the two halves and tucking the ends into my slacks.

There. That didn't look so...

Crap. I looked like I'd done snow angels in a muddy puddle.

I'd just have to wait for it to dry and hope I'd gotten the stain out.

Washing my hands, I splashed some water on my face and

surveyed my reflection. Topaz eyes stared back at me, asking what the hell I was doing.

"Good question, frenemy," I told my reflection.

My eyes were too bright—on the harried side of energetic. My hair was on my side today though—apparently the only thing. The thick blonde mass formed natural barrel curls if left to air dry. I'd recently visited the salon and let my stylist put fresh highlights through the weighty length. Which was ideal timing because there was no way I could afford his prices on any of the jobs Tommy had circled in the paper.

Not liking what I saw in the mirror, I dried my face with more paper towels and left the toilet.

A weedy man cut me off as soon as I re-entered the seated eating area.

"Our toilets are for paying customers only," he informed me, looking directly into my eyes.

I pulled up short. "I didn't use your toilets. I just had to get a stain off my shirt."

He grimaced. "Our water. And did you use paper towels?"

My fists clenched. "Are you serious? Tell me Montgomery's is not that stingy."

"We're a business, madame. Not a charity," he sneered.

I'd show him madame. My brows crept up as my hands came to my hips. I fixed him with my most quelling expression—one learned by studying my grandmother.

"Is that so?" I asked haughtily.

The weedy teen watched me with a bored expression. "I already said so, didn't I? You need to buy something before you leave."

"Or what?" I snapped, tossing my hair.

He sneered again. "Or I'll call the police to escort you to the station. For trespassing."

Seriously? Outrage swirled in my chest, and I did my best to keep a firm hold on it. Being arrested might hinder my efforts to get a job. And I had no bail money.

Why was this guy targeting me? I'd been into the city plenty.

People were usually full of smiles and sunshine. Had I just encountered the only three assholes today?

... Or was it because I hadn't arrived in a black car with tinted windows and a chauffeur?

I deflated. "Fine. What's your cheapest item?"

His eyes sparked in triumph. "Our ice cream. It's 100 percent organic."

"You mean the supplier you use is called Organic."

The teen's guilty jerk confirmed that was the case.

"I'll take one then." I waved him off.

He pointed at the nearest queue. "Our meal artists will be happy to serve you."

My jaw dropped. Now I had to wait in fucking line? This kid was outrageous.

I noted the smirk on his lips before he turned to berate the next person exiting the toilet. That had to be how *Montgomery's* made their money. Using their toilets as a Venus flytrap to catch the innocent.

I stood in line, stewing in the injustice of it all. The irony of supporting the same corporation I'd just judged others for supporting didn't escape me. I glared at the back of the weedy teen's head. Greasy hair and a pimply neck. He probably only exerted his power here because he was bottom of the food chain in high school.

The thought made me feel a tad sorry for him. It also cut through my anger.

The teen's back was to me...

I skirted my gaze to the automatic glass doors and back.

Didn't need to tell me twice.

"Stop her," the teen shouted as I bolted for the door.

I burst free and dashed down the stone steps, my pack thumping against my lower back. Luck was with me and the green man signal was flashing to cross to the next block.

Shouts rang after me, but I didn't look back as I sprinted past the waiting cars.

Fuckers weren't getting my money.

Uneasiness crept up my spine as I put more distance between me and *Montgomery's*. They wouldn't send coppers after me, would they? For something as small as that? There had to be cameras in there. They'd have a picture of my face.

I shook the thought away and dodged around a corner, lunging for the entrance alcove of a building.

Panting, I waited for five minutes in the alcove, but no handcuffs clamped down on my wrists.

Win. Hopefully.

I wiped sweat from my forehead, stepping aside as a young man entered the doors at my back. He smiled nervously at me, two sheets of paper in his grip.

"Dropping off your résumé?" I asked him, still breathing hard. I really needed to get back to the pool.

"No one ever gets a call from Live Right Realty, but can't hurt to try, can it?" His lips crooked in a lopsided smile.

This was *Live Right Realty*? "Oh, I'm meant to be dropping my résumé here too."

He held open the door, and I strode into the lobby, flashing a smile. Dark hair and dark eyes. Not my favourite combo, but I liked his style—a tight black tee and dark-blue jeans kind of guy, though I could see he had the ability to slip into a suit and tie without effort.

Aside from Tommy, he was the nicest person I'd encountered all day.

"You didn't know you were in their building?" His dark eyes twinkled.

I lifted a shoulder. "Long story."

"I saw you running out of Montgomery's."

Shit. Hoisting my pack, I answered, "A misunderstanding."

He laughed quietly, and I joined in as we entered the elevator. Tall, dark, and handsome pressed Level 44.

My ears popped as the lift shot up.

"I'm Rhys, by the way," he said, sticking out his hand.

He was totally getting his flirt on. In an awkward, adorable way. "Basi." I shook his hand, making sure to linger a few seconds too long.

"Doing the résumé rounds today as well?"

I nodded, exhaling. "Sure am. It isn't going so great."

His eyes roamed my body and my brows crept upward until I realised he was staring at the ex-coffee stain covering my stomach.

Fuck. I had a massive wet patch on my shirt. I was meant to wait until it dried.

Ding!

The buzz of a bustling workspace reached into the elevator.

"Shall we?" he asked, tilting his head.

I swallowed, thinking of my last encounter. "Let's do it."

His dark eyes gleamed, and it wasn't hard to guess where his mind had taken my comment. Which I might not be completely averse to after knowing him better.

Unlike the pet store, I wasn't assaulted by the smell of roadkill when I stepped into the reception area. A small plaque on the front bench desk read *Live Right Realty*. Behind the desk stood several admin staff.

Several *beautiful* admin.

What the hell did they eat for breakfast? Their skin was flawless, their hair gleaming. Each of them rivalled my height except their willowy frames belonged on the catwalk or in an exquisite painting.

"Can I help you?" the closest admin said when we stopped in front of the desk.

A quick peek at Rhys told me he'd noticed the beauty of the reception staff and was robbed of speech.

I took the reins, smiling for all I was worth. "Hi, yes. Thank you. I'm Basi. I saw your job advert in the paper and wanted to drop my résumé off for consideration."

The words slid out of my mouth just fine, but after last time, I didn't dare celebrate.

The ethereal woman held out her hand.

"Oops, hold on a second," I blurted. "It's in my pack."

Rhys recovered and handed his over silently.

The woman scanned the front page. "Thank you, Rhys. We'll be in touch."

When he turned away, she slipped the résumé beneath the desk. A second later, a whirring sounded.

Hold the front door.

Did she just shred his résumé?

She turned her smile on me at full wattage. She totally did!

I slid my résumé free—the one that cost ten cents per page to print. "How many people are you looking to hire?" I asked, not handing it over.

The woman dropped her gaze to my bag and up again. "*Elegance.* I love that brand."

I frowned. *What?* "My pack? Thanks."

Her eyes travelled my frame, lingering on the massive wet patch on my stomach. I breathed thinly and stilled as she studied me. The woman's eyes were bright blue. The kind of bright that was impossible to look away from—not a thought I could ever recall having. As she perused my manicured nails, silky hair, and ensemble, I could almost see the twin beams of her gaze on each body part.

"Is that *Alastair* body wash I smell?" she asked.

This was officially becoming weirder than my run-in with Jenny at *Purrfect Pets*. But weird in a scary way.

I blinked. "You can smell that?" I suppose I washed three times yesterday, and once more this morning.

The receptionist hummed. "Lemon myrtle is my favourite scent. What did you say your name is?"

"Basi," I answered, leaving off my last name. I'd left it off my résumé too. Though Tommy said that slip might cost me professionalism points.

The name Le Spyre was well-known in this city. I refused to use my name to secure a job. If a realty firm knew who I really was, they'd use my connections, and I'd be right back where I started—playing the fucking rich game.

"Basi...?" she prompted.

Not happening, lady. I widened my smile and passed her my résumé. She immediately flicked through, pausing on my details on the front page as she had with Rhys.

"Orange," the woman said so quietly that I was positive she didn't intend for me to hear.

This was getting stranger by the second. The other two admins had now stopped what they were doing to watch us.

I'd had my fill of unusual shit today. "I'll leave it with you," I said, the curve of my lips brittle. "My email is on there if you wish to get in touch with any questions."

The woman slowly lifted her head.

She shot a glance at the other two and turned back. "Actually, Basi. Your résumé looks perfect for what we're looking for. Could you interview on the spot?"

They wanted me to interview? *Now?*

"You realise I have no job experience, right?" Stupid thing to say when I wanted a job, but the oddness of her behaviour raised the hairs on my arms. Something about the keenness of her eyes made me want to sprint for the lift. My heart pounded from close proximity to her which couldn't be possible. Could it?

Had she guessed who I was? Surely not. She probably just thought I was rich and had connections—the reason for forgoing my last name in the first place.

I hesitated.

Where was Rhys? A quick glance told me he was long gone.

Shit.

"Selling a house is much less about job experience than people experience. The right *kind* of people experience. Your social and extra-curricular portfolios are impressive."

I'd made sure to only include those I'd participated in during high school. Normal people didn't help to organise charities and high teas for the wealthiest families in the Southern Hemisphere—even if I refused to attend them.

Her comment went some way in alleviating my concerns that she was just after my network. Maybe I'd read her wrong.

I really needed this.

"Thank you," I said demurely. "An interview would be great."

She peered at my pack again. "Are you free now? It would save you a trip back from Orange."

Her eyes were so hard to look away from. Such a bright blue. Enthralling. Looking at them nearly drove lucid thought from my mind. I didn't like the vibes she was putting out, but the woman was offering me the first scrap of hope I'd had all day.

"That would be great," I lied, tearing my gaze away to fix on the diamond necklace at her throat.

I darted a look up again.

Her lips curled, revealing a row of straight, perfectly white teeth. "Perfect."

4

I stumbled out of *Kyros Sky*, fingers pressed to my temple. The main receptionist—apparently in charge of hiring and firing as well—hadn't asked anything other than what I assumed were normal interview questions, but I felt wrung out, my brain full of clouds.

Hold on.

Where did the sun go?

I entered *Live Right Realty* just after midday. Didn't I? Now, it had to be at least 6:00 p.m. Thinking back over the interview questions, I couldn't recall the process lasting very long.

Maybe I spent more time in the *Montgomery's* toilet than I realised.

"You're losing it," I muttered. The craziness of today was hitting all at once. Hopefully it hadn't shown in the interview—though my gut twisted at the thought of actually working with the beautiful women upstairs too. They were just so… intense.

I circled my fingers on my temple, lifting my other hand to mirror the soothing gesture on the other side. I groaned at the small pleasure. If I was back at the estate, I'd be on the phone to my massage therapist, stat.

Wheels screeched.

The breath choked in my throat, and I whirled as a car hurtled straight for me.

This can't be how it fucking ends.

The sleek black car screeched to a halt an inch from my kneecaps, and my heart hammered as my mind stuttered over my imminent death and miraculous survival of the last few seconds.

The driver door opened, and only then did I process that I'd somehow walked into flowing traffic. What the hell was wrong with me? I almost died.

I almost died.

Pure adrenaline coursed through my veins and I slammed both hands on the bonnet of the car that was far more reminiscent of the place I'd run away from than my current situation.

"You almost ran me over, you compensating-for-something jerk!" I turned to look at the driver.

And stopped.

Hormones and ovaries.

He'd left the door wide open, ignoring the honks from the line of cars extending behind. Though summer reigned, the towering man wore a knee-length business coat. Beneath it, I glimpsed a three-piece suit and a slim black tie.

If Rhys could have slid into a suit with ease, this man could slide *out* of one even easier.

Swallowing hard, I pulled my hands off his bonnet.

After a lifetime amongst the elite, I knew power when I saw it. This man had it. Not only in his muscular frame that was apparent through the coat. Not just in the ticking of his jaw. He came from powerful lineage—an inheritance that was the work of many generations. I could detect it as easily as the sinking sun.

Or a urinary infection.

My face hardened.

He stopped when we were almost toe to toe, and I tipped my head back, feeling my curls brush the small of my back.

His eyes. *Bright green.* So insanely bright. Kind of like the receptionist's in *Live Right Realty.*

"Compensating for something?" he asked in a rumbling voice.

Huh?

Oh... *right*.

The unstated subtext of his comment implied he didn't have anything to compensate for. No matter how much I agreed, arrogance drew out the worst in me. The urge to apologise disintegrated.

I looked him up and down, wrinkling my nose. "Seems like it."

His eyes flashed and he stilled.

Predator.

The only word I could think of to describe the man's sudden change.

My heart pounded anew. He was big. Like, athletic and two heads taller than me. Something about the guy sent my body into overdrive. My mind screamed at me to run.

But he was an ass. Asses didn't get the satisfaction of seeing me afraid.

I held his gaze, planting my feet. My hands landed on my hips.

The flash subsided and the corners of his lips twitched. "You realise that you ran out in front of my car."

I did. "The green man was flashing."

The man hummed and cocked a brow at the pavement. I did the same, realising we'd created a spectacle. Pedestrians lined the road on either side. We'd stopped the traffic in this lane and the one next as people slowed to gawk.

More pertinent was the fact that I was the *only* pedestrian on the road. Which I assumed was his point.

Running a hand through my hair, I blew out a breath. "Whatever. Thanks for not killing me." I really should be grateful about that. Oh, well. I wasn't fucking perfect.

Pivoting on my heel, I resumed crossing the street, weaving between the gawking lanes. All four lanes were now slowing to catch a look at the drama.

"Where are you going? I'm talking to you," the man growled at my back.

Seriously? *Growling?* No one actually did that. Well, except that one Caveman, but he was just overzealous in fulfilling his roleplay.

Under different circumstances, I might have flirted shamelessly with Black Tie in the hopes of loosening his tie, but he was a douche bucket. I wasn't attracted to asshats. Scratch that. I *was*, but they were for one-night stands. Nothing more.

Safely atop the opposite pavement, I lifted my middle finger overhead, calling, "Sit and rotate, buddy."

"Don't tempt me," the man answered, gaze set on my face.

Uhm, did he just imply what I thought he'd implied?

I recovered, shouting, "I'll trim my nails then."

Montgomery's bright green sign caught my attention as I turned away from the hot piece of bastard. More *importantly*, my gaze snagged on the weedy teen opening the door.

Crap! I'm back here?

His eyes landed on me. Shock registered one second before the teen bellowed, "Stop her."

Fuck!

Legs and arms pumping, I zig-zagged through startled pedestrians. One ear on the teen's nasally commands, I kept the other on the snapping calls of the driver I'd left in the middle of the street, for some reason feeling he was the larger threat.

Which made no sense at all.

"You're sure you didn't notice anything weird about their eyes and smiles?" I pressed Tommy again.

She shook her head, appearing nonplussed. "Nope. I've dropped my résumé off three times. They're fucking gorgeous. Every one of them—which I suppose is kind of strange... Do you think they wear contacts or something?"

Pretty sure my imagination was on the fritz and I was dreaming up monsters under the bed. Rhys hadn't seemed to notice anything astray either, apart from the beauty of the receptionists.

"Are you sure you want to work there if the staff gave you the heebie-jeebies?" Tommy asked, snatching up the last fish taco. She'd paid, so I let her have it.

We were in a pub on the waterfront. Twenty years ago, the decor would have amazed. Now, it was tired and worn. But the food was good, and so was the strawberry mojito I'd downed.

Lips pursed, I turned my focus inward at her question. The head cloudy experience of earlier had dissipated now. Nearly being flattened by an expensive car would do that to a gal. Looking back, I was certain most of the staff's strangeness was in my head. After pet store Jenny, coffee sasquatch, and the teen with a power complex, I was just twitchy and stressed.

"My options are few. I mean, I've blown any chance at being hired by Montgomery's."

Tommy choked, spraying red onion and coriander across the table. She quickly chewed the rest of her mouthful and swallowed. "I would have given money I don't have to see you hauling ass down the street."

Hardly fun at the time, but I added my throaty laughter to her breathy one. "I'm so glad there weren't witnesses. Well… except *Rhys*." My eyes slid to her.

Tommy's ears all but pricked up. "Rhys? Do tell."

"Boy-next-door type. Tight black tee. Good manners."

The corners of her mouth tugged down. "Ah well, could be worse."

I flicked some of the masticated onion and coriander back at her. "No one's attractive to you at the moment except alternative musicians."

She conceded the point with a small smile, sipping her watermelon mojito.

"Plus." I continued. "Rhys was the warm-up. You should've seen the specimen who almost ran me over."

Watermelon mojito sprayed across the table.

I eyed the droplets covering the empty platter. "You should practice keeping stuff inside your mouth."

"You were almost run over?" she screeched, drawing the attention of the nearest table of college guys.

"Oh, yeah. That happened," I said, ducking my head. "Guess I should have started with that."

She slid off the stool and rounded the high circle table. Ignoring my protests, she patted me down.

I batted away her hands. "Jesus, ruffian. Get your damn paws off me. I'm fine."

Ignoring me, she returned to her stool once reassured I wasn't an inch from death. The college guys at the table over threw wide smiles our way.

With practiced movements, Tommy scanned them and picked out the most miserable one, winking.

I let my hair fall forward to hide my grin.

"I thought you'd met someone," I said when she'd finished her first round of flirting.

She flicked her jaw-length chestnut hair back, blasting Mr Misery with another lash-batting come-hither. Poor guy didn't stand a chance.

Tommy cleared her throat. "I have. But it's casual."

"You only do casual." Which concerned me. She was the same age as me—and had never had a boyfriend. Not even a two-weeks-when-you're-thirteen one. I was fine with her having fun as long as my main girl didn't have some commitment problem.

"*Exactly*," she announced. "Anyway, you were telling me about nearly dying from hot guy."

I thought of the man who'd approached in slow motion as though we were in some kind of perfume commercial. Or maybe the slow-motion part was just my dirty mind. *Wowsies*, he was truly the hottest guy I'd ever seen. Talk about instant ladyboner.

Then I remembered his superiority complex and scowled. "I didn't nearly die from *hot guy*—though he'd agree with you."

"So he was *really* hot then. And rich."

"I—" I squinted at her. "How did you know he was rich?"

"It's your ironic caveat. You hate the rich world, but you're attracted to rich men."

"Wash your mouth out."

Her chestnut gaze danced. "Am I right or am I right?"

"Rhys might not be rich," I grumbled. Though I *had* envisioned him in a suit. Did I have a complex?

Tommy sighed. "For what it's worth, what happened to you at that party with Business Guy when you were seventeen has probably made you hate them. Rich guys, that is."

I sipped at my mojito before remembering I'd necked it in the first five minutes. The straw made a bubbling sound of complaint as it encountered thin air.

I know, buddy. I know.

This was one of those days where I would've kept them coming, but I wouldn't do that on Tommy's dime. She helped her father pay all the bills at home—including the bill for her pop in the dementia ward of Bluff City Retirement Village.

"I dislike rich guys because I've never met one who wasn't an A-hole," I shot back. "That arrogance in guys sets my blood at boiling point. Though he *did* have a three-piece suit on. With a slim tie. That, if he *wasn't* a jerk, I might have had the urge to loosen."

Her eyes glazed. "Oh yeah. I'm there now. And are we on a white leather sofa or poolside? Is he wearing anything else? What are *you* wearing?"

Laughter trembled on my lips. She always made me feel better. "You need to message your guy tonight for an urgent sleepover. But back to the job thing. I'm not going to worry about it. From what you and Rhys were saying, it's a miracle I even got an interview. So I won't hold my breath—I'll keep an eye on my emails and keep applying for jobs in the meantime."

"Check now," Tommy said, drawing out her phone—another of my hand-me-downs.

"*Chh*, like they've already emailed." I still reached for the offered phone, entering her passcode.

She made eyes at Misery again as I logged into my email.

"Are you going to get his number?" I murmured, waiting for the page to load.

She hummed. "He's on thin ice. I've given him the *look* twice. He's either not into me or not confident. I'll give him one more go and then cut him loose."

I chuckled, but it faded as my eyes snagged on the top email in my inbox. "*Whoa.* I have an email from them." I read the subject lines of the other emails. There was one from my grandmother that I wasn't touching. The others were from companies I purchased products from in the past and now they felt they could email me for the rest of my life.

Tommy rounded the table. "Open it." She slapped my arm.

"Ouch. I'm doing it." I clicked on the email and scanned the contents in mounting disbelief.

I turned to Tommy, my mouth slightly ajar. "Are you reading what I'm reading?"

She recited, "*Dear Miss Basi, thank you for your interest in the trainee position at Live Right Realty. We were delighted with your résumé and interview and would like to offer you the position.*"

The email went on to detail the payment structure and duration of the traineeship.

"Thirty thousand for the year," I said, glancing at Tommy. I spent that much in a week sometimes. Okay, a lot of the time. "Is that good?"

She grimaced. "No. But it's a traineeship. When you complete the training, your salary will go up. By a lot usually. I earn thirty-seven thousand a year. Plus, this says that you'll receive a 1 percent commission bonus of any house you secure."

"Is that normal terminology for real estate? Secure." It sounded weird to me. Though my work experience was limited to large-scale, international businesses to be fair—none of which involved realty.

Her face was as blank as mine.

I chewed on my lip. "I have almost no money. I need to take this job."

"You have nearly three thousand dollars, Basi. That isn't *no money*," she said drily.

What? My pocket change? I hurried to shove down my confusion, feeling that this might be a Y S I S moment.

"Yes, of course," I said hastily. "But I have to get a place to live."

Tommy nodded. "True. You'll need to pay a bond and get a few things for that. *Cheap* things." She glanced at me.

I waved her away. "I know, I know. I'm going to email Live Right back now. It says that I'll start the day after tomorrow if I accept the role."

"Basil..."

At her odd tone, I glanced up.

She hesitated. "This isn't coming from a jealous place, so don't mistake it for that. It's just... I know a bunch of people who've gone for that job. No one ever gets it. You said the receptionist was looking at your pack and digging for your last name. Are you certain she didn't put two-and-two together? What if she only offered the role because you're a Le Spyre?"

I lowered her phone to the table.

Tommy's face flushed. "Oh, I've gone and done it. Sorry, my love. Ignore me. I wasn't there. You should trust your gut."

"No," I said slowly. "You have a point." She wasn't saying anything I hadn't thought myself.

I stared at the phone in my hand—at the empty reply tab I'd opened. "There aren't any pictures of me online and very little information. Daniel and the rest of our security team ensure anything that does pop up is immediately taken down. The only connection Live Right would have is my first name and that I own an expensive pack. A background check won't yield anything."

"I'd just hate for you to be drawn back into that game," she said in a hushed voice.

Rock and a hard place. Somewhere I hated to be—except for that one time with the Caveman.

"If I stay at Live Right for a week or two, I get money for that time, right?" I asked Tommy.

She nodded.

"Then I'll work there for now and keep interviewing to find something else. If I feel like they're using me for my estate connections, I'll jump ship. I can resist for a couple of weeks if they pressure me."

"A solid plan," Tommy declared. She threw Misery a third look.

He didn't budge.

"And he's out," my friend said, wrinkling her nose.

I held back a snicker as I typed a quick reply to the receptionist who'd signed off the previous email with the name Angelica.

Brr. Her name was as cold as her eyes.

Hitting Send, I'd hovered a finger over my grandmother's email for barely a minute before a reply from *Live Right* came through.

"Angie doesn't muck around," I said, impressed by the sadness of her life. It was 8:00 p.m. Woman had to be a workaholic.

I read aloud. "*Miss Basi, welcome to the team. We are glad to have you aboard.*" I scanned the rest of the email. "She said that we'll go through details on Wednesday. What details?"

My friend slurped back the minty dregs of her drink. "Bank account number, tax number, address. That kind of stuff."

As she spoke, my face slackened. "What?" I croaked. "I don't have any of those things."

Tommy answered between slurps. "Of course you do." She took one look at my face and stopped slurping. "You don't know your bank details and tax number?"

Mutely, I shook my head. "I have credit cards that draw on the estate. I've never had a real job before." Hysteria entered my voice. I gripped the table. "What if I don't have a tax number? How long do they take to get? Where do I get one?"

"Basi. *Basi.*"

Tommy rounded the table again and clicked her fingers in front of my face. When I fixed on her chestnut eyes, she threw money down on the table and shouldered my pack.

"Come on, lovely," she said, dragging me off the stool.

I trailed after her, panic holding me tight. I'd spent all day being shat on by people and now I miraculously had a job and might have to turn it down.

"You have an address," she said as we walked. "Just use mine. We can go to the bank tomorrow morning and open an account for you."

There was just one problem. "Can I use a fake name?"

"Nah, that's illegal. Pretty sure."

I sighed. "What if there's not a single bank owner in Bluff City that I'm not on first-name basis with? They'll recognise my name."

Tommy swore. "Ah, crap. Sir Olytheiu. I forgot about him. *Dang*."

He owned the largest bank here, yes. Not the only one.

I straightened suddenly. "I could use your bank details for the job."

She shot me an amused look.

"No, seriously. Your middle name is Beatrice. What if I use your last name? Then I'll use the initial B? Would the bank process that and put the money in your account?"

Her expression turned contemplative.

"It would probably work," she said. "I'll have to check if using my tax number will mess with my tax bracket because your salary coming in will be classed as a second job. I used to work two jobs, but the total only made up what I earn now. And my second job was taxed at a higher rate than the first."

A pain stabbed over my left eye.

"How much of that did you *not* understand?" Tommy asked after a beat.

"From tax number to higher rate," I confessed. Rich people had teams for all this fiddly shit.

She cracked a grin, but her eyes were serious. "I'll look into it tonight. We'll check how long the tax number application takes. In the meantime, you can call the tax office and see if you already have one. That would make everything easier. I don't mind lending you my bank number, but I'd rather not do the same with my tax number unless we have to."

I was putting her in a tricky situation. I didn't know just *how*, but clearly I was. "Sorry, Tom. I didn't consider it might drag you into trouble. I'll figure something out. Truly. I'd hate to mess with your... bracket."

She threw her head back, laughing. "Y S I S, bitch. That was a bad one."

Yep. I really had no idea what any of that stuff meant.

"Plus, I said *we*, didn't I?" Her expression was ferocious. "*We've* got a whole day to figure it out. It'll be okay, Basil. Promise."

I appreciated that big time considering I felt about as emboldened as a sober karaoke singer right now.

"I love you," I told her, sighing heavily.

"Loves ya, too, babe," she answered, flashing a carefree smile.

Was this how the poor lived? How did they just keep going when the entire world was against them? How did they have any fight or laughter left?

I released a breath, forcing away the dregs of my panic. This job business just became exponentially more complicated, but I'd come so far already.

I had to keep going.

5

I stopped outside of 47 Wreath Street and gave it a once over. The rental left a lot to be desired. Put another way, there wasn't a single desire it fulfilled. Aside from possibly being the first place I'd rent of my own accord.

The house had no grass to speak of—the owner had elected to fill the garden space with concrete instead. The grey slab showed mould where water must pool when it rained. The paint on the weatherboard cladding was cracked and chipped worse than Tommy's home. Her place looked like a freakin' palace compared to this joint.

The one thing it had in common with her home was the orange roof.

"You here for the viewing?"

Hand gripping my throat, I whirled to the man behind.

The condition of the house reflected the condition of the owner. Sweat beaded on his upper lip. The stubble on his face passed five o'clock shadow three days ago. Food stains dotted his shirt, and the top button was open, displaying a rug of hair a mouse could get lost in.

I cleared my throat. "I am."

He grunted and pushed past. "Come on then."

Nice and polite. What a keeper.

Trailing in his wake toward the entrance, I peppered him with the list of questions Tommy made me memorise. "I understand the house is ready for tenants immediately?"

The man unlocked the door and wrenched it back violently. The sound of metal on metal rent the air, accompanied by a crunching of, what sounded like, something structurally significant. He tugged twice more and managed to get the entrance halfway open.

"That's what the notice said," he answered me, offering no explanation for the state of the stubborn door.

I soldiered on. This is why I'd listened to "Skyscraper" by Demi Lovato before coming. "Whiteware is included?"

"Yeah."

Great...

The man led me into the lounge, and I eyed the blue carpet, wondering which parts were stained and which were the original colour.

The state of the brown and orange kitchen didn't bother me. I had no idea how to use an oven or how to prepare food. It did contain a fridge—which I opened per Tommy's orders.

The man's lip curled. "It works."

I flipped him an arched look and reached to flick the power switch. The light inside blared to life and a soft whirring sounded. What noise did fridges make?

Not a clue.

Flicking the switch off, I followed the guy across a dark hallway to the laundry—equipped with a washer—and through two bedrooms. One had housed a smoker at some point. If I took the place, I knew where I *wouldn't* sleep.

The bathroom wasn't as horrible as expected. In fact, it was the nicest part of the house. I smiled at the shower-bath combo. Looked like a new toilet too.

I flushed the toilet, obeying Tommy because she'd sense if I didn't.

"Want it then?"

Should I refuse based on his manners alone? The temptation was strong, but I'd been taught that emotions had no place in business.

I hummed, slowly walking back through the apartment. "How much is rent?"

"Two hundred a week. As said on the listing."

Tommy said that price was outrageous for Orange.

Snorting, I turned. "We both know it isn't worth half that much. So how about eighty dollars a week?"

His scowl twisted, but his eyes gleamed. Was I really so easy to peg as the rich brat? I'd borrowed Tommy's clothes, so it wasn't my outfit. What was giving me away? My hair? My nails?

"One hundred," he said. "Each week. Payment on Sunday by 10:00 a.m. In your letterbox. Not a second late."

I'd been schooled not to accept more than eighty-five, but it was only fifteen dollars difference. "I accept. I'll move in tomorrow, so I'll pay for five days only." It was kind of strange to do mental calculations without a string of zeros attached to the end, but I managed. "That's seventy-two dollars."

The man's chins wobbled as he laughed. "That ain't how it works, sweetheart."

"You realise I'm *considering* becoming your tenant? I'd advise against calling me sweetheart again."

The smile slid off his ugly mug.

"You'll pay the entire week or wait to move in on Sunday," he told me.

I tapped my lips, considering that ultimatum. "Okay, I'll move in on Sunday. Lose out on seventy-two dollars. I have somewhere to stay. In the meantime, I'll search for a different place."

I turned to leave.

"Wait."

The smile didn't spread across my face, but it sure wanted to. This joker was a harmless puppy compared to my grandmother, though her manners were about one thousand times better. She knew how to introduce herself for starters.

He held out his hand, looking like he'd sucked on a lemon. "Fine. Seventy-two dollars for this week. One hundred otherwise. And I'll need a month's rent as bond. *Up front.*"

It said as much on the listing.

Taking my time, I wandered through the lounge and kitchen again, peeking into the laundry once more. *Can I live here?* Envisioning myself relaxing on a sofa and drinking wine on a Friday night in this place would take a stronger imagination than I possessed.

When I ran away, it was to escape and to choose the rules of *my* life. I'd expected to start at the bottom of the ladder. I *wanted* to start at the bottom to better understand the world's problems. That sentiment didn't extend to punishing myself unnecessarily—now I knew that sleeping on the streets really was as bad as it sounded.

Tommy helped me figure out that after tax, I'd have over four hundred dollars to spend or save each week. The rent for this apartment took a quarter of that sum. Twice that amount would push the limit once I took food and transport into account.

This hovel was within my budget and available now, but would living here be unnecessary punishment?

I belatedly remembered another question. "Utilities are included?"

The man cursed under his breath. "Yes," he grated.

Bastard would have charged me extra for them if I hadn't asked. What a dick.

Did Tommy rattle off any other questions?

... If she had, I couldn't recall them.

I inhaled slowly—ignoring the musty, smoke smell saturating the carpet and coating the walls. I could spend a few months here. After that, I'd have a better grasp of what week-to-week costs were; maybe some savings up my sleeve.

"I'll take it," I told the man. "And I'm Basi by the way."

"Clint. Bond."

Huh? His name was Clint Bond?

His grubby hand shot out.

Oh my god, he wanted the bond? That's how he asked for things?

Don't give the guy an etiquette lesson, Basi. It's too late for him.

I smiled and hoisted my pack higher. "Thanks for showing me the house, Clint."

I ambled to the half-open front door and squeezed through the gap.

"I thought you wanted the place," he snapped.

I smiled sweetly. "What did I say earlier about treatment of a potential tenant?"

His face turned purple.

Still I waited, letting him suffer.

Fixing him with a cool look that extended into awkward length territory—for him anyway—I fished in my pack for the stack of cash. I pulled out the wad and leafed through until I found four crisp one-hundred-dollar bills.

"Here," I said, holding it out.

I glanced at his face and frowned at the direction of his focus. On the wad of money. *Crap.* Maybe bringing it out like that wasn't wise. I shoved the stack into the zip pocket and swung my bag on again.

He blinked and inspected the money in his hand.

"Keys," I pressed.

My tolerance had officially expired.

Clint dragged his eyes off the money. "The keys will be in the mailbox at 7:00 a.m. tomorrow morning. You paid for five days this week."

That one was my bad for haggling him down, but my shifts at *Live Right Realty* were 11:00 a.m. to 8:00 p.m. I'd have time to move in tomorrow, so Clint could go screw himself.

"That's only fair," I said grandly. "Thank you for your time, Clint."

Asswipe.

I strode in the direction of the bus stop, feeling more in control of this situation than I had since sleeping on the streets. I officially had my own apartment. I'd get five days' worth of pay for working this week. More than enough to pay rent.

Which meant that the two and a half thousand dollars in my zip pocket could go toward kitting out my new place.

It was time to shop.

I attempted to straighten my ill-fitting charcoal pencil skirt as the bus lurched to a halt. People trickled off and the bus resumed its slog. Mid-morning, and I'd already spent a full day's energy moving my new purchases from Tommy's to mine.

Mine.

I beamed. Who knew there could be such joy in outfitting a house that belonged to me? Well, a rental.

Tommy surveyed my purchases last night with a critical eye, nearly critically enough to deflate my high. She'd worried over the lack of contract for the apartment and the absence of keys. Once assured that I'd accounted for expenses until I was paid by *Live Right*, she'd relaxed. My grandmother had trained me in estate affairs since I started high school. Sure, there wasn't the same margin of error to play with, but the principles had to be the same in the peasant world as they were in the rich world.

A girl with lopsided pigtails waved from where she sat next to her grandmother. My heart twisted slightly in my chest. Once that could have been me and my grandmother.

I snickered loudly, drawing the attention of an old man. He smiled and returned his attention to reading the paper.

On second thought, swap the bus for a private jet, the pigtails for an intricate braid, and insert clothing I had to keep pristine at all times. But the relationship was real. I loved my grandmother. She was all I had after my parents' helicopter crashed over the Maldives. My parents were both only children and so I had no cousins, no aunties, and no uncles. The only relations I had were from my grandmother's generation and mostly deceased. If I had any alive, I'd never met them.

Truly I wanted to be out here living like this. But things ended on an ugly note with my grandmother, and that didn't sit right with me.

I hadn't read her email yet. I could guess what it would say—an order for me to stop being narrow-minded; that people would kill to be in my position. My only relation understood me on so many levels, and yet didn't in fundamental ways too. When we discussed anything other than my inheritance and *responsibilities*, we could spend hours talking.

I might have hurt her by leaving, and perhaps I should have handled it differently—sat her down and explained why I was going. In a rational way she'd have respected.

Tonight, I'd read the email. But I had to get through my first day at *Live Right Realty* before that.

I tugged at the pencil skirt again, pulling at the hideous white blouse tucked into the high waist. The outfit was the least hideous I could find at *Jamieson*, an outlet store Tommy got some of her clothes from.

The prices were so cheap I couldn't believe it. Upon further inspection, the quality of the material was so shoddy, the prices seemed outrageous. The garments wouldn't last more than ten washes—yet another way the system squeezed money from the poor while ruining the environment. I bought a few outfits I could mix and match out of necessity, but from now on, I'd save for classic pieces of higher quality that would last years.

I glanced out the window, zoning out as the bus passed through Orange, Red, and Pink. This bus only serviced those three suburbs, and sure enough, before heading into Purple, the bus turned inward to Grey.

Skyscrapers soon loomed overhead, their tops impossible to see from where I held on to my rung.

I was only concerned with one scraper.

Kyros Sky.

I'd spent two days pushing down memories of my interview on Level 44 of the building. Not an easy feat when my imagination had taken the interaction with Angelica and twisted it beyond recognition. I'd woken in a cold sweat last night after a nightmare where the receptionist asked me a list of personal questions, and I'd answered every one of them without hesitation.

Weird.

And inaccurate. The stress of figuring out peasant life was getting to me, and whatever my sentiments on Angelica, I was on a one-way street now. I couldn't *not* work there with bills to pay.

The bus lunged to a stop, and I followed the other city-goers exiting the back door.

I'd disembarked at a different stop today. This morning, I looked up the route from here to the skyscraper on Tommy's phone, but the inability to double-check directions on the spot was fucking disconcerting. Honestly? I usually just hopped in the car and left our chauffeur to figure everything out.

Montgomery's was visible at the far corner on my side of the street. Ha! I knew where I was. Take that, world.

I crossed the street up this end just in case weedy teen was doing the security rounds outside the fast-food chain. By 10:40 a.m., the elevator of *Kyros Sky* was shooting me upward.

10:40 a.m. was okay, right? Not too early?

Being punctual was a professional quality—my grandmother was a stickler for it.

Chill out, Basi.

Exhaling a final time, I smoothed my blouse and skirt again, and hooked my thumbs through my bag straps.

"You got this," I whispered to myself.

The doors opened, and a smile was already plastered on my face. I'd expected the same bustle and murmur from Monday.

The smile slid from my face.

The place was a ghost town. No one stood behind the desk.

I'd just taken on a fucking rental. And the thousands I'd spent on furnishing it. *Shit.* I mean, there was enough money for food and transportation for the rest of this week. But nothing at all for next week.

I'd made a terrible mistake. I'd—

"Basi. I'm glad you made it," Angelica strode from an office to the left of reception.

My heart galloped. In relief—or so I told myself. It was possible that I'd *really* downplayed how uncomfortable her eyes made me feel. The bright blues fixed on my clothing, scanning me from head to toe. When she returned to meet my gaze, her expression was empty of disgust or disappointment.

After her attention to my expensive items on Monday, I was happy to note her reaction to my cheap outfit. Tommy was wrong, I wasn't hired for my connections. That was a win.

"Good morning, Angelica. Am I early?"

I was.

She smiled, and I noted the dark smudges of fatigue beneath her eyes. Kind of surprising that I could make out any facial detail within ten centimetres of those blazing orbs.

"No, no. The other staff usually schedule house visits and clients for the first half of the day. They come into the office later."

Oh... "Realty businesses don't keep normal work hours?"

"Not us," she said, her eyes flashing in anger.

I froze for a full five seconds.

Angelica blinked a few times, and I sucked in a ragged breath, heart pounding in my ears.

Holy fuckery, Angelica was terrifying when she lost her temper. The woman tilted her head, and the ferociousness drained from her face, allowing me to unlock somewhat.

"I just meant that waking up later must be nice. I'm a night owl," I forced myself to say.

If she pulled that shit again, I was leaving. I didn't even understand why she made me feel so scared, just that she did. Except I couldn't leave now. I'd used my money to outfit the rental and had rent to pay on Sunday.

Fuck. I'd backed myself into a corner.

"A night owl?" The concept seemed to amuse her. "I can relate to that."

Probably the only thing we had in common.

She recovered the brisk manner from two days prior.

"There are a few things to sign before I start your initiation," the woman said.

Ugh. This was the bank account and tax number part.

A long call yesterday, with a long enough hold time that I swore I visibly aged, got me through to the tax office. They'd confirmed I had no tax number. After a transfer to another department, I'd discovered that a tax number took three to six weeks to process and I'd need two forms of identification and proof of address. I had *one* form of ID—my learner's driver's licence. I only sat the stupid test so I had something to get into clubs with.

"About that," I said, my gut churning. "I wrote down my tax number, but I'm in the middle of moving, and for the life of me, I couldn't find the bit of paper."

Tommy had dutifully jotted down her bank account and tax details for me this morning. While she did that, I searched and found that what we intended to do was tax fraud—with consequences neither of us could afford.

Just like Tommy not to say a damn thing. I wasn't putting her in that position. I'd have to file for a tax number as soon as possible and delay *Live Right* in the meantime.

My gaze dropped with the lie, but a peek upward yielded surprising results. Angelica looked amused again.

The slight quirk of her lips was gone in a blink.

My brows wrinkled at her smooth expression. Had I seen amusement? Maybe it was a trick of the light.

"Don't worry about any of that," she said, flashing a smile.

I swallowed at her teeth.

I felt... *threatened* by her teeth. What the hell? Was it because they were so white? I'd visited Bali a few times and been harassed by monkeys for food. To them, smiling was a sign of aggression. Which meant that if her smile got my back up... I was a monkey.

But what did that make Angelica?

"Basi?"

Crap. "Um. Don't worry?" I asked weakly.

Her head was tilted again. "We pay in cash."

"Really?"

"You're required to pay tax yourself, of course. You're a contractor—except we pay you annual leave, sick, and grievance days. It's easier for the books if we pay in cash."

I registered the term *contractor* and very little else. What did the term contractor mean? I associated it with builders and the like. *Dammit.* This was the definite downside to being rich enough to afford teams who handled the nitty-gritty. Was contracting workers a normal way of paying people in the realty industry?

I'd ask Tommy tonight—but this twist of events might work out perfectly.

"You don't need any of my details?" I asked, patting my pack. "Because I've got the rest of them right here."

Call me Bluffing Basi.

Amusement flashed in her eyes again. This time I was certain of it. What was so damn funny?

Angelica gestured to a stack of papers. "Just a few details to get to know you. That's all."

6

“This is the staff room,” Angelica purred, gesturing around the huge room.

More like a school cafeteria, really.

“You’re welcome to put food in the fridge and use the kettle for hot drinks.” She continued.

“Great,” I mumbled.

How many staff did they have? The room was massive. It had to take up a quarter of Level 44, yet we were still the only people in the building after two hours of forms and awkward chit-chat.

True to her word, I hadn’t needed to present any important numbers. Not even my driver’s licence. As such, I was now Basi Tetley.

The forms were just a series of tedious personality questionnaires because Angelica liked the team to be close. If the others were like her, I could safely count myself out of social events.

Angelica showed me the bathroom and supply rooms next. Level 44 was wrapped around the elevator. Aside from the open reception area and the staff room, the rest of the level was divided into offices.

“How many people work here?” I finally asked. There were a lot of rooms.

"One hundred."

I must have made a sound of surprise. She smiled—I seriously wished she'd stop. "Live Right Realty is the largest and most profitable realty business in Bluff City."

I was duly impressed. "I didn't know that."

Bet my grandmother did. Nothing happened in this city without her knowledge.

"We get great results." Her voice dropped into a fervent tone I'd otherwise associate with Sir Lancelot making an oath to a fair maiden.

By now, the way my heart thumped in her presence had wrung every bit of energy from me. I was too tired to be on edge anymore, and it wasn't even 2:00 p.m. Just from being *near* my boss.

That was messed up.

Wasn't it?

"*This* is your office," she declared, pushing open the door to a room in the far corner of the level.

The office contained a marble desk, flat-screen computer, three black leather chairs, and a sleek standing lamp. The charcoal walls were bare.

I'd definitely been shoved in the corner. But I was a trainee. What was more, that's where I preferred to be in this establishment. "It's perfect. Thank you."

She showed tooth again. "It's Live Right tradition to hang pictures of the homes you secure. Yours are empty for now, but I'm sure they'll fill up in no time."

Secure. There was that strange term again.

With a dainty twist of her wrist, Angelica consulted her *Foffz* watch. "Time for lunch."

I kept my sigh of relief contained. I wasn't hungry, but time away from my intense boss would be a welcome change.

"Is two hours enough?" she asked, light confusion showing on her ethereal face.

How old was this woman? She only appeared late twenties at

most. How was she the owner of the largest realty business in Bluff City at so young an age?

Wait... was she asking how long I *wanted* for lunch? On *Truth Ranges,* the nurses had half an hour for lunch, and the surgeons got an hour. But no one chose how long they wanted.

"Whatever's normal," I murmured.

She searched my expression. "Two hours. If that's not enough, please tell me."

What kind of job had I nabbed that I had a two hours *minimum* lunch break?

I wasn't one to look a gift horse in the mouth. "I can work with that."

"Then take a moment to get settled in. I'll expect you back at 4:00 p.m. to introduce you to the rest of the team."

With a final baring of teeth that had me forcing back a shudder, Angelica left the room.

The greater the distance between us, the better I felt. Which had to be in my head, right? Crap, I was losing the plot. My shoulders sagged, and the slight headache I hadn't detected dissipated.

My breath filled my lungs instead of occupying my throat.

I'd never had such a physical response to a person, and I had no idea how to interpret it. Why did she scare me so much? Was it because she literally held my future in her hands?

I didn't think it was so simple.

The feeling of being a monkey hit me again.

Something about her was predatory and seriously set off my warning instincts. Or maybe it was because I was used to being top of the food chain and didn't know how to handle the reverse.

Either way, a bad sleep as I tore between excitement and nerves and stress was now messing with my imagination.

Or perhaps I really was a monkey and less evolved than her.

I'd be cute with a monkey tail.

I swung my pack onto the desk and riffled through the contents, unsure what Angelica meant by *settle in*. I had half my leftover money in there, glasses, a spare top in case I met with another coffee disaster.

And a pen.

"Ha!" I extracted the pen and set it upon the desk. I glanced around the office. My office. "Mine."

My new favourite word.

Officially settled in, I headed for the elevator, thankfully not encountering Angelica on the way.

Two hours seemed a long time and I had no idea how to fill it—until recalling that I needed to keep looking for jobs. I couldn't quit *Live Right* until I had the proper numbers and documents, and if the first two hours of this job were anything to go by, I'd switch jobs as soon as possible. I couldn't ever recall being so tired in my life.

I purchased a roll of bacon and avocado sushi, proud of myself for locating a cheap food option. Finding a newspaper was a harder task. Eventually, I found a place tucked inside an underground mall with books, magazines, and lotto tickets.

A stack of newspapers sat on a table just inside the door.

I hadn't accounted for the newspaper in my budget, so I waited until the cashier was distracted and slipped on my thick-rimmed glasses, riffling through the paper until I found the job notices.

The pet job was still up. Jenny had unrelenting standards, so that was a given.

The newspaper run and tomato factory job were gone. I peeked at the cashier to make sure she was busy and scanned the page again.

Nope.

Nope.

Nope.

A cleaning job caught my eye. *Ugh*, it was for an address in the estates. I wasn't cleaning the toilet of anyone I knew. A notice for a janitor job in a public school was printed beneath it.

That might be an option.

I cursed my decision to leave my pen at the office. If I hadn't left my phone at the estate, I'd snap a picture. What the hell did poor people do in this situation?

The cashier looked over, and I hastily closed the paper.

Could I be a school janitor?

I'd never cleaned anything other than my hair and body. I did love my shave, wash, and hydrate routine, yet somehow I suspected washing my body and cleaning toilets were different things.

I read the price of the paper. Two dollars and fifty cents. I'd budgeted more than I would need, about fifty dollars more, in case an emergency came up.

Hmm, no, I wasn't willing to spend two dollars fifty for a potential janitor job. I wasn't sure it was for me.

With a quick nod at the cashier, I strode out, smiling at how much a few days had changed me. I'd gone from sleeping on the streets to being a renting, working woman in four days. *And* I'd turned my nose up at purchasing a newspaper. Go me.

The feeling of being precariously out of depth hadn't disappeared, but I had a few handholds. And I'd only nearly died a couple of times. My encounter with Licky Lips was born of a foolhardy decision. Plus, I *may* have stepped out on the street into flowing traffic, but I was still inclined to blame the encounter with Black Tie on *him*.

Because his attitude sucked.

If I ever saw him again, I'd be sure to tell him. Maybe after removing said black tie.

I waited until 3:57 p.m. to re-enter *Kyros Sky* and return to Level 44. That was how much I dreaded feeling like a monkey again.

Four hours to go. Totally doable. And tomorrow? Well, I'd worry about tomorrow when it came around.

Ding!

The buzzing murmur from Monday greeted my ears. The other staff members were here. *Thank Zeus.*

I straightened my pencil skirt.

"You must be Basi," a woman behind the desk said.

I couldn't be certain, but she looked like one of the admins from yesterday. Her eyes were also bright blue, but she didn't have the same terrifying effect as Angelica.

I echoed her cool tone. "I am."

I was fluent in all three dialects of bitch—passive-aggressive bitch, sly bitch, and confrontational bitch.

"Angelica is gathering everyone in the staff room."

I nodded and quickly deposited my bag in my office before walking to the staff room.

The murmur of conversation swelled as I drew closer. Right until I reached the door.

It cut off.

Everything and everyone.

Off.

My eyes widened. What was that about? My instincts said that one hundred people had been talking about me and somehow knew when I'd arrived to stop talking. But that was... crazy.

I stopped in the doorway.

"Basi," Angelica greeted.

I looked at her and the same pounding heart I'd had all morning while in her company hit me all over again.

Then I glimpsed the other staff.

Bright eyes.

Looking at me.

Air wheezed in my throat.

My mind *stalled.*

Eyes like hers. The lot of them. *Bright. Burning.* Not all blue. A few greens. Some almost violet.

No one smiled, and the currently disconnected part of me was grateful because seeing their teeth would have tipped the terror surging unchecked through my body and mind into mindless territory.

No one spoke a word and sweat beaded on my forehead. My palms slickened with perspiration. My blouse stuck to my chest like I was in the tropics. *Oh my god.* My legs were shaking.

I had to be sick.

The symptoms started three days ago and became worse at random intervals... except for those times when I wasn't, well, here.

Why were their eyes all so piercing?

Whatever the answer, I'd bitten off more than I could chew. Admitting that was easy as I stared back at one hundred heartbreakingly beautiful people who made my heart want to shrivel and die.

Whatever this breeding programme was, I was officially out of my depth.

"Basi?" Angelica's face swam before me. "Are you alright?"

Looking at her was easier than peering at the one hundred staff.

"Alright?" I squeaked.

Someone laughed under their breath.

"There are a lot of us," she said in apology. "I had no idea you suffered from stage fright."

Stage fright.

I stared dumbly at her, regaining enough of my senses to guess what I looked like. Rational Basi, the tiny amount of her present, demanded I get my shit together. Because I looked like a fool.

"Stage fright," I managed to repeat.

"Come with me," Angelica said kindly.

I was ushered to a chair that thankfully didn't face the gathered group. Profile to them, I kept my gaze averted to the cupboards lining the nearest wall.

"Everyone say hi to Basi," Angelica said softly.

For the most part, the staff had kept quiet during my meltdown which seemed weird in its own right. At her words, they chorused, "Welcome."

My eyes popped at the collective effect of their voices.

Predators.

I'd had the thought prior in regard to Angelica and had it again. There was no other way to describe their musical, silken sound. I gripped the undersides of the chair I sat upon, begging my bladder to stay full.

Someone laughed again, and a faint strain of anger edged in around my fear.

"Basi Tetley is our new trainee and will stay with us all year."

Angelica continued. “For the next week, she will shadow Katerina to learn the ropes. Basi, would you like to say a few words?”

If I did, there was a strong chance I’d vomit or piss myself. Mutely, I shook my head.

“Stage fright,” she explained to the others.

That wasn’t what I felt. I might be ignorant of a lot of things, but I wasn’t delusional. Something else was going on.

I clamped my lips shut as bile surged up my throat.

I couldn’t stand it any longer.

“Basi?” Angelica asked when I bolted to my feet.

“Bathroom.”

The same fucker laughed again.

My cheeks burned in mortification, and yet I was so terrified and frozen that the loss of dignity didn’t otherwise touch me.

“Of course. Katerina will meet you in your office soon.”

Great. I won’t be there.

I moved stiffly out of the room, eyes focused on my goal. The door. Outside and down the hallway, I dragged in a sobbing breath. The air couldn’t get in my lungs fast enough.

Had I inhaled once in that room? I must have, but it didn’t feel like it.

My head swam and I pressed my hand against the wall as I panted, tears squeezing at the corners of my eyes.

After this morning, I knew distance would help, so I slid my feet forward in a heavy shuffle. Slowly, my head stopped spinning, but a pounding headache took up residence and remained.

What the fuck were they? Hypnotists? A hypnotist *mafia*? It would explain their bright eyes and the wariness I felt.

But so many of them? And all working in realty?

That didn’t add up.

Unless that was how *Live Right* became the largest and most profitable realtor in Bluff City. And how Angelica became so successful at such a young age. Those bastards hypnotised people to make a sale.

The legal implications of that were *huge*.

I made it to my office, blood returning to my limbs, and the ease of my movement coming back. By then, I knew that I'd stumbled on something illegal.

Big time illegal.

I'd gone from one cage to another. And I had to get out now.

Returning to my office door, I peeked down the hallway. People were leaving the staff room. *Damn.* In normal circumstances, I'd take my stuff and leave without explanation. That wasn't possible if they suspected that I'd guessed something about their illegal activities.

Ding!

The elevator sang out, announcing someone's arrival.

I could see the reception from here, but the lift was tucked around the corner.

"Kyros," Angelica greeted.

Wait. The high-rise was called *Kyros Sky*. Was this *the* Kyros?

Hopefully he'd keep Angelica busy. She was the most likely person to prevent me from leaving.

A man approached the front desk, and I squinted at his frame.

Tall. Wearing a three-piece suit. Baby-making hormones, he had the sexiest ass I'd ever seen on a man. It wasn't a body part I tended to catalogue on males, but on him? I could suddenly understand the urge to *fondle the globes of his ass* like in *Fernando's Eighth Ab*.

Broad shoulders tapered to his hips. I'd always been a sucker for the upside-down triangle on men. And boy-oh-boy did he *wear* that suit.

In fact, it looked like he'd be adept at sliding right out—

I pulled up abruptly. The man turned at the same moment, talking to someone behind him.

Fucking fucker!

It was Black Tie.

"The new trainee was just introduced to the staff, sir, per your instructions."

My jaw dropped.

"Will she be a good fit?" he asked, deep voice reaching my ears with ease.

Angelica didn't hesitate to answer, beaming. "Absolutely."

Squeaking, I retreated into my office in an arm-waving mess. My limbs were still funky from the staff meeting and I fell on my ass.

Sir.

Per your instructions.

This wasn't happening. That man out there was Kyros—for whom the building was named. Which wasn't important in the slightest. But he was the *boss* of this business? I'd assumed Angelica was top dog.

This was really bad.

This wasn't happening.

I crawled across the carpet for my desk, certain my legs couldn't bear me. After a day from hell, crazed instinct was finally in the driver's seat. It wanted me to get under the desk so the earthquake called life could collapse this high-rise on my dumb head. Instinct also didn't want me to crawl around to the other side.

A shortcut was best.

The space at the front of the desk was narrow, but I could make it under.

I slid my arms in, turning my head sideways to get it through.

"Basi?"

I froze, ass in the air. Could she see my lacy black G-banger through the slit in the back of my pencil skirt?

Please don't be here.

"I was hoping to introduce you to the CEO of Live Right..."

Black Tie was with her *now*? Or standing in reception? My mind latched onto hope—

A masculine voice rumbled through the office. "It appears we came at a bad time."

That. Mother. Fucker.

He already knew who I was! There was no missing the gloating tone.

I didn't respond to Angelica, consumed with sudden rage. An entire day's worth of fear turned into a furious missile. Target: Kyros. He'd set this up somehow. I was part of a prank. They'd all worn contacts to freak me out.

My fingers shook with the urge to wrap around his neck and squeeze. However, my *immediate* predicament was how to extract myself from beneath the desk. To slither forward or to shuffle backward? I opted for forward to gain a second to collect myself under the desk.

Sliding onto my stomach, I pulled myself through the small gap.

Footsteps rounded the table, and, flat on my stomach, I eyed the black leather business shoes as Kyros came to stand in front of me.

Freens.

Of course he'd wear the most expensive shoe in existence.

I pulled my legs through and crouched under the desk, waiting for him to move away so I could crawl out and try to get through the next painful conversation.

The bastard *sat.*

In my spinning leather chair! Right in front of where I crouched. Was he trying to outmanoeuvre me? I'd been pushed to my limits today.

He'd just pushed me past them.

Teeth barred, I shuffled forward on my knees until I was between his open knees and stood as quick as possible. I refused to give him the satisfaction of lingering in that position.

There wasn't any way to free myself from the triangle his legs made with the desk. Not without touching his thighs or climbing over his legs.

Seething, I met his bright green gaze.

I should have listened to that errant thought two days ago. The one that drew parallels between his eyes and Angelica's. Reality wasn't the only bitch. Hindsight could fucking join it.

He didn't bother to hide his smirk. "I'm sitting."

Kyros spread his hands wide.

What was he on about? I scowled, my churning anger mounting.

"What was the other part?" he asked. It was the rhetorical kind of question.

"Ah. Yes," he purred, the sound deep and menacing. "You told me to sit and rotate."

Understanding shot through me in one bolt of pure wrath. I tracked his movements as he pushed the seat back so he was free of my legs.

As I watched, he rotated three times in the spinning chair.

My chair.

I'd only felt hate once in my life. And it was at my rich *friends* for nearly destroying Tommy.

He stopped spinning but didn't stand. His eyes met mine again, and I met him head-on. Hair the colour of toffee only made his meadow-green eyes brighter.

The urge to physically attack him surprised me—not being prone to violence. I tapered it though, remembering my theories on the illegal activity happening on Level 44. I couldn't play this wrong. Not if something dodgy was going on.

"Cute," I replied. "And you are?"

A gasp sounded from behind me. *Shit*, I forgot Angie was here.

The man rested back against the headrest. His eyes glittered as he searched my face. My eyes catalogued his smooth skin—just on the golden side of beige. His neck begged to be free of that damn tie.

"You know who I am," he replied.

He turned his attention to rolling up his white shirt sleeves. His three-piece suit was Air Force Blue—one of my favourite colours on the opposite sex. The giant's tie was slim again, and the same black as his shoes. A huge watch adorned his left wrist. Otherwise, his only accessory was a gleaming silver tie pin.

I watched as he rolled his sleeves, wondering if it might be the most attractive thing I'd seen in my life.

A shame he was... well, *him*.

Hopefully Angelica would enjoy the show because I wasn't standing around to be humiliated any longer. I turned away as he started on the second shirt sleeve. Shoving my pen in my bag, I drew the drawstring and swung it onto my back. The man behind me had stilled—the leather of the chair wasn't squeaking anymore.

Those observations only served to demonstrate how acutely aware of his movements I was.

Dammit.

"Is Katerina ready?" I asked Angelica, who stood open-mouthed in the doorway. Her eyes flittered between me and the hulking idiot at my back.

She nodded.

"I wasn't finished speaking with you," Kyros said. His calm tone didn't fool me. He wasn't used to being ignored. I could smell entitlement from a mile away.

I rounded the desk and only turned to face him when nearly at the door. Smiling, I lifted both brows in polite enquiry. "Yes, sir?"

The frown that graced his face was a tiny win, but I'd happily take it.

Kyros stood slowly, and I took in his towering height. He would loom over me, and I wasn't a short gal. My lower stomach clenched against my will at the sight of his powerful frame. It'd look great hovering over me in bed.

He rounded the desk and stalked across the room, oddly graceful for a person of his height. "You might be interested to know you didn't scratch my car."

My anger was draining away with every second. That's how exhausted I was. Even though this asshole was playing games that made me want to spit fire and grow talons, I just couldn't summon more energy.

I was utterly spent.

"I'm glad," I replied, shifting my gaze to the computer behind him. Some of my hair slithered over my shoulder, swinging to partially cover my face.

I could feel him watching me, but honestly, I just wanted to close my eyes, to sleep and wake to find this was a nervous nightmare before my first day of work.

"Angelica," he said sharply. "Miss Tetley has had enough for the day."

Have I ever.

"S-She has? But of course, sir."

Poor Angie.

"She is to have the rest of the day off," he ordered. "Have someone drive her home."

That roused me.

"No," I objected.

"Yes," he said coolly.

My hands were on my hips before I knew it. I stepped closer to him, breathing thinly as I tipped my head right back. "*I said, no.*"

Any person who had ever known me knew not to mess with hands-on-hips Basi. This tiger was a wild one. Angelica resumed her shocked gasping as I silently dared the bastard in front of me to disagree again.

I would end him.

His eyes took on a glittering quality, and his fingers twitched in my direction, but he fell short of actually touching me.

Wise male.

"Can you make it home?" he enquired softly.

Ah nuts, I hadn't expected kindness.

The fire left my eyes and I averted my gaze again. "Of course I can."

"Then we'll see you tomorrow at 12:00 p.m.," he said in the same quiet voice. On second thought, it wasn't kindness at all. Kyros was cooing to the monkey in the room to earn its trust.

Motherfucker.

Angelica whispered, "She works 11:00 a.m. until 8:00 p.m., sir."

"12:00 p.m.," he repeated, green eyes flashing over my head.

Shit, son. Don't take it out on Angie.

I stepped away from him, my weary heart thudding pathetically. Though his eyes didn't blaze as much as Angelica's, he was scarier by far than the woman behind me. He made her look like a field mouse.

If my body wasn't so exhausted, I'd be struggling to cope in his presence.

What the fuck was going on in this place?

"12:00 p.m.," I echoed wearily, hoisting my pack.

I wouldn't return to Level 44 of *Kyros Sky*.

Not for a million dollars and a fucking crown.

7

My head pounded.

No. That isn't right.

The pounding was outside of my head.

I sent my new duvet flying, scrambling to answer the insistent knocking. I half fell off the bed, weaving on sleep-drunk legs to the door.

"Basi. If you don't let me in in five seconds, I'm calling the po-po."

Tommy.

Her voice almost undid me.

I unlocked the door and wrenched with all my might. I had no idea how I'd managed to get inside last night. Arriving home was a blurry memory.

Tommy shoved from the other side and sidled through when we managed to prop the entrance a quarter way open.

Her lips were pressed together. "What the actual fuck, Basi? Where have you been?"

I yawned and beckoned her to the kitchen. "I was exhausted after work yesterday. I crashed."

"I came around at nine last night. And again at eight this morning. I thought something had happened to you."

Seeking comfort myself, I padded across the orange lino and hugged her. Her arms wrapped around me.

"What happened?" she asked.

What happened? I had the worst day of my life. And I was trapped really bad. I'd trapped *myself*. I rushed in to renting this shitty place and buying a heap of stuff, thinking I had normal life all figured out.

But I was a fucking rich moron.

Now, I'd been sucked into an illegal business with criminals who openly intimidated me. Even worse, I couldn't leave without *really* becoming homeless.

Except I could barely admit that much to myself.

Whatever I said about not needing anyone's approval was a big, whopping lie. I needed Tommy's. She was always so self-assured, possessing the confidence that came when a person knew how to look after themselves. That side of her had always awed me, *inspired* me.

"Yesterday was hard," I said hoarsely.

"Hard is an understatement. You must've slept twelve hours."

Twelve hours. "What's the time?"

She checked her phone. "Just after nine. Lucky I woke you, huh? You can't be late for your second day of work. Don't suppose you bought an alarm clock when you got all this stuff?"

Nope. Because that was a practical item that would make sense.

"I don't have to be at work until 12:00 p.m. today," I said, swallowing my fury—every bit of it aimed inward. Despite my doomed financial situation, I was still determined not to return. Tommy didn't need to know that though. Not until I could cope with admitting my failure to her.

She rubbed my back. "Oh good. We can ride the bus together."

Basi, you idiot.

"We can." I agreed, my insides twisting.

"Two besties going to work together. This is just what you wanted. Look at you go." She beamed at me, then sniffed the air. "Before we leave, you need a shower. Big time." She pulled back. "How about you go do your routine and I'll head home to dig out my old phone. I don't want any repeats of what happened last night."

I nodded obediently, rendered silent by her unwarranted praise.

"I'll be back in a tick," she said.

I lingered in the kitchen after Tommy left, my mind shaking with the severity of my situation.

For no other reason than she'd told me to, I traipsed to the shower and turned the nozzle. Pulling off my new pyjamas—something I'd purchased as a reward for securing a job and apartment, what a joke—I tested the water.

Just shy of scalding.

Perfect.

I stepped into the shower bath and let the hot water pour over me. The heat seeped into my soul, soothing the pieces that it could. Maybe it could restore whatever broke inside me yesterday.

I doubted it.

The fear-filled memory of walking into the room crammed with bright-eyed criminals left me gasping. I forced the recollection away, focusing on the streaming water.

My breathing steadied again, and I pushed my wet hair behind my ears.

"You're not a monkey," I whispered.

Turning on autopilot, I shaved the areas that required shaving, foamed my body in my lemon myrtle wash, and dried before moisturising.

I wrapped one of my *new* beige towels around myself and stared at the woman in the cracked mirror. On good days, we got on. Most days, we tolerated each other. Today, we hated each other. Yesterday morning I marvelled at the excitement of setting up my first apartment. Now, each item was a sore reminder of my ignorance. As an heiress, I'd represented a tiny percentage of the human population. The vast majority lived *this* way each day from birth to death. Normal life wasn't a cute little Monopoly game. It wasn't the same as running a multi-billion-dollar estate. There were all sorts of hidden costs and forms and timetables. The *rules* were different, and I had no idea what they were.

How would I ever understand it all?

Gripping the lip of the vanity, I listened to thuds and bangs coming from the kitchen. Tommy was back. Or I was being robbed. Probably the latter.

I sighed.

Tommy expected me to go to work today. I felt like a coward for omitting the truth, but I couldn't handle more than the shit-heap currently piled upon my shoulders. That included telling Tommy and witnessing her reaction. My friend wouldn't judge or criticise me. She wouldn't even pity me.

Tommy would be 100 percent furious on my behalf. She'd go into mumma bear mode. Because she saw me as someone in need of protection. Because I was incapable of caring for myself, despite all my talk that I wasn't like other rich morons.

Shame. Embarrassment. I couldn't tell which I felt in greater quantity.

I'd go with Tommy to *Kyros Sky* today. When she left, I'd head straight to the news agency, buy a paper, and apply for the janitor's job. I'd come clean about everything once I had a win to share.

Hopefully.

"Quick, your toast is getting cold," Tommy hollered.

That got me out of the bathroom. My arms shook—and no wonder. I barely ate lunch yesterday and didn't eat dinner or breakfast.

"Toast?" I sat on the stool, still wrapped in the towel. "I have that?"

"Y S I S. You don't buy toast. You buy bread and *make* toast," she said, snorting. "And no, you didn't have bread. I made this at home."

I picked up the floppy peanut-butter-covered toast and polished off it—and its sacrificial twin—in six bites.

Tommy's eyes widened. "Hungry much?"

"Didn't have dinner."

She clicked her tongue. "I need to teach you to cook ASAP."

Probably shouldn't bother learning. The rate I was going, I'd be back at the estate before the week was out.

"Turns out, I didn't need to hand over bank details or tax numbers. Live Right pay in cash," I said.

"What?" she demanded. "They pay under the table?"

No idea what that was. "I'm a contractor. I still get annual leave and stuff, but they said I have to pay my own tax. Is that normal?"

A deep frown marred my friend's face. "Not for that type of work. I'd expect a wage and commission or salary and commission. I'm unsure of the exact ins and outs of contracting, but that sounds dodgy as fuck, Basi. Was there anything else weird they said?"

Where do I begin?

A hysterical laugh bubbled up my throat. I clamped my lips together to keep the crazy inside. I wasn't telling her about the bright eyes or nearly pissing myself in the staff room. That would remain my mortifying secret for all time.

"You know that guy who almost ran me over?" I brushed breadcrumbs off the counter as Tommy extracted two peppermint tea bags from her jeans pocket.

The kettle was already boiling—the one kitchen appliance I'd purchased. My stomach growled. Peppermint tea would be perfect for my aching head. I felt hungover.

"Yeah," Tommy replied.

"He's the owner," I said.

"Owner of?" Her eyes rounded. "Of Live Right? No way!"

The business name made me mentally flinch. "Not just the realty place. The entire building. His name is *Kyros.*"

She whispered, "*Kyros Sky.*"

I sighed. "Yup."

"Spill, bitch. Did he clear the desk with one powerful stroke and have his wicked way with you?"

What? "Jesus. No!"

"Lame," she muttered, focusing her attention on the front ties of her black top. The garment would look medieval on anyone else. With dark jeans on, she just managed to look sexy with a capital S.

If only she knew the whole story.

I'd throw her a bone. "He came in while I was bending to get under the desk."

Tommy didn't ask why I was bent over, just waved me on.

"He came in. Sat down. And then he said," I lowered my voice, "*I'm sitting. What was the other thing? Oh, yes. Sit and rotate.*"

Amusement lit her gaze.

I crossed my arms. "He spun in my office chair."

"No way. That's hilarious."

"Hardly," I scoffed.

Tommy patted the air. "Calm your farm, I'm on your side."

Damn straight she was. "Then he started rolling up his sleeves."

Her face screwed up. "Why?"

"Dunno."

"Nice forearms?"

"You better believe it. Anyway, he'd pissed me off. I grabbed my bag and went to leave."

Tommy slid my steeped peppermint tea across the bench toward me. "To be clear, you didn't have sex on the desk?"

I cradled my drink, drawing forth the smirking image of his face. "I can safely promise never to go there. I've never met such an arrogant fucker in my life."

Taking a sip of her drink, Tommy fluttered her lashes above the rim of the mug. "This Kyros is your boss, yes?"

"Correct."

She cackled in glee. "This is gonna be epic."

"No, it won't," I snapped.

Tommy lowered her drink, chestnut eyes searching my face.

I blew out a breath. "Sorry. Yesterday tuckered me out, and I'm crabby."

"Forgiven. I remember starting full-time work. I slept and ate for at least a year. It'll get better, I swear. Your body just gives up at some point and you forget what relaxation feels like. Plus, it's the weekend in two days. Starting mid-week has some perks."

Two days was an insurmountable task when it came to *Live Right*. I was sticking with the plan I formulated in the bathroom.

"Before I forget. Here's my old phone." She drew out a piece of junk I knew well. It was the reason I'd gifted her my phone last Christmas. The phone she'd had was an archaic beast.

"But." She hesitated, pulling out the sleeker model I'd gifted her.

My eyes narrowed. "Don't you dare say what you're about to say."

Wisely, she slid the sleeker model back into her back jeans pocket and picked up the beast again. "The battery lasts an hour. You can only call and text on it. But it's something at least. You really worried me last night, Basil."

"I'm sorry," I mumbled again, taking the phone. The beast felt far more like a bludgeoning weapon than a phone, but I was careful not to make fun of it. Tommy saved for a year to afford this thing.

"What does this part do?" I asked, pointing to the bulky posterior of the phone.

Tommy choked on a laugh. "That's the battery."

My lips parted. *Oops.* "Well, shit."

I followed her into peals of laughter which, I'm not gonna lie, felt almost therapeutic. I held the beast phone to my forehead in a mock salute. "Thanks, Tom."

"You're welcome. Now, go get dressed, you big ol' grown-up head. I'll meet you at the bus station in an hour."

Ugh. That.

I walked her to the front door. She'd left it propped open—couldn't blame her.

Tommy squeezed halfway out the door and stopped to look back at me, squealing, "I can't believe we're going to work together. This is the start of something great, Basi. You'll see."

When she left, I pushed and grunted until the door closed, resting my forehead against the cracked paint of the wood.

Fuck.

"Theodore wants to meet up after work today," Tommy said, peeking at her skinny phone that could take pictures. Unlike *some* phones.

We'd just walked past *Montgomery's,* Tommy holding the ends of her khaki cardigan wide to *protect my outlaw butt* from the weedy teen.

Every step took me closer to *Kyros Sky. My* palms were already slick with sweat.

"Who's Theodore?" I asked. "Wasn't his name Dean?"

"Dean who? Theodore is the total hottie who came into work yesterday making business enquiries for his dad's catering company."

"Tell me everything. Right now."

Tommy snorted. "That's all I have. It's only been a day. Except... I've never felt the floor disappear from under me before. And I did when I saw him for the first time."

Uhm, oh my god. That was an admission and a half from my bestie. "Is this one for keepsies then?" I stole a look at her.

She tucked her phone away and rearranged her cardigan. "Early days, Basil."

"Hypothetically speaking, if you still liked this guy a lot after a few weeks, would you have the exclusivity discussion with him?" I'd wanted to quiz her on this subject for a while.

Tommy bit her lip. "I don't know. I like things to be new and exciting—that weightless feeling at the beginning of a fling. I don't want stuff to get old and boring."

Tommy's parents divorced when she was young. Her mother left Bluff City and rarely contacted her. Was that what bothered my friend? She thought once the honeymoon period was done that people no longer cared for each other?

"I see what you mean," I admitted. "Though relationships change, Tom. The first few months is all infatuation that doesn't mean much, even though he's all you can think about at the time. After that, things get deeper, slower, and you really get to know the other person."

"You're basing that off your one relationship with Ricky Pikar when you were nineteen?"

I smiled. "Yes. And *Fernando's Eighth Ab.*"

"Marjory never stood a chance," Tommy whispered, licking her lips. "He had *eight* abs to start. Then there was that twist at the end where he had ten."

Husky laughter bubbled up my throat. How the hell was I capable of mirth when the high-rise of doom was looming ahead?

"But Serious Street." I caught her hand and tugged her close. "Don't look at relationships as permanent. Look at them as an exploration or experiment. If you don't like it, then maybe relationships aren't for you right now—or at all. That's fine too."

She brushed a strand of short brown hair off her cheek. "Theodore may be a terrible lay. I won't hold my breath just yet."

"That's my girl."

I eyed the alcove of *Kyros Sky*, trying to keep my breathing steady.

"How many levels to this obnoxious fucker?" she asked.

My lips twitched. "The man or the building?"

"From what you told me the man only has one. The building."

"No idea. I'm on Level 44."

She entered the alcove. "Let's check the elevator numbers."

Uh.

This was the part where she left so I could escape.

I hurried after Tommy, watching as she pushed the call button. We stood in silence as the arrow pulsed, the whoosh of the lift akin to the downward rush of a guillotine.

Ding!

That ding was creeping up the rankings of my most hated sounds.

The doors slid open, and I stared at the beauty within before cursing long and hard in my head.

It was one of them. A fucking bright eye.

"Basi," she greeted, stepping out into the lobby. "We didn't get a chance to meet yesterday. I'm Katerina. You'll tag along with me for the next couple of weeks."

A glance at Tommy confirmed she was open-mouthed and staring at the goddess before us. And Katerina had nothing on Angelica or *him*. Her eyes didn't seem as intense. Muted somehow.

My heart raced, but my head wasn't pounding in her presence like with Angelica.

"Hey," I said, aware I had a charade to play along with. "It's nice to meet you."

Tommy slid a look at me, waiting for an introduction. Smiling widely, I slipped inside the elevator and studied the numbers.

"Sixty-six," I muttered at her.

My friend's brows shot up. There were a lot of high-rises in Bluff City. But even I hadn't been in one with so many levels.

"Are you ready to go?" Katerina asked, glancing between the pair of us.

Tommy eyed me, a wrinkle appearing between her brows, but I wasn't dragging her into this mess. No way. I was already cursing myself for using her last name on my forms. None of this, whatever this *was*, could come back on her.

I swung my hair back. "Sure. I'm ready."

To Tommy, I said, "I'll catch you tomorrow. You can tell me how your date goes."

She blinked a few times, and her obvious hurt kicked me in the smalls. This type of interaction rubbed at scars she'd carried for a lot of years. But I'd rather hurt her a little by having her think I didn't want to introduce her to my fancy friends than to actually bring harm to her door.

Tommy forced a smile. "Will do. Have a good day, Basil."

Some of my tension drained away. "You too, girl."

I focused my attention on Katerina, whose narrowed eyes showed sharp intelligence. *Yikes.*

The woman pointed to an entrance in the far corner that I hadn't noticed. "My car is in the garage."

Here was the moment I'd waited for. Tommy was gone. While Katerina's presence wasn't ideal, she was just one person. Freedom beckoned from mere steps away.

"Will we be at home visits for most of the day?" I asked, rushing through the maths in my head. Two days of pay could extract me from my predicament. For another week. One day of pay would only allow me to pay rent.

She cocked her head. "We'll come back for your lunch break and go out again until later. There will be research to do in your office for the last hour of the day."

In other words, today would be nothing like yesterday.

Every fibre of my being had resisted return. And yet now I was here...

I had to do it.

Eight hours of misery and I'd be about to afford rent for this week and the next. It was time to toughen up.

"Sounds good to me." I lied.

I followed the woman into a low-ceilinged dark garage that appeared to occupy the entire ground floor. Row upon row of shining cars greeted my eyes—ruby reds, titanium, and black hues. I wasn't a car enthusiast, but I could spot a rich car from a mile away. Everyone in this skyscraper was loaded.

Katerina led me to a royal blue car that I nearly had to crawl onto the passenger seat of. With a graceful twist, she eased onto the driver seat.

"Nice wheels." I pulled my pack free and shoved it by my feet.

She patted the steering wheel. "I purchased this with the last commission I earned for securing a house."

I brushed aside the urge to ask what securing meant. I wasn't sticking around. I didn't care. It was slang for their illegal dealings. "Nice."

Without warning, Katerina zipped the car out of the park. The back tyres slid on the polished concrete, the rubber squealing.

My hands splayed against the window and dashboard in reflex. "Holy sh—"

"I like to drive fast," she said apologetically.

No kidding. I was thrown to the left as she left the garage and entered traffic, slotting between two trucks. Reaching for my seat belt, I clicked it in place. "I can see that. While I'm in the car, would you mind driving slower?"

"You don't like the way I drive?" Her voice dropped.

My heartbeat rocketed. "It's not that," I blurted. "I get car sick. I wouldn't want to barf all over your Italian leather."

Her cute upturned nose scrunched. "I see. I'll go slow."

She made it sound like I'd asked for a kidney. "Thank you."

Slow turned out to be just over the speed limit—preferable to her audition for *The Fast and the Furious.*

She gave me a rundown as we left Grey. "We're heading to a house in Green this morning. It's owned by an elderly man."

"He's looking to sell?"

Katerina frowned, and the action drew my attention to her lips. Did she get injections because they were impossibly full and soft? Normally injections made lips look puffy and painful, but she was pulling it off.

"That's what we're hoping," she answered.

I processed that. "He's unsure?"

"They always are."

Was this sage advice for the new trainee? It felt like she was saying something more with her words.

She followed the signs to Green and we screeched through street after street of emerald roofs. I'd visited this suburb a few times. They had cute winding streets with Instagrammable brunch spots. Grandmother and I had visited a few of them.

"You're shadowing me," Katerina said. "I'll introduce you, and if the client talks to you, just answer politely. Otherwise, leave the business talk to me. Watch and listen. Tonight, I want you to take notes of everything you recall. There's a kind of *script* we loosely adhere to."

"I can do that." It was a shame we didn't start with this yesterday. Today was already miles better than Wednesday.

She slowed down when we reached a quiet corner in Green. The street sign read *Gentry Street*. Turning, she soon eased the car into a sweeping driveway with neat hedges.

"We have to drive slower on the street of sale in case a client is watching," Katerina explained, baring her teeth.

I nearly chuckled at her bitter tone, except she was out of the car in a blink.

I extracted myself from the car and hurried after her. I caught up at the front door and she shot me a disapproving look. I grimaced a fake apology and spun as the front doors were pulled open.

"Mr Hartly," Katerina said, smiling at full wattage.

The man paled. The staff at *Live Right* needed to stop smiling.

"Might we come in to continue our talk from the other day?"

Did the wolf use similar words when trying to get inside the houses of the three pigs?

The man swallowed and glimpsed at the screen door sitting between him and Katerina. I could almost hear him processing that the screen was flimsy and wouldn't keep her out.

He nodded and pushed the screen ajar. His watering blue eyes rested on me and his shoulders visibly eased.

Not just me then.

Though I wasn't having as much trouble with Katerina. Which made about as much sense as being afraid of teeth.

The man shuffled through the wide hall, almost side-on. He wasn't comfortable with my mentor at his back? Poor old man had to be eighty or more.

I stepped in front of Katerina so I was between Mr Hartly and her.

Monkeys had to stick together.

There were a lot of strange things going on in my life, but the simple fact that I just inserted myself between two people—because my gut identified one as a fucking predator—should have sent me off the deep end. Except the work hangover I'd woken with was still rampant. It was almost like I was in some kind of autopilot survival mode. Either that or I'd given up on my situation.

I had zero idea what was going on aside from my hypnotist mafia theory. And I wasn't stupid enough to open Pandora's box. I'd go with the flow until the end of the day, get my money, and get the hell away from them all.

Next time, I'd apply for the stupid paper run.

Mr Hartly led us to the lounge and eased onto the sole La-Z-Boy. Letting Katerina pass me, I caught her warning glare. This time I didn't apologise. I connected far more with people of Mr Hartly's age, being raised by my grandmother and her close-knit circle of friends.

Katerina walked to the sofa facing him and sat. I followed and perched at the opposite end. A low table sat between us and the older man, and I could tell he felt better for the buffer.

"Thank you for seeing us, Mr Hartly," she said. "This is my trainee, Basi Tetley. She's an up-and-coming star at Live Right Realty. Are you okay with her being here?"

"Y-Yes," he wheezed, watery eyes begging me not to go.

I smiled, and his brow cleared a smidgen.

"As you know, Live Right is interested in purchasing your property."

Hold the phone. We were buying *off* him? Not brokering a sale between him and a buyer?

Mr Hartly blinked several times. "Yes. I'm not sure I understand—"

Katerina dipped her head at his half question and interjected. "House prices in Green are forecasted to continue dropping over the next year. Lower house prices wouldn't usually be an issue, except no one is rushing in to buy the bargains—and they haven't for several years. In short, the house market is crashing, Mr Hartly, and Live Right wants to stop that happening."

Was that a normal thing for real estate companies to do?

Mr Hartly was a step ahead of me. "So you're buying a heap of houses so the properties don't become worthless?"

"Correct," she said. "And by doing so, we're preventing thousands of owners from losing money on investments."

"Then what?" he asked, eyes narrowing.

Phew. Go Mr Hartly.

"Then when the population *does* start buying again, we sell the houses back to the public for the price we paid," she answered smoothly.

My doubt was echoed on the old man's face. I wasn't sure I swallowed any of that.

His bushy brows climbed. "I'm meant to believe a business of Live Right's magnitude isn't profiting from this at all? Why would any business take such a risk? You people must be forking out millions."

Yeah, I was on his side. Her sales pitch was shit. Large businesses were after everything they could get, and having met the owner of *Live Right*, I felt *extra* safe agreeing with Mr Hartly. Kyros didn't strike me as the charitable sort. Everything he did would have a benefit for him. My theory was based entirely off his shoes.

Katerina's voice lowered. "This is a small city as you know, and although we are governed externally, we're a self-sustaining economy. The small scale of that economy has its drawbacks in that our revenue base is smaller. It makes us more sensitive to change in any industry. Unlike a lot of *other* small economies, our largest industry isn't agriculture—it's real estate. So, Mr Hartly, the riskiest course of action—for Bluff City *and* for a realty company—would be for us to do nothing. We need business to continue *being* a business."

Ferocious though she looked, her words rang of truth this time. While my training surrounded international business, I'd heard my grandmother and her friends talk enough on the subject to know Katerina was correct about the drawbacks of an economy of our size.

Mr Hartly glanced around the room. "I bought this home with my late wife. We raised three children here. None of them live in Bluff City anymore though, and this place is too big for me to take care of. I have to hire gardeners and cleaners to keep up with things. I mean, I have savings, but the pension isn't big enough to cover all the costs, you know? I need to sell..."

I knew what he wanted to say. Katerina's Cheshire smile was making him hesitate.

She'd told me to keep quiet, but I couldn't. "You don't want your home to become involved in anything bad."

Blue beams trained on the side of my face. *Eek*.

Mr Hartly faced me.

"*Yes*," he whispered. "How do I know this isn't a scam? I've never heard of a real estate company buying up properties out of the goodness of their heart. It's like that email I got last week—some Norwegian prince who wanted to give me a million dollars."

I cracked a grin. "I get those too."

The wrinkles at the corners of his eyes deepened.

My heart raced under Katerina's attention. Bracing myself, I turned to her, managing not to flinch under her blazing look. She didn't appreciate my impromptu script, I could gather.

Who cares? I wasn't sticking around, and I wouldn't let her bully this man into a sale.

"What can you tell me about Live Right Realty?" the man asked, darting a look at Katerina, who'd smoothed her expression into pleasant blandness at his attention.

I could fill a book with my experience. "Not much, I'm afraid. I only started yesterday."

The blue beams were back on me. Was she displeased I hadn't lied?

Well, Katerina could join her boss in the act of sitting and rotating.

"But," I added—because I also didn't want to swim with the fishes, "the staff all have nice cars. Which I guess means they're good at their job."

The man scratched his chin. "I don't know if that's a good or bad thing. Where are you from?"

The estates. "Orange," I answered.

He hadn't pegged me as rich?

Day made.

"A nice, honest girl then." He nodded as if that had confirmed his opinion of me.

I guessed girls from the estates were mean and dishonest then. Which was fairly accurate, really. I just liked to believe I wasn't one.

"I try my best," I said, casting my gaze downward.

He shifted his focus to Katerina, who I could feel simmering beneath her smile. "Live Right hired a girl from Orange?"

Katerina leaped at the chance. "If a person possesses the professionalism we pride ourselves on at Live Right, they get the job, Mr Hartly. We don't discriminate."

Sure. Anyone with messed up eyes and teeth was welcome.

His lips pursed. He was considering her offer, I could tell.

Katerina could too.

"Last time we spoke, you decided to have your house valued privately. Can I ask if you went through with that?"

"Sure did," he said, opening a small drawer in the table between us.

He extracted a file. "Bought this place for sixty thousand in the eighties. It was worth ten times that amount two years ago—now it's worth eight. This was always our retirement plan." His eyes misted.

Old people nearly crying was a new one for me. The elderly in my life were fucking ferocious on every front. The idea of them crying was almost laughable.

He passed the folder to Katerina, and she scanned the contents.

"All is in order here. Our own evaluation returned a figure of four hundred and fifty."

"If I'm selling to you, I'll be taking five hundred and ten thousand," he said, setting his jaw. He paled again when she stilled.

"Five hundred and ten thousand?" she repeated in a low voice.

I darted a look between them, wondering if I'd have to leap in the middle and save Mr Hartly's life.

He stumbled over his words. "I don't know what it is you big folk are doing in that tower, but there's something you aren't telling me. You can pay five hundred and ten thousand or you can get out and I'll sell to a good, honest person."

Power to Mr Hartly. He wasn't backing down.

Katerina's tight-lipped expression made me wonder if that was the norm. Or was she intimidating him on purpose in some kind of realty bluff? Every so often, real estate agents came to the estate, but they never behaved like this—if they managed to get through the gate at all. My grandmother would skin them alive if they tried.

Sitting here, witness to the old man's fear, and Katerina's scare tactics… it really was as though she was the mafia and Mr Hartly just an innocent citizen. *Was* Kyros a godfather? Bluff City had an undercurrent of crime like any city. Had I stumbled upon the above-ground face by accident? Were they all on drugs? Did that explain the weird eyes?

Weariness piled on my shoulders. This uncertainty was exhausting.

"I must speak to my supervisor," Katerina said, tilting her chin.

Poor Mr Hartly was sweating up a storm.

She stood in a graceful movement that startled both of us. "I'll be right back."

Fuck me. If Katerina came back with a gun, I was out of here.

As soon as she left the room, Mr Hartly spun to me. "Is she scamming me?"

Did I think she was scamming him? *Yes.* But not with the money side of things. Part of the explanation she gave him rang true, but the rest didn't. Like him, I could sense there was more than they were divulging. Something bad. And, as I'd already pegged, something highly illegal.

Katerina could be listening to this conversation.

Which was why my answer to him was a cool lie. "I believe they mean to prevent the market from crashing. The forecasts in Green really aren't looking good. You'll be in good hands with Live Right, Mr Hartly."

He sighed. "I'm glad. I want to do right by the memories I've had in this house. I want others to have a chance to create such memories too. I may have lost the love of my life, but someone else is with their one-and-only right now, and the thought of them in this house brings me great comfort."

I was going to hell.

Katerina glided back in like the criminal swan she was. "My supervisor cleared me to accept your offer on one condition."

Mr Hartly tensed.

So did I.

This was the part where he signed over his soul, or Katerina cut off an ear.

She opened a folder of papers and twisted the top of the fountain-tip pen, holding it out to him.

A wolfish grin crossed her face. "We need you to sign today."

8

I sat at my office desk typing useless notes. I resisted the urge to insert what I'd really witnessed, unsure of what security Kyros had in place. They couldn't know that I suspected they were an underground mafia of some description.

Today passed without major incident. I still felt wrung out and ready to collapse in a heap—but I'd started the day feeling like crap too. Parts of the day were even interesting. I'd learned that when *Live Right* referred to securing a house, they meant buying it. As for the script Katerina referred to, I'd returned to the car expecting to be scolded. She'd congratulated me instead. The anger. The call to the supervisor. It was all a bluff. It was *Live Right* policy to close the deal the same day.

Which seemed dodgy as fuck.

So I hadn't asked why, but the question had plagued me all afternoon.

I glanced at my phone—henceforth known as Beast—plugged in to charge so the battery didn't go dead every hour.

7:00 p.m.

One more hour to go.

... Unless I returned tomorrow.

This morning, I was adamant I wouldn't return. After *that*, I was certain this was my last shift.

But the day spent with Katerina wasn't terrible.

More than that, a few quick figures had shown that if I finished out this week, I'd have enough money for food *and* transport next week. I'd have all next week to find another job. At lunch, I dropped the last three copies of my résumé off to prospective jobs. One for a position at *Jamieson*—the outlet store where I bought my crappy clothes. Another was for a cashier gig in a fruit store, and the other was for the janitor position. I would literally take *any* other job.

Angelica knocked on the framing of the open door. "How was today, Basi?"

Now was the time to bring up quitting and payment.

I ignored the fear-filled reaction of my body. I was becoming better at compartmentalising it. Otherwise known as being too exhausted to react.

The memory of my hasty budget forecast swam before my eyes.

Dammit!

"Good, thank you," I said firmly.

Her brows lifted. "I'm glad to hear it. I wondered if yesterday overwhelmed you. We have a lot of staff and they've known each other for a long time. But you'll be part of the team in no time."

Awesome. I couldn't wait to be best friends with everyone. "Will most days be like today?"

She smiled, and I blanched, caught unawares.

"Most days, for the next two weeks, yes," Angelica said, taking a step into my office. "After that time, you will operate on your own with a set caseload. I believe Katerina talked you through our process?"

"She did. The visits after lunch were preliminary visits." Which I'd learned were essentially cold calling houses in a bid to get a foot in the door.

"Perfect." Angelica beamed.

My stomach lurched. The sushi roll I'd eaten was considering making a guest appearance.

"You'll be an adept hand in no time." She cooed at me just like Kyros cooed last night. I was still a monkey.

"Once you complete the tasks Katerina set you, you are most welcome to call it a day." With another terrifying display of teeth, she left the room.

If that wasn't incentive to get my work done, I didn't know what was.

Earlier, Katerina presented me with a list of addresses we'd visit tomorrow. I was meant to research them in a system called *Monocle.*

I double-clicked on the icon, and a login tab appeared.

Katerina didn't give me a login. I clicked Enter but was denied.

Shoot. I wanted out of here.

Standing, I smoothed the fronts of my slim fit pinstripe trousers. A thin cream boatneck sweater completed the look. My boobs looked awesome in it.

Striding across the room, I beelined for the reception, glancing around. I really didn't feel like talking to more bright eyes, but I wanted out of this tower more.

"Miss Tetley." A deep voice sounded behind me, and I whirled, hand gripping my throat.

Kyros exited the elevator doors.

I hadn't heard the usual *ding.*

His meadow-green eyes fell to where my hand rested, and I breathed thinly as he swallowed. In a suit again—charcoal this time—he dipped his gaze lower to my breasts. My chest inflated as though he'd forced air into my very lungs. It made it look like I was preening under his attention. Which I was *not.*

My body and mind were on the same page, right?

Right?

"What do you want?" I snapped, turning away to collect myself.

"I'm your employer, Miss Tetley. Don't speak to me that way. I do not tolerate insubordination."

I scanned the reception area anew. Seriously, where did everyone go? Not that I could blame them for avoiding the jackass at my back.

"That's laughable." I glanced back over my shoulder. "You stared at my ass yesterday. You stared at my boobs today. Then there was that little strip tease you did rolling up your shirt sleeves. Or do you treat all your *employees* that way."

He was silent.

I sighed, scanning reception. "Angelica?" I called. "Katerina?"

Anyone?

"Do you require assistance?" he asked. The clip of his business shoes was muffled by the carpet, and only a faint scuff was audible.

I tensed, every muscle in my back drawing tight. How close was he?

And who spoke like that?

Unfortunately, the polite question unsettled me. A battle of exchanged barbs, I'd expected. Helpfulness, not so much. This was the second time he'd switched tactics and used kindness to make me uncomfortable. I'd have to remember that.

Not that I expected to see him again after tomorrow.

Unable to bear him at my back, I faced Kyros, hands on hips. "*Monocle* requires a login. I don't have one. I need to do research on tomorrow's targets."

"Come. You can use mine for now." Without waiting for my reply, he gestured to my office.

Balling my hands at his order, I focused on the end goal. On the way home, I'd get a salad from a little eatery I discovered next to the underground mall. Then I had a date with my cheap and crappy bed.

Kyros stood aside, waving me ahead.

As soon as I moved in front of him, my hackles rose. I didn't like having my back to him *at all*. A gasp lodged in my throat, and I lengthened my steps to put distance between us.

"Are you okay, Miss Tetley?" he asked, deep voice rumbling.

Was he *laughing* at me?

Ignoring the question, I hurried across the room and sat in the desk chair. My discomfort dissipated, and after a shaking inhale, I pointed at the login box still on my screen. What did I say about hindsight before?

I shouldn't have taken the chair.

Kyros rested a large hand on the back of my office chair, right above my head. He leaned forward to grip the computer mouse—or crush it.

But my mind was on other things. Like his torso brushing my shoulder and the unyielding line of his jaw. I closed my eyes, battling with my ovaries, and trying to recall the fear of thirty seconds ago.

He smelled fucking incredible.

I'd never encountered the cologne before, which surprised me. I inhaled, and the earthy, citrus scent filled my head. I usually noted people's choice of fragrance. But never before had someone's natural musk mixed so effortlessly with the product meant to enhance and entice the sense of smell.

It had to be custom made.

I opened my eyes as he straightened, studiously ignoring the way my thighs were squeezing together. It had been a *long* time. I'd gone off rich boys—the ones I knew anyway. While on the estate working here-and-there for grandmother, I'd only spoken with male employees, all of whom were my seniors. There hadn't been many nights out with Tommy in recent months either—working six days a week would do that to a person.

Our gazes locked.

Not a fleck of brown disturbed the intense green of his irises. His face was carved from stone, lips wide and full, and currently pressed together. He disapproved? Interesting considering he'd instigated our nearness.

I frowned, realising how hard we were both breathing.

How close he was.

How my body wanted him, though my mind most certainly did not.

With colossal effort, I dragged my eyes to the screen again. *Monocle* sat open. I wheeled my seat forward, dislodging his grip on the back.

"Thank you," I said. *Fuck.* I sounded like a porn star.

Ah, well. Some things couldn't be helped, but they *could* be ignored. For instance, I wasn't blind to the rise and fall of my chest, and I highly doubted a man with eyes as keen as his would be either. But I could refuse to act on it.

And would.

He lingered, and I refused to look at Kyros, scanning the computer screen instead. None of it registered. Not one bit.

"I'll leave you to it then," he said. The gravel in his voice was the alarm clock every heterosexual woman wanted to wake up to. A bolt of heat shot straight through me, and I jolted at the ferocity.

Whoa, that's a new one.

I grunted through it. "Yep. Bye."

"Good evening, Miss Tetley."

Only when I heard the elevator *ding* did I drop my head into my hands.

Holy shit.

My body just boycotted me, both in terms of fear and desire.

What *was* that?

I stared vacantly at *Monocle*, frazzled mind scrambling over the encounter from the moment Kyros had exited the lift.

Just my luck to run into him at the end of the day. From what I could gather from Katerina, Kyros hardly ever showed on Level 44.

He must have come looking for something.

Except... I saw him arrive, and he went straight to the elevator after our conversation.

Which made it seem a whole lot like he came down here to see me.

Katerina zipped into the towing zone out the front of *Kyros Sky* and shoved the car into park.

I'd returned for the third and *final* day, unsure if I was dumb or brave.

Her eyes fixed on the entrance. A couple lingered there. Only one had bright eyes, so the other had to be a monkey like me.

My mentor scowled at the pair.

"You disapprove?" I asked. I thought they looked pretty darn cute.

She hissed. Like, a legit cat hiss.

In one and a half days, I was over any surprise at her vocal abilities. Katerina made a whole heap of unusual sounds: rumbles, growls, hisses, and a weird gurgling hum when she was happy.

Don't think about it. You're halfway through the day already.

I couldn't fuck it up.

"They shouldn't mix," she snarled.

Say what? Because I couldn't help myself, I blurted, "Why?"

Katerina's face worked and she shot me a veiled look. "Because they're bad for each other."

I stared.

Nope—not getting involved. I pushed open the door and climbed out of her car. "See you at six."

Per her request, I'd complete my two hours of research after lunch today instead of at the end. We had a target in Black this evening that Katerina was nervous about—or so I gathered from her flagrant thwarting of the speed limit.

I slammed the door shut, swinging my pack on. I was on my third and final outfit, a hugging navy blue dress with a square neckline. The dress fell to just above the knee, and I'd layered a puff sleeve white blouse beneath. Despite its *Jamieson* origins, the dress fit quite well.

I set off in the direction of *Sister Sushi*, digging around for my loyalty card. This was only my third lunch break, but the makings of routine made me feel a part of the Bluff City hustle. At lunch, I was just another working woman grabbing a bite and looking in the paper for a better job when the cashier wasn't looking. Because she was dirt poor.

Perfectly normal.

"Miss Tetley."

The world hated me.

Kyros leaned against the corner of his skyscraper.

I slid my eyes in the direction of my beloved sushi. I probably couldn't ignore him—I'd stopped for too long.

I cursed long and hard in my head, then skirted to join him against the tower so traffic could pass by.

"Kyros." I rushed in an undertone, "What are you doing out of your tower? Don't you know how dangerous it is down here with the common folk?"

He'd tensed at my urgent tone, but relaxed, shooting me an annoyed glance.

I snickered, watching the crowds of Bluff City citizens enjoying their lunch break. "Anyway, lovely to see you. I'm just on my way to get food, so..."

I managed a single step.

"How are you finding the job?" He shoved both hands in his pockets.

I'd buy a magazine with that on the front cover, but it was incredible how easily he conveyed that he'd rather be elsewhere.

"Small talk, Kyros?" I tilted my head back to meet his gaze, feeling my hair swinging across my shoulder blades.

His eyes followed the silky slither of my butter-blonde tresses. My hair was the ultimate wing woman. Except my hair didn't consult my head, just my reproductive organs. Which had never been a problem before this man.

I had to admit that Kyros's hair was no two-dollar shop wig either. The sides were shaved, and the top middle section longer. The toffee-coloured strands were styled back, not a lock out of place. It was a modern style that could make or break a person.

The jerk pulled it off.

He pushed off the walk and straightened, cutting off my view of the good people of Bluff City. "Small talk. Straight talk. Loud talk. No talk. You don't seem to like any of it."

Searching his face, I didn't immediately answer. His comment implied that he'd tried several different approaches with me. Flattering, I supposed, but we hadn't talked that much. And those few interactions were tense with a capital T.

I was well aware of my attractive physical qualities—not deluded enough to think men would fall in love with me after a single come hither. Then there was his obvious reluctance to be in my presence.

Consider me confounded.

"Maybe it's the person I'm talking to." The words would bounce off his swollen ego anyway.

He dipped his head to mine, and my palms slickened. I gasped for air as he pushed closer again. The space between us disappeared.

Cloying. Heady.

"You're attracted to me," he stated.

Yep. Ego to spare.

"*Physically*," I managed to puff out, enjoying his answering surprise when I didn't deny his accusation. "Neither of us are mentally, emotionally, or spiritually attracted to the other. Our bodies may want each other, but one in four odds aren't enough."

His attention on me was so intense that a whine slipped between my teeth.

"What gives you the impression that I'm only physically attracted to you?" Kyros leaned against the building again. "And, if that is the case, surely one in four odds is enough to satisfy our urges?"

Warmth pooled low in my stomach. *Whoa, Nelly*, I had urges alright. And no doubt he could satisfy each one several times over.

A one-time thing was tempting. Extremely so. If Kyros wasn't connected to, well, his illegal tower, I wouldn't have hesitated for a second.

This was my last day at *Live Right Realty*.

I refused to take any part of it with me.

"You don't like being near me, Kyros. I don't know if the conversation is painful for you or if you've taken a dislike to me. Really, I have no idea why you're punishing yourself by talking to me. With all that said, it is definitely against my will to be near you, so that should answer both your questions." Smiling, I swung my pack to the front and dug for my glasses. He'd turned my hunger for food into hunger for time between the sheets, so I'd go to the agency first to read the paper.

I slipped my thick-rimmed glasses on and dropped the case back into my bag. When I looked up, his mouth was slightly ajar. He blinked at me.

Whatever.

I glanced down the street again.

"Basi, is that you?"

I searched for the speaker. A real smile widened my face. "Rhys? Hey!"

Rhys scanned me head to toe. "You got the job?"

I shrugged a shoulder, remembering my *boss* was behind me. "Seems like it."

He wore suit pants today. Shirt untucked. Not neat and tidy like Kyros. Casual and comfortable. "You got a job too?" I asked.

"Sure did. Got lucky with a car sales yard." Rhys stared over my head, and when he looked back, I made a face only he could see, darting my eyes pointedly to where Kyros lurked.

Amusement flitted over his handsome face. "Are you heading out for lunch?"

He was going to save me from Kyros? *My hero.* "I'd planned to. Sister Sushi."

"The bacon and avocado roll?"

"I never knew that sushi combo existed. I'm obsessed." I laughed, and Rhys sucked in a breath at the husky sound.

His eyes darkened. "Join me then. My shout. You can tell me about your job. We can swap war stories."

Hells yes! I was on a budget. If I ate a few rolls on his dime, I wouldn't need dinner. And Kyros just made me hot and bothered. I'd redirect that heat to the boy next door. He wouldn't lead me directly to hell without passing GO.

"It's a date." I smiled archly.

"Miss Tetley." Kyros's rumbling voice vibrated through me. "You have work to do."

The outrageous words took a few beats to register. "You're fucking me?"

"Not yet."

He couldn't say that. That wasn't legal... was it?

"My break is two until four." I protested.

"Is there a problem?"

I jumped at Rhys's voice. *Shit*. Forgot he was here. The amused glint in Kyros's eyes suggested he might have noticed.

His eyes hardened, settling on Rhys for a beat before returning to me. The warning was clear. And though Kyros's assholery made me want to throttle him, I had to remember all the dodgy shit happening in his tower.

I smoothed my expression, turning to Rhys. "Apparently something has come up. How about I grab your number? We can head out another time. Maybe this weekend?"

His cheeks reddened. *Adorable.*

I pulled out my pen, batting my lashes. "I have no paper. You'll have to write on my arm."

He chuckled. Rhys reached for my hand, flipping it over to slide calloused hands up my forearm. *Mmm.* I shivered. That slow stroke was a promise of hidden talents. Consider me pleasantly surprised.

Rhys took his time about jotting his number on my skin—which I doubly appreciated because I knew it would be killing the butthole behind me.

"Thanks." I met his eyes.

"Talk soon, Basi," he replied.

After that forearm play, I was game for more than talking. What was it with forearms lately?

Rhys was swept up into the stream of pedestrians and quickly lost from sight.

"Are you done playing with the boy?"

If he expected me to back down, he could think again. Rich people had zero qualms about speaking their minds. I whirled on Kyros. "You just cock-blocked me! That's low."

He grinned.

Had I expected an apology? Not for a second.

"Don't complain when I return the favour," I said savagely, stomping back in the direction of the tower.

Straight into a passer-by.

This time the coffee splashed down my arm.

Kyros darted out a hand and gripped my forearm as I found my feet again.

"So sorry," I gasped at the person through the pain of hot coffee on my skin. *Ouch.*

The young man wasn't looking at me though. He stared at the man still gripping me. Breathing hard, the male dropped his gaze to the ground, entire body trembling.

Crap. I was shaking too.

Looking at Kyros would evaporate me into the same submissive heap. And that was a fucking crazy thing to even *think*. Yet the truth of it was infallible in my mind.

"Kyros," I murmured without budging. My knees trembled on the verge of collapse. "I stepped into this man, not the other way around."

His hand slipped down to my wrist, but he shifted it back to circle my forearm.

I sucked in a breath. "I'd like to wash the hot coffee off my body. Just when you're ready."

That did it. Grunting, Kyros tugged me toward the alcove of *Kyros Sky.* The man crumpled in a heap behind us, and I followed, eyes wide.

What the hell was happening?

"You need to watch where you're going," he snarled.

Air lodged in my throat. "No kidding." I managed to choke out.

He released me, and I darted a look up as my body stopped shaking and my breath evened out.

This was getting out of control. I'd yammered on about spiritual disconnect and *blah blah*, but there were huge issues between us. One, his illegal fucking skyscraper. Two, whatever the hell he was. Because normal people couldn't do that.

Normal people didn't make other people want to cry for their mothers.

"Kyros," I started, approaching the subject like a grown-up. "I'm gonna need you to stay the fuck away from me."

Well, it started out good.

He scoffed, and anger flashed deep inside me.

I scowled. "I'm serious. I don't like this possessive bullshit you've got going on. You've gotten in your head that we should suffer each other's company, and I have no idea why. I don't care, and I don't give a single fuck if you're my boss. Cut the immature games and leave me alone."

I pushed the elevator button, then studied him again. "Struck speechless. It's a good look on you."

Gloating would be my downfall one day.

Ding!

Ding ding ding all freakin' day. Couldn't wait to bust this joint.

Five hours left.

I stepped inside and the lift doors began to close. Leaning against the back bar, I couldn't help stealing a peek at him.

The muscles in his neck were taut, but his meadow-green focus left mine to trail down my body. Gaze lowered around my middle, he smirked just as the doors sealed.

Pervert.

Or did the coffee get on my clothes after all? I did a quick scan.

Clear.

Then I noticed black smudges all the way up my right forearm.

"You shitty bastard," I whispered.

Rhys's number was gone.

9

Twenty minutes left of my last day at *Live Right*.

Katerina had just dropped me off after our last prelim visit, so I was on cloud nine—even after Kyros's dick move. *Double* dick move. He'd cock-blocked me *twice*. Normal people respected societal boundaries. Love and sex weren't games.

I'd said I wasn't interested. Hell, I'd given him a statistic of why things wouldn't work. Some people just couldn't take no for an answer, but after tonight I'd never see him again.

My body was in mourning over that. My womb wept for the night that could have been.

Fickle little thing.

I pulled out Beast and opened the only number on there.

I typed:

Plans tonight? <3

The phone was so old I had to click the number nine four times to get an S and forming the love hearts I like to tag onto the end of every text was a nightmare. Though I'd found a cool game on here called Snake. Each time the snake ate a brick, it gained the brick on the end of its tail. I had to dodge the tail as it grew longer and keep eating bricks. On my amended break—4:00 p.m. to 6:00 p.m.—I became addicted.

Beast vibrated.

I have wine

I smiled at Tommy's reply, answering,

Thank duck for that. <3 <3

D didn't take as many clicks as F.

See you after your shift, lovely!

I sighed. Tonight, I'd tell Tommy about all the crap this week.

With careful consideration, I'd realised that resigning face-to-face with Angelica could be dangerous. I'd email her tomorrow. It felt like the coward's route, but I was past the point of caring. She and Kyros could deal. Or not.

Not my problem.

Before I left, I needed my pay. Packing up my belongings, I stacked the folders of properties I'd researched that afternoon to drop at Katerina's desk.

Angelica stood at reception.

"Hey, Angelica."

"Basi. Are those files for Katerina?" She stretched her hand out.

I passed them over.

"Ready for the big weekend?" she asked.

She did small talk about as easily as the Tin Man did yoga.

I smiled. "Just a quiet one for me."

"I find that hard to believe. You're a young woman. Isn't there a significant other in your life?" Her eyes danced, making my stomach churn.

"There would be," I snarled. "But Kyros rubbed his number off my arm."

Oops. Clearly not over that.

Her mouth popped open. "He what?"

I was nearly free. I didn't want to get into a Kyros discussion. "Don't worry about it. Total misunderstanding."

About personal boundaries and appropriate behaviour.

"He shouldn't have done that."

To her credit, though Angelica would probably play the part of rug for the boss man, she looked pissed on my behalf.

"Before I leave, could I get my pay for the week?"

She blinked rapidly. *Whoa.* Really, really fast. That was creepy on an exorcist level.

"Pay?"

I glanced around. "For working this week? You know? My pay."

"Oh." She laughed lightly.

I laughed with her. This conversation was hilarious.

Not.

"We pay fortnightly, Basi. It was on one of the forms you signed. We're on the alternating week right now, so you'll be paid next Wednesday."

All I heard was *next Wednesday.*

"Fortnightly," I repeated, heartbeat thundering in my ears.

"That's common practice for most businesses. The payroll is a big job."

Her words faded to white noise as my stupidity slammed home. This wasn't happening.

I'd assumed people got paid weekly. Yet thinking back, I had nothing to support that assumption. *Nothing.*

My breath always came fast in Angelica's presence, but hysteria now worked its way up my throat.

What was I going to do? I had fifty-five dollars to my name. Not enough for the rent I had to pay on Sunday.

"I—" Licking my lips, I said, "Could you make an exception? I didn't realise pay came fortnightly. I need to pay rent this Sunday."

Those words cost me everything to say.

That's how I knew I was still a fucking rich brat.

Pity lighted her eyes. "I'm sorry, Basi. The company is strict on pay. We had problems a while back with double-paying due to advances such as this. Please understand, the payroll is a huge job. One person doing this kind of thing is easy to accommodate, but yours is the tenth request this week."

"Just once, Angelica?" I pressed, leaving my dignity at the door. "I promise you'll never hear me say these words again."

I hoped to keep that promise. After three days in the real world, I'd learned there were any number of rules I had no idea about.

She stepped back, face firm. "I feel for you, but I can't make any exceptions."

My world imploded like a pyramid of cards.

Turning away, she paused by the desk. "I meant to say I have meetings until 4:00 p.m. on Monday. The others will be in after midday." She slid something to me along the desk. "Here are the keys to the front door, and an electronic tab for the elevator, so you can get onto this level. The tab will disarm all the alarms too."

On autopilot, I reached forward and took the keys.

Then Angelica was gone, and I was left—once more—in a trap of my own making.

I entered the air-conditioned *Toggles a*nd strode to an empty cashier, attempting to look confident. Clint expected rent at 10:00 a.m. tomorrow morning, and I was seventeen dollars short. After a sleepless night, I had three plans to tie me over until Wednesday.

"Hi," I said with a sheepish smile. "I need to return a few things."

The cashier frowned. "Why? Are they damaged?"

I shook my head. "No. I've changed my mind. They aren't... right."

Without a word, the teenage girl pointed at a sign overhead.

Toggles does not offer refunds if the customer changes their mind.

A store credit can be offered at cashier discretion.

A store credit? I considered it. Could I pay Clint in *Toggles* vouchers?

Doubt it.

"Thanks," I said dully, grabbing my bags again that I'd lugged all the way from Orange instead of paying four dollars for the bus.

"Good luck," the teen said with a sad smile.

Awesome. I looked pathetic too. I should have cited damage as the reason—though the cashier would have checked.

... Maybe I could ruin the stuff a bit and go back in when she went on lunch break.

Nearly at the exit, I turned to scan the shop floor. My gaze snagged on a group of staff. The young woman I'd spoken with was whispering to the others.

As one, they turned to me.

Dammit! Didn't need to read minds to figure out the subject of their conversation. There went that plan. I hurried out of the store.

My stomach grumbled and gurgled.

Time for plan two.

Each day this week, I'd walked by a blood donation centre that passed out a thirty-dollar grocery voucher to donors. I had to eat. I'd skipped dinner last night and couldn't go another day. I had a healthy appetite, but I'd exercised unusual restraint since leaving the estate, and didn't have any energy stores at this point. A thirty-dollar voucher would cover food until Wednesday—I'd make it work. Even if I had to eat those noodles that took two minutes to cook in boiling water.

The attendant at the blood donor centre ushered me to the only free seat, where I filled out a form. I had to show my ID, so I used my real name.

Her eyes widened slightly when her gaze skimmed over my surname.

"Right this way, Miss Le Spyre," she said in hushed tones.

I'd never be free of it. "Just Basi, please."

"Of course," she stuttered. "If you could lie down on this bed. An attendant will be with you in a minute."

No doubt they'd be told who I was.

I deposited my *Toggles* bags on an empty chair and hoisted up onto the medical seat. It was more comfortable than my bed.

I flopped my head to each side.

Tubes ran into the wall, disappearing from sight. Is that what they'd hook me up to? My mind summoned the presence of giant vats behind the walls, filled with blood—though I was pretty sure donated blood came in individual plastic pouches. That's how they did it on *Truth Ranges* anyway.

"Miss Le Spyre," a man said.

I squinted at a middle-age male nurse. "Just Basi."

"Of course. I'm Nurse Tim. There are a few questions before we start."

I tuned out, nodding and answering when I had to, and sitting still as he strapped a Velcro band to my upper arm and pierced my vein.

I watched the dark red surge down the tube to where it disappeared behind the wall to whatever lay beyond.

"Good veins," he murmured.

Why did nurses say that? I mean, I was sure large veins were easier to stab, but I found it hard to take compliments to my venous system. "Thanks."

"You know..." Tim started.

I knew that tone of voice.

"—the donor centre is a community-funded centre. This year we're short of our goal. If we don't reach it, we'll have to close down. Thousands of people rely on our centre to survive."

The curse of the rich. Always being asked for money.

Each year, I gave to charities with causes I felt strongly for—led by my grandmother's example. I wanted to help those in need. But when places like this learned who I was, they saw a dollar figure. It got really old.

"I'm sorry, Tim. I don't have any money to spare."

"Oh… I must have misread your last name."

"Le Spyre is my last name," I answered, hoping against hope he'd drop it. "I don't have any money to spare. I hope that the donor centre reaches its goal though. It's a great cause."

My effort to soften the blow fell on deaf ears.

He pressed his lips together, sticking a plaster over the small wound. "There you go. All finished."

Nurse Tim turned to leave.

I died a little inside. "The grocery voucher?"

The nurse wasn't quick enough in hiding his accusatory look. "What? The incentive?"

Contempt filled his words. *That* I wouldn't put up with. Sitting, I fixed him with a direct look. "You give the voucher to people who donate blood, correct?"

Tim averted his eyes and ducked out of the curtained-off space. A minute later, ferocious whispers erupted on the other side. Even with the coincidental timing, I heard enough to confirm I was the subject.

Swallowing hard, I stood and picked up my *Toggles* bags.

Shoving back the curtains, I had the minute satisfaction of seeing the gathered group of nurses jump.

Face impassive, I scanned them all.

Tim approached with my voucher, holding it out.

"Thank you, Nurse Tim." I took the voucher and dipped my head like a fucking queen before turning to leave.

Just get outside.

"You could change thousands of lives in one second with the money you have."

I halted at the woman's voice.

"You rich people have no idea." She continued.

No, we didn't. But in this regard, the woman really was barking up the wrong tree. I channelled my inner grandmother, still facing the exit.

"Do you know how the rich stay rich?" My tone could have peeled paint.

For the first time this week, I was the predator.

"They keep the rest of the world poor and *compliant*," I finished. No matter how much I disagreed with their tactics, the truth of the statement was incontestable.

Head held high, I walked out...

... Leaving my battered spirit on the floor.

9:50 a.m.

Clint would be here any minute. Only the plan at the donor centre worked out. So I was onto my last idea—to bluff like this city was named after me.

I had my pack on with all my important stuff, just in case he took the keys. I'd have to ask for help from Tommy to shift the stuff out and highly doubted Clint would give me the day to get it done. The bastard would make me arrange a time and probably charge for it.

But I had a few negotiation points up my sleeve. I hoped.

Turned out Clint was punctual when it came to money collection. At 9:59 p.m., he rounded the corner.

"Good morning, Clint," I greeted, careful not to sound falsely bright. Nothing irked my grandmother more.

If you have to get out of a tight hole, don't look like an idiot doing it.

No skin off my back. I'd looked like an idiot more than enough lately.

"Morning," he grunted, wiping his nose on his sleeve.

Coming from him that was almost good manners. I would have liked to reward his behaviour with rent money. *Alas.* "How would you like $150.00 for rent this week?"

A momentary greed was wiped out as suspicion lit his face. "You can't pay."

"Turns out my job pays on Wednesdays every other fortnight. To be fair to you, I'm offering to fork out $150.00 for the next two weeks."

His chins wobbled as he laughed. "I knew a rich bitch didn't have a hope of getting the cash together."

The tables would not turn. "Clint, I've warned you about that kind of talk before."

"You think I give a fuck? You've stayed free in my house for four nights and can't pay rent. I'm out of pocket."

Rise above, Basi.

"I have forty-three dollars to give you now as a good faith payment." I needed the rest for the bus until Wednesday.

Clint wiped his nose again. "Rent just increased to $175.00 each week."

Don't stomp. Don't put your hands on your hips. "That's not happening and you know it. Work with me, Clint. You get to keep a great tenant. I don't have to lug my stuff to a new place. And I *will* do that, unless you compromise."

He darted his eyes past me.

My heart sank. *Bad move.* Shouldn't have mentioned having *stuff*.

He rounded on me. "Give the keys."

Clint was a bottom feeder. I hadn't failed to notice that in our interactions. But I never would have come here if I believed he'd try to intimidate me. We were on the *street.*

... The empty street.

He shoved my shoulder, and I stumbled back more shocked than hurt.

"Keep your fucking hands to yourself," I gasped. I put the key between two of my fingers and made a fist.

Clint had a good double-chin-shaking laugh at that. Every trace of mirth drained from his face, a greasy contemplation taking its place. Ironically, my heart was beating nowhere as fast as it had at *Live Right* during the week. In fact, I regarded the slimy man almost impassively. Yet I'd be a fool to disregard the very real danger just because his eyes weren't blazing.

"The keys, bitch," he snarled. "Or we're going to have a problem."

The words *do you know who you're messing with*, balanced on the tip of my tongue. I refused to let them past.

"I'll need time to get my stuff out," I told him. Neither of us missed the tremor in my voice.

A slow grin spread across his face. "Consider that your rent payment."

My jaw dropped. Like fuck it was. I didn't dare tell him the contents of the house were worth far more than my rent payment.

"And I'm keeping your bond."

"No you won't," I spat back.

Clint rushed me.

I'd always assumed I'd have time to defend myself from a man of his hulking size.

I managed to stab him with the key once. He shoved me back, following quickly to deliver an eye-ringing slap. The ground seemed to slope, but as the ground raced toward me, Clint kept a ruthless hold around my upper arm.

I half crawled, half stumbled to remain upright, blinking through the ringing in my head.

"You little slut," he growled. "Listen good. You never paid me a bond. We never had a contract. You never stayed here. Got it? Come back and I'll slit your throat."

I whimpered as my bone screamed in protest of his increasing grip. He was going to snap my arm.

"I won't." The sob left me.

"Keys," he hissed in my face. "Now."

Through blurring eyes, I stared into his beady eyes, lodged too close together. Lifting the hand with the keys firmly lodged between my knuckles, I dropped my gaze.

Clint loosened his hold.

I jerked my knee as hard as I could upward, crushing his junk. Shouting, I sliced the pointed edge of the key across his flabby cheek.

He howled, stumbling aside, hands cupping his crown jewels.

And I ran.

I ran.

And I didn't stop.

10

I'd been assaulted.

My pride was forgotten. The time to involve Tommy was now. I needed help to fight Clint and get my stuff back. There might even be an agency or something that could help me. Tommy would know who to approach because I sure as fuck didn't know the rules of this world.

The problem being that in the throes of panic, I ran for twenty minutes straight. I was in Pink now. That's how far adrenaline carried me.

Beast! I could call Tommy! Yanking the phone out of my pack, I stared at the blank screen, clicking the power button.

Nothing.

Sighing, I glanced around the intersection. I'd never been to Pink. I could only recall driving through the place to get somewhere else. I went to Tommy's in Orange, Green for brunch, and Blue and Black for high-end shopping, dining, and entertainment. I'd been to Red once, too—to a club with Tommy.

It was midday, and I had no idea where I was. The memory of the sprint here was a blur.

I dabbed at my cheek and nose, checking for blood. There wasn't any, but my face fucking hurt.

"Excuse me?" I called to a younger woman carrying a few plastic bags.

She glanced up, her eyes widening as she backed away.

Crap. I probably looked like a zombie. "Can you point me in the direction of Orange?"

Still backing away, she flung an arm out.

"Thanks!" I started back for Orange, my pack thumping against my lower back. At least I had the presence of mind to take the crucial stuff out of Clint's apartment.

I'd go straight to Tommy's. She'd ring her father and he could get some friends together. I'd have to crash at their house for another week. Maybe more. No doubt he'd tell grandmother. But rushing into things had only brought trouble and regret to my door thus far.

I had to stop being so fucking naive and ignorant. This wasn't a cute game of *Sims*. There were rules and complexities I was ignorant of that were getting me into trouble.

Trouble like finding myself *legitimately* homeless with fifty-five dollars and the remains of a grocery voucher to my name until Wednesday. I worked for some kind of mafia godfather and was trapped working in his illegal tower because of my financial situation. I'd lied to Tommy most of this week.

Where did the chaos begin and where did it end?

Absorbed in berating myself, it took a few minutes too long for the purple roofs to register.

"Purple." I gasped.

She pointed me in the wrong direction! Or had I misinterpreted her flailing arm for help?

I sank down onto the curb, my insides quivering as panic tried to push me over the mountain top so I could free-fall down the other side.

I wanted my grandmother. I needed my grandmother.

Beast couldn't go on the internet—when the stupid phone

deigned to work—so I hadn't checked my emails since leaving the estate. The work computers only contained *Monocle.*

The public library. I lifted my head.

I could use their computers. Tommy helped me get a card when we went to type up my résumé.

I was closer to Grey than Orange at this point, and my soul craved contact with someone familiar. Someone who could protect me for a night. A person who would set me on the right path.

For me, that was either Tommy or Agatha Le Spyre.

Wrestling with the urge to give up, I set off for the skyscrapers of Grey—their tips visible over the rise of a hill.

The library was a popular place on the weekends, apparently. Waiting in line for one of the four computers gave me time to recollect some of my reason though. With greater reign over my mind, I could see that shock had me in its vice-like grip. Tendrils of desperate fear still curled around my chest.

"Number seven," a librarian called.

I stood, and an elderly lady waved me over to the third computer.

The internet was surprisingly fast and too quickly I was staring at my grandmother's email in my inbox.

She hadn't emailed again, but that wasn't her style.

Delaying the moment, I deleted my junk mail and read another email from Angelica apologising for our conversation on Friday. She hoped I understood company policy about the advancement of funds.

I hoped she understood that I was just physically assaulted and robbed because I hadn't had an extra seventeen dollars.

Then again, it wasn't up to *Live Right* or any business to pull me out of financial trouble. It wasn't even the responsibility of my family or friends or the system. I had two feet to stand on like everyone else.

Just click the damn thing.

Squeezing my eyes shut, I tapped the mouse icon on the email from Agatha Le Spyre.

Squinting through one eye, I skimmed over the email.

I love you, Basilia.
You will always succeed.

My forevermore love,
Your Grandmother

A burning slammed the space behind my eyes. Tears had remained in the background for days. The urge to cry was so fierce it overwhelmed the throbbing heat from the slap I'd received.

I breathed deeply, resting my head on the desk.

Don't cry.

There was a time for tears. And that was when a child's parents died. *Then*, a person was allowed to cry their tiny heart out.

I sucked in breath after breath and, in those agonising moments, came as close to crying as I had in twelve years.

When I'd regained control, I read the email again, swallowing back the surge of emotion a second time.

How had she known I'd need this?

My grandmother was fucking magic. That was how.

I came in here needing her. Guidance. Love. Somehow she supplied that in two short paragraphs that she sent the night I left the estate.

My heart swelled.

I re-read her sign-off. *My forevermore love.* It was something she started saying after my parents' death.

Lifting my head, I trailed my gaze over the first paragraph again, drinking her words in.

You will always succeed.

My grandmother believed in me. Even though I'd left her and refused to be part of the rich bullshit. She was still rooting for me.

In my eyes, the two sentences in the top paragraph were linked.

I would succeed because people loved me.

As soon as I could afford to, I'd go see my grandmother. Before, I'd seen that as admitting defeat. Not anymore.

Smiling even if the gesture didn't quite reach my soul right now, I typed out an email to my only relation.

Grandmother,
I caught the bus the other day
and lived through the experience.

My forevermore love,
Your Basilia

Logging off after, I caught the glares of those who'd been waiting their turn for the computers.

How long had I sat here for?

I nodded to the elderly librarian and left the building, gaping at the twilight sky. That explained the glares.

Butterflies erupted in my gut.

It would be dark soon.

Call me a coward or call me smart, but I wasn't walking to Orange by myself at night. Clint's grip on my arm was an all-too-recent reminder that I could be overcome in a matter of seconds. He could still be out there. Maybe he'd called some friends in to help.

Fool me once, shame on you. Fool me twice, shame on me.

I'd catch the bus back. Wasn't like I had to pay rent anymore.

The library stop was the place I'd first hopped off with Tommy, so I headed there and waited.

... And waited some more.

When the librarian from earlier walked by, I smiled politely. She hesitated before approaching. The woman's hair was confined in a bun at the nape of her neck—in a similar manner to my grandmother's preferred style. That was where the similarities between them stopped.

"The buses stop at 4:00 p.m. on a Sunday," she said, grimacing. "Or are you waiting for someone?"

I didn't know what the time was. Clearly after 4:00 p.m.

Was I waiting for someone? Nope.

Did I have a plan? *Nope.*

She rested a hand on my shoulder. "Do you need help getting someplace, dear? Do you have somewhere to sleep?"

At least I didn't look rich anymore. I must have skipped by the downtrodden nine-to-five-job appearance and proceeded straight to homeless.

Licky Lips probably wouldn't know me.

"Dear?"

I focused on her. As it turned out... "I have somewhere to go."

I waited in the small mall where I stole sneak peeks at the paper each day.

When 9:00 p.m. came around, I rode the escalator to the surface.

Stars twinkled high above, night in full stride.

The city was well lit, but I stuck to the shadows where possible, the memory of Clint all too vivid. My mind was convinced he or his friends lurked behind every corner.

Caught between fear and dread, I stopped in front of *Kyros Sky,* the key and chip that gave me access to Level 44 burning in my hand.

I'd waited until well after closing time, and Angelica had said no one would be here until midday tomorrow, but there was still a risk I'd get caught.

Until I reunited with Tommy, I was homeless. Sleeping on the streets was the very last resort. I could have tried the homeless shelter recommended by the librarian—my response hadn't satisfied her that I had a plan. But *Live Right,* despite the alarming people and their maybe illegal agenda, was my first option.

I preferred the devil I knew.

Slotting the small silver key into the front door, I made sure to lock it behind me. Expecting sirens to howl at any second, I passed the electronic chip over the pad next to the lift.

Months spent in hotel rooms had taught me that much.

I used the chip again inside the elevator and pushed button 44.

My hell.

My salvation.

After the token *ding,* I crept into the reception area, one foot at a time.

No alarms went off, and my insides slowly unclenched.

It was just for a night. For safety. I could charge Beast too. Though I wouldn't text Tommy until morning or she'd come to get me in the dark.

Right now, I was within four familiar walls. I could make do until morning.

I crept into my office, leaving the door ajar in case I had to make a silent getaway.

Crawling under my desk, I opened my pack.

A change of clothes—thankfully work clothes—glasses, purse and cash, grocery voucher, phone and charger, razor, toothbrush, and paste, body wash, and moisturiser.

My list of belongings had increased by a partial grocery voucher and a phone that preferred the early 2000s. Should I laugh or cry about that?

It had to be near ten at night. I was usually a night owl, but not after this hellish week. Not after today.

Yawn after yawn besieged me, yet sleep remained a flittering and distant sonofabitch. Instead, branded on the backs of my eyelids was Clint's ugly mug.

I shuffled onto my other side and tried to find a better spot to nestle my head atop my pack. I was using my spare set of clothes as a blanket.

It was fucking cold in here.

Clint. Toss.

Clint. Turn.

Clint. Clint. Clint.

At first, I thought the muted thud was in my head. I'd been replaying the part where I'd run. The muted thud was my bag rising and falling against my back.

I only froze when someone laughed.

My eyelids flew open.

Holy fuck.

Someone was up here.

I wasn't alone.

The woman laughed again. A lover's laugh. A man echoed the sound in a deep baritone, their conversation a mere murmur of indistinct words.

I covered my mouth. *Shit!* This was bad. I mean, I could explain the situation. And would. But receiving a key and then using your workplace as a bedroom looked really bad.

Where were they in the building?

Removing my makeshift blanket, I eased out from under the desk and crept to the door, glad I'd left it ajar.

One of them had turned on an office light beside reception.

I recognised them. It was the young woman and man that Katerina had so strongly disapproved of being together. They'd snuck up here for pretty obvious reasons. The man, somewhere in his thirties, had her pressed against one of the reception benches. Her mini skirt was hiked, one of her feet hooked around his calf.

Who came to work to bang anyway?

At least it looked as though they'd picked their romping spot. I just had to keep quiet and wait for them to go. They had no reason to come into my office—I hoped.

"That's it, baby. You know you want it," he panted. "I trust you."

Jesus. Sexy talk was anything but when I wasn't part of the action.

I cast one last amused glance their way but stilled, squinting.

What the hell?

The office light was catching on the woman's teeth. Her fucking long teeth. The man tipped his head to one side, baring his neck, and—

Jerking violently, I slapped both hands over my mouth as the woman bit into his neck. One of her hands came up to push his head even farther to the side. The other clamped his body against her own.

She drew on him, slurping, swallowing, gulping.

She was drinking his blood.

He moaned, his hips moving against hers. The Bright Eye didn't reciprocate, and his movements weakened. The man's hands clawed at her back, slipping away to the soundtrack of her gurgling swallows.

The monster followed him to the ground, snarling as she ripped into his neck anew.

He stopped moving.

Eventually, she stopped too.

I couldn't blink or think. I couldn't even inhale. Frozen to the spot, fear pulsed unchecked at the thought I was next; that this *vampire*—for that's all she could be, as impossible as that concept was—was thirsty for more.

A switch flicked within her. One moment she was a snapping animal. The next she was screaming bloody murder, shaking the man's corpse.

The man she killed.

"Ryder," the vampire moaned. "No. *Come back*."

She bit her wrist, dripping glistening ruby droplets into his mouth.

I couldn't look away. Terror—*shock*—demanded that I watch until death found me.

She sobbed over her dead lover. Her meal. "Kyros will save you."

Gathering the man in her arms with no perceivable effort, the young woman raced to the emergency stairs, disappearing in a whoosh of air.

I knew then what my mind hadn't fathomed on my first day at *Live Right*. Part of me had understood they weren't human—that they were *other*. My brain had rationalised my reaction to their predatory grace and features and anger.

Not anymore.

I was mentally and physically adrift.

Barefoot, I padded into reception. A pool of blood stained the light-grey carpet, illuminated by the office light. I stared, wondering if I had that much blood inside me.

Continuing to the elevator, I calmly waited for the lift to heed my call.

Ding!

I smiled at the sound and entered, pressing G for the ground floor.

The doors began to slide closed.

Across reception, a door slammed off its hinges, soaring through the area to crash into the wall to my right.

Kyros stopped in front of the bloodstain by reception.

And in the light, his teeth lengthened to fangs.

And in the light, his eyes flooded black.

In the light, the monster lifted his gaze to find me lurking in the shadows.

I waved as the doors sealed.

11

I leaned against the railing in the elevator, ears popping on the speedy descent.

Around level twenty, my numbness parted enough for panic to find me at last. It was a quiet panic to start—a seizing, a stalling... a pained clenching of my insides. My lungs emptied like bagpipes.

They wouldn't fill!

Eyes widening, I gulped. Try as I might, air wouldn't flow past the top of my esophagus. I splayed my hands over the back wall, seeking purchase.

Ding!

The street. I had to get to the street.

I staggered out of the elevator.

Splintering wood exploded in a deep boom. The door to the garage was pushed off its hinges, crashing against the far wall of the lobby before slapping to the tiles.

Kyros stood in the frame of the destroyed doorway, his snarling breaths heavy. How did he get here so fast?

"Spy," he growled.

Black dots crept across my vision, yet I still had room to be confused by that single word he uttered.

My knees gave way, my mouth opening and closing like a fish out of water. I'd been frightened to death? That's what it felt like.

Impossible.

Yet it wasn't.

I'm dying.

I was a gazelle caught in a lion's sight and all I could do was accept my fate. I wavered in kneeling, the monster's seething silhouette blurring.

His footsteps echoed closer.

This is it.

A hand brushed my hair back and, in a menacing voice that would haunt me to the end of my days, the vampire whispered low, "You're not going anywhere."

He sat me up and gripped my chin, shaking my face a few times. I was limp as a doll. My eyes somehow met his.

That was all it took.

I couldn't look away. His eyes were so very green. Now, they blazed into my very soul and the control I'd always had over my mind and body disappeared.

"Breathe," he commanded.

My chest lifted, the expansion of my ribs dragging air into my lungs.

After that, my body remembered how the job went, but spent, I sagged forward against Kyros. He stood and let me smack against the cold tiles.

"How long have you been in their pocket?" he snapped over me.

I sucked in breath after painful breath. Not a single crumb of energy remained within me.

On my back, I stared at the man glaring down at me. Not a man. A *vampire.*

Kyros stopped, tilting his head as he contemplated me.

"You're not dying before I know what you've told them." The words ripped from his chest like a tiger's furious warning, and he crouched to pick me up in much the same way the woman had picked up her dead lover.

This time he took the elevator.

I was moving farther from the street. Away from humans. I was going to die—that was clear. But Kyros's words finally squeezed through my brain.

He thought I was a spy?

For who?

Scrap that thought. Only one thing mattered.

"Not spy," I rasped, my head lolling.

His jaw was clenched so hard it was a wonder his teeth hadn't shattered. "You were caught on Level 44 in the middle of the night. Tell me, who did the blood belong to? It wasn't one of mine."

The blood puddle by reception.

The woman sprinted up the stairs with her boyfriend, and Kyros came down after. I'd assumed he came *because* she went to find him.

"I saw you on the cameras standing in reception. Don't deny it, human."

He'd seen me staring at the liquid remains of Ryder.

Ding!

The doors opened and Kyros began to run. Or whatever this was. The halls blurred in a mess of grey and bright lights. I moaned, clutching at the front of his crisp white shirt.

He came to a brutal stop, and I clamped a hand against my mouth. Theme parks were my jam, but nearly dying had pushed my body to its limits.

Shoving nausea back, I was flopped onto a metal chair. Kyros strapped my arms and legs into restraints on the framing. The thought of me escaping was laughable. I couldn't have moved at all—except to fall on my face.

But if he'd strapped me here to make me panic, then mission accomplished.

"Kyros," I pleaded, trying not to jerk on the restraints. "This is a misunderstanding." The words slurred together.

He strode to a cabinet and removed a vial.

What the fuck was that?

I tugged at my restraints with the strength of a newborn kitten. "No."

Blurring back, he plunged the needle into my thigh.

I screamed as life exploded within me. Energy, too much energy, seared through my veins. It couldn't get out. An itch under my skin. I thrashed to be free. The desperation to move hit my mind in a clamouring chorus of bells. A thousand voices chattered in my ears.

Adrenaline injection.

"Kyros, let me go," I shrieked. "Get me out."

He gripped my hair, wrenching my head so I arched back over the chair. "What did you tell Clan Fyrlia?"

Tears of pain stung my eyes, but my muscles coiled at snapping point. "Tell who?"

"Who do you answer to?"

"Please," I sobbed. "I don't know what you're talking about."

His top lip curled, revealing dreadful fangs. A whimper left me.

"Then again, they would have ensured you couldn't reveal anything. No matter, I can work around that."

My legs attempted to bounce up and down. My hands formed tight fists. *Loose, tight, loose, tight, loose, tight.*

I shook my head to clear my tripping vision.

He dipped his head to catch my gaze.

I couldn't have looked away if I'd tried.

"What were you doing on Level 44 tonight?" he demanded. His deep voice ricocheted through me.

My mouth moved, words flowing freely. "I got kicked out of my apartment for not paying rent. I went to the library. It was dark when I left. The buses had stopped running. I was scared of walking in the dark. Angelica gave me a key last Friday. I decided to sleep under my desk."

He hissed a string of words over his shoulder, and someone answered.

There were others in the room.

I was frozen to his will but could still think despite being unable to do anything about it. Maybe these people could help. I'd yell for help when I could.

"Continue," he said, face showing his disgust.

"A woman came to reception with a man. I wanted to check where they were so they didn't find me. I thought they were just having sex, then she bit him." My body shook anew. My feeble human mind was trying to put the world back together again, but like Humpty Dumpty's shell, there was not a chance in hell of it happening.

"She bit him and didn't stop. He died. She picked him up, saying you could help." I continued against my will.

His grip tightened. "No one came to me."

"His name was Ryder," I gasped.

Footsteps. "Sir?"

The monster's meadow-green eyes didn't budge from mine. "Did you give her keys?"

"I did, sir. She was to open on Monday because of the meetings you scheduled for me."

It was Angelica.

Was she a vampire too?

I choked on a whimper.

Kyros's lips pressed together. "She was kicked out of her apartment today. What do you know of that?"

"She asked for payment on Friday evening for the hours worked. I said no, as per our policy. She mentioned that would render her unable to make rent."

Every word from her lips seemed to make him angrier. I wouldn't have any hair left by the end of this.

Though I'd be dead, so that didn't matter.

"Deana?" he asked.

My body didn't react, held immobile in his power. Or maybe his eyes. The eye contact appeared crucial to rob me of control. I didn't know how the vampire was doing it, just that I couldn't escape the snare of his gaze.

"In her room, sir."

I couldn't see the man who spoke, but he continued. "With a dead human. A man called Ryder who she'd been seeing for some time."

More footsteps. Another voice. I could only see the person's business shoes.

"There was a bag under her desk, Kyros. It contained clothing and toiletries," Business Shoes said.

"Fuck," Kyros muttered.

He shifted his gaze and removed the hand from my hair. It was almost more painful to be free.

My head slumped forward, my entire body trembling. The first burst of the adrenaline injection had dissipated, but the uncomfortable wired feeling under my skin was still present.

"I think she's telling the truth," the same man said.

Kyros stood before me, his stance wide. "We can't know that. She could be under their blood compulsion. Unless we break through it, we won't know for sure."

Angelica hovered just behind him. "Sir, if Miss Tetley is telling the truth, and she has only just discovered we exist, she'll need to be compelled by blood regardless. Or be dealt with."

There it was. The declaration of my doom from the same fucking woman who'd hired me.

My ragged inhales and exhales disturbed the pregnant silence.

You will always succeed.

I had to try.

For my grandmother's sake. For Tommy. They'd never know what happened to me.

"I won't say anything," I managed, the lingering adrenaline shaking my voice.

Everyone but Angelica laughed quietly.

"Why do they always say that?" Business Shoes asked.

My head snapped up. I glowered at the sandy blond. "Because I want to live, you fucking dumbass."

The room hushed.

Angelica hummed. "They don't usually say *that*."

The man scowled at her, and she smirked.

Kyros stepped closer, and I slammed back against the chair, fully craning my neck as he approached. He was a demon. *A beast.* A soulless evil. He—

"There has been a mistake, Miss Tetley," he said, crouching to undo my shackles. He took my shaking hands in his after. "If not for your own mistakes, and for a disobedient young member of my clan, you would not be in this position. Yet here you are, and now we must proceed. You have said that you wish to survive. Noting that, there's one path forward. Blood compulsion is a permanent insurance that you won't bring harm to my people. If you go through with the compulsion, it will guarantee you don't share the secret of our kind. You'll live, with restrictions."

"Which are?" I found myself asking the monster.

Business Shoes snickered. "Is she negotiating?"

Angelica's brows were climbing too.

"You will work for me until I determine whether you're trustworthy or not. If not, you will undergo a further compulsion to mute you regarding anything to do with *Kyros Sky* and *Live Right*—not only your knowledge about our race. Let me tell you from experience, Miss Tetley, secrets can destroy relationships unlike anything else and so destroy you in the doing."

Angelica and Business Shoes exchanged a glance.

Kyros's eyes remained locked with mine, but he didn't seize control of me as before. "You will stay in this tower for the duration of your trial. *Those* are the restrictions."

The choice wasn't hard. I was strapped to a chair and the alternative was death. "What is the duration of the trial?"

Business Shoes cracked another smirk.

"However long I decide." Kyros reached over and undid my restraints.

I rubbed my raw wrists. "I accept."

"Very wise," he said drily.

Angelica cleared her throat. "Twenty minutes until the dice roll, sir."

What that meant, I had no clue. Maybe all vampires gathered for Yahtzee on a Sunday night. High-pitched laughter caught in my throat. I doubled over, snorting and choking.

Vampires playing Yahtzee. It was in my head now. *Shit.*

Ringing hoots erupted from my lips, and I cradled my stomach, slithering down on the chair until my head rested on the back.

"Is she okay in the head, Kyros?"

"No."

It wasn't enough to hunt me and torture me. No. He had to insult me too. Loathing ripped through my weary body as the laughter siphoned away.

"Fifteen minutes," Angelica announced.

"Let's get this over with." Kyros bent down.

I slapped at his hands as he made to pick me up. Unsurprisingly, that stopped him not one single bit. His arm circled my back, the other beneath my knees.

"Sir," Angelica said slowly. "Surely you don't mean to complete the blood compulsion yourself."

"She's right, Kyros. That's a job for someone else. You need your head in the game tonight."

"I can try to smooth the incident over in her mind," Angelica said, darting a look at me.

The vampire holding me considered her words. "There is none more skilled to do the job, but the incident is traumatic. Her mind won't let go of what happened."

"Let one of your seconds do it." The sandy blond cut in.

"If someone from Fyrlia has compelled her to be here, then my blood will break through all holds but one."

Both vampires bowed.

I kind of felt like a fox pelt or something. Kyros wasn't affected by my weight in the slightest.

My head lolled and laughter gurgled in my throat.

"She needs rest," Angelica said. "Her heartbeat is all over the place."

"I assure you, Angelica, I'm perfectly capable of discerning the same," Kyros said, his eyes flashing.

She cast her eyes downward immediately.

His hold on me tightened. "Conrad, alert the other seconds that my veto is nullified for the duration of the seventy-two-hour thrall. Their majority vote will override mine during that time. Call Gerome and Lionel to the tower as an extra precaution."

"Consider it done."

"Angie. Check Miss Tetley's phone and text those she's in contact with. A story to cover the next three days."

She bowed. "Yes, sir."

"Everyone. Out."

I watched a row of people file out of the room. We'd had quite the audience.

When they were gone, Kyros sat on the same seat he'd just tortured me in, cradling me in his arms.

There was a block in my brain. I must have short-circuited in the last few minutes. My mind felt like a scratched, warped music record.

Because I should be struggling to get away. Spitting fiery words at him at least.

I was just so deathly tired.

But I was certain that, if I lived through this, the hate would return. In full force. And never ever fade.

For now, we stared at each other in a strange acceptance of what just happened.

"I'm going to drink from you," Kyros stated, breaking the calm.

I didn't say anything.

"Then you will drink from me."

I wrinkled my nose.

His eyes narrowed. "I have not elected to compel someone in a long time, Miss Tetley."

Was he offended?

"You expect me to thank you?" I rasped.

After a beat, he conceded that with a tiny dip of the head.

I rested my cheek against his shoulder, eyelids heavy. "Will it hurt?"

Will I die?

"I will minimise the pain as much as I am able. There will be a pressure in your head. That is the compulsion where I must set the restrictions we spoke of."

"'Kay," I mumbled. What other answer was there?

Later, if I lived, I'd deal with the mental fallout of this night from hell.

He sat me up and forced my legs apart so I straddled his thighs. I dragged open an eyelid to glare at him.

"It's easier this way," he murmured, vision tunnelled on my neck.

Sure it is. "No sex, Kyros. I mean it. If I want sex during the compulsion, I won't be in my right mind."

He cast me a strange look. "You won't want sex during the exchange."

If I had energy, I might have been embarrassed. Maybe paranormal novels weren't an accurate Vampire 101.

"*That comes after*," he hissed.

I opened my mouth, but Kyros shoved my head to the side, inhaling the base of my neck. He groaned deep in the back of his throat, chest rumbling under my fingertips.

I squeaked at the sharp pinch as his fangs sliced into my neck.

My thighs clamped around his legs.

I screwed my eyes shut, panting as a whispering pressure built in my head, *mounting*. A deep voice bounced between my ears, and it echoed back and forced in the confines, doubling back on itself, crisscrossing until I thought I'd pass out.

A plug was pulled and the pressure faded in a flooding rush.

With one last, lengthy draught, Kyros's fangs retracted. I jolted. The pain was worse coming out than going in.

"Conrad," Kyros called. "Be ready to intervene if necessary. I don't want to bed this human."

Didn't everyone leave the room?

Blood rolled over my collarbone, and the huge vampire dipped his head, licking upward over the bite he'd created.

He kept licking, a rumble vibrating in his chest almost like a purr.

"Is that it?" I whispered, unsure if it was wise to interrupt a feeding vampire. I wouldn't get between a dog and its bone.

He kissed the bite and lifted his head. Heat filled his meadow-green gaze. A few strands of toffee hair had separated from his always neat hair and flopped over his forehead.

Something hardened beneath me.

"No!" I said, squirming on his lap. No sex during blood compulsion, my ass. That was a definite erection.

"Your turn," he said. There was a dreamy quality to his voice.

Not breaking our stare, Kyros bit his wrist and pressed the dripping wound against my closed lips. In a burst of speed, he leaned forward on the seat so I was forced backward. His free hand whipped between my shoulder blades to support my arched position.

"Open," he snapped in annoyance, shaking his wrist against my mouth.

I parted my lips.

Thick soup tasting of rust and salt trickled into my mouth, and I gagged—at the texture more than anything—though I wouldn't be licking any rusty fences to replicate the taste in a hurry.

A growl ripped from Kyros's chest, and I tensed, swallowing obediently until he yanked his wrist free.

He licked his wound, and I watched it seal from beneath hooded eyes.

Were we done—?

Fire filled me in a wall of red.

The suddenness drew a gasp from my lips.

Oh my god.

I squirmed on his bulging lap, my shocked gaze flying to his. I clutched his shirt in both hands, moaning slightly.

"This is the after part?" I keened, everything from the waist down clenching.

He ran his hands up my thighs, thumbs close to the apex of my thighs. "Powerful. *Exquisite.*"

I crept my fingers up his neck and lifted high on my knees to bring our faces level.

"We didn't want this before," Kyros reminded me, voice still dreamy.

"*Mmm,*" I answered, lowering my mouth.

A door crashed open and a male spoke. "Sir."

Kyros's hips were grinding into my core from below. When had that started? He didn't stop in response to the voice, but a terrible snarl filled his chest, spilling over. I didn't care. I began to rock on his lap, desperately seeking my own release.

"Sir, the dice are about to roll." A woman interrupted this time.

Kyros's eyes flashed, and he squeezed his eyes shut. "When?"

"One minute, sir."

He swore long and hard.

Not as hard as some things.

"Do you need assistance separating from her?" the woman asked.

A bead of sweat trekked down the side of his face.

Clasping my waist, the vampire bodily lifted me, striding to the door. *Him.* I needed him now. I'd always need him. The world could fall to ruin around us and none of it would matter if he was inside me.

My hands finally found what they were looking for.

Kyros moaned as my fingers brushed the front of his suit pants. His mouth crushed down against mine.

"Thirty seconds, sir."

"*Fuck!*" he seethed.

I was passed to another.

Whimpering, I reached for Kyros as Angelica took me in her arms.

"Confine her," he said, muscles straining with some inner battle. "Post a guard at her door. Female. The human isn't to leave the tower."

And then the vampire was gone.

12

Vampires existed. It was my first thought upon waking in a room with no windows. How the fuck did I fall asleep after that?

Did the monsters even call themselves vampires? The term felt inadequate to describe the terror Kyros could induce—like calling a panther a kitten or something. Pop culture had ruined the term.

I rolled onto my back, lost in what I'd gotten myself into. My mind and body didn't know what to feel first. I'd felt soul-numbing disbelief when my parents were ripped from me and the two building blocks intended to guide me through life were crushed.

I'd felt bone-shaking shock when Clint hurt me for a quick buck.

The disbelief and shock that ripped the rules of the *world* apart was different altogether. I'd always stood on the world beside everyone else, and it was a given that the *rules* of the earth I lived on would remain the same. That gravity would keep me grounded. That I would not fly without man-made machines and devices. That without my head, I would die. That I would age. They were rules people rarely spoke about, and yet those unspoken rules created a safety net; an anchor that helped every person on this planet centre themselves.

In the space of a few minutes, my world had been blown to

smithereens. I had no sense of up and down. My only tether to earth *now* was that Kyros let me live.

For *now*.

He'd mentioned that if I failed this trust trial thing, he'd compel me further, but there was no mention of death. I felt it was implied—due to the fact they drank blood.

My exhale shook its way from my lips. Vampires existed. One killed her boyfriend in front of me. Kyros had guzzled my blood like I was a strawberry mojito. And I—

Oh my god. I drank vampire blood! My hand flew to the bite at the base of my neck. I couldn't feel any raised bumps, but the area was tender.

Curiosity spurred my despairing ass from the bed.

I shuffled to the edge of the mammoth bed and stood. White spots flooded my vision, what blood I had left filling my legs.

"Whoa," I rasped, feeling behind before sitting heavily on the mattress. I closed my eyes until the dizziness faded and squinted around the room to get my bearings.

A blaring blue light—the *only* light in here—caught my attention.

2:00 p.m.

Was I dizzy because I slept, what had to be, nearly twelve hours? Or was it that last night I was drained of a crucial pint or two?

After the events of the last two days, I should feel wrung out. But fear filled me with a crackling, erratic energy that I didn't know how to process.

Someone knocked at the front door. "Miss Tetley?"

I leaped to my feet again, dizziness forgotten. Okay, maybe I wasn't as cool and calm as I thought; much more like an on-edge rabbit who could ignore the world as long as she remained in her burrow. Or her prison cell.

I didn't recognise the woman's muffled voice. I didn't have to, really. I was in *Kyros Sky* and anyone in here was surely above me on the food chain if bright eyes were an indication of their race.

"Yes?" I squeaked in response.

"Are you well?" The woman's faint voice trickled through heavy wood and across the five metres between me and the door. My prison cell was actually pretty big. The massive bed occupied the corner farthest from the doorway, and two other doors branched off the room and were closed. That's all I could make out in the alarm clock's blue glare.

Was I *well*? A high-pitched squeal left my lips.

"Miss Tetley?"

"Sure. I'm right as rain," I said, choking on a chuckle. Oh fuck, I'd lost the plot.

"... Very well. Let me know if you need anything."

Yeah right.

My prison cell had a guard. Which, upon second thought, I'd known. Angelica brought me here and spoke to another female vampire, and Kyros had ordered her to post someone outside the door.

Kyros.

Groaning, I turned for the closest shut door. Hopefully one of the two contained a bathroom. I didn't want to leave my burrow.

Pushing open the door, I felt along the wall until I found a light switch. Soft light flowed through the space. A bathroom.

Win.

I whistled low. They treated their victims well—a claw bath, double overhead nozzles in the shower, and fluffy white towels.

Sinking onto the toilet, I left the *rules of the world* dilemma unresolved and moved on to problem two of one million—the blood compulsion.

I had to grab Tommy, her family, and my grandmother and get the fuck out of Bluff City. Oh man, that might not work. This city couldn't be the only place with a vampire infestation. Which meant I had to get out of the tower, away from Kyros and *Live Right*, and alert my loved ones so they were on their guard always.

Or would that put them in more danger? The last thing I wanted was for them to go through the same thing I was going through. Moaning low, I slid from the toilet to the cold, graphite floor of my burrow.

I was going *legit* insane. Like, living in a tree where pants were optional and tree bark sustained me *insane*.

Only one cure to insanity existed.

Shave, wash, hydrate.

Peeling myself off the graphite, I swept the bathroom counter for the necessary supplies. In my haste, the objects on there—a hairnet, body milk, shampoo and conditioner, soap, and a tiny comb—went flying to the cold ground. The neatly rolled hand towels followed.

I had soap and moisturiser, but if I couldn't complete all three parts of my sanity ritual, the whole thing was pointless. Sometimes hotel rooms—which this seemed to be—had little razors. Returning to the bedroom to continue my search, I halted in the doorway. Light streaming from the bathroom illuminated the silver logo of my *Elegance* pack.

"Mine," I snarled, leaping on the bag in a frenzy.

I recalled Kyros checking out my homeless story by sending a pleb to check my office. Someone thought to bring it here for me—Angelica, I assumed. Thank Zeus's left nut all my stuff was in there.

I drew out my sanity pack and cradled it close, scuttling back the way I came.

Turning the shower settings to scalding, I remembered my reason for leaving bed in the first place.

I turned to the mirror to study my neck.

Dark smudges circled the space under my topaz eyes. My eyes ranged from orange-brown on a good day, to muddy brown on a bad day. It was a muddy brown kind of day. My silky butter-blonde curls weren't looking so silky smooth—the locks plastered against my face and neck.

I swallowed, peeling the tresses back from the right side of my neck.

No marks.

Huh. I don't know what I'd expected—two small wounds. Maybe a tattoo of Kyros's face? The spot was tender to touch. No way could I forget the feeling of his fangs slicing into me. I tilted my head to the left and angled toward the light, shivering at the memory of the large vampire exposing my neck last night.

There. Faint yellow bruising. It would be gone in a few days at most. He'd accelerated my healing somehow. Is that what he did with all the licking?

Warmth flushed through me at the thought of what nearly transpired between us after the blood compulsion. The warmth lasted a split second before fury followed in its slipstream, shredding all trace of lust in its path.

That was more like it. I'd known the hatred would come back.

He'd nearly killed me. With *fright*. And then saved my life only to interrogate and hurt me. Now, his blood was in my body, and my blood in his. That felt more invasive and violating than if we'd had sex. Sex would have been a one-time thing. With him anyway.

This blood compulsion?

... He'd been inside my head, controlling me while drawing my life force into his mouth one greedy guzzle at a time. But for Angelica's interruption, neither he nor myself could have stopped us from having sex.

I scowled at myself in the mirror. "Hussy."

Quickly stripping, I stepped into the hot shower. A sigh left my lips as water pounded over my head. *Mmm*, good pressure. *Kyros Sky* had one thing going for it. Because it sure wasn't the owner.

I let go of as much of the last two days as possible. Minutes passed, maybe hours during which I remembered the episode with Clint. It seemed so insignificant now. What Clint did to me had obeyed the rules of the world I'd known. I'd take a run-in with him over Kyros any day.

My breathing slowed.

My shoulders eased.

Only then did I pick up my razor with something akin to reverence.

And began.

Losing myself to the task as I inspected my body for hair. Then I foamed the lemon myrtle blend all over my body. I returned a second and third time, trying to rub Kyros's fingerprints off my body.

I wouldn't be rubbing Clint's away, it seemed. Ugly purple bruises marred the skin of my upper arm, but I hadn't noticed any bruising on my face from his slap at least.

Remembering the state of my hair, I ducked out of the shower to grab the shampoo and conditioner from the floor.

After two shampoos and two conditions, the heat in the shower had my head swimming. The crackling, erratic fear I'd felt since waking had dissipated somewhat and I was feeling appropriately tired.

Time to face the world again—after hydrating of course.

I wrapped a towel around my body, tucking it in over my breasts, and wrapped a second towel around my head.

Legs shaking, I crossed back to the main room and flopped onto the bed.

Jesus, how much blood did the leech take? I wanted to sleep again.

How did the blood compulsion even work? It was meant to stop me talking about vampires, but how foolproof was it?

Kyros failing occurred to me for the first time.

Vampires exist. I imagined Tommy in front of me as I tried to say the words aloud, only managing an intelligible gurgle. With my finger, I tried to trace the words on my leg as though writing it for her. Nope, couldn't even budge my hand. I couldn't think of any other ways to test my constraints, but I could assume the blood compulsion worked. Which was magic.

And impossible.

But it was real.

Shuffling off the bed again, I squeezed as much moisture from my hair and used the tiny comb from the bathroom to work out the knots. Drying my arms and legs, I returned to my pack to don the only clean underwear I had—my black G-banger and lacy bra. Another sign the universe was having a field day with my life. This was a day for underwear that stretched over half my stomach, a hole-ridden tee, no bra, short shorts, and woollen socks.

Pushing aside my longing for all of the above, I picked up my moisturiser. A hazelnut-sized dollop was enough for both legs. I put much more than that on my hands today.

As I worked the scentless blend into my arms and torso, I returned to my attempts to break the blood compulsion even though I was on the fence about telling my loved ones about vampires, leaning toward not. That aside, the bastard had pillaged my mind. Pure self-respect wouldn't let me accept that without a fight.

Hey, Tom, Twilight is real, but Edward's hair is better. Nope. The words choked in my throat.

I opened my lips again. *Fangs, super speed, mind-control stuff. What do you have?*

Spelling the word backward proved futile too. The bastard had me trussed up nice and tight. What a dick.

I squeezed more moisturiser onto my hand and propped my foot on the edge up of the leather bed frame to work it into my smooth legs.

"*Let me in.*"

I froze, my muscles coiling to run at the voice rumbling through my door.

Three words spoken by *him.* That's all it took to undo the careful ministrations of the last hour or two. Fear took me first. Anger close behind. Loathing curled my fingers into claws while terror begged me to hide. In a strange twist, the heart-pounding part was the easiest to manage—I'd already had three days of managing that at *Live Right*. It made me realise how muted Kyros was until last night. How dull his eyes had appeared in our prior interactions. When he'd dropped his human act, I'd nearly expired on the spot. Literally.

It had to be a power thing. Kyros was definitely in charge around here, so I assumed he was the strongest. At least in his clan. Which meant there were other clans—who he didn't get along with judging by his accusation that I was a spy. Maybe I could use that to my advantage, but the rebellious thought seemed overly ambitious considering I couldn't talk about a single thing to do with vampires.

At least my sanity routine had shown me what I needed to do next. I had to get myself to safety and to protect my loved ones. To do that, I had to keep the vampire leader happy.

Which meant not irritating him.

Which meant I couldn't show a lick of my anger around him. Anger, I could hide. Fear, not so much.

"Sir, you gave orders that you were not, under any circumstances, to gain entry into Miss Tetley's room."

I tensed at his furious answering snarl.

That was all it took for the vampire guarding me to open the door. For the first time, I considered that the guard wasn't there to keep me in, but to keep Kyros *out*.

Fuck.

The vampire, dressed only in low-riding black sweatpants, strode in the room. I caught a peek of a white-faced young woman before he slammed the door shut.

He looked straight at me.

Then stilled.

Not like a human—or a crocodile waiting to ambush prey. He went as still as stone, his eyes riveted on my ass.

My eyes widened. "Shit."

I was still in the *leg propped up on the bed while wearing my G-string and bra* pose like I was starring in a porn film. I hastily lowered my leg.

Kyros's eyes went to my breasts as they bounced with the change of position. *Really, body?* I swung my wet hair to cover my chest, and his chest rumbled.

I couldn't win.

His eyes went to the area between my thighs only clothed in a scrap of sheer black material. My face didn't need to present for what he had in mind. Which was probably why he ignored it. *Practical.*

My heart sputtered in my chest.

Why wasn't the vampire speaking or moving? What was he

planning? I blew out a shaking breath, noticing how perfect his gold-tinged skin was. My fingertips itched to run themselves over the smooth plains of his chest.

He took a step forward, and a gasp left my lips as the wall of fire from last night slammed into me hard enough that my knees folded.

I sank onto the bed, body trembling with the sudden heat.

"Kyros," I pleaded. "Stay back."

Last night, I wasn't able to reason through the cloud of lust whatsoever. Four metres separated us where last night there was none. Whatever this fire was, distance helped to keep my mind clear. He couldn't come any closer.

Kyros had snarled outside the door, but now his voice held that dream-like quality—just like last night.

"You're testing the blood compulsion," he said softly.

Oh crap, he could feel that? My terror over his sudden presence here subsided somewhat—though the burning flood sweeping through me didn't leave room for terror if I were honest. An ironic mercy.

"Don't do that again. I don't like it." The vampire took another step forward. "It woke me."

"Kyros, no. Don't come any closer." I scrambled back into the far corner of the huge bed, as far from him as possible.

His nostrils flared, and his eerie voice drifted to me. "There are two things you should never do in my presence, Miss Tetley."

I moaned as he took another menacing step forward.

"Never give me a direct order." His lip curled, and he bent forward like a lion about to pounce. "And never, *never* incite my predator by running or turning your back."

Kyros tensed, and I used the last scrap of my reason to edge into the corner and hug my knees to my chest. My legs quivered from need, but a sob left my throat. The blood compulsion had done something to me. I didn't want this, but I was about to forget all of that.

My gaze trawled over the bed to his body—to the V that

disappeared into his low-riding sweat pants. Sweat broke out on my forehead as I resisted the urge to wrap myself around him.

Loungewear never looked so good. His usual suit had forewarned me he was muscular and toned. The reality was better. So much better.

My greedy fingers itched to run up the ridges of his abdominals, starting at the area where a small patch of hair disappeared into the waistband of his pants. Each of his arm muscles was defined, the veins just visible. By the same token, he wasn't wrestling-man muscular. His neck wasn't thickened. His arms didn't have to hover away from his body to accommodate massive lats. The monster was strong and powerful but possessed an inherent grace that was more terrifying than anything else.

One moment Kyros stood by the corner of the bed, and the next he was crouching on the bed, his feet either side of mine.

My mouth rounded at the display of speed.

And that was it.

Fire consumed me.

We reached for each other at the same time. He pulled me forward as I rose to my knees. Our bodies made delicious contact and I let my head drop back from the sheer bliss of it. This was like nothing else.

Nothing else.

I gripped his shoulders as he gathered my half-dried hair and forced my head back. I arched in response to the kisses he was pressing up my neck. He growled when he reached the spot he'd bitten last night.

I licked my lips as his mouth moved along the tops of my breasts. *Oh, fuck.* My shaking mounted, and he purred as I gasped his name.

"Kiss me. Now," I breathed, trying to pull his head up.

His purr morphed into a ripping snarl. Meadow-green eyes snapped to mine, blazing. A promise of death in every contour of his beautiful face, he trailed his nose up over my jaw to my temple, inhaling deeply.

"What did I just tell you, little human?" he asked in his dream-like voice.

My hands slid down his hard torso and a surge of warmth low in my stomach eradicated the terror that was trying to work its way to me.

I fluttered my lashes at him. "I wasn't listening. You'll have to tell me again."

His eyes blazed anew. "Naughty girl."

Kyros fitted his mouth over mine in a kiss that demanded more than I'd ever given. Before I could process the feel and taste of him, he was gone.

I blinked at the thin air where he'd been, the fire within me draining away and leaving me cold.

My gaze flew to the doorway.

Two vampires held Kyros against the far wall. His furious snapping filled the room, and some of my terror returned.

His fangs had descended. When did that happen?

I fell back onto my butt, huddling in the corner, hands around my knees again. It happened again. I'd lost my mind when he got too close. This time he'd kissed me. Trailed his lips over my body.

I lifted both hands, squeezing my head in a bid to erase the last few minutes of my life. The lingering lust was fucking with my head. Why did he feel and taste so damn good?

"What's wrong with me?" I whispered.

Kyros's ripping growls were lessening.

"There's nothing wrong with you," one of the massive vampires holding him back answered. "The three-day thrall after blood compulsion has this effect. Sometimes."

He turned to the woman who'd guarded me prior to Kyros's arrival. "Next time inform us immediately."

She fell to her knees under the power of his wrath, which was thankfully aimed away from me. "Yes, sir."

Next time. That was the only part I was interested in.

I had no idea who he or the other vampire were. But the one with the shaved head had given me an answer, so I braved another question.

"Will I be safe from him?" My voice trembled. "What's to stop him coming back again before the three days are up?"

The other vampire, the one with long jet-black hair cracked a grin. "You *want* to be safe from him?"

I'd never hated anyone more in my life. I abhorred Kyros. "Yes." Thankfully I was too shell-shocked to spit the word.

The vampire shot the other bodyguard an amused look. "Turns out the avoidance isn't one-sided."

Kyros had kept his gaze on the ground since the other two vampires ripped him away. Now, he lifted his eyes to where I cowered in the corner. A shadow flickered over his face, and I shuddered at the sight.

"Gerome, Lionel, I need the two of you to get out of her room or I'll attack you," Kyros said, his voice edged with the promise of violence.

The one with a shaved head hesitated. "Are you sure, brother?"

"Leave, Lionel," he roared.

I screamed at the sound. I couldn't help it. Panic seized in my throat. My hands still gripped my head, and I squeezed my eyes shut. "Everyone get the fuck out!"

In a beat, I was standing in the middle of the bed. I picked up the closest pillow and launched it at the trio. "Get out. *All of you*."

Kyros caught the pillow, his expression impassive. It didn't stop me launching another pillow missile which landed at his feet.

"Not a bad view," Jet Black said, folding his arms as he watched me.

... Reminding me I was in my underwear. My hand dropped to my sides as I glanced around for my discarded towel.

He continued. "If you're not going to try your luck, brother, mind if I have a go?"

Plaster exploded.

I dropped to the bed, covering my head. The explosion of plaster didn't stop, and after a few ragged breaths, I peeked over my arms to find the source.

Kyros had attacked Jet Black. He'd tackled his brother through the front wall, leaving hardly any of it behind.

No.

Absolutely not.

Fighting vampires was where I drew the fucking line. The males moved in a blur, smashing through the walls and doors that I knew one misplaced blow would end my life.

I wanted to live.

I *would* live through this.

Hopping off the bed, I wobbled on weak legs to the bathroom to wait out their fight. Closing the door, I caught sight of my stricken expression in the mirror. Sighing and ignoring the shouting and snarling outside, I crossed to the shower.

Might as well start my sanity routine all over again.

13

I belted out "Hands to Myself" alongside Selena Gomez.

Kyros's tantrum had destroyed two of the four walls of my first room. When I left the bathroom a couple of hours after his impromptu visit, the three males were gone and the female guard calmly escorted me to new quarters. The short march down the hallway had confirmed that this level of the tower was a hotel of sorts or filled with small apartments. This room was the mirror image of my last one.

After all the excitement and about three showers, I'd slept most of the last twenty-four hours. *Then*, I twiddled my thumbs for a time in an attempt to be a good prisoner.

I wasn't used to sitting still.

A few hours earlier, boredom drove me to turn on the TV. Unfortunately for my neighbours—if I had any—I'd found a top hits music channel with subtitles. I did pretty well resisting the urge to sing along until Queen came on.

If those fang fuckers were going to leave me in here for another day and a half, it would be spent in the spiritually healing activity known as karaoke.

I glanced at the alarm clock as my buddy Selena finished up and the channel introduced the theme of the next half an hour.

11:00 p.m.

Phew, time flew when I had Avril Lavigne, Muse, and Destiny's Child for company.

The piano intro for "Let it Go" came on, and I squealed, lifting my shampoo mic to my mouth.

I had a secret crush on *Frozen*.

I sang at the top of my lungs through the first verse and entered the chorus with gusto.

The hairs on the nape of my neck rose and I choked back the next line.

I wasn't alone.

Suspecting Kyros, I whirled.

Angelica stood in the doorway. Her mouth was pursed, and her arms folded as she leaned against the framing.

I narrowed my eyes as her lips twitched.

Her voice strained. "I think that 'I'm a Survivor' was your best cover."

She was laughing at me. Which was okay. I only sang to cheer myself up. I wasn't one of those cool kids that practiced all week to wow crowds on a Friday night.

Even though her eyes were as bright as the others, and I'd always been scared of her, my brain didn't connect Angelica as a vampire for some reason, so it was easier to relax in her presence.

"Given recent events, I had reason to put my heart and soul into that one," I said drily. I chucked the shampoo microphone on the bed.

Her face dropped.

Oh? Was bringing up the reason for my imprisonment impolite? How crass of me to keep hanging onto it like it only happened thirty-something hours ago.

She lowered her arms. "Your guard just called and begged to be relieved of her post."

I snickered. Bet she called during "Brave" by Sara Bareilles. I couldn't sing that high, so I just picked any old note that felt right. "How many heard me singing?"

"Every vampire in the tower."

What? I knew these people were fast. I had wondered if their other senses were heightened, too, with the way Kyros sniffed my neck. "Good hearing much?"

Her eyes flickered in confusion. "Oh, do we have good hearing? Yes. Excellent hearing. Though the old and powerful amongst us are able to tune out disagreeable sounds with more ease than the younger members of the clan."

She'd just labelled my karaoke as a disagreeable sound. I was onto her.

"I guess vampires don't like loud noises at all then." The words slipped from my mouth. My jaw dropped. "I just said vampire!"

"You're in the presence of a Vissimo."

"Huh?"

"That's our name. Vissimo."

"Right. *Vissimo.*"

I could say that too!

Hold on. I frowned. "Kyros compelled me so I couldn't talk to his enemies though. Can I talk freely around any vampire?"

"Beyond general terms, probably not. However, silencing you completely would make things difficult while you're living alongside us." Her gaze landed on me. "You'll likely find it impossible to repeat sensitive or specific information to those below a certain rank. Or outside of a certain location. I'm unsure what exact restrictions Kyros put in place, but those are the common variations."

Whatever they were, it sounded like there might be wriggle room. Good to know.

I tucked the information away for later. "How many of you are there?"

"In this tower? Two thousand."

Shitty fucker! *Two thousand?* That catapulted my escape attempts from hard to impossible. I'd definitely have to leave Bluff City to avoid that many. There was only one place I *could* evade them, really, and that was the estate I'd left. With that said, I'd only return there to grab my grandmother and skip town.

But the more I knew, the better equipped I'd be to protect my loved ones.

Angie was very verbose this evening considering my position as Kyros's prisoner. I wondered how much information I could squeeze out of her.

"Do all Vissimo live in towers?" I asked.

She cracked a grin. "No. But we all live with members of the royal family. In this clan, all sub-clans do live in towers, excluding those who live in the core clan with the king and queen."

So Kyros ruled a sub-clan connected to the core clan ruled by his mother and father. Like a club with satellite branches. "Are all sub-clans ultimately ruled by the king and queen?"

"Correct. The work of each sub-clan supports the cause of the overall clan."

I puzzled over that one, putting it aside for now. There were far more pertinent questions to ask.

She stepped inside the room, and my brows lifted at my lack of reaction to her. My heart wasn't thumping in her presence at all. Kyros had scared the fear of less powerful Vissimo out of me, apparently. Or maybe it was the three-day thrall. Maybe that screwed with my usual reactions and thoughts somehow.

"I'm sorry, Basi," Angelica said, dropping her gaze. "I never wanted any of this to happen to you."

"Then why did you let it?" I asked her, voice hard.

Whoa, some part of me held a grudge against Angelica. I clamped onto it. "You hired me. Why?"

If she'd shredded my application like Rhys's, I wouldn't be in this mess.

Her bright blues widened before she collected herself. "A mistake, I grant you. Not because of anything to do with you though. In recent years, we've caught some unwanted attention from humans for never hiring them. I got the sense you were on your own and thought we could trial the addition of a human to the team to quash rumours."

How odd to hear myself referred to as a human. I mean, that's what I was. But she said it in the same tone I used for farm dogs.

"This has fucked up my life," I told her, sadness flooding through me. I could never go back to the ignorance I'd known.

I turned from her to switch off the TV.

Her head drooped. "I know. Nothing can undo what you have been through. But I wanted you to know I am very sorry that's the case."

Exhaling, I closed my eyes.

I'd never been good at forgetting, and I found it hard to forgive until that happened. I'd always carry scars from what happened a day and a half ago. But she didn't need to know that. "I hear you."

Facing her, I caught her small smile.

"Then I can reveal my secondary purpose in coming," Angelica said, clasping her hands behind her back. "I thought you might like to see around the place."

See around the place? I didn't want to leave my burrow... yet knowing more about the layout would help me bust this joint.

"Sure," I said, smoothing my black pencil skirt and crappy white blouse.

Angelica followed the movement of my hands.

She grimaced. "I didn't think about procuring you clothing. Things in the tower have been rather hectic with—"

"—Kyros having tantrums?" I enquired. Actually, I'd been thinking about how both sets of my underwear were drying in the bathroom. I had a bra on though, no one would ever know I was going commando on the bottom half.

Her mouth rounded. "Miss Tetley, he can hear you."

What? Even a little conversation like this?

Had I farted recently?

I shrugged a shoulder. "He shouldn't listen to conversations if he can't handle what he hears."

I was full of puff, but bravado was the only thing carrying me since someone drank my blood.

Angelica seemed to grasp I was full of shit. "Regardless. I would usually have had someone collect your belongings by now."

My belongings were Clint's belongings by this point. He'd probably sold them already. "Don't bother. I'll make do."

"It's no trouble to have someone visit the address you provided."

Tommy's address. "No," I snapped.

She frowned.

Shoot, I did not want her to go to Tommy's house. I ran a hand through my hair. "Crappy couple of days."

Her brow cleared. "Understandable. But I'll drop off some of my old things later for you to pick a few outfits from."

She made it sound like I was never leaving. Perhaps I wasn't. "That would be great. Thanks."

"How about we get you out of this room?" Her nose wrinkled as she peered at the carnage behind me.

I walked out after her, drawing the door shut, and noted the number on the door. *615.* Sixty-first floor? Just my luck. Could I beat an elevator to the bottom? The lift only beat Kyros to the entrance alcove from Level 44 by a few seconds, but if I'd run from the elevator, I could have made it to the street. From Level 61, I could apply the same logic. With a minute head start, I'd beat him to the bottom. If I timed my escape for the middle of the day—when Kyros had professed that he'd been sleeping—there'd be a ton of workers around on their lunch break.

It was something to go on at least.

Time to find out as much as I could about Vissimo. "So, how do you know Kyros?" I asked.

She flashed me an inquisitive look, then faced forward. "I'm his aunt."

What the hell?

I'd assumed older age equated to more power. I really needed to leave everything I thought I knew about vampires at the door. "How does that work?"

A smile warmed her voice. "The usual way, I imagine. Kyros's mother is my sister. Also, one of my men is the king's nephew."

There was so much weird in that sentence. I trailed after her, digesting, and then followed the path of lesser evil. "You have multiple, uh, men?"

"Normal for vampires. Both men and women have harems. We have low fertility rates."

So they just had bulk sex. I'd never pegged Angie for a sexual deviant.

Wait, wait, wait. "You guys are *born*? But you're dead." Weren't they?

She stopped in front of the elevator.

I eyed it.

Bingo. My escape route.

"Not dead," she replied, expression serene even though I'd essentially just called her a corpse. "Vissimo exist on the brink of death. Our hearts beat very slowly. We can conceive, but it is rare."

"Why?" I blurted, before wondering if that question was as insensitive as in the human world.

Ding!

I hadn't missed that piece-of-shit sound. Should have taken the ding for the bad omen it was when I dropped off my résumé.

The elevator doors opened, and I entered after her.

Level 61. I'd been right.

"Humans find it harder to conceive when their bodies are under undue strain—obesity, malnutrition, stress. Nothing is more intense than existing on the brink of death—more stressful to the body. No matter what our minds yearn for, our bodies are in constant state of battle. You'll find that most Vissimo traits can be explained if you remember we continually exist in those frantic moments before death." She pushed number fifty and we descended.

I saw a hole straightaway. "Kyros is strong."

"We are never stronger than when our lives are threatened," she said. "Nor faster. Our senses are heightened, every part of us ready to fight."

"I'm following you," I said after a beat. "But there has to be an element of magic. Like, how do you guys exist?"

The elevator slowed and dinged again.

Angelica's delicate laughter rang like chimes as we left the lift.

"How do *humans* exist?" she challenged.

"Depends who you ask."

Angelica gestured down a wide hall to the right. "There is a Vissimo clan whose existence is dedicated to exploring our origins. But alas, nothing concrete. However, it is really no more of a mystery than the presence of humans. A mouse looking at you would think you possessed magic too."

If a mouse could think like that. And I'd been demoted from monkey to mouse.

"I guess so," I mused aloud. My mind needed a few minutes to process that. "How many clans are there?"

"Twelve."

"How many vampires?"

"More than two hundred thousand during our last census."

They had a census. "Is that a clan thing then? To have a purpose? You mentioned a clan who is interested in Vissimo origins."

She smiled as we entered a cafeteria. "Correct. Each new clan forms around a powerful alpha male who is titled king when he has more than five thousand Vissimo under his care. When Vissimo join his clan, they also join his cause."

What was the reason for *Kyros Sky* then? What on earth did their cause have to do with rolling dice and owning a real estate agency that only purchased properties and didn't appear to sell them?

"Are there queens too?" I frowned. "How does that work with the harems?"

"If a king chooses a queen from amongst his harem, she gains royal status. Any young she has born of the king gain automatic royal status too. With regards to children from his harem, a king can choose which babies he wishes to grant royal status to. These royal children enter into the king's care and that of his queen."

"Whoa, mothers give up their children just like that? Are they still allowed to see them?"

Angelica's lips twitched. "Their offspring become royal, Miss

Tetley. The granted status announces to everyone the child is extremely powerful. It's considered a great honour—but only a king has the power to separate a mother and child. A few decades after harems became the mode, another clan released evidence that it was best for the birth mother to remain completely apart from the royal family. It was easier for her, the queen, and most importantly, the child, in the long run."

That seemed so cold. My human mind couldn't compute. "So in *general*, babies stay with their mothers?"

"They do. And the mother declares who the father is."

I exhaled slowly. "Right. Sounds like drama waiting to happen to me." Wouldn't everyone just fight over the babies?

Angelica glanced at me. "It's not. Usually. Her word is law."

The hall opened into a huge space dotted with hundreds of tables.

"If you are hungry, come to Level 50 to eat," she said. "The food is free and available twenty-four hours. Though everyone is at their work stations upstairs right now." She pointed out how everything worked, but I barely listened, my mind on our previous conversation. Which was saying something because I hadn't eaten since the world imploded around me.

My situation stole away every speck of my appetite though I *did* eye a rack of wine with longing.

Wine, I could go for.

"Don't worry about laundry or cleaning," Angelica was saying. "Our Indebted handle that. Just leave any dirty clothing out. It won't get lost and will return clean."

Her showing me all this stuff was nice and all. That she'd take the trouble to do so surprised me—especially because I didn't think guilt was the only thing driving her to reach out. I mean, I doubted I could repeat anything through the constraints of the compulsion, but she was practically pushing a Vissimo guidebook into my hands. Was the guidebook Kyros-approved? He was in control here, and while there might be a faint strain of favouritism for Angelica, she answered to him with sir, not Kyros.

"Angelica?" I asked her softly in the hopes two thousand other vampires in the tower wouldn't hear. "How long will he keep me here?"

The corners of her mouth turned down, her expression grim. "You'll return to work the day after next. Once the effects of the thrall fade."

Return to work. Escaping from there would be easier.

"Will I get my phone back then?" I asked.

"You will. I told your friend that you went camping with work colleagues for a long weekend."

Tell me she didn't. Tommy would be fucking frantic. Me? Go *camping*?

I swallowed back dread over that tidbit. "The thrall doesn't affect me unless Kyros is too close, right? I'll be okay with my phone now."

I had to do damage control ASAP.

We returned to the elevator and she pushed the call button.

"Miss Tetley, you just sang to a television with a bottle of shampoo in your hand for three hours straight. Females experience the aftermath in a different way to males—often symptoms mimic those we experience during PMS."

She had to be screwing with me.

Her earnest expression didn't fade, and I considered her words. I didn't get bad PMS, if truth was told. Tommy said I was always a moody bitch and that didn't worsen during my period.

"And males?" I asked, wondering if asking for my phone a second time would make her suspicious.

"Protectiveness, as you have seen. Violence, if another male draws too close. Extreme lust. He won't think of anything else but you for the full seventy-two hours of the thrall."

I lifted my brows. "I see."

Angelica had used the word protective. I knew of another P word that could describe Kyros.

Possessive.

But I was haunting his every waking moment, which was good to know. Except that fucker wasn't allowed to fantasize about my body.

She slid a look at me. "Kyros emptied your level and sent all male Vissimo to rooms on the first ten floors. Some are sleeping five to a room for the duration of the thrall."

Ding!

We entered the lift again and my heart pounded as she jabbed Level 66. The top floor.

"You said that existing on the brink of death explained most things about your kind." I ventured. "How do you explain the compulsion thing?"

"Very good," she murmured. "That is what the clan researching our origins centre their research on. It is considered the anomaly in our make-up. There are those of us who liken compulsion to human hypnotists, a skill heightening by the constant adrenaline coursing through our bodies. Others say that because blood is our life force, we have greater control over it."

Humans needed oxygen, food, and water to live and we had no magical command over them.

She spoke again. "My personal thought is that Vissimo simply evolved that way. Snakes have venom, birds have flight, some animals can change the colour of their skin to camouflage with their surroundings. Each of those qualities is magical, really—a physiological change which enables them to survive. In my mind, our compulsion is an extension of that concept; we evolved in such a way to protect ourselves or to secure a meal."

Sure, a massive fucking extension.

Though I would no sooner compare humans to a shark, so perhaps I shouldn't compare humans and Vissimo—no matter that we looked similar.

"Why do you guys have a cafeteria when you drink blood?" *Oh my god,* did they serve blood down there? Was that even wine I saw?

Angelica laughed at my expression. "*Brink of death*, remember? We have large appetites. However, we cannot survive without blood donors. How much depends on the age of the Vissimo."

Ding!

I stared between the doors as they slid apart and gaped at the multitude of blurring vampires on Level 66.

"Are you ready to learn about the cause of Clan Sundulus?" Angelica asked. She stepped out of the lift and turned with a grace I'd never possess.

Her head tilted as I lingered in the elevator.

There was a challenge in her eyes. Something I'd never seen in her expression. Then again, I had a feeling a lot of people underestimated this woman. She was one of those quiet people who somehow always got what they wanted.

The question was: What did she want?

The last time I entered an area filled to the brink with vampires, I'd nearly pissed my panties. Seeing vampire Kyros in his full glory might have put the weaker vampire into perspective, yet I knew the coming moments were about to be very uncomfortable.

Did I need to know what happened on Level 66 to escape? Probably not.

Did I need to play along until I escaped?

Absolutely.

"Why not," I replied, smoothing my skirt before stepping out of the elevator.

14

A cold wall of fear slapped me the second I entered Level 66. Knowing my reaction to their group presence was natural made things much easier—in that I could take a moment to acclimatise without someone sending me off to the looney bin.

The elevator doors whooshed closed at my back—my exit gone—and my heart rate tripled. I squeezed my eyes shut, breathing in rhythm with the thundering in my ears. I remained this way until the pounding faded, and then dared a look at my surroundings.

In the staff room, I was the sole focus of one hundred Vissimo, but on this level, none of the several hundred vampires in sight paid me any mind.

"What the..." The words left my lips as the vision before me registered.

"From 10:00 p.m. to 3:00 a.m., you will find most of Kyros's sub-clan on the top three levels of *Kyros Sky*," Angelica said. She'd waited quietly while I tried to avoid a survival meltdown.

The floor was circular, obstructing my view of the whole floor. *Kyros Sky* was one of those towers that had a disc up the very top before the steeple. Now I knew the space ship appearance wasn't for the 360-degree view—but to accommodate the masses of Vissimo up here each night.

A huge monitor covered the wall in front of me. A rectangle image with different coloured blocks filled it. Some of the blocks were flashing—whatever that meant. The monitor occupied the only wall I could see. Otherwise, glass-walled meeting rooms filled the outer perimeter of the level. The glass rooms were filled with small groups of vampires who appeared to be in the midst of animated conversation.

The wide expanse between the inner wall of the tower and the outer glass rooms was arranged into rows of compact work stations. Each station contained a monitor set upon a dark-grey standing desk. Vissimo occupied every single one, their eyes fixed on the screen, fingers typing in a blur.

I'd barely given the appearances of the staff at *Live Right* a thought beyond their bright eyes, but I looked closely at the monsters surrounding me.

The vampires varied in hair and eye colour and ranged in height from a head shorter than me to well over six foot—both males and females. At the moment, with hundreds of them in the same straight-backed position before the computer screens, a new element of fear crept over me.

The only thing scarier than a mindless beast was a cultured one.

I pivoted to Angelica. "Some kind of illegal underground stock exchange?"

The nearest Vissimo scoffed.

Angelica rested her eyes on them, and they quickly smoothed their expression, returning to work.

Angie is totally a dark horse.

"Understand, Miss Tetley," she said in a firm tone, "our clan prides themselves on obeying and operating according to human law. It is the difference between us and our... competitor. While they may commit crimes against humans to play the game, we do not sink to their level."

She said competitor like I said dog poop.

Which I'd stood in by accident it seemed.

I clasped my hands behind my back. "I see."

She couldn't seriously be telling me that they were legit? Like, *legally* legit.

God, I needed wine in my veins.

"Shall we?" she asked, gesturing to the rows of work stations.

I glanced at the huge monitor with the flashing blocks of colour again, trying to connect the dots.

Nope, nothing.

Shrugging a shoulder, I weaved between the stations after my fanged tour guide.

"How old is Bluff City, Miss Tetley?" she threw back over her shoulder.

Her question surprised me. But everyone knew the answer to that thanks to the stupid Bluff City anthem we were forced to learn in primary school. "Ah, 149 years old."

"Correct. One hundred and *fifty* years ago, my sister—then not yet a queen—had two kings in her harem. When she fell pregnant for the first time, both kings granted the child royal status, as is their right, and claimed the baby for their own line. The qualities of our blood make human DNA tests ineffective, and though my sister was adamant the child belonged to *our* king, her declaration held no legal weight in such an instance. When the child was not given up to him, the second king declared war on our clan."

This was just like *Truth Ranges*—except vampires. My first observation would be that having two kings in your harem was always going to lead to this, but I remained mute.

Angelica paused outside an empty meeting room. "It is the creed of all Vissimo clans that vampire lives be protected. With our low fertility rates, we cannot needlessly kill each other. We would have long since been extinct if we had listened to our baser, violent instincts."

Yeah, and they would have taken a chunk of humankind with them.

She faced me. "It was decided there would be no battle—of the usual kind—to resolve their dispute. Around that time, a game was popular amongst Vissimo."

"Was it Yahtzee?" I said before thinking better of it.

A slight wrinkle appeared between her brows as my personal joke flew right over her head. "We live on through the ages, Miss Tetley. Games between friends and family help the decades go by."

This was the part when she told me about vampire Twister afternoons each Sunday, I knew it.

I forced my urge to snicker away, clearing my throat. "Right."

She narrowed her eyes on my twitching lips, and I pressed them firmly together.

"Please continue," I managed.

Angelica quirked a brow. "The game was called *Ingenium*—a battle of intelligence and strategy. At its root, two or more vampires would purchase businesses on the same street and engage in a contest of commerce until only one business was left standing. This concept then extended to other things: circuses, apartments, car manufacturing—any industry you can think of."

It sounded a whole heap like vampires were using earth as a game board. Honestly, the short span of my mortal life made that seem like a waste of precious time, but clearly Vissimo lived a long time. I'd assumed they were immortal, but maybe I shouldn't. Hardly anything else had proved true. "The two kings decided to settle their dispute by playing *Ingenium* with Bluff City." The words left my mouth as I had the thought.

"Well done, Miss Tetley."

I rocked back on my heels. *Holy shit.* "Don't tell me that Bluff City only exists because of this game?"

She shrugged a shoulder. "It was a small porting village when the battle first started. Due to its position, the village would have always developed into a city, but we certainly accelerated its natural path."

Turning from her, I stared blankly around the bustling room. This section of the level was just like the area outside the elevator. The Vissimo worked at their standing stations—or in small groups within the glass meeting rooms. Were they *all* focused on tasks designed to help this clan conquer Bluff City?

"How does one of the kings win?" I asked after a full minute.

"When they own Bluff City."

Of course. Stupid mouse question.

I took in a slow breath, exhaling just as slow. "That's why you buy houses and never sell."

"Yes, but it is not quite that simple. Follow me. The dice are about to roll."

She'd said the same thing two nights ago—I only remembered because she stopped Kyros and I from bumping pelvises with the words. His need to witness the dice roll had overwhelmed his urge for an uncontrolled romp in the torture room.

I checked my watch. "They roll at midnight?"

"Every night, yes. Tonight is our turn. We can only move—make purchases and sign contracts—in the twenty-four hours after our king rolls."

My mouth dropped open. This was incredible. Unbelievable. "That's why you always try to get contracts signed on the same day!"

Angelica smiled, and I shuddered. Her teeth were too much with the sheer masses of Vissimo around. My palms broke into a fresh round of clamminess. If I was staying here, I had to get better at managing my reaction to them. Sure, pure exposure helped, but the sweating was kind of gross.

Puppies, puppies, puppies.

That just made me think about Angie snacking on a sausage dog. A bead of sweat rolled down the side of my neck.

We continued between the grey standing stations. Ahead, the work stations stopped short to make way for a giant glass tube set in the centre of the walkway. It reminded me of those inside skydive places where people could fly around.

No one stood near the tube, but Angelica led me to stand directly before it. She shot a look over her shoulder to a glass room and her lips curved.

I tried to peer into the meeting chamber as well, but she squared her shoulders, blocking my view. *Huh*, what was she up to? Knowing dark-horse Angie, something shady.

I glanced back to find Vissimo were leaving their work stations to gather around the huge glass cylinder. The male vampires clearly visible around the other side shifted their attention from mine as soon as our gazes met.

... Okay.

Angelica set her eyes on the smooth concrete floor inside the tube. I did the same. This was where they rolled the dice? Did the dice fall from the ceiling or something?

Angelica said in a whisper, "There are nine sub-clans in our clan. Each is ruled by one of the nine royal children."

Cutting her an incredulous look, I said, "You're telling me Kyros has *eight* siblings? I thought you guys had low fertility."

"Remember that not all the king's children are born of his queen."

Oh, right.

She continued. "Each of the sub-clans controls an industry within Bluff City—entertainment, agriculture, food, education, retail, finance, health, and manufacturing. Kyros handles the largest industry—real estate, renting, and leasing."

Ingenium was far more complicated than I thought. When she said the winner had to own the city, I assumed she just meant the houses. This was a contest of economy on an immortal scale. I couldn't even fathom how fucking complicated all the pieces had to be. Complicated enough that two thousand vampires worked in just one of the industries.

"I don't get why you need dice," I said. "If you go every second day, what's the point of them?"

She arched a perfect brow. "There are two minutes to go. Watch and see."

I faced the tube along with everyone else, swallowing several times to control my leaping heart and surge of nausea. Before, the vampires had kept their attention on the monitors. Some had to be looking at me now.

Murmuring broke out at my back and fresh beads of sweat broke out on my forehead. Something was happening back there, but instinct told me that if I turned around to face the Vissimo behind, things would go from bad to worse really quick.

I refused to piss or vomit.

Heat swept over me. A heat I couldn't fail to recognise.

"Fuck!" I choked. Shoving one instinct as another tried to force its way in, I spun on the spot, eyes searching for him.

He leaned against the glass wall of a meeting room—the one Angelica had smirked at before. The door sat wide open, and I tore my eyes from Kyros's black three-piece suit and matching tie as a string of vampires filed out after their boss. They halted, peering at Kyros and then the glass tube in confusion. One by one, their eyes fell on me.

Each of them scowled, and I gasped as my chest seized in terror.

I only recognised the male with the sandy hair from their midst. He was in the torture room on the first night.

Kyros took a step forward, and I automatically edged sideways as the heat between us crept higher.

"Where are you going?" Angelica murmured, eyes downcast.

Shooting a glare at her, I said, "Are you shitting me? You knew he was up here. The thrall is still going. What were you thinking?"

Angelica wasn't stupid. Which meant she had her own agenda.

I fucking hated being part of political games.

"You're perfectly safe with this many Vissimo," she said under her breath.

Sure.

I kept edging around the glass tube until I stood on the opposite side to Kyros, where the heat was manageable.

I stared back through the glass at him. He'd left the wall and stood just outside the glass across from me. The yearning to jump him was a simmer deep in my stomach, but even that had me feasting my eyes on the sloping angle from the tips of his shoulder to his hips. He was just so damn *symmetrical*. I couldn't say that I'd ever had that thought before—because it was a pretty weird one—but shit, I bet a protractor could prove me right.

I let my gaze roam over his chest to his full mouth, and higher to his eyes.

The vampire's lashes were downcast, his meadow greens on me. Well, *part* of me.

Kyros lifted his focus from my breasts to my face after a few seconds.

Such a charmer.

Fuck you, I told him with a narrowing of my eyes.

His green eyes blazed, and I recognised the flaring anger as the desperate longing clawing at my insides. I blinked as his eyes shifted over my shoulder.

Movement erupted behind me.

Jumping, I glanced back and watched as the Vissimo who'd stood directly behind me ran.

I stared at Angelica.

What's happening?

"Males," she said, the amusement plain in her voice.

Oh, right.

They were putting space between me and them. Because of *Kyros.*

Sigh.

I peered to the other side of the glass tube where Kyros loomed, realising that side contained only female Vissimo. I'd been there just a minute ago, so the males had purposely arranged themselves far away from me to accommodate their boss's... mood.

Oops. Guess I went and messed that up.

The females filed to my side without a word, rearranging themselves so the male Vissimo running around the level so they didn't get too close to me could gather behind their boss.

Not a single one stood closer to me than Kyros. I rolled my eyes and, too late, saw the man himself was perusing me again.

Thankfully, the view of him was obscured as an image filled the glass tube. In the middle of the tube, two gorgeous men stood facing each other. A way behind each man, two women sat on thrones, and on the floor between the two beautiful men rested two dice.

It seemed to be a live stream from wherever the kings rolled each night. The image was so clear I felt like I was in the room with them. Only the lack of sound reminded me that wasn't the case. *Creepy.*

"Each night, the kings and their queens gather to roll the dice," Angelica murmured in my ear. "The dice are weighed and carefully checked by a member from an impartial clan each night beforehand."

That was a lot of effort. I guess the clans had no reason to trust each other. I'd paid attention to everything Angelica told me, but all the information was tinged with incredulity. I'd lived in Bluff City my entire life. If she was right, and I really was watching the kings of two warring vampire clans play a game that had spanned one hundred and forty-nine years, then I'd been part of a game *my entire existence.*

I'd hated living within the elite world. But I'd merely existed in a rich game *within* a bigger, uglier game.

Bile rose up my throat, and Angelica shot me a look.

"Are you okay, Miss Tetley?"

She could sense something was up. I shook my head, swallowing hard. "So did your king choose your sister for his queen after the dispute so all her children would be his?"

Angelica nodded. "And fifty years ago, King Mikael also chose a queen."

I focused on the royals in the live stream. Kyros was related to one of them. Picking out his mother was too easy. She had the same meadow-green gaze, currently fixed on the Vissimo I assumed was her husband. The king had jet-black hair and blue eyes—like the bodyguard who'd gone head to head with Kyros in my first room. I could see hints of ruddy-brown in the king's hair, too, a subtle likeness to Kyros's toffee hair colour.

He was larger even than Kyros by at least a head. Was that an age thing, a blood thing, or a protein shake thing?

I shifted to look at the other royal pair.

The second king's skin was olive, an obvious contrast to the other king's golden brown. The main difference was the upward slope of his almond-shaped eyes. His queen had the same shaped eyes, though her dead-straight curtain of blonde hair and bright violet eyes were a stark difference to her lover's hazel and dark-brown combination.

"The kings aren't related?" I asked for confirmation. They didn't look it.

The vampire beside me shook her head. "Kings rarely are."

The queens—both of them, took my breath away. The word exquisite came to mind. So graceful and untouchable. Like they'd break into a thousand pieces if I spoke too loud in their presence. But once I had a moment to blink through my initial response to them, I found my eyes continuously drawn to Kyros's mother.

There was something magnetic about her, even through the cameras capturing the dice roll.

"They've done this each day for one hundred and forty-nine years?" I asked.

Angelica didn't tear her gaze from the tense scene. "No. We have two days off each month."

Their work standards hadn't changed much in one and a half centuries—or their union sucked.

"King Julius is about to roll," she whispered.

The female Vissimo at my back hushed. Even with my human ears, I could have heard a pin drop.

King Julius stooped to pick up the dice, holding one in each of his massive hands; hands that could probably crush my little mouse head. I shivered. I never wanted to meet this guy face-to-face. He was one scary mothertrucker.

He let his hands swing back and then whipped them up to shoulder height. As the dice left his fingertips, he bent over, adding a fierce backspin.

The dice spun in the air, too fast for my eyes to track. I shook my head, refocusing as the two cubes started their fall to the stone flooring that the kings stood upon.

Both kings zipped back to sit in the empty thrones beside their queens.

It only took a moment to see why.

The dice made contact with the stone floor and the vampire-strength backspin on them sent the cubes catapulting. They careened over the chamber, bouncing off the floor and furniture.

I winced, imagining how loud it must be in real life.

"If the dice hits a member of the royal family, there's a re-roll. But King Julius has the best roll," Angelica promised.

A few females at my back murmured their agreement.

I absorbed that, craning to watch as the dice slowed and eventually toppled onto their sides.

"Seven," I announced.

Gasps rang out. Angelica shot me an amused look.

I started as the live stream showing the kings and queens disappeared and a screen with the flashing colour blocks descended from the ceiling. Kyros was visible through the glass once again, and his hooded gaze held me in its grasp before he removed a small remote from his interior waistcoat pocket.

Damn.

I sucked in a ragged breath, pushing back at the growing inferno low in my stomach, but it was no good. The lusty embers were there to stay until either Kyros or myself had the sense to put more distance between us.

Somehow I gathered that he wasn't the retreating kind.

Given the differences in our tooth length...

I stepped back onto someone's foot.

I grimaced my apology to the glaring Vissimo and quickly shuffled forward again, biting down on my lip to withhold the yearning whimper that wanted to slip out.

Kyros's voice rumbled through Level 66, but I couldn't miss the slightly strained undercurrent.

"As our human guest has already announced," he said, "today's number is seven."

Was that his job? My bad.

I glanced at Kyros, who had the remote lifted in the direction of the screen with the flashing blocks of colour.

I concentrated on a shifting red dot. The dot moved seven times in response to Kyros's command on the remote until it landed on an orange block. The entire orange block wasn't flashing, just most of the squares within it. What did that mean?

Were the blocks specific colours?

Oh!

"Yeti schlong!" I pressed my nose against the glass. "It's Bluff City."

The image was a simplified map of the city. The colour blocks were the various suburbs. And the squares within them must be the individual houses within each suburb.

I recalled the path of the red dot as Kyros clicked on the remote. The dot hadn't moved around the perimeter of the city, it zig-zagged. There was a set path the vampire clans followed with the roll of the dice, just like snakes & ladders or Monopoly.

Shit!

The humans here weren't only unaware victims of some ancient supernatural game; our city was set up like a game board.

"Fuck me," I blurted.

"Miss Tetley," Kyros said.

I glanced up and choked as a wall of heat slammed into my body. He'd taken a single step around the glass tube. That was all it took. Heat flashed in his gaze and he visibly shuddered.

Yep, he felt it too.

But the vampire didn't retreat. Was he serious? A pissing contest?

Kyros spoke from between clenched teeth. "Kindly keep your observations until after the debriefing."

Oh. "Yeah, sure. I can do that. Continue."

His furious snarl ripped through the level, and my knees nearly gave way. I'd swear to whoever was listening that Angelica *laughed* under her breath.

She was fucking crazy.

And so was I.

I'd given Kyros an order.

His body shuddered and he bent forward, looking ready to bolt straight through the glass tube to rip my throat out. Though he wouldn't manage that with the pheromones we were putting out.

Honestly, I wasn't against humiliating Kyros in some way, but I really didn't want to get hot and heavy with him on the floor of Level 66 in front of hundreds of vampires.

Or at all.

That ship had well and truly sailed.

Except if he came any closer, that's where we'd be going.

"Continue, if you'd like to," I forced myself to say, dropping my gaze to the floor. *You bastard.*

His snarling cut off abruptly. Someone needed to introduce the fucker to meditation. Maybe he could hire someone to massage his earlobes full-time too.

"I will," he hissed.

I hovered still and quiet like a good little human, while Kyros rattled through the debriefing. Most was hard to interpret, but his stream of orders made me realise just how intricate this operation had to be. Roll forecasts, statistical probability for future rolls and for the movements of the enemy clan, budgeting, rental price fluctuations, and population trends. My initial impression was closer than I intended. This really was somewhere between Wall Street and a real estate empire.

"Begin," Kyros announced.

If I hadn't felt the lust bordering on panic, too, I would have believed his cool and calm act.

Organised chaos ensued as the gathered Vissimo beelined for their stations—their reactions had to be pretty automatic after one hundred and forty-nine years.

Angelica turned to me. "At ten past midnight, team leaders strategize with their group for an hour. Between one and one thirty, Kyros meets with team leaders to hear their reports and recommendations for the day. Two until three, the nine leaders of the sub-clans meet here to discuss the group strategy. Three to three twenty, Kyros presents the final game strategy to King Julius for approval."

When she paused, I asked, "Then what?"

Angelica tilted her head back, lips curving. "And then our turn really begins."

She made it sound like what I'd just witnessed was high tea compared to an ice-hockey match.

"Angelica," Kyros snapped.

He'd been speaking to a small crowd. Which only went to show that I was completely aware of him. *Dang it.*

I undid two of the buttons of my blouse, certain my clothing had somehow become smaller in the last hour. I was overheating big time.

The horde of female Vissimo behind me was gone, so I slid a foot back, sighing at the instant relief.

I took another.

And a third.

So much better.

"Yes, sir?" Aunty Angie replied.

At her innocent tone, I stopped my retreat and pinned her with a glare. The dark horse was up to something sly. Since her agenda clearly involved me, I very much wanted to know why she was pushing Kyros's buttons by bringing me up here during the thrall. And when I figured it out, I'd derail her plan immediately to teach her not to involve me in the future.

A growl slipped between his teeth. "My office."

I snickered despite myself. "You're in trouble, Angie."

His green gaze snapped to me, and I froze, barely clamping down on a squeak. A fucking *squeak*. My grandmother would fix me with a quelling look over the rim of her teacup if she knew.

"What were you saying, Miss Tetley?" Angie murmured.

The quiet ones always came out on top. "I'm going to put space between me and the—" I cut off, deciding the word *jerk-off* may not be wise to use "—*him* before there's a repeat of last time."

I shouldn't have said it.

The moment I did, the painful simmering surged to outright flames. I could only remember the joyous second we'd reached for each other in my hotel room the other day.

My wing-woman hair slithered over my shoulders as I tilted my head to Kyros. A hooded look revealed that he'd walked farther around the curved glass, eradicating my small retreat.

"Save me," I hissed, shooing the woman toward her nephew with the last scraps of my sanity.

She grinned but obeyed.

I was wise enough to consider the two rules Kyros gave me down on Level 61. I'd already broken one rule tonight by delivering a direct order. I couldn't turn tail and run. He'd be on me in a second.

I backed away like we were locked in some medieval scene where he was the bored king, and I was a joker who'd just recited thirty minutes of knock-knock jokes, keeping my eyes trained on his tie.

I kept going until the glass tube—and the vampire—were out of view. One more day of this torture and I was free. Relatively free. I'd still have to stay in the tower, but that wouldn't be so bad with the better escape opportunity from working on Level 44.

Crap, was this how Stockholm Syndrome started?

"Thank fuck for that!" I tipped my head back as my shoulders sagged with the outpouring of tension. The heat drained away, but the ache between my thighs? That was there for good.

Great.

A few of the nearest Vissimo females laughed quietly at my fervent outburst. Some shot me flat looks too. I pursed my lips as I contemplated their underlying animosity.

Was it because they fancied Kyros for themselves? They could have him.

Maybe it's a superior race complex.

A woman to my left muttered to a vampire on her left. "*My Heart Will Go On.*"

Oh, right. The karaoke.

I coughed. "I apologise for the singing. I didn't realise how good your hearing was. I'm going through some stuff..."

I fidgeted on the spot before catching a small smile from a rock-goddess brunette with the biggest blue eyes I'd ever seen.

"You're in the thrall," she commented, lifting a shoulder.

And that meant what exactly?

I soldiered on. “In my opinion, I captured the essence of Celine Dion perfectly in the second verse.”

A couple cracked smiles. Some of their expressions were downright adoring which seemed kind of strange.

... I’d still take it as a win.

A tiny win.

Which had to be another Stockholm thing because who was I kidding? I was ducked with a capital D.

15

"Do humans usually sleep on the floor next to photocopiers?"

I nuzzled into the surface under my cheek and frowned. Why was it so hard? I didn't like it.

"It is night-time for humans, sir."

The voice belonged to Frangelico. *Mmm*, loved that smooth hazelnut liquor.

I dragged myself upright. "One cupcake shot, please."

Through bleary eyes, I squinted at a group of the most incredible specimens this world had to offer. They loomed over me. One of the women looked like she could sing flowers into existence and one of the men could probably flatten a village with a flex of his biceps.

"Spare the villagers," I slurred, jabbing a finger in his direction.

A blonde in a pantsuit folded her arms. "What's she saying?"

"I have no idea," Angelica said, tapping her trembling bottom lip.

"I'm onto you, Frangelico." I propped a hand against the wall.

I lifted my other hand to the wall on the other side. Felt different. I glared at the grey plastic.

A photocopier?

I was in a narrow corner space between a photocopier and a wall.

What the hell?

My mouth bobbed as I remembered waiting for Angelica. The level had been in so much chaos, I'd stood in this corner. Then sat. Then fallen asleep.

Ugh.

Rubbing my eyes, I threw off the remnants of sleep.

"Cute, isn't she?" a woman chimed. "Like a kitten."

"You can't have one," a man answered in silken tones.

The pantsuit woman cut off their conversation. "I still want to know what she was saying before."

"Frangelico is an ingredient in a cupcake shot," a man with jet-black hair said.

I knew him. And the guy with the shaved head. They were acting as Kyros's bodyguards during his thrall. Were they his brothers too, perhaps?

"But why should Neelan spare the villagers?" Pantsuit asked.

She wasn't the first to try deciphering my delirious just-woke-up ramblings. I'd *said* the words and had no idea what they meant.

"I fell asleep," I declared gravely as I tried to claw my way up the wall. No easy task in a pencil skirt. *Shit*, half of my blouse buttons were undone. When did that happen? I only undid two of them earlier.

Cheap, crappy *Jamieson* clothing!

"Here, let me help you," a man purred.

Accepting defeat, I took his hand. What were the odds I could get my blouse buttons fastened without anyone noticing?

Without any *vampires* noticing.

A sudden heat shoved the thought aside, burning away the last dregs of sleep.

"Kyros is coming closer," I gasped, digging my nails into the stranger's thick forearm.

My head snapped up to meet Kyros's gaze no more than fifteen metres away. His eyes were riveted on where I clutched the male Vissimo's arm.

"Get away from me," I breathed.

Slowly releasing the man, I edged away until my butt hit the back wall of my corner.

"Wise move," the man muttered, snorting.

That was about the last thing I'd do if Kyros was looking at me with murder on his mind. This guy had a death wish.

"He really has lost his head," Pantsuit announced, crossing her arms and surveying Kyros. "I didn't think it possible."

Jet Black replied, "Told you so."

"You're one hundred and twenty, Gerome," she snarled. "Quit saying *told you so*."

"*You're late.*" Kyros hissed the words, stalking closer. A pitiful whine slipped between my teeth as the fire ramped up a notch.

My body hadn't forgotten our early encounter, and the fire was borderline painful.

But I had nowhere to go. I was literally backed into a corner.

The one with the shaved head, Lionel, ignored his brother. "Don't you find it fascinating that she doesn't want him? Usually it's the other way around."

"His last compulsion was thirty years ago though," Gerome said. "And with a vampire. Perhaps that's it. He has the hots for humans."

The others grinned.

"She's had a lot to process in the last few days," Angelica interrupted, frowning at the vampires.

No kidding. Angelica seemed to have forgotten she was a massive part of that shitstorm.

"Please take this talk somewhere else," I panted at them. "And take Kyros with you. Now."

"Did she just give eight members of the royal family an order?" an auburn beauty asked, tossing daggers with her blue gaze.

I closed my eyes briefly.

These were Kyros's siblings. All eight of them? *Of course* they were. Because the world was playing a fucking endless joke on me.

Suddenly, their bickering made perfect sense.

"She said please, but it was definitely a command. Are you used to ordering people around, little woman?" The closest male who'd helped me up was facing Kyros—perhaps not completely stupid after all.

I glared at him. "I'm hardly little—"

My knees shook as I really *looked* at his face. I gasped, tracing over the flawless beauty of his features. Two ocean eyes burned out at me from beneath sandy locks. The waves had a slight flick at the ends—the kind that made half the heterosexual female population long to run their hands through the waves and the rest want to take a pair of scissors to cut a few centimetres away.

My thoughts exactly echoed those I'd had nearly five years ago when I first met him.

It was Business Guy! *Fuck.*

I'd recognise him in a dark room.

Every scrap of bitter embarrassment I'd experienced the night he rejected me at the opening ceremony pushed forward. I was going to die of mortification on the spot.

How was he even here? And a vampire?

My cheeks flamed as surely as I was seventeen again and left without a partner in the middle of the dance floor, posed to kiss with my eyes closed.

Ugh.

"What's going on with her?" Pantsuit asked. "Her heart just went into overdrive."

The man frowned at me. "Do I know you?"

"Nope," I blurted, fidgeting on the spot.

Kill me now.

"Is she attracted to Rory? Jesus, I think she is," Lionel said, choking on a laugh. "You're screwed, bro."

They were the last words anyone uttered.

A roar rent the air.

I turned from the figure of my teenage embarrassment to Kyros just in time to witness as he shifted his weight to rest on the balls of his expensive business shoes.

My fate was tied to Rory's. He was too close!

Lunging forward, I shoved Rory out of my corner, surprised when the vampire stumbled away.

I should leap out of the tight space too. The thought came a split second too late. Panic had me in its grip, and I jumped back in the nook, pressing myself against the wall.

I screamed as Kyros *appeared*, slamming his hands against the walls either side of my head. He gnashed his fangs inches from my face, but fear slid from my body, a white-hot burning covering my frame like a gold guild.

We reached for each other.

My blouse was already half undone and he ripped it clean off my body. I jolted as though he'd electrocuted me. Foreign hands gripped at his arms, and Kyros whirled in a blur, lashing out with a hand clawed.

I needed him.

"Kyros," I panted.

He tossed me over his shoulder, and the air left my lungs as he jumped.

Faces blurred beneath us, and then he was landing, knees bending slightly, already swinging me upright.

I stumbled, but desperation sharpened my balance.

Hands working overtime, I yanked at his tight waistcoat. I only managed to send one button flying before he took over. His hands blurred as he moved between his clothing and my pencil skirt, tearing them to shreds

"*Brother*," someone shouted.

"*Are you seriously trying to reason with him right now, Lionel?*" A female.

I didn't care—as long as she didn't come near Kyros. If she did, I'd tear her face off.

A terrible low growl trembled in his chest, the carnal sound a deadly siren call. I pressed my body against his, slipping my leg between the vampire's thighs.

His terrible snarl cut off, and we moaned at the same time.

In sync, I wrapped my legs around his hips as he lifted me. One large hand supported me under the ass, his other hand splaying over my shoulder blades as he lowered his hot mouth to my breasts.

"Kyros?" I said uncertainly as he ground into my core.

His green eyes flashed down to mine.

I was feeling too much. I was afraid. The flames would consume me. They *were* consuming me.

"*One... two... three!*" a voice boomed.

Four pairs of hands grabbed at Kyros, wrenching him backward. Caged in his arms, I went flying with him. Still, I could feel only lust when his fangs descended mere inches from my face.

Kyros flipped us and landed lightly, setting me gently on the ground before blurring away.

Other arms clamped around me.

The person ran, cradling my body close to theirs. I kicked and screamed, but as the woman ran, my urge to escape steadily dwindled. My trembling legs stopped quivering, and my gasping pants slowed to steady breaths as the heat drained from my lower stomach.

The cold longing that filled the empty space was so strong it resembled a cramp.

That was nothing but the bitter, bitter cold filling my mind as awareness returned.

I was set on my feet and swayed on the spot, just managing to stay upright. I threaded my hands through the hair at either temple as the dizziness from the blurry piggy-back ride faded.

Sound blasted through the level—ripping snarls from Kyros, and a few yelling voices that I couldn't place. That noise was just audible over the swelling murmur of hundreds of people.

... No.

Please no.

Please tell me everyone wasn't still here.

I peered down the length of my naked body. Only my skirt remained. Well, the *waistband*. The skirt itself hung in one long piece over my butt like a tail.

We'd lost control.

Kyros had attacked Rory. My hands shook, and I slid them free of my hair, lowering my arms to my sides.

I lifted my chin to look at the crowd of Vissimo on Level 66.

Stations had been thrown everywhere. Monitors and keyboards lay upended and papers littered the ground. The *workers* seemed torn between watching me and the crashing at my back—Kyros's doing, I assumed.

When the onlookers caught sight of me standing there, more and more seemed to decide I offered the better odds of entertainment.

Sickly embarrassment trickled through me in an oozing roll, and the instinctual fear that mass numbers of Vissimo caused began to mount within me.

"Okay. We believe you now, Gerome," the woman behind me said. She'd carried me away from Kyros.

It was the snobby auburn one.

Then her words slammed into me.

This was a fucking *set up?*

Molten rage mixed with my mortification and fear, and a burning set in behind my eyes. I swallowed hard as Kyros's snapping faded.

God, we'd ripped off each other's clothes in front of all these people.

And his siblings orchestrated it.

I couldn't look at him.

Reaching behind, I undid the zipper of my skirt's remains and let the garment fall to the floor. Sometimes the only way to get out of the mess was to go further into it.

I kicked the shredded skirt aside with no idea where my blouse was.

Keeping my chin raised, I scanned the Vissimo before me. I was standing by the elevator at least. I didn't know where Kyros had carried us or how far Auburn ran with me after, but my exit point was close.

I was buck naked in front of hundreds of creatures with fangs, and I'd come face-to-face with the person from the most embarrassing memory of my teens. Yet as I stood humiliated in front of an entire clan of Vissimo, my only crushing, bitter thought was that I could never escape this place. Or *Ingenium.*

I'd left one game and joined the master edition through sheer stupidity.

Anger exploded in my chest, scratching at the swirling cavern of mortification and fear and lust until it mastered them.

I scowled at the gathered vampires, and in an icy voice I'd never used but heard many times, I said, "Don't you all have work to do?"

Hint: It was a rhetorical question.

The lot of them scrambled, and I could only silently congratulate their wisdom in not hesitating. Holding onto my fury, I pivoted to face the group consisting of Kyros, his eight siblings, and Angelica.

Angelica.

I fixed my gaze on her first.

The slight smile on her face faded at my condemning look. I let her see my humiliation, my confusion, and my devastation. With my narrowed eyes, I told her this was her fault. She brought me up here tonight—either to mess with Kyros herself or as part of his siblings' game. *She* lured me here after apologising for the shit I'd gone through in the last week.

Which rendered her apology to less than worthless.

"Shame on you," I said softly.

She hung her head, breaking eye contact.

I spun on my heel for the lift and pushed the call button.

Turning back, I sought out Kyros at last. Only anger allowed me to meet his eyes after what nearly happened. I'd happily tear off a man's clothes in a private room with someone I'd *chosen*. Never in public like this. *Not* with him.

Never with him.

He stood in the midst of his four brothers—Gerome, Lionel, Rory, and Neelan. Honestly, I didn't fucking care what any of their names were. Not after what they just did to me.

Kyros took a step forward. "Miss Tetley—"

"Stay where you are," I demanded in the same icy voice.

He halted, not a snarl in sight at my order.

"Good boy." My survival instincts were out the proverbial window; every ambition to hide my hatred and make my escape easier was gone. So there was no voice of reason to stop me from showing Kyros just how much I loathed him. Not just for the twisted things *he* had done—for the twisted things those under his power had done too.

Every bit of it was his fault, and I didn't hold a scrap of that sour hatred back.

Ding!

Funny how quickly that sound had switched from annoying to life-saving.

"Deal with your siblings." I flung him another order.

Auburn opened her trap. "What did she just—?"

I clicked my fingers at her and she cut off. "Shut your mouth, Auburn."

Pantsuit laughed. "I like her."

Whatever.

"Someone get her some fucking clothes," Kyros roared. He clamped his lips shut, breathing hard.

Man, I was so, *so* over this.

"She has an excellent body," Rory said, tilting his head and smiling. "Her breasts are full and pert."

"Bro," Lionel whispered.

Rory's quick peek at Kyros's heaving shoulders was enough to shut him up.

I stepped into the elevator, pushing the button for level fifty, instead of sixty-one. This bitch needed wine and lots of it. Most of the Vissimo in the tower had already seen me naked. There would be a nude stroll to the cafeteria before I returned to my room.

Leaning against the back bar of the lift, I maintained my cool glare before ten shocked Vissimo faces.

"See you later, assholes," I said.

I couldn't even summon the energy to be concerned it was 9:20 a.m. and I was nursing a massive hangover at the same desk I'd been sleeping under before vampires existed.

Two and a half bottles of wine had seen to my current state. I hated wine hangovers—tiny demons were dancing a tango in my temples, I had the mouth dries, and my stomach ached from the acid overload.

I'd passed out yesterday afternoon after a full morning of drinking. I vaguely recollected having the bright drunken idea to just walk out of the tower at some point. I'd woken early this morning back in my bed, so I guess the idea never got to the action part.

Several hours of vomiting and a second exhausted sleep had led me to this moment

Work.

Did a concept like work even matter anymore? I couldn't summon the energy to care if so.

I'd discovered two railings of clothing inside my room this morning. I didn't care who might have come in and seen me in my sorry state. I didn't give a single shit about any of these monsters. I just pulled the tags off a hugging white dress with a thin yellow belt, flats, and new underwear—recalling the fatal decision to forgo panties before the trip to Level 66. Even with the temple demons dancing a tango in my head, I'd had the presence of mind to grab my pack, shoving everything inside, including my dirty laundry. If opportunity presented itself, I was out of here.

I groaned.

Should have stopped at bottle two last night. I had almost no memory—everything was there until I put on the robe to walk to Tommy's house. Then nothing.

Dammit, I hadn't had a hangover this bad since Caveman, and seeing as no one had come in to tell me what to do, I might as well continue sitting here clutching my pounding head.

Beast vibrated on the desk.

"Yuss," I mumbled, picking up the phone, careful not to dislodge the charge cable.

Ten percent in twenty minutes. Enough for the phone to turn on.

"Please let that be enough for you to stay awake," I begged him.

Beast chimed in a furious trill.

You don't seriously expect me to believe that?

I groaned. There were about one hundred messages from Tommy. As expected, she'd believed Angelica's camping cover story not one bit. I'd never camped in my life.

Basi, where the fuck are you?
I went to your place and saw a bunch of guys moving your shit out! Wtf!

My gut twisted.

Not that I could have done a thing to reassure her, but I hated that Tommy spent the last three days freaking out. And Clint could have hurt her if she'd confronted him.

Please answer me, Basil. I'm so worried :(
All the worst things are running through my head right now.

I opened a new message having decided two days ago how I'd handle the cover-up. That I was about to lie to my best friend just added a fresh layer of bitterness to my predicament, but her safety was paramount.

Tommy, I'm so, so sorry :(
I got in a jam with Clint and he kicked me out. I went glamping with work so I had somewhere to sleep for a few days. I hated every second of it.

I have so much to tell you, babe. <3 <3
I'm back at work now—crashing at the tower until I get paid and can get a place again.

I'm safe, I promise. Love you <3 <3 <3

I hovered my thumb over the Send button. Fucking hell, the burning behind my eyes was back. I wanted my bestie *bad*. I could only tell her about Clint and losing my stuff, and I'd have to make up a bunch of lies about glamping, but my soul needed her.

I fired off one last line:

I miss you so much, Tom. <3 <3

I gathered together what strength my hangover had left me with and hit Send.

A second later, Beast vibrated.

[Message auto-sent to security recipient. Please do not reply to this message]

What did that mean? Had Tommy's phone credit run out?

I read the message again.

Wait.

My jaw dropped. Those *fuckers*. My texts were being monitored by their security!

I cursed aloud, a filthy word that would have made my grandmother swat me—even though I'd learned all the words from her and Dame Burke.

"Is this a bad time?"

His voice plagued my nightmares and dreams. I was out of my spinning chair and pressed against the full-length window behind before registering that lust hadn't overtaken me.

I didn't budge, looking across the office at Kyros.

His throat worked, and his green gaze darkened. Regret? Pity? Shame? Who knew.

"The thrall is over," I stated. Of course, or I wouldn't be back at work and my white dress would already be the latest clothing sacrifice.

Kyros inhaled. "It is. You're safe from me now. Considering my behaviour, I wanted to see for myself that you were unharmed."

"How nice of you," I answered sarcastically.

Not a speck of anger entered his expression. "You will be here for the foreseeable future, and I don't wish for you to feel unsafe in my tower. Being human, none of what happened is natural to you."

"Your apology is worthless," I informed him. Not that he'd actually said sorry. "None of what you did can be undone."

I would remember standing naked in front of all those vampires for the rest of my probably short life. And that was only if I forgot him torturing me. The list was a mile long by now.

His eyes darkened again. "A long time has passed since I last compelled someone with blood, and that was with a Vissimo. My arrogance led me to underestimate the effect of a blood compulsion with a human. I should have put more safeties in place. I realise that humans are more conservative than—"

I snorted loudly. "You think I was humiliated because I was *naked*?" Had he even been there? I lost my mind up there, the end result being that I nearly had sex with someone I hated.

Nudity was the least scarring part of what happened.

Kyros searched my face and inhaled. "Let me assure you that you have nothing to worry about. I'm just glad no real harm befell you."

Real harm?

Real harm. "You mean that we didn't manage to have sex in front of hundreds of people?"

He maintained eye contact. "Yes."

"If your siblings had their way, things might not have worked out that way."

"They have been dealt with. And Angelica."

I doubted the punishments for royal family members would be harsh. I stared at him only seeing someone I detested with every part of my being.

When he didn't show a flicker of remorse, I exhaled, channelling my grandmother. "Is that all, Kyros?"

He came here to apologise, did a piss poor job of it, and didn't even know what he was apologising *for*. He should have started at frightening me to death and finished at refusing to put distance between us because he didn't want to lose face in front of his stupid clan.

Looking at his handsome face hurt my chest. I'd kissed that cruel mouth without realising I'd lost myself.

I never wanted to feel that again.

"There's another matter to discuss," he said tersely. The vampire strode across the room, his phone in the air.

Frowning, I edged forward and read the screen.

"Who is Tom?" he asked in that rumbling voice of his.

Mother. Fucker.

"You *are* monitoring my phone," I accused, rounding the desk to put space between us. The thrall was over, but I wasn't willing to push the boundaries.

Kyros slipped the phone back into his waistcoat. "This is a separate security matter."

His bullshitery was incredible. "You're joking me. What if the person I text was called Annie? Would it be a matter of security then?"

I had the satisfaction of seeing his green eyes narrow.

Shaking my head, I turned my back to the vampire.

"*What have I told you about turning your back to me?*"

I leaped and pivoted in one movement, my heartbeat ramping.

His eyes had brightened to blazing, something I assumed was associated with his temper.

"I didn't warn you for fun," he snarled. "I warned you because if you listen, you *may* stay alive. My predatory instincts are heightened when you turn away. I am an *alpha*, Miss Tetley. My reaction to a direct challenge is incredibly hard to suppress."

My hands balled and the demons in my temples upped their tango antics. "Three days ago, I found out the world is not the world I knew," I told him flatly. "Since then, I've discovered that the city I live in is not the city I've known since birth. *And* I've been trying to protect myself from a horny vampire. Forgive me if some things are slipping through the fucking gaps, Kyros!"

I threaded my hands through my hair and—to hell with it—screamed. "Jesus Christ!"

I spun away from him, squeezing my head as though it could force the last week from my brain.

Strong hands tugged at my wrists, easing my fingers from my hair.

Kyros tugged me to his chest, but I wrestled to break his hold.

"No," I gasped, panic gripping me. I shoved against his chest and he stood back from me, eyes wary.

"Don't touch me, you fucking monster," I said, hating the tremble in my voice. "Don't ever touch me again."

His chest rose sharply.

"Very well," he said in the quiet following my outburst.

This time *he* was the one to put the desk between us. The vampire planted himself near the doorway, crossing his arms. "You've lost weight."

Huh.

My mind tripped over the subject change.

"When did you last eat?"

Not since you sank your fangs into my neck.

I needed to eat. I was feeling faint and dizzy and my hangover was far worse because I'd had nothing in me to soak up the alcohol.

"Kyros, I'm a big girl. I'll eat when I want to eat. I don't know if being alpha includes force-feeding your clan. But I'm not, and will never be, part of your clan."

A growl rumbled toward me, dark and menacing. His face worked until the sound faded away.

Kyros fixed me with an expectant look.

I threw my hands in the air. "What?"

"I'm waiting for you to tell me who Tom is."

I rubbed my temples, closing my eyes. "This isn't happening to me."

"People generally find it easier to answer my questions, Miss Tetley."

"Is that because you're an annoying ass?"

He growled, almost too low for me to hear. "Out of consideration for what you went through yesterday, I've allowed you to speak in such a way to me. Do not push your luck, human."

My head throbbed as I tossed my hair back. I wanted him gone. "Tom is a friend."

He growled. "What kind of friend?"

"How is that relevant to protecting your clan and family?" I growled right back.

"... It's not." He sounded surprised by the admission. "If you would humour me, Miss Tetley. I'm still feeling some effects of the thrall."

I opened my eyes. "The thrall is over. I don't feel anything anymore."

Anger swept across his face.

Poor baby, did I hurt his oversized ego?

"I find your question downgrading and possessive. But that's about been my experience of your kind so far, so if I tell you who Tom is, will you leave?" I asked.

He considered that and nodded.

"Tommy is female. We do not have sex."

Kyros hummed, watching me. "I never asked whether you had sex or not."

Sure. Like that isn't your real question. "You said you'd leave."

"I was always going to leave," he replied, smirking. "There's one more thing I wish to make clear."

Clenching my teeth, I didn't respond.

"Angelica took it upon herself to show you the inner workings of this tower. You are limited by the constraints I put on your mind, but I wanted to tell you why I can't let such information get to our enemy. I hope that it might help you to understand why I acted toward you in what must seem a brutal way."

It didn't just seem brutal. It was brutal. The torture part at least. Kyros should have kept his distance on Level 66, but neither of us were in control once he got too close. He was just faster and stronger about doing something with his lust than me.

"The clan we battle against, Clan Fyrlia, are brutes without a moral code."

I tried not to laugh my little monkey-mouse head off at that.

"Nearly all crime in Bluff City can be linked to their clan. Most Vissimo clans have made strides to become cultured over the centuries, cultivating ourselves so we are not animals to better ensure our survival. Fyrlia has not. They can act the part if needed, but behind closed doors, they are savages."

Was Kyros aware he just described himself?

"If we lose *Ingenium*," he continued, looking out the window, "the consequences are severe. For my family. And for our people who will be forced to join Clan Fyrlia. If I or those in this tower come across as ruthless, it is because of what we stand to lose."

Friends, family, and a better world were the only things worth fighting for, in my opinion. But to put any of those things at risk over a *game* was something I couldn't abide. I didn't give a single shit about the consequences of losing *Ingenium* and how he used that as an excuse to treat me as he had.

"I hear you," I replied. *I won't ever forgive you, bastard.*

His eyes narrowed, but he straightened after a beat. "Very well, I shall leave you to your day."

Finally.

Kyros strode to the door and, with a mind of their own, my eyes slipped down to his ass, outlined in his pinstriped suit.

My mouth dried and heat stirred in my stomach.

He'd said the blood compulsion thingy still affected him, right? I still had some of it in me too.

"Perhaps coming to speak to you was a mistake."

Kyros looked at me from the doorway, one hand on the frame. The care with which he made the movement made me realise how easily he could destroy this office, this skyscraper, and this city. I'd witnessed his strength.

"I just wanted you to understand." Kyros finished.

Never more serious, I met his weary green eyes. “If you’d asked, Kyros, I could have just told you understanding this is the last thing I want right now.”

“What do you want?” he said low.

Kyros hadn’t given me empathy or a real apology, but he had given me honesty. I rewarded him with the same. “I want to wake up and discover you don’t really exist.”

His lips pressed together.

Were his breaths deeper than before? I couldn’t tell.

We stared at each other. Then Kyros jerked his head in a tight nod.

“You will find your appointments for the day in *Monocle*,” he told me, gesturing at the computer. “You’ll be able to create your own login when it opens this time. Vampires usually sleep from 3:00 a.m. to 1:00 p.m., but you’ll work 9:00 a.m. until 5:00 p.m.—human hours.”

The last part flowed in one ear and out the other.

“Appointments?” I said weakly. “Like preliminary visits?”

Outside of the tower?

My breath caught.

“Yes, like preliminary visits,” he said shortly. “The addresses are stored in the software, and there’s a white car in the garage parked closest to the elevator. It is yours to use for site visits. Keys are in the ignition.”

Holy. Shit.

This wasn’t happening.

I was totally, totally out of here.

16

The thing about the loan car was I only had my learner's licence, but a tiny thing like not knowing how to drive wasn't coming between me and escape.

The flashy bit of white metal from Kyros came equipped with GPS—luckily, because Beast didn't lower himself to that modern shit.

Two small scrapes later, but no crashes, I pulled over outside 77 Bard Boulevard—a two-bedroom house in Orange.

The high-pitched whine of metal rang out from outside, and I jerked on the wheel.

"Crap!" I kept forgetting how wide the thing was. I mean, it wasn't my car, but if this was my getaway vehicle, I wanted to keep it nice.

I sighed, turning off the car—it took me ten minutes to find a button in the middle of the dashboard that turned the stupid vehicle on. Turned out *the keys are in the ignition* wasn't a literal instruction.

"He's made it too easy," I told the dashboard.

It didn't answer back. So that was good.

The one thing I wanted was to drive to my grandmother. Kyros had given me a car, the keys, and hadn't set any restrictions—aside from the mind compulsion. I didn't have a guard tracking my movements. I supposed people could be watching me, but if they were, I couldn't see them.

The street was otherwise empty of cars and people.

... Kyros had offered me my escape on a silver platter. It was too easy by far.

"He's testing me. Or he knows something I don't." I groaned and thumped back against the headrest.

An entire morning spent researching my two afternoon prelim visits while I knocked back glass after glass of water had lessened my headache, but my eyes felt scratchy and my body weak. The hope that fuelled me after hearing about the car had siphoned away.

I really had to eat. A visit to *Sister Sushi* was in order. I had fifty-five dollars to burn. *And*—I straightened in the deep, plush seat.

"I get paid today!" Today was Thursday. I should have been paid yesterday. Angelica had kept herself scarce since our last encounter.

I'd have to hunt her down to get every cent owed.

Except that would require going back.

Which I wasn't doing.

Or had Kyros known I'd be back for the money? The guy was a games master for a living. Why should I assume this ploy was anything less than another game? Was giving me a car actually a test—or had he just banked on me *thinking* it was a test?

"Oh man, that's getting too crazy," I spoke to the car again.

Thumping my head against the black leather headrest once more, I grabbed the file for 77 Bard Boulevard and swung the door open. Tucking the small remote that I guessed passed for a key these days in my bra, I walked up the steep driveway.

The car beeped at my back and I spun.

No idea what that meant. Had it self-locked? I winced at the long scratches down the curb-side tyres and body.

The small scrapes weren't so small. "Oops."

I grinned at the thought of the damaged car sitting in the garage of the tower until someone told Kyros.

"I told you people, I'm not interested in selling!"

Yelping, I gripped the base of my throat, spinning to the house.

A curtain twitched behind the front bay windows.

"Get off my property before I call the police."

I ducked my head, catching a glimpse of smeared bright-red lipstick and beady blue eyes behind the curtain.

"I mean it!"

From the woman's attitude, I could assume this wasn't really a prelim visit. Not like the first approach visits I'd been on with Katerina. This woman made it sound like *Live Right* bothered her constantly. They'd sent me to someone who hated them.

Fine for me. I hated them too.

"Okey-dokey, Mrs Gaughton. I'm leaving right now," I sang out in the direction of the window—cracked open a sliver.

The curtain twitched again. "Good. Stay away or I'll get an order."

An order, huh? If she was going to bluff, she should research the terms for five minutes. "Sure thing. I'll make a note on your file that you're not to be bothered again."

Could I do that?

I set off for the car again. Maybe I could pull over in a quiet street and take a nap. As I picked my way down the steep driveway, I spotted a wilting lavender bush in her tiered garden. The whole garden looked sad if truth be told, but I always noticed lavender wherever I went because it was Grandmother's favourite.

She hung lavender dry beads in her wardrobe and her clothes carried the scent. When she took her green tea in the afternoons, it was always in the lavender terraces. That was the only estate garden my grandmother tended to—the singular hobby she pursued around managing the estate's finances.

I glanced back at the curtain. It rippled. Mrs Gaughton was watching to make sure I left.

I hesitated, then called, "You're overwatering your lavender, did you know? My grandmother said you should only water them when the soil is dry up to your first finger knuckle."

There was no reply.

"Okay, good luck with it," I said.

Naptime.

I could swing by my old apartment and see what the state of things were. At this point, my stuff seemed a lost cause and not worth my time, but my second appointment was at three. I had time to kill.

"Wait!"

I peered back up the driveway. The tiny old woman had left her window station to squeeze her head through a crack in the front door.

"Yeah?" I asked.

"I can't get that lavender bush to take off. Do you have any other tips?"

Ugh, apart from lavender being drought resistant and hard to kill? I actually did know a few things. My grandmother was most relaxed in the west gardens, so I gravitated there to be in her company at 4:00 p.m. most days. "I know that you shouldn't have pruned it now. You should get it done before summer or if you—"

"*Yes, yes*, but don't shout it at me. I have to write it down. Come inside." The crack widened.

I tucked away my smile at her sudden change of heart but glanced at the car, thinking of that nap.

Eh, I didn't really have anywhere to be.

I walked up the driveway. "Sure, why not. Do you have peppermint tea?"

She swung the door wide and stepped aside to let me in. "Think I have a few bags leftover. I buy it for when my sister visits from Frankton Gorge."

I slipped inside and waited on the worn cream carpet as she shut the door. "I love Frankton Gorge. Bluff City is so flat, it's nice to be in the green hills sometimes."

Mrs Gaughton cackled. "Especially with those wineries."

Wine.

My stomach roiled and I blanched.

"Are you okay?" the woman, mid-sixties from her file, asked.

An excuse hovered on the tip of my tongue. Then I remembered *Live Right* could go suck a big dick.

"I got plastered last night. A couple of bottles of wine. I'm hungover."

Mrs Gaughton snorted, patting my forearm before dragging me through the house. "Can't say I envy you that. Two weeks ago, I overindulged in my extended Sunday lunch and was in a sorry state. Have you eaten?"

I glanced around the house as she led me into a cramped kitchen with a round table in the middle of the space. Pretty nice for Orange, really. Some of the rooms were on the tiny side, but the place was in good repair. Nicer than Tommy's.

My stomach lurched again.

Tommy hadn't replied to my messages before I left the office for lunch. Beast would be dead in my pack by now, but I'd text her again as soon as I could, even if that meant Kyros reading my texts.

"Nah, not today," I admitted. *Or maybe four days.*

"A bit of grease to line the stomach then," she declared, and got to work in the kitchen. "I always do the same on a Monday."

"Sounds like your extended Sunday lunch is a party," I said with a small laugh.

"Just a bottle of Shiraz and a few vodkas. But sometimes they go down so smooth, I add an afternoon cap or three."

Mrs Gaughton got wasted every Sunday.

Withholding my grin, I took a seat at the table and within minutes had my hands wrapped around a piping hot peppermint tea. The woman whipped around the cramped space in a frenzy, pulling out cheese, onions, butter, and bread. She slapped everything together and set the sandwich to fry in a pan. Whatever it was, it smelled freakin' delicious.

Only then did Mrs Gaughton yank open a drawer to pull out a floral notebook. The word *garden* was scrawled across the front in black marker.

"I need everything you've got on lavender," she spat. "It's the third one I've planted in the same spot. At this point, it's personal."

I puzzled over her ferocity for a second before closing my eyes.

"Right, let me soak up everything my grandmother says about them." Overwatering was the main thing. And well-drained soil.

Keeping my eyes closed, I pictured my grandmother—dressed in one of her token skirt suits—ambling about the lavender terraces. And I began to rattle off everything I could recall about lavender.

At some point, the older woman slid a plate in front of me, and I opened my eyes to eat the cheese and onion toasty, chewing on the deliciousness when Mrs Gaughton was furiously writing down a tip.

"You don't think the lavender will die because I pruned it too early?" She studied her notes.

"No idea," I replied. "You'll have to wait and see with that one."

She hummed, tapping the pen against her red lips, spreading the smear farther. "I'd love if the bush was thriving by my sister's next visit."

"You have the one?" I asked. "I don't have any siblings."

Standing abruptly—I was learning everything was that way with her—Mrs Gaughton placed her notebook back in the drawer and lingered at the bench, cleaning the pan and setting the kitchen to order once more.

"Yes, just the one," she answered eventually. "She'll visit in two weeks."

I smiled at the yearning in her voice. "That sounds lovely. I hope the lavender plays game for you."

She turned and smiled. "So do I. If it does, it will be thanks to you."

"I'll have to drive by and check on it." I winked, getting to my feet.

I followed her back to the door, checking my watch. Shoot, I'd spent more time here than I thought—I had twenty minutes to get to my second appointment.

"Don't just drive by, Basi." She glowered. "You're welcome to come in. If you have any tips on marigolds, I'd planned to replant a bunch of those next week."

I wondered why she didn't give up when she so clearly had a black thumb. "Thank you, Mrs Gaughton."

"Please call me Mrs Hannah, dear."

My heart warmed. She really was a lovely woman. Eccentric, but completely adorable. I missed my grandmother so much that any old woman was endearing to me right now.

"Thank you, Mrs Hannah. I might take you up on that visit."

It wasn't until I was bunny hopping my loan car down the road that I realised I hadn't brought up the house once. Husky laughter tumbled from my lips. If Kyros was going to lock me in a tower, I'd be the worst fucking employee ever.

Because I was going back.

After a few hours to mull the coincidental turn of events, I'd decided giving me the means to escape was certainly a test. Kyros wanted to see if I was a flight risk. He probably had safety measures in place, and if I ran and they caught me, that was it.

I had to out-bluff him.

That meant figuring out what his edge was before I escaped. Kyros had an ace up his sleeve or he wouldn't have let me out of the tower. A quick search of the work system, *Monocle*, had shown I had appointments tomorrow afternoon and next Monday, so I'd be out of the tower again. Knowing that, running at the first chance felt like a bad idea. I'd screwed up too much lately, and most of my fuck-ups had resulted from rushing into things.

Not this time.

I'd take the first opportunity for a *successful* escape. Kyros had said that failing my *trial* would result in further compulsion. I had to be smarter than I'd been so far.

The next address was in Orange too. Which I suppose made sense—the clan had landed on Orange last night which meant they had twenty-four hours to get as many contracts signed in that suburb as possible. The GPS took me past Tommy's place, and my heart jerked in the direction of her familiar home.

God, I could go inside, crawl under her covers, and never come out again.

Except I couldn't.

I couldn't do so many things because I was in another fucking mess. One that I wasn't sure would ever end. I knew about vampires now. That couldn't be undone ever.

Turning one of the levers by the wheel, I narrowly avoided a honking car as I turned onto Friar Close. The indicator kept switching damn sides! I turned off the windscreen wipers, and ripped the wheel right, narrowly missing someone's hedge.

"Shit," I said, choking on a laugh.

Driving was pretty fun. Though a quick look in the mirror by my head told me the hedge hadn't survived intact.

Crap.

I gunned it to the end of the street around the curve of the close to 190 Friar Close. Hopefully the owner of the hedge didn't see me. Better get this prelim over and done with quickly just in case. This visit was probably to another person *Live Right* had pestered before.

Grabbing the house file, I leaped out of the car and strode along the short driveway.

I whistled low. Double garage in Orange. What a rich guy.

I knocked a few times and retreated, arranging my face into a smile.

A minute passed, and I slid a foot toward the car.

The door swung open.

Dammit.

"What do you want?" a lean fifty-something asked. His tone was polite, but the tightness around his eyes told me he didn't appreciate the visit one bit. Mr Yersaw retired three months ago and was a widower—or so *Monocle* said.

His face fell. "Oh, are you one of those blasted Live Right people?"

Yep, they'd visited him before. I opened my mouth, but he rushed on.

"Bad time. I'm watching *Truth Ranges.*"

My eyes rounded. "You are? What season?"

He faltered. "Seven?"

"Before Macy Lane breaks her finger while fixing the roof tiles during a storm or after?" I gasped. "Shit, spoiler alert. So sorry!"

Mr Yersaw's mouth twisted. "Don't worry, I've seen every episode and keep up to date."

"I'm usually the same, but I've missed an entire week," I confessed, grimacing.

He blinked and then consulted his watch. "It's 3:20 p.m."

We looked at each other, faces slackening.

Every Thursday at 3:30 p.m. something happened that every self-respecting *TR* fan tuned in for.

"*Truth Ranges* omnibus!" we chorused.

17

"Hey, Basi?" A hand shook my shoulder. "Hello?"

My surroundings came to me and I bolted upright. "Frankenstein!"

Mr Yersaw frowned down at me. "Huh?"

I was sprawled across his couch. *Dang*, I'd fallen asleep during the *Truth Ranges* omnibus. "Transportation."

He mouthed the word, eyes scanning my face.

I glanced around, trying to kickstart my brain after the nap. I'd intended to stay for a couple of episodes—not the entire thing—but now another show was on, *Harkies Hullabaloos*—a cooking show following elderly divorced women who travelled the world on motorbikes.

"Sorry," I said when I could trust my mouth. "I speak nonsense when I first wake."

The skin around his eyes crinkled. "Had a friend in the Navy who used to do the same."

"I apologise for falling asleep," I muttered. "I got really, really drunk last night and I'm nursing a hangover."

He returned to his seat. "Is that why your shoes are cream and your dress white? My wife used to say they shouldn't be worn together."

I blinked down at my flats which clashed with my outfit. "Yep, that's why."

"I never was one for drinking. Didn't like the person I became with it."

Neither had I last night.

"But I hope you had a good time with your friends," he added when I didn't reply.

My lips twitched. "I drank by myself in a hotel room."

"Always thought that was the way I'd do it, too, if I took up alcohol," he confessed. "Though that seemed a lot like being an alcoholic." The middle-aged man coloured. "Not that you're one—an alcoholic."

My grin widened and I held up a hand. "Mr Yersaw, I'm not offended. Don't worry, it was a one-off. Kind of. Happens a few times a year, tops. I should be going though. It has to be getting late."

"7:00 p.m.," he told me. "I didn't know if I should wake you. You were out to it."

Yeah, no wonder. I hadn't taken good care of myself lately. My stomach was begging for food again, and the last few hours of sleep was the best I'd had all week. "Thank you so much for letting me watch the omnibus with you—even if I fell asleep." I gave him a lopsided smile.

He smiled tentatively.

Mr Yersaw's eyes slid to the file I'd chucked on the seat next to me. "You know. Watching TV with someone was nice. I retired a few months ago, but when I imagined retirement, I was travelling the world with a friend or catching up on a million hobbies. All I've done is sit in this house. As soon as I retired, my body decided to fall apart."

I listened patiently as he rattled off his list of ailments.

"I'm beginning to hate this house." He finished.

My heart panged. "No one likes feeling trapped. But maybe you'd like the house better if you got out of these walls for a while? Did some travelling."

"No," he said firmly. "Last week, I went to an RV sale yard. I want to drive something like that around—a new place every other week—for as long as I want. Weeks, months, or years. The rest of my life. They have convoys you can join, did you know? I could meet people."

"Sounds like fun," I said. "Why don't you do it?"

"I need to pay for the RV." He gave me a pointed look.

That blows. "That's a real shame. Is there anything you could do for cash?"

He peered at the file. "I have an asset."

I caught his second pointed look. Oh. *Oh!*

"You want to sell your house? If so, I can certainly help you."

Excitement lit the man's face. "You know, I hadn't planned to sell for another fifteen years. I can keep up with the maintenance and I've lived here since I scraped together the house deposit thirty years ago. But I guess the last three months have shown me that I've spent my life working. I'll be dead in thirty years at best. I need to do something now."

Okay, shit. I was maybe about to sell a house.

Shaking back my bed hair, I picked up the file and perched on the seat. "If you're looking for something right now, you are talking to the right woman. Live Right has a same-day signing option."

All prelim files came with a valuation and a few contracts with different values on them.

"You're kidding?" he said, slumping back on the two-seater. "*Today?*"

"If that's what you want, I can make it happen. But are you sure you're not rushing into this?"

Good one, Basi. Talk him out of it.

He stared vacantly, then frowned at his hands. "It's the opposite. I should have rushed into living a long time ago. This world just made me think I couldn't."

His words hit me with force.

"What's the offer?" Mr Yersaw said firmly.

Blinking, I opened the folder. "Well, we had your home evaluated two months ago for four hundred and sixty thousand," I said, reading the bottom number of the valuation range as Katerina had taught me.

Mr Yersaw considered that, and sighed, "Should have sold five years ago, but I could buy four brand-new RV's with that. My Navy pension would be enough to cover travel costs. I'll take it."

... He would?

"Uh, uhm." I shuffled through the contracts. "Let me just see..."

The man burst to his feet, pointing at the cooking show on TV. Four women were racing down a country lane on their Harleys. "Why not? Anyone can start at any time, right?"

Wasn't that what I'd tried to do when I left the estate? My voice was soft when I answered him, "Yes. I really do believe that, Mr Yersaw."

"Where do I sign?" he said with a nod.

"You haven't read the contract," I said weakly.

He paused in the act of searching for a pen.

"Is it a good contract?" he suddenly asked, glancing at me. "You seem like a nice person, but I guess this house is all I have. Shouldn't be stupid with it."

Angelica had assured me their clan operated and obeyed human law to the letter. Still, I was securing someone's home so they could fulfil their retirement dream. "How about you take a seat and we go through the contract together?"

I drew out the back contract and read the value print on it. "And Live Right would be delighted to offer you five hundred and ten thousand for your home."

Take that, Kyros. You fucker.

Smirking as a gobsmacked Mr Yersaw took a seat, I began reading through the contract with him line by line.

I blew my hair out of my eyes. Long hair was really annoying sometimes. Like when I rolled over at night and the strands somehow got trapped in my armpit. Or like when my hands were handcuffed behind my back.

"Just take me to the station," I told the officer who'd dragged me out of the car and was now pushing me ahead of her. Jail was the perfect solution to all my problems.

"You're an employee of Kyros Sky," the woman grunted—like that explained why they weren't locking me up like a normal person.

A second officer was pulling my scratched-up loan car into the garage. He parked beside the police cruiser I'd ridden in. Man, I'd really done a number on the white car.

Fun while it lasted.

The female officer had called ahead to the tower, so I had no hope of giving the po-po the slip and burying the whole episode.

The middle-aged male officer joined us, and both police tensed as the door to the lobby opened.

I blew out a loud exhale as Kyros bore down on us dressed in the same pinstripe suit he'd worn to visit me this morning.

"Officers," he greeted, extending his hand.

The police officers didn't hesitate to shake it. They hadn't even shaken *my* hand when they saw I was a Le Spyre.

Why wasn't I surprised that Vissimo had a friendly relationship with the police? *Sticking to the letter of the law,* my butthole.

Kyros turned to me. "Explain."

I clamped my mouth shut.

His jaw ticked as the silence extended.

The female officer intervened as the air between us crackled with unspent tension. "Basilia was caught driving the wrong way down a one-way street, sir."

Power to her, she didn't so much as blush in his sexy presence. Unlike her partner.

My mind had snagged on another problem.

I'd had to show the officers my learner's licence with my *real name* on it.

Shit! If these vampires found out who I really was, that would lead them directly for my grandmother.

"Basilia," Kyros said slowly, sliding me a veiled look. "That's what Basi stands for?"

"Nope, Basil," I quipped, shifting my arms. Hard to look dignified in handcuffs. The metal was cutting into the underside of my wrists something chronic. "What'll it be, officers? Three months in jail? Life? Let's get a move on."

"Further to that," the female officer sent me a quelling look, "Basilia then produced her learner's licence. I'm sure I don't need to tell you that driving without supervision on a learner's licence is against the law. In addition, we received two phone calls today regarding complaints of a white car that we believe she is responsible for."

It must've been the hedge. What else did I do?

"I accept the consequences of my actions," I said gravely.

Last week, I'd be pooping my white dress and cream flats over being arrested. Today, I knew vampires were real. Sue me. Giving a shit about any of this was hard.

Kyros stepped closer to me, whispering, "Yes, you will."

He turned to the officers. "Would the police department consider a warning this time? I personally guarantee there will not be a repeat."

A warning? "I'm a criminal," I blurted. "You don't want to even know the things I've done. Bad stuff."

No one paid me any mind.

The officers exchanged a look, but the woman clearly wore the pants.

She opened her mouth. "Miss—"

"Basi will do," I said hastily.

Everyone stared at me.

A deep frown marred the space between Kyros's brows.

"We're friends after that ride, right?" I aimed the joke at the female officer. "First-name basis..."

Her partner whispered in her ear, "Did you do a drug and alcohol test?"

She nodded mutely and forced her attention to Kyros once more.

"I'll agree to a warning. This once. You've never failed to come through for the department before."

I liked this woman. She was one of those *I'm comfortable in my skin and don't need to shout to garner respect* people.

But I'd like her more if she arrested me. Did the police know vampires existed? Did this pair know Kyros had fangs and a bad temper?

"My thanks," Kyros said, dipping his head like a fucking prince—which I guess he was.

He looked at me, and I looked back.

"Thank the officers," Kyros growled.

Oh, right.

"Thank you for setting me loose on Bluff City so I can commit crime again," I told them. Really, I just bent the rules. I looked up the one-way before driving up there—and I drove as fast as possible in case someone came around the corner.

Was it my fault Grey was a maze of one-ways?

The officers scowled at me, but the male eventually reached for the keys at his belt.

Kyros held up a finger. "Removing the handcuffs isn't necessary."

I spluttered. "Like fuck." My wrists were sore—and my shoulders. I'd never considered myself a computer-era sloucher, but the pain across the fronts of my shoulders said otherwise.

The woman slid a look my way and jerked her head at her bitch as I continued spluttering. They hopped into their cruiser and drove away.

I swore. "There goes my respect for the police."

Kyros's cool expression dropped the second the car left the garage. "We'll continue this discussion in my office, Miss Tetley."

Authority brought out the worst in me. "Is this like a principal's office thing or a kinky thing?" I awkwardly displayed the cuffs.

"It's a *you seriously fucked up* thing," he replied, eyeing the cuffs as though that could change.

There went my plans to quietly slip into my room without any contact with *Vissimo*. But I'd wrangled my way through the interaction without the coppers letting my real name slip, so that was a win. Now I was tied to Kyros through this blood compulsion, I absolutely could not let him find out who I was. The thought of what he might do to Grandmother to get her estate made my stomach churn.

I waited until he was nearly back at the garage door. "I agree to the cuffs, but you'll need to get my stuff out of the car, if it's not too much trouble?"

Kyros stilled before slowly facing me again, a snarl slipped between his teeth.

I wiggled my fingers, displaying the handcuffs again.

"What?" I widened my eyes. "It wasn't an order."

He blurred to me, and I only managed to stand my ground because my brain hadn't processed his arrival until several seconds later. The vampire lowered his head to mine, and I turned my face away.

Not quite touching me, he dragged his nose from my jaw to temple, inhaling deeply like the night he drank from my neck.

"Playing power games with me is a very bad idea, *Basilia*," he purred.

I kept my head turned. "I don't play games, Kyros. I loathe games. I left everything I'd ever known to escape them. And don't call me Basilia. Only one person calls me Basilia."

"Maybe I should call you Basil then," he said sarcastically, straightening.

I tilted my head back to meet his gaze, annoyingly aware that I still had bed hair from the nap on Mr Yersaw's couch. "No, not that either. Another person calls me Basil and it's not you. You can call me Miss Tetley and that is all."

Stepping around him, I strode to the door. "If you grab my stuff, could you not forget my pack? And there are two files."

My lips twitched at his quiet growl. I had this *no orders* thing down pat.

A shriek left my lips as I was picked up and cradled in an iron grip. The air rushed around me, and I was only aware that we moved with incredible, mind-boggling speed. He'd run with me once before, *that* night, but I'd been near death at the time.

One of his sisters ran with me last night too. Her speed was nothing on his.

I shifted higher to peer over his shoulder, gaping at the stairs circling away before my very eyes like a swirling kaleidoscope frame. I settled back in his arms, and in less than a minute, I was deposited in a metal chair.

Kyros chucked my bag and the files on the floor.

"Couldn't wait for the elevator?" I enquired.

He leaned forward on the armrests, crowding me. My heart pounded as his fangs descended.

"When you taunt me," he rumbled, "I will react. I am an alpha *Vissimo*. Unless you'd prefer I latch onto your femoral artery, you can fucking deal with the outbursts."

I shrugged a shoulder. "Not a worry. That was kind of like a rollercoaster ride."

He reeled away, swearing.

The room registered. It was the huge chamber where he'd tortured and bit me. Air lodged in my throat, and I scrambled off the chair.

Or tried to.

My knees gave way, and twisting to avoid landing on my face, I forgot my hands were cuffed.

I cried out as my entire body weight forced the metal into my wrists. Face screwed up, I rolled off my hands.

"Fuck." Kyros crouched down and sat me up.

He reached around and there was a sharp pinch before the cuffs fell away.

I hissed, drawing my hands around to inspect them. "Ouch."

Kyros inhaled and stilled. "You're bleeding."

"I guess you'd know." My voice shook from the lingering pain. I flipped my trembling hands and eyed the blood dripping from both wrists.

The breath caught in Kyros's throat, and I snatched my hands away.

He was showing fang again.

I pulled my knees to my chest, and he jolted, meeting my eyes. As I watched, the dreamy quality left his green orbs. He gathered me again—because I didn't have legs anymore, apparently—and tried to set me in *the chair*.

"No," I shouted, kicking out.

"What's wrong with you?" he snapped, placing me on my feet.

I pushed away. "I'm not sitting in that chair."

"Why not?"

Of course he wouldn't remember a small thing like terrifying a human to death. Spotting another chair, I walked to it. *Leather. Tall back. Comfy.* Spinning it, I plonked myself down. It was huge—I could probably sleep in this thing.

Pulling my legs up, I peered at Kyros. "Alright. I'm ready."

A flicker of resignation crossed his face. "Where were you going when the police caught you? Your shift ended at 5:00 p.m. It is now 9:20 p.m."

Cold relief swept through me. Letting me go *was* a test. "I left my last visit late."

In a burst of speed, Kyros eradicated the space between us, slamming his hands on the armrests either side of me. One of them cracked.

"Do not *lie* to me, Miss Tetley."

My chest rose and fell, and several pounding heartbeats passed before my tongue unlocked. "It's not a lie."

He pressed closer, gaze lowering to the blood dripping down both forearms. The dreamy quality began to seep in again.

"If you have Band-Aids, I can handle this," I whispered.

His nostrils flared. "It's fine."

I didn't have to speak. My doubt was louder than words.

Kyros ran a hand through his toffee strands, releasing a breath. "Perhaps that's best."

In a blink, a first aid kit was on my lap. I shook off my reaction to his speed and opened the bag, riffling for a Band-Aid.

"You were leaving the city and the police caught you," he stated as I ripped the packaging off a large Band-Aid. I'd clean the wound later. Maybe. *Nurse of the year.*

I sighed. "Look, you apparently think I was running. I don't know what to tell you. I was buying your clan a house. You're welcome."

He'd been pacing, fangs descended, but pulled up short. "You... secured a house? You had two prelim visits."

"If that's what you call being given the dreg properties."

"What one did you secure?" He crossed to where he'd thrown the files down in a temper and crouched.

He thumbed through Mrs Gaughton's before picking up Mr Yersaw's.

"109 Friar Close," he said in excitement, standing with the file.

Kyros grinned, and I studied his reaction. Had he ever done anything but smirk in my presence?

The vampire held the file up in the way I held out strawberry mojitos for cheers. "We've been after this property for fifteen years, Miss Tetley."

"You've been bothering Mr Yersaw for fifteen years?" *Poor guy.* No wonder the tentative man was driven to call me a *blasted Live Right person*.

The vampire game master laughed, inspecting the file in glee, and I sucked in a breath. *Whoa*, remembering that I was filled with his favourite juice was hard when he laughed like that.

He lowered the file. "This doesn't excuse the fact that you drove on your learner's licence and were arrested in a company car."

The words doused the small fire in my ovaries.

Kyros set the file on the desk behind me and perched on the edge, swinging my chair to face him. "When I offered you the car, why didn't you inform me that you couldn't drive?"

Because I was on a one-way ticket outta this asylum.

I hung my head. "I was just so embarrassed I didn't have my full licence."

"You can lie better than that."

His comment startled a laugh from me.

I straightened and switched tactics. "Why would I? I wanted to have a few hours away from this insanity."

"This isn't insanity, Miss Tetley," he replied. "It is our way."

Their way sucked. Literally.

I pressed my twitching lips together.

His jaw ticked. "Am I to assume the damage to the car can be explained by the fact you cannot drive?"

I lifted a shoulder. "Sorry 'bout that."

Kyros rubbed his jaw.

"Do I test your patience, Kyros?" I peeked up through my lashes at him.

A flicker of annoyance showed before he caught my impish expression. He cast me a flat look that told me how impressed he was.

He stood again, taking Mr Yersaw's file with him. "What about 77 Bard Boulevard? Any luck?"

"*Mrs Gaughton*," I corrected. Did he really think of the humans in Bluff City as addresses? What a douche. "I worked on her for a couple of hours over a cup of tea. She wasn't having any of it."

But her lavender bush will soon be thriving.

He glanced up. "You got inside her house?"

"I did." Pursing my lips, I glanced at the exit and began shifting toward it.

"Sit down, Miss Tetley. We aren't done."

"It's getting late," I told him, huffing as I sat. "Better get to Level 66 for the roll so you don't miss it."

Kyros held my gaze as he called, "Angelica."

Three seconds passed before his aunt stepped into his torture-chamber office.

"Sir." She bowed.

"Please assign Miss Tetley to your problem cases henceforth."

My jaw dropped. "That's not fair."

"I have a damaged car and only my goodwill with the police saved you from a black mark on your record. That you apparently didn't care about in your bid to be locked up. Do you really think jail could save you from my reach?"

My mouth snapped shut, and his eyes glimmered in triumph.

Dick.

"It will be done immediately, sir." Angelica cast a quick look at me. I crossed my arms, firing off all the fuck-off signals I knew.

She didn't try to apologise.

Good.

"My pay is a day late," I informed her.

"It's waiting in your room. Did you get the racks of clothing?"

I gestured to my white dress, standing. "As you see. And I get a commission for buying a property."

After surveying my cream flats, she turned to Kyros, face lightening. "What one?"

"109 Friar." He grinned again.

"Well done, Basi," she said, moving closer to hold out her hand.

I stared at it until she drew back.

"Miss Tetley—"

I stomped my foot. "Get to it, Kyros! Jesus. Anyone would think you're purposefully dragging this out. I'm tired and hungry."

His green eyes dropped to my feet. "Did you just stomp your foot?"

Dammit.

"No. Now please say whatever you feel that you need to say so I can leave."

"One day that mouth of yours will get you in trouble," the vampire told me coolly. "You mistake me for a far more lenient man."

You're not a man. You're a beast.

I waited, edging toward the door.

He took the seat I'd vacated. "You'll be driven to each appointment by one of my Indebted. They will teach you to drive. I cannot spare anyone else."

"You're teaching me how to drive?" My scowl faded.

Kyros quirked a brow. "No, I'm not. One of my Indebted will."

"One of your minions will teach me to drive?" My voice was tiny.

He frowned. "Why are you acting stranger than usual?"

No one except the estate butler had ever offered to teach me to drive.

"Thank you." I beamed at him.

He stared blankly like I was a book written in sugar-high toddler.

"You're welcome?" Kyros asked.

I looked at the door and groaned as curiosity overtook my hunger. "What's an Indebted?"

"Vissimo who have broken vampire law. They lose clan status and become mercenaries who work to pay off their debt. Only then can they rejoin our society."

"Just to be clear, these criminals will teach me to drive?" Was he nuts?

He spun in the chair to face the desk. "Most are second or third generation Indebted. They're no trouble. Contrary to what you might expect, they are far less likely to act out than the rest of the clan."

Oh, great. *Perfect.* That made me feel tons better. Though if the punishment for human crimes wasn't confined to the wrongdoer and spanned generations, I might be compliant too.

I grunted. "That it?"

"That it," he grunted back, attention on the large monitor on his desk.

Did Kyros just make a joke?

A grin *and* a joke in one night.

Next thing, a pig would fucking fly.

I strode for the door. First stop, Level 50. Then bed. Even with my three-hour nap, I was beat.

"Miss Tetley?" Angelica's voice halted me.

She continued. "I thought you might like to know a woman named Tommy came by the office today."

I tensed.

That wasn't ideal. The last place I wanted my bestie turning up was *Kyros Sky*.

"And?"

"She wanted you to be informed that she'd return at 9:00 a.m. tomorrow."

I swung the door open and muttered under my breath, "*Fuck.*"

18

Ding!

I ran on tiptoes to my open office door, listening for all I was worth. Not that any of the staff came to the office at 9:00 a.m.

"Hello?"

Crap, crap, crap. It was Tommy. She'd really come.

I took a steadying breath, smoothing my white pantsuit. The sober evening in my hotel room last night told me one thing—most of Angelica's hand-me-downs were white and royal blue.

I ran over my lines. Lines I wasn't sure I could say around the compulsion. I successfully wrote them down last night, but that could mean anything.

Showtime.

I stepped into the hall. "Tommy."

She whirled from the reception desk to find me. My eyes drank in the sight of her, and my legs coiled with the need to go to my friend. But if I *did*, she'd drag me out of here by my hair.

Tommy ran my way, and I strode to meet her halfway.

She threw herself against me, and I wrapped my arms tight about her. My heart pounded against my chest and I rested my cheek atop her head. Too many times in the last six days, I'd thought I would never see her again.

"It's only been a few days, right? I feel like I haven't seen you in a month." I joked to cover the blissful agony of seeing her.

She tried to pull away, and I tightened my hold. As soon as Tommy got free, the interrogation would begin and I'd have to start lying.

"Dammit, Basi. Let me go. I'm going to yell at you."

"Shh." I lifted a leg to wrap it around her. "Ouch! You *pinched* me."

Tommy didn't apologise.

Pointing at my office, she said, "That yours?"

I nodded and hung my head as I followed her inside.

"What the actual fuck?" She whirled on me as soon as the door was closed. Nice of her to be considerate about my workmates and keep this in-house. If only she knew everyone could hear.

"Shit really blew up," I stalled.

Tommy balled her fists. "I don't hear from you all weekend. Then I get some bogus text about camping that you didn't send. There weren't any heart emojis."

I had to stop using those.

"I was minutes away from calling your grandmother."

"Tell me you didn't," I blurted.

"No," she exploded. "But only because you finally deigned to reply."

Thank fuck for that.

"I asked Angelica to text you," I told her, relaxing somewhat when the vampire's name left my lips without issue. "I was swamped after the run-in with Clint."

She was too smart to completely take my decoy. "We aren't done with your glamping story by a long shot, but I want to hear about what happened with that bastard."

I shuddered at the memory. "I was stupid last week, Tom. I thought I got paid weekly, but it was fortnightly. I fell short on rent money. I tried to negotiate a better deal with him, but I accidentally mentioned I had stuff in the house. He took the keys—"

"How did he take the keys?" Her eyes narrowed.

My lips pressed together.

"Strip, Basi."

"No." I fended off her grabby hands.

"If he fucking laid hands on you, I'm going to take a baseball bat to his motherfucking head!"

Yikes.

"Okay, okay. He grabbed me. I broke free. I ran and got lost. When I settled down, it was getting dark and I'd ended up in the city. I was too scared to walk back to yours in case Clint found me. I wasn't thinking straight. The buses had stopped and my phone was dead. I had the key to work and decided to sleep here. But Angelica hadn't left yet. When she heard everything, she invited me away with some of the other staff for the weekend. When we returned, Kyros offered me a place in his tower until I get on my feet."

"I want to see where Clint grabbed you." She'd calmly listened to my rambling. Which meant she didn't believe a word. My girl was clever.

Her life could depend on me being cleverer.

Relenting in this instance, I shirked my white blazer. The silk blouse I wore beneath the white blazer was royal blue and sleeveless.

I held my arm out for Tommy's inspection. She cursed when her eyes fell on the bruises. They'd faded from angry purples and reds to blues and yellows.

"I'm going to take an axe to his head. God, Basi. Why didn't you come to me? You know Father and I would have helped."

The hurt in her voice made me want to crawl under a rock. At least this answer was an honest one. "I just took off in a random direction, half out of my mind with terror. I've never run so fast in my life, Tom. I asked for directions back to Orange, but I must have looked insane. The woman I asked hauled ass and I mistook her arm swing for directions. I was in shock. And then the city was in sight."

She released my arm, and I tossed my blazer onto the desk behind her now the game was up.

Tommy scrubbed at her face. "I feel like I've failed you big time. I promised to help you figure this out, and I haven't done any of that. You were assaulted."

"You can't be responsible for me. I should have come to you when I couldn't pay rent, but I was too ashamed after buying that stuff for the apartment. I couldn't face you."

"You can always come to me, Basil. Always," she said softly. "I'm more offended that you thought you couldn't."

The last week had changed me. Because as we faced each other, I admitted something I'd always been too proud to speak aloud. "You're so capable, Tom. I wanted to be like you. When I couldn't, I felt stupid."

And still did—even though being stupid shouldn't mean shit when vampires existed and controlled me.

"... Is there more you aren't telling me?"

Goddamn, she had a Basi Emotion Radar. "I've just missed you. Being around strangers for a few days has made me weepy."

She snorted. "The day you're weepy is the day I win the lottery. Back to the glamping."

I held up a hand.

Tommy choked on a laugh. "Okay, Grandmother."

Staring at my hand, I realised she was right. My grandmother totally did that. "Oh my god."

When had I started copying her?

Tommy opened her mouth, and I held up a hand to stop her again, smiling wryly.

The truth was, my friend wasn't a dumbass. She knew me better than almost anyone in this world. So I wasn't going to treat her like a dumbass and crap on our relationship.

"Tom, do you remember my fourteenth birthday when Harriet stuck that note on your back? I grabbed it off as soon as I saw it and told you the note said *gorgeous*."

Tommy rolled her eyes. "Such a terrible liar. I fished it out of the bin later and read it."

The note had said *poor, ugly bitch*—because rich teens were about the meanest people out there.

"My point is that I lied to you to protect your feelings."

She stilled. "What are you telling me, Basil?"

I had to be careful. "I'm telling you that if you ever need to know something important, I'll tell you. If I don't always tell you everything, it's nothing to do with who you are—because I will always love you. You were worried when I didn't get in touch, and I wish I could promise never to do that again—but Beast might have other plans."

I felt quite good about how successfully I'd buried a warning message in babble.

My friend didn't immediately reply. She searched my face with her keen chestnut eyes. Had she read between the lines enough there? I was protecting her. I didn't want Tommy to feel I was in danger because she'd do something about it—with the axe she apparently had.

My friend glanced away, scanning the room.

Was she searching for cameras? *Shoot.* Perhaps I wasn't as subtle as I thought.

Tommy was nearly bang on—there were ears on this conversation, but the vampires didn't require cameras and microphones to listen in. Which is why I'd tiptoed around the mention of the estate.

"So you're living here?" she said at long last.

"Up top, yeah. It's about one thousand times nicer than my apartment."

"And the clothes?"

I peered down. "Angelica's hand-me-downs. I lost my stuff to Clint, remember?" *And a vampire tore one of my two outfits off me and let his minions see me naked.*

"You're coming to live with me."

"No, Tommy. I don't want to put you out." I shut my mouth as tears sparked in her eyes.

"Something's going on," she whispered, rubbing her forehead. "You're in trouble, I know it. And you're in it deep. And you won't let me help you. Or I can't help you for some reason I don't understand. You're coming with me right now, Basi. Fuck this job. You had a bad feeling about it from the start. I'll support you until you get more work. We'll figure it out. Just please come with me."

A tear slipped down her cheek.

Tommy wasn't a blubberer. She did cry. But not easily. And I'd done it to her.

I stared, at a loss of what to say. What possible reason was there to refuse her plea?

A knock startled us both.

I turned as the door opened to admit Kyros.

I *knew* he'd listen in on this conversation, but I hadn't expected him to butt in.

"Get lost," I mouthed, faced away from Tommy. I didn't want him to meet my friend or vice versa. No way.

He pushed the door open wide, and I scanned him from head to toe before remembering I hated him.

Kyros was in his usual suit get-up—a shiny charcoal number today—but his hair was mussed and his blinks were slow. Had he'd rolled out of bed and rushed down?

"Miss Tetley," he said, voice husky.

Definitely asleep before coming here.

"Kyros," I greeted, widening my eyes in a blatant hint to piss off. I heard Tommy's grunt as I spoke his name.

He ignored my hints, passing a paper to me. "Your tenancy agreement. As discussed, you'll have a discounted rate for three months. If you choose to stay beyond that, we will renegotiate."

With Tommy at my back, I felt safe giving full force to my withering look. I glanced over the paper. It seemed like a legit tenancy agreement—but what did I know? The estate had a legal team to handle all contracts.

The paper was snatched from my hands.

"And this is?" he asked sleepily. Mussed-up Kyros was cute. It had to stop.

Think of him slicing his teeth into your neck. The heat in my stomach unfurled.

That's more like it.

I rushed through the introduction. "Tommy, meet Kyros, my boss. Kyros, meet Tommy, my best friend."

He stepped closer and reached around my body, hand extended to her. Doing so necessitated him brushing against me, and Tommy would pick up on that without fail.

Kyros was playing more games.

I put space between us as she shook his hand briefly.

She handed me the agreement. "That's a good price for renting in Grey. Your wage covers it?"

"I made sure of that," Kyros said, frowning slightly.

Tommy hummed, studying the vampire much like I used to when I'd had no clue he could kill me in a second.

"Guess who sold a house yesterday?" I said to divert her attention.

She smiled and lifted her arm for a high five. I grinned and slapped my palm against hers.

"Miss Tetley..."

I cut a glance at Kyros, inhaling sharply at the menace on his face. He crossed to me at human speed and lifted my arm, green eyes riveted on the blue and yellow bruises there.

Tommy hovered behind him, and I could only feel relief. Because if she'd seen Kyros's blazing eyes at that second, she would have known he was *other*.

"Who the fuck did that to you?" he asked. His low voice shuddered its way through my body.

If Tommy wasn't in the room, I would have said Kyros himself did it up on Level 66.

"A man named Clint," my friend answered.

My heart sank. "Tommy, no."

Clint was a bottom feeder, but Kyros fed *on* humans. I may have felt murderous toward Clint at the start, but I didn't want anyone hurt on my behalf. Not when the punisher had powers the human didn't. And not when it was Kyros. He wasn't getting any more involved in my personal life.

"He was her landlord. The one who chucked her out and stole her stuff," Tommy ignored me to say.

Crap. Kyros wasn't home right now. His eyes were fixed on the bruises.

The silence extended.

Aiming for subtlety, I reached for the bottom of his charcoal waistcoat and tugged.

He lifted his head. "I'll deal with it."

Uh. "Not necessary. I've handled... *it*."

"She hasn't," Tommy piped up, sidling around Kyros. It didn't take a genius to see why. Her eyes were going full tilt between me and the vampire. A smile curved her lips.

"No," I told her. "Absolutely not. One level."

"But is the one level the penthouse?" she asked, her smile widening to a grin. "Because, if so, that's the only level a gal would ever need."

Heat crept into my cheeks. No, I *wasn't* a blusher.

Kyros eyed my face and murmured, "Am I missing something?"

"Yep," Tommy replied. "Probably not for long though."

"Alright, time for Tom to go elsewhere." I shooed her out of the room.

"He's ducking dot," she mouthed. At least that's how I chose to interpret it.

Aloud, she said, "Wait, I have a couple of things to say to you."

Dang. "Go on then," I huffed.

"First, if you ever try this shit again, I'll kill you so no one else can."

I choked on my husky laughter. "You are such a psycho."

"Love is a dangerous thing," she replied, widening her eyes to highlight her craziness. "I might get confused if you test me. *Second*, you owe me a date. Tonight. It's Fri-yay. We're hitting the clubs to consume adult beverages."

I wanted to go.

So badly.

Without consulting Kyros, I couldn't say yes. Backing out on plans with Tommy so soon after disappointing her wasn't an option. "I..."

"You already had plans to go out with Laurel, didn't you?" Kyros interjected smoothly. "If you're worried she won't like more company, I assure you she's one of my most sociable employees."

"Oh." Tommy's face fell at the news we'd have company, then she perked up. "It will be nice to meet one of your workmates."

No, it wouldn't. Who the fuck was Laurel?

"If you think Laurel would be okay with that," I mumbled over my shoulder to Kyros.

"I've known her a long time. I'm sure." His eyes glinted.

Fucker. He was going to order one of his minions to like my friend.

"I'll meet you here at 9:00 p.m.," Tommy said, winking at me. "The strawberry mojitos are calling our name, girl."

"Text when you arrive." I'd meet her downstairs. "Beast will endeavour to pass the text on." *And Kyros.*

She rolled her eyes. "I hope the commission you made from selling a house is enough to get an actual phone."

"I don't. I set a new high score on Snake this morning."

"Trust you to get involved with a shitty game like that."

"Shitty game alright," I agreed in a dark voice. Just not the game she thought.

Tommy propped up on her toes to kiss my cheek. "Catch you later, lovely."

I wrapped my arms around her again and stole as much of her Tommy-ness as possible. "Miss you already."

She patted my arm, searching my gaze again, a wrinkle between her brows. Then she looked past me once more, bobbing down to mouth, "*Seriously ducking dot.*"

Ugh.

Waiting until I heard the *ding* of the elevator taking Tommy away, I closed the door and turned to Kyros. "Thank you."

I met his direct gaze briefly and tried to sidle past him.

He whipped out an arm, barring the way, his forearm resting against my stomach. "Why didn't you tell me about that human? Clint."

"You heard me telling Tommy *before* you interrupted our

conversation." The glimmer in his eyes confirmed his ears were *that* sensitive. "Is that why you rushed down here?"

"I came down because she wasn't swallowing a word you said. Now, she thinks you're in the middle of a sordid affair with your boss and reaping the benefits."

It occurred to me to be angry over that. I ruined my outrage by snorting. "Just so you know, I wouldn't sleep with my boss to get benefits."

"You were going to lunch with that boy, Rhys, for a free lunch."

What the hell? "How did you know that?"

"I'm one hundred and forty-nine, Miss Tetley."

I rubbed at my cheek. "I was planning to do that. Touché."

He didn't budge, waiting.

I sighed. "I didn't tell you about Clint because it's none of your business."

"Do you live in my tower?"

"Who even says that?"

"People with towers."

Fell into that one. I humoured the egotistical maniac. "Yes, Kyros. I live in your tower."

"I protect those who live in my tower."

I shook my head and pushed down on his arm like it was a ticket barrier before striding to the desk. "Not me."

He followed in my wake. "What was your last address?"

Yeah right.

Sitting down, I opened *Monocle.* "Hey, why have I got appointments today? It's the other clan's turn today. We can't sign contracts."

Kyros waved a hand. "Only the actual purchase and signing of contracts have to happen on our turn."

"What if I do a prelim and butter someone up and your clan doesn't land on the right suburb for ages? Do I just string the client along?"

"Essentially. It's part of the game. We need to be ready to move at any moment. We have entire teams dedicated to predicting the probability of the next rolls. Those probabilities influence the appointments we schedule for you, amongst other things."

I had a feeling the *amongst other things* part could fill fifty books. I eyed the vampire. Kyros wore passion well. The sight made my stomach flip in a girly way, not with the intense lower stomach tightening attraction I'd always felt around him.

"And good try," he said, leaning on his closed fists.

"I'm not giving you Clint's address. You'll eat him."

Kyros jerked. I had a second to wonder if my number was up before he threw his head back. Laughter boomed from him in waves.

He found *that* funny.

Looking heavenward, I returned to *Monocle*, ignoring him.

My first visit was to a young professional couple in Green. I tried to recall the game board on the monitor upstairs. Surely Green was only a few moves away from Orange. Was the probability of rolling a three or four very high? Or was I being given the improbable cases because they assumed I'd suck?

Likely.

"If that made you laugh, you need to get out more," I informed him, typing in the address of my first appointment. I had three today.

"You think?" he said in that voice that never failed to rumble through me.

"I *know*."

Whoa, this couple in Green was on fire. Twenty-seven years old and both were orthopaedic registrars, mortgage paid. No kids yet, but that could be a selling point. If they planned to have kids, they could be on the lookout for something bigger. Or when they became orthopaedic surgeons, they might want a house in Blue or Black because they'd be loaded and society was programmed to think the goal in life was to have the biggest house possible.

Kyros murmured, "There's not a lot of time off in *Ingenium*."

I cast him a quick look, unsure how to interpret the admission. "A lucky thing you're passionate about it."

"You think I'm passionate about this battle?"

Some might say battle, some might say Yahtzee.

The memory of his grin when I'd given him the news about 190 Friar Close popped into my head. "Yes, I believe you are."

He perched on the desk. For the first time in our acquaintance, I didn't mind him staying.

Kyros watched me closely. "This game is all I've ever known."

I clicked on the most recent valuation of the property in Green, skimming the contents. "That's bound to happen when you're one hundred and forty-nine and the game exists because of you." I glanced up in time to catch his surprise.

He didn't speak.

Was Kyros finally rendered speechless?

In a moment when I should feel victorious, I just felt bad for him. The battle between the two clans wasn't his fault—it wasn't even the queen's if harems were an established part of Vissimo culture. It was the fault of two possessive jerk kings who couldn't see that the important thing was the health of the child and not who the baby belonged to. To grow up knowing thousands of people worked each day *because* you'd been born. And then to start playing the game, too, never knowing anything else...

Yes, indeed. Call me conflicted. Call me any number of things. I, Basilia Le Spyre, pitied the man I hated.

His throat worked.

I returned to my screen, opening the notes section to type out a few points of interest. "For the record, you look nothing like the other king. You have your mother's eyes, but the same skin tone and hair colour as King Julius."

His chest lifted. I only caught it because I was paying such close attention. Which dug at my pride well and truly.

"King Julius has dark hair," Kyros said after a beat.

Strands of my hair fell in front of my eyes and I tossed the blonde tresses back. "He has toffee undertones. If I can see them, you surely can."

Kyros stood for a while, hands in his pockets. "What were you thanking me for earlier?"

Whoa, subject change much?

I tipped my head back to peruse him. "For reassuring my friend when I couldn't."

He nodded. "I see."

"Good for you. Now get out of here. My boss is a vampire and has an attitude problem."

"I was thinking we might get through one civil conversation too," he said drily.

I opened the next file. "I hate to disappoint you."

"*Mmm*, maybe that's what I like about you, Miss Tetley. And thank you."

Lifting my head, I stared at the spot where Kyros had stood a second earlier.

What for?

19

I swung my door open and studied Laurel—my guard, driving instructor, and paid friend. I spent most of the day with her guarding me while on prelim visits.

I grimaced at the Indebted's get-up. "You can't wear that. The only person who can pull that look off is Jessica Alba in *Dark Angel*."

Kyros wasn't wrong about Laurel—five minutes in her company had told me she was the most human Vissimo I'd met.

"What's wrong with it?" she demanded, staring down at her black leather ensemble, complete with gloves.

I snatched up my second-choice outfit off the bed. "Put this on. Then people will know you're not in the club to assassinate them."

She smiled, showing many white, gleaming teeth. "But I am."

I swallowed, reminding myself not to get too comfortable. Even though she watched *Truth Ranges* sometimes *and* ate sushi.

So far, there were only ticks next to her name.

"It's blue," she stated, surveying the outfit.

"Yeah, I was only given white and royal blue clothes."

"Kyros's favourite colours," Laurel said, peering at the two racks.

I scowled. "They're what?"

"Who gave them to you?"

Angelica.

Who had yet to apologise. Seeing as she'd delivered the clothing mere hours after her part in humiliating me, I had to conclude she wasn't sorry whatsoever despite her sheepish act.

I wasn't sure after the Level 66 stunt, but the colours of the clothing confirmed my suspicion.

Kyros's aunt was playing matchmaker.

Which made zero sense. Kyros and I had mad lust. Nothing more. Actually, a lot less than nothing. So many walls sat between us after a week of knowing each other that I shuddered at the thought of how many would be there after two.

"Never mind who," I replied, setting my jaw. "Change."

Laurel erupted into a blurring flurry. Leather smacked me in the face, but when the vampire stopped, she was zipped inside the royal-blue tube dress. She pulled her long and dead-straight black hair forward over her shoulders.

"Respect. Changing that fast must be super handy."

She surveyed me. "You look good. Blondes always look good in white. Brunettes look like demons trying to draw innocent people into their lair."

My laughter was polite only—was that what she did though?

Beast chimed, and I leaped across the bed to reach him.

I hope you're wearing sexy underwear for me.

I grinned extra wide at Tommy's message, knowing Kyros would read these messages.

I typed back:

If underwear doesn't cover me from belly button to mid-thigh, I'm not interested.

Ha! See how he liked that visual. I plugged Beast back in. I wouldn't take the archaic device with me tonight. The fucker would just die.

"What's so funny?"

Kyros would be imagining me in granny undies.

I cleared my throat. "Tommy's here. Let's go."

I slipped into some nude heels. I couldn't see a brand name, but quality heels were like walking on clouds. These were cloud shoes. Grabbing my one hundred bucks for the night, I tucked the cash into my bra like the classy woman I was.

The white number I had on was a cold-shoulder dress—a full tight sleeve covered one arm, while the other was bare. The garment ended slightly above mid-thigh—when I stood still, so it would be perfect club length when I hit the dance floor.

Laurel put her black combat boots back on—which looked pretty fucking good with the blue dress—so I remained silent, and we beelined for the elevator.

Ding!

"Do you go out to nightclubs all the time?" Laurel asked as we stepped inside.

I rearranged my bra. I was too poor for a stick-on bra these days, so I'd worn a normal bra and tucked the strap on the bare shoulder side of the dress away so it couldn't be seen. "Used to. With Tommy."

"Why has she got a man's name?"

"Why don't you ask her and see what she says?" I tipped my head back, letting the soft ends of my high ponytail tickle my back.

"That sounds like a trap."

I smirked. "What about you, Laurel? You go out much?"

She shrugged a shoulder. "Not really. I work a lot."

Said every Vissimo ever. Royal families aside, I felt kind of sorry for everyone involved in *Ingenium*.

"I know you're on the job tonight, but I hope you can still have some fun."

Doubt entered her voice. "Maybe."

Ding!

The doors had barely opened, and I was squeezing out to embrace my night of freedom. Tommy pushed off the opposite wall, looking killer in a rose-gold cami tucked into a leopard-print mini. If I wore that, I'd look like I charged by the hour. Tom looked adorable and elegant.

"Pulling it off," I informed my friend.

"I wasn't allowed to wear leather, but she can wear leopard print," Laurel said, frowning.

I waved between the two. "Laurel, this is Tommy. Tommy, Laurel."

Tommy stepped forward. "Basi believes that only Jessica Alba from *Dark Angel* can wear black leather."

Laurel snorted. "That's exactly what she said."

I caught Tommy's approving look. She was already team Laurel. But then my bestie accepted anyone who was decent to others, which was part of why I loved her.

"Where are we going?" I asked, itching to step outside the tower for a few hours of normalcy.

"I figure we're both poor, so we should organise our crawl around happy hours." She led the way out of the tower, glancing back. "Laurel, you'll have to slum it with us tonight."

She threw Tommy a small smile. "I don't have much money anyway—I'm paying off my father's debt."

"Oh, I'm sorry to hear that. I pay for my pop's retirement village bill and help with my father's mortgage, so I feel ya. It's a hard gig."

Laurel threw her an inscrutable look. "Thank you. It is hard sometimes."

Tommy cracked a grin. "Thank me by enjoying yourself tonight. And helping Basi to enjoy herself. She either loses the plot or takes forever to loosen up."

"What! I do not."

"She's uptight," Laurel agreed.

Given current events, I was allowed to be a little fucking tense.

Tommy hummed. "Always has been."

I whacked her arm. "Don't gang up on me."

"Loosen up and we won't."

After consuming three bottles of wine recently, I really wasn't ready for another bender yet.

We passed *Montgomery's* and Tommy grabbed my hand soon after, dragging me down an alley.

I peered at a flickering street lamp as we passed. "Oh my god, I slept here once."

Laurel made a sound in the back of her throat. "You what?"

Tommy scanned the area. "You're kidding me. Here?" Laughter bubbled out of her. "I still can't believe you did that."

That Basi lived another life. "I didn't know it was near a club. And to be fair, it was more that I accidentally dozed off from sheer exhaustion."

Live music pounded out of two metal doors down the very end of the alley. A bouncer stood guard but ushered us in without checking IDs. It did make me wonder how old Laurel was though. Her eyes weren't blazing, which I associated with greater control. Kyros's didn't blaze unless his emotion was heightened. Angelica's eyes glowed a bit.

Was Laurel stronger than Angie?

I tore my eyes from the vampire as she slid me a curious look. *Shit*, I couldn't let my guard down around her. Laurel belonged to Kyros—was literally Indebted to him. She'd repeat anything of importance. And who knew what her orders were when it came to me.

"Shots!" Tommy roared.

It was a shot night? *Crap*.

After knocking back a tequila, I settled into shouted conversations with the others over the acoustic band. Familiarity at last—even with the guest Vissimo. Tommy always had great work stories and had Laurel in stitches recounting the stains she'd found on the sheets that week. I could feel tension draining from me.

My best friend was magic.

I sipped at one of my two rum and Cokes—a happy hour deal I had to take advantage of on my budget because turned out I couldn't afford strawberry mojitos anymore. That didn't sting as much as I thought it would. Perhaps this moment was a munched version of what I wanted when I left the estate. In most ways, my independence was less than it had been. But this, buying a drink with money I'd earned, was cause for a small celebration.

Maybe a big one… "I need something with a faster beat," I shouted. "Let's go to *Cooks*."

"But I'm laying groundwork," Tommy complained.

I rolled my eyes at Laurel. "She's after musicians at the moment."

"So miserable, so in need of guidance," my friend said, smirking over the lip of her glass.

Laurel wrinkled her nose. "You enjoy that?"

"Right now. You like a big, strong man?"

The vampire shrugged. "More than one. But always stronger, yes. I like to be thrown around."

I choked on an ice cube. Laurel was up in a flash, pounding on my back. The ice cube flew across the table.

The vampire resumed her seat, folding her hands in her lap.

Never mind that I'd nearly died, Tommy was busting a gut over the comment.

"Laurel, I think I love you already," she declared, holding up her vodka and cranberry—rich bitch. "See you shrews at the bottom."

"But I'm still on my first drink," I objected.

The others ignored me.

Ugh.

I knocked back the rest of my first drink, and by the time I'd finished my second rum and Coke, the others were grabbing their things. I slid off my stool and hurried after Tommy and Laurel, winking at the bass player. Maybe Tommy was onto something with musicians. Though he was about the most un-musician looking musician ever.

Dammit, he was wearing a tie. I really did have an ironic attraction to the guys I professed to dislike.

We left the alley and weaved around a few blocks to a nightclub I'd been to several times. Tommy began speaking to a guy on the way, and I waggled my brows at Laurel.

"Does she know him?" she asked.

I considered that. "Tommy feels the mating call constantly."

When I last spoke to her, she was considering serious steps with what's-his-name.

"Tommy," I yelled. "What happened to that guy you've been seeing?"

The man she was speaking to glared at her and made scarce.

I snickered at her dark look.

"You vage-blocker," she said grumpily.

I watched the dude wobble away. "He was hammered. You weren't getting anywhere with him tonight. And don't avoid the question."

She slid a look at Laurel. "His name was Dean, and I nipped it in the bud."

What about the Theodore guy? Didn't she ditch Dean for him last week?

Still, I took her hint. My friend barely spoke to me about this stuff. Laurel was accepted but not tested.

"Sure. Shit happens, right?" I replied. "I'd buy you a consolatory drink, but I'm skint."

"Never thought I'd see the day," Tommy said as we arrived at the next place.

I fell quiet, burningly aware of Laurel's presence. Now was not the time for Tommy to forget I was Miss Tetley for a reason.

The bouncer asked for our IDs, and I made sure to angle mine away from certain vampire eyes.

His eyes fell heavy on me. "The VIP area is open, Miss—"

"That won't be necessary," I said smoothly.

Nodding, he pulled back the red rope and let us pass.

"This is more like it," I shouted as we descended into the underground club. Flashing neon lights filled the space, lasers blasting in swirling designs over the black walls. Below us, happy masses pulsed in time to the thumping beat.

A pleasant buzz had spread through me during our walk, and I was ready to dance.

Priorities though.

We squeezed our way to the opposite end of the dance floor, and I leaned over the bar, crossing my ankles as I bent them up in the air to lean forward. These were cloud heels, but my feet still appreciated the break.

"How much are your tequila shots?" I asked the bartender.

Tommy started laughing. I choked on one myself, knowing exactly what she was laughing at. *Bitch.*

The bartender drawled a smile. "For you? How about one on the house?"

"What about my friends?" I purred. Yes, *purred.*

Thank you, rum.

He inclined his head—clever fellow. "Of course, beautiful."

I winked at him. "Then I graciously accept."

Tommy bumped me with her hip. "Did you just say grashioushly?"

Laurel's eyes were alight. "She did."

The alcohol didn't appear to have affected the vampire one bit, but I was glad she was having fun. Even at my expense.

We threw back the free shots.

That D-floor was mine.

Tonight, I was dancing away a week's worth of shit and a lifetime's worth of shock. Laurel and Tommy were hot on my heels, and as the music switched over to a thrumming, seductive beat, we all began to move.

"Holy shit, Laurel's got swagger!" Tommy yelled in my ear.

I hadn't known hips moved that way. I wondered if Kyros's could move like that too.

Bad!

He was part of the issues I was dancing away. Lifting my hands in the air, I let my ponytail swing to one side and began to move with the music. I honestly wasn't much of a dancer unless super drunk—maybe I *was* uptight—but at sixteen, I'd scoured YouTube and had twenty moves I mashed together in random order. I knew them well enough now that I guess it was my own kind of dance.

Tommy, like everything she did, danced in unique elbow-popping style and nailed it.

Laurel bumped and grinded like she'd just left the set of that dance movie with far too many sequels.

The song ended and shifted to a faster beat—a remix of a Drake song. *Hells yeah!* Tommy herded me toward Laurel, who'd drawn a ring of men around her like fucking moths to a flame. The vampire peeled out from between them.

They sandwiched me, hips wiggling against mine.

I rolled my eyes at them, standing ramrod straight.

"Uptight Basi. Uptight Basi," Tommy screamed in my ear between hiccups.

Laurel took up the chant.

Scowling, I wiggled my butt once and shoved my boobs in Laurel's face to satisfy the hussies. They didn't let me go until the song ended, so the effort was wasted.

Another remix came on.

"*No*," I hollered, forming a cross with my forearms. "I'm not dancing to this shit."

Tommy was already snapping her arms like a crocodile while singing "Baby Shark" at the top of her lungs.

"Baby Shark" could fuck right off.

Laurel was doing it too. A *vampire* dancing to "Baby Shark."

I categorised the sight.

"Nope." I backed away double time. *Out of here.* I'd find my bartender again. Maybe slide my number over.

I didn't have a pen or paper, *but I could get creative.*

Reaching the bar, I leaned across so I could kick my heeled feet up again and give my toes a break. Even cloud shoes had a comfort expiry.

"Give me tequila," I bellowed to no one in particular.

Large hands appeared on the bar either side of my raised hips.

I *hated* being hit on by drunk guys. In general. There were exceptions. But for the most part, I hated it.

Lowering my heels to the ground, I spun so my back was against the bar, my eight out of ten scowl at the ready.

Green eyes slammed into mine.

My breath hitched. "What are you doing here?"

I didn't yell the words, but he heard me anyway—being a damn vampire and all.

Why the fuck was Kyros in this club?

He leaned forward. *All* the way forward.

True, I didn't have his hearing, but my listening ability wasn't bad enough to necessitate him brushing his lips against my ear.

A shiver wracked my body at the contact.

"I get two days off every month," he spoke over the pulsing bass. "And someone recently told me I need to get out more."

Yeah, I didn't mean he follow me. This was my night away from him.

Swallowing, I glanced at his body as per my usual. It was impossible not to—some vampire trick I was sure because I'd never had a problem pretending physical indifference. My gaze lingered on his bare forearms. He'd rolled up his sleeves and ditched the waistcoat and tie. The top two buttons of his shirt were undone.

"Right. I didn't mean here specifically," I managed to say. "Is there a reason you're standing so close?"

His eyes hardened. "I thought I'd be a gentleman and cover your ass—that every man and several women have been looking at for the last minute."

"Perhaps I want them to look," I shot back, hands landing on my hips. "It's my body. Don't cover it without my say so."

Kyros's gaze dropped to my breasts and hips, then lower.

I grabbed his face and forcefully redirected his gaze to my face. Correction: he let me redirect his gaze.

My skin tingled where I touched him and my chest rose in shocked surprise. Warmth pooled deep in my stomach and his green eyes flashed as he inhaled.

I severed contact and whirled back to face the bar. What the hell was that? My hand crept up to my throat as I tried to steady my erratic breathing.

Hoping the bartender might be around so I could ignore the

vampire at my back, I glanced up and looked straight into Kyros's eyes in the reflection of the mirrors lining the back wall of the bar.

His gaze heated me from the inside out.

I couldn't look away.

My topaz eyes were huge, bright from the alcohol—my face pale.

Kyros stepped closer and his warmth seeped through the thin material of my dress. His green gaze dropped to where my hand rested against the base of my throat. Curling my fingers, I lowered my fist until it rested over the valley between my breasts.

Kyros caught my gaze in the mirror again, and sighing, I leaned back against him. The medium of the mirror made me feel like I could look my fill, forbidden though it was, like the glass was no man's land—a place where we could meet in peace.

It filtered my hate for the man pressed up against me, leaving only the attraction I'd denied since first meeting him.

His lips brushed against my other ear and I shivered anew, knowing he was close enough to feel my reaction this time.

Kyros's deep voice rumbled through me. "Can I buy you a drink?"

My aching body begged me to say yes.

"Strawberry mojito, wasn't it?"

How did he know that?

I turned around in the cage of his arms again, tipping my head back. "It's really messed up that you're hitting on me, listening to my conversations, and reading my texts."

The words bounced off his ego. "After the little show you put on draping yourself across the bar, I can confirm the last text wasn't true. And you told me about strawberry mojitos when I found you passed out in the elevator after you raided my wine cellar."

My underwear was much smaller than I'd described, true. But that wasn't important—other than the fact we were both thinking of the lack of barrier now.

"You put me in bed? Weren't we still under the thrall?"

"It had just ended."

"Shit. Sorry about that." I'd hoped my first guard had retrieved me.

He moved to my other ear. "Was there a reason you were in the elevator?"

I dropped my gaze and peered along the bar at the throngs trying to get a drink. Whether instinctively or not, the humans avoided a good metre either side of the games master.

His finger under my chin drew my gaze back. His eyes were so hard to look at when his control slipped—which I couldn't fail to notice was a lot around me.

"You haven't answered my question," he said, during a lull in the music.

"Which one?" I hadn't replied to his offer of a drink either.

I bit down on my lip in response to his growl.

I fanned my lashes down. "Why are you really here, Kyros? You're nearly one hundred and fifty years old. I don't want you here. *You* don't want to be here. We don't even like each other."

"I like you just fine, Miss Tetley."

I blew a strand of my ponytail off my cheek. "I'd hate to see how you treat people you dislike."

His face dropped. "I sincerely hope you never have to see that. You're frightened enough of me as it is."

Kyros reached for the strand of hair I'd failed to blow off my cheek. He drew the butter-blonde curl back to the rest and then ran his hand down the length, right to the silky ends. He pressed his hot palm against the base of my shoulder blades.

He was really close. I was sandwiched between him and the bar, except this was a sandwich—unlike Tommy and Laurel's—that I was becoming more okay with.

I didn't want to be okay with it.

He'd hurt me.

I placed a hand on his chest. Kyros caught it in his free hand. I turned my face away again, and he used our clasped hands to draw it back.

"*Beautiful Basilia,*" The vampire ran his nose up his favourite track from my jaw to temple. He was inhaling the scent of my blood, I assumed, but the sensation set my body alight.

What had he done to me to make me hate him? I scrambled to remember it all because I knew it was bad.

Kyros captured my mouth with his, nudging my head up in the same movement to grant easier access. A sigh left me at the feel of his lips, firm and commanding. *Warm with promise.* I'd never been kissed by someone with obvious experience. I tipped my head farther back to deepen the connection. He didn't waste time. A low snarl left him as he wrapped his hand in my ponytail and ran his tongue along the bottom of my top lip.

I gasped at the intimacy of the action, slipping my leg between his strong thighs. He leaned closer, pressing me against the bar. I arched back over the lip and kept contact with his lips. Not even his lips—his *tongue*.

What was this?

Ice poured over me and I shrieked, bumping Kyros's nose with my forehead.

His hand shot out, gripping a college guy by the throat.

I grabbed at Kyros's forearm, spluttering from the cold. "It was an accident."

His eyes blazed.

Not good.

I turned and nabbed some napkins from the bar, dabbing at the wet patch down my side. Beer by the smell of it. The dress was a goner. "Kyros. It's fine. Let him go."

His eyes snapped to mine. A packed nightclub wasn't the best place to rile his vampire. "Please," I added quietly.

He released the guy, who had the sense to scramble away as fast as he could.

"Basil," Tommy slurred, edging next to me. "We need more drinks. Don't we, Loz?"

Laurel danced behind her and nodded obediently, sliding a look at Kyros.

Tommy noticed him for the first time. "Hey! It's one level."

"One level," Kyros mouthed.

He shot a veiled look at me. *Ah nuts*, he'd put it together. Was he remembering the penthouse part too?

His lips curled.

Yep.

Tommy's comment was all the reminder I needed to regain my composure. So maybe Kyros had three levels. So what? That wasn't enough. I needed all sixty-six. And that was *if* I swept the needle in the thigh, the threats, the blood compulsion, the top-level nudity episode, and a whole bunch of possessive shit under the rug.

Which I wasn't doing.

"He was just leaving," I said, avoiding his gaze.

Laurel's eyes glittered.

"*He* isn't," Kyros countered. He jerked his head at Tommy. "She's going to be sick soon."

She was. I only knew that from experience, not from enhanced senses or whatever he was using. My night was over, and not a second too soon.

"Come on, Tommy babe. We gotta get you home."

I looped one of her arms over my shoulders. "Laurel, could you give me a hand?"

Kyros halted the Indebted vampire's movement with a look. "You're done for the night. I'll see they get home safely."

The vampire dipped her head—a concession to our surroundings, perhaps. I got the feeling she was used to bowing far lower to him.

She lifted her head and stared directly at me.

I shrugged a shoulder, unsure what she was looking for. Had I snapped out of the lust cloud? My brain had. I couldn't speak for the rest of my body.

Or was she checking I was okay with the change of plans? Not like I had a choice. Neither did she.

Her eyes glittered again before she strode off into the crowd.

Kyros wasn't driving me anywhere. "I'll—"

He picked Tommy up. "Miss Tetley, for once, don't argue. You have no way of getting your friend home. Swallow your pride and accept my help."

Whoa, someone was shitty the tongue thing ended.

Kyros started for the exit, and I hurried after him, slipping into his wake. The crowd parted for him and we crossed from one end of the club without stopping or altering our path once.

His car was directly outside.

Of course.

I reassured the bouncer we were okay as Kyros rested a lolling Tommy along the back seat, shutting the door carefully.

He was driving the same car he nearly ran me over in. Had I expected to one day be sliding into the vehicle? Nope. Though at the time, part of me definitely hoped for it.

"Where does she live?" he asked as I buckled up.

... *Shit.* "Can she stay in the tower with me?"

"No."

He already had her address; he just didn't know it.

Fuck! Sighing inwardly, I rambled off Tommy's home address, extending my legs and crossing them at the knee.

Kyros pulled away from the curb, pausing every few metres to allow small groups of unaware drunk twenty-somethings to cross the road.

I stared out the window, hands twisting on my lap.

"I won't hurt your friend," he said so softly I wasn't sure I'd heard right.

I turned to stare at him before returning my window vigil. Kyros sounded like he believed his words—good on him. He would absolutely harm my friend if she got in the way of *Ingenium*. And that's what I hated about games. They weren't real, and yet real people got hurt when others played them.

People like Tommy.

People like my parents.

People like me.

He increased the speed as we turned onto the one-way out of

Grey toward Orange. *Just.* Kyros drove far less like Katerina and far more like a seventy-year-old.

The vampire broke the silence. "You may be interested to hear that Clint left town."

What? He'd dealt with that already?

My mouth dried. "That isn't street talk for you murdering him, is it?"

His expression darkened. "Clan Sundulus does not break the law. He was simply encouraged to leave everything he owned and leave within the hour. He won't be back. Your belongings were transferred to a storage cage in the lower levels of the tower. I'll make sure Angelica gets a key to you. And the bond you paid is in your room."

Encouraged to leave. That had to be illegal despite his reassurance.

I took a steadying breath. "... Thank you, I suppose. I'd rather you hadn't interfered at all if I'm honest."

"It is my duty to care for those in my tower."

We'd argued about this before. I wasn't part of his damn clan. I wasn't in his tower by choice, and therefore didn't fall under his protection.

Too tired to fight, I leaned my head against the cool glass, watching as we merged onto the freeway.

Tommy let out a sudden snort. The silence after lasted until Kyros took the off-ramp for Orange.

"Do you really hate me so much?" he asked, his tone curious. No more invested than if he was watching a science experiment.

Did I hate Kyros?

I frowned and shifted.

Yes.

... Then there were parts of him I could appreciate. His passion. His vulnerability in the face of a battle being fought over his existence. That he was indirectly teaching me to drive—even if he probably just offered to slip me a guard while I was outside the tower.

"I don't know you, really," I replied, staring at the beer stain covering my front. I hugged my arms around my stomach.

Kyros turned up the heat, but I wasn't that kind of cold. No heater would warm up the part of me that had frozen. That *he* froze.

"I don't *want* to know you," I added. "I might have come across any Vissimo—your siblings, your parents, or one of your workers. Any of them might have done the things you did to me—nearly frightening me to death, strapping me to the chair, and pumping me full of adrenaline. They might have compelled me with a blood exchange."

"But?" he asked, guiding us at a sedate pace through the uneven streets of Orange.

I was surprised my words hadn't angered him.

"It wasn't anyone else," I clarified. "You did all of those things. You hurt me. You scared me. At the centre of every bad thing that has happened to me recently is your face."

The sound of our breathing and Tommy's soft snores filled the tiny cab of his overpriced car.

"Don't kiss me again, Kyros," I said wearily, resting my forehead against the cool glass again. "I don't want you to touch me. Not really."

20

I was certain most people didn't spend their weekend receiving driving lessons from vampires.

At this point, I had no idea what the rules of my tower trial were. He'd let me out clubbing—albeit with a guard. And he let me out for driving lessons and prelim visits. I took that to mean I could go anywhere if Laurel was with me. If it was up to me, I'd be spending the day snuggling with Tommy while watching a movie, but she had work today. I'd called an hour ago to make sure she made it to her Saturday shift.

Laurel had a firm hold on my keys as she led the way through the garage. "I'll take you out to *Gerry's* parking lot."

"Who's Gerry?"

Laurel cast me an amused look. "*Gerry's* is a hardware store."

Oh. Right. Couldn't say I'd had the pleasure. "You go to *Gerry's* a lot?"

She nodded.

By now I'd cottoned on that the Indebted really were mercenaries. They got paid to do the things Vissimo didn't want to do. Who knew what that really entailed. "For stuff to kill people with?" I asked.

"Rarely. Tools for interrogation, yes."

Again, *legal*, my butthole. Pretty sure any mercenary job that necessitated a trip to a hardware store was as illegal as it got. Kyros was full of it.

A wrinkle formed between my brows. "How does it make sense that you're being punished for your father's crime and *commit* crimes to pay off the debt? Messed up."

Laurel stumbled and shot me a *real* look.

Funny how drinking with someone accelerated the friendship process. On closer inspection, Laurel wore her father's debt, *her job*, like a cloak. The cloak was straight-backed and professional, though friendly and occasionally sarcastic.

Then there were times the cloak came off, and I saw the young woman she could have been without being born into servitude. Actually, I kept forgetting she was probably old. *Old* woman.

Laurel inhaled sharply and peered at the closest camera as we reached the car—a silver one parked in the far corner. Yellow L plates occupied the front and back windows. A few scratches marred the sides.

I'd been given their trash car for driving lessons.

The car's lights flashed, and I slid into the passenger seat, tossing my full pack down by my feet. Never knew when an escape opportunity might present itself.

I wasn't worried that Kyros might be listening. He shouldn't eavesdrop if he didn't want to hear me starting a rebellion. "And for a race who supposedly reveres children, how does it make sense to make them slaves? That's whack. Plus, I thought this clan operated legally."

"This clan does," she said quietly. "The Indebted don't."

Huh, so that's how they got around the pesky law. Using Indebted to do the dirty work was the same as Kyros personally breaking the law in my book.

Laurel didn't respond to my first observation. It didn't take a genius to figure out why. But her silence was enough agreement for me.

I pursed my lips. "How old are you? If that's not offensive to ask."

I watched as the vampire's face shut down—the cloak had descended again. She turned the key in the ignition. This car had a key *and* an ignition. *Old school.*

"Two hundred and eighty. Indebted for half of that," she answered as the engine thrummed.

"That's disgusting," I announced, making her jolt again. One hundred and forty years in servitude.

"My father went berserk and killed ten children and their parents. It was a heinous crime. This is how Vissimo punish such crimes."

"The punishment should be confined to the person, not their children," I said, my heart clenching at the thought of her continued servitude. That was messed up logic right there.

"The crime wasn't confined to adults. Why should the punishment be?" she replied in a wooden tone. "And it is just the eldest child who inherits the debt."

Just the eldest child. How nice of them.

I could tell Laurel didn't believe the words coming out of her mouth. She'd learned to say such things to appease others.

"I have twenty million dollars left to pay off," she said, pulling out of the park. "Another century and I should be free."

I reached out and placed my hand over hers on the wheel. I didn't speak, squeezing her hand.

The cloak dropped and—*whoa*—a red tear, *blood*, slipped down her cheek. She dashed it away so fast my brain tried to convince me I hadn't seen it.

Clearing my throat, I leaned back in the seat. "Minimum wage much?"

She inhaled. "Depends on the job. The more dangerous, the quicker you pay off the debt. Being Indebted has a high mortality rate. I choose to live—which comes with longer servitude and lower pay."

"I hope you're getting paid a flat mil for this driving lesson then. It's unlikely you'll make it to the end of the day."

Laurel snorted. "Nonsense. A car crash couldn't kill me."

"Oh good," I said politely.

How *did* they die? Seemed bad manners to ask—so I'd save the question for Kyros.

We reached the exit of the garage, and she indicated right.

A man stepped in front of the car.

Laurel cursed and slammed her foot down. We weren't travelling fast, but the car screeched to a halt.

The car settled on its back wheels with a jolt and I exhaled, lowering my hand from the dashboard.

"What an idiot!" I shouted at the man.

"Basi," Laurel said in undertones.

Squinting, I looked again.

Oops.

It was Jet Black. One of Kyros's brothers. Gerome or Lionel, I couldn't remember which.

He beckoned to Laurel, who killed the engine and exited the vehicle without a word.

Crap, did I get her in trouble by airing all my opinions on Indebted? My eyes widened as she passed Kyros's brother the key. With a cursory glance at me, Laurel strode past the car and into the depths of the garage.

Jet Black clambered in.

"Kyros and his fucking sports cars," he grumbled. "Who wants to be crammed into a tiny piece of metal? Big engines, big cabs. That's what I'm about."

I didn't doubt that. My interactions with Jet Black were thus far confined to him pushing Kyros's buttons, him fighting Kyros, and him throwing me under the bus on Level 66.

"What are you doing?" I demanded.

He shifted around in the car seat to look at me.

Kyros was bigger than him, and yet his brother appeared squished into this car where Kyros didn't seem to have any issue getting into his. Jet Black's eyes were bright blue like his father's. He was muscular and tall like all the male Vissimo, but on a whole other scale to those I'd seen. Did the royal blood give him an extra boost?

All Kyros's siblings were more somehow—whether more muscular, ferocious, or beautiful.

I'd been half asleep, and then half out of my mind after the Level 66 thing, but I recalled his eight siblings were scary as shit. This one, however, had a boyish quality to his features that made me want to relax. I didn't trust it. I'd seen those deep-sea fish with the dangling light—angler fish. Their teeth were fucking sharp.

The warmth Jet Black exuded was a trap.

"I'm taking you for a driving lesson," he said, blue eyes twinkling.

I folded my arms over my seat belt. "That's Laurel's job."

"Not anymore."

I didn't get paid enough to deal with these alpha fuckers on the weekends. "Will she still get compensated?"

"No. She isn't doing the work."

I clicked the button to release my belt and opened the door. "Then I'm not going."

He grabbed a loop of my white jean shorts and tugged me back into the seat. "Fine. She'll get paid."

I arched a brow. He'd agreed too easily. He was always going to pay her. "Double."

Jet Black laughed. He wore hugging khakis and a tight tee. His shoulder-length black hair was confined at the nape of his neck. "I'm feeling generous today. Sure, why not."

Her wage probably just went from twenty-five dollars to fifty.

"Why am I in the driver seat?" he asked. "I know how to drive. Let's switch."

Uh.

"Laurel was taking me to *Gerry's*."

"The fuck is Gerry?"

Rich people ignorance. "A hardware store…"

His high brow cleared.

Kyros's brother had his mother's skin tone. If any of the Vissimo I'd met were to fit the physical idealism of a vampire, it was Jet Black. Personality not so much—if he was really this playful.

We switched places, and I set myself up behind the wheel, pulling in the seat. I'd learned where that lever was on Thursday.

He waited until I was settled. "It's nice to meet you, Basilia. My name's Gerome."

Not Lionel then. "Just Basi."

"But the police called you Basilia, correct?"

I thumped the wheel. "Does Kyros tell you guys everything or do you hack the cameras?"

"Maybe we hack security. Maybe we have spies in his tower. Or maybe he tells us everything, and we do the same in return."

Was I meant to pick an answer? "I can't imagine why he would tell you guys, what with the stunts you pull. Why are you really teaching me to drive?"

His blue eyes glinted, mouth quirking on one side. "Why not? I could be feeling charitable. It will be a good chance to know you better."

I snorted. "Sure."

"Kyros is the eldest, and he works too hard. We like to fuck with him."

That sounded more like it.

Gerome whipped out his phone. "Picture!"

The flash went off, and I blinked. People still used flash?

I leaned over to look at the picture. "Take another one."

"It's just going to Kyros," he murmured, thumbs moving rapidly as he typed out a message.

It was a bad picture. Surprising both of us, I snatched the phone. "Let me take it."

"Give my phone back, human."

"*Shh*, it will screw with him more if I take the picture, *Vissimo.*" And I knew my best angle.

"True. Take it."

I held the phone up on selfie mode and pulled a duck face. Gerome glanced at me and did the same.

Okay, I looked hot now. Which shouldn't matter because Kyros was on the receiving end. I shook my head.

Should've let Gerome send the double-chin picture.

"Alright," the vampire said, plucking the phone from my hand. "Start driving."

Twisting the key, I started the engine. In the white car, I'd barely been able to hear the motor. This one, not so much—but it was no roaring public bus.

I waited as Gerome finished his message to Kyros.

"He'll come down here as soon as you send that," I said, wondering if I could pull out onto the street in time to avoid him. Surely Kyros wouldn't run at vampire speed down through Grey.

"Nope. It's our weekend off for the month. We go to our parents' place."

"You should join them."

He slid an amused look my way. "Trying to get rid of me?"

"Yes," I said honestly. "I really want to learn to drive, and I have a feeling you're not going to take this seriously. Exhibit A: Letting me drive in Grey."

He slid the phone away. "Why so eager? Driving isn't that fun."

I gripped the wheel. "It's not about fun. It's about knowing how to do it like everyone else."

"What's the point of knowledge if you can't have fun too?" he countered. "Plus, you've already driven in Grey according to my big bro, and my motto is sink or swim."

"Why is that your motto?"

"Biggest risk, greatest reward, most fun." He widened his eyes dramatically. "Drive! The speed limit here is 60 kilometres. Slow down at orange lights. Stop at the red. Indicator is on the right side of the wheel—usually."

Yeah, I already knew the indicators changed sides. "Fine, but please pay attention. I want to do this right."

He studied me, some of the boyishness fading away. "You're full of surprises, Basilia."

"Just Basi."

"What about *Basil*?"

He must have hacked security. Unless Kyros repeated shit word for word. I ignored Gerome and edged the car out of the garage entrance. I waited until a string of cars had passed by—ignoring Gerome's snigger—and pulled onto the one-way street. *The right way.*

"Indicate for three seconds before switching lanes," he instructed, not watching the road. "Get over to the far left lane sometime in the next four blocks."

His phone chimed and the vampire read the message, chuckling as he tapped out a reply.

I wasn't going to ask what Kyros said. Not after last night.

I'd fallen asleep in the car and woke as he carried me to bed—after telling him *not* to touch me. What's more, my hands had been bunched in his shirt and I knew for a fact I gave him a sleepy smile before realising who carried me.

Lucky I wasn't a sleepwalker. Who could tell what I'd get up to?

Indicating for three seconds, I began to drift across the empty lanes. "Now what?"

"Stop!"

Shrieking, I slammed on the brakes. Except it wasn't the brake. The car shot forward as I twisted on the wheel, panic choking me.

A hand whipped out to grip the wheel. The car steadied. After blitzing past another block, I had the presence of mind to take my foot off the accelerator and find the real brake.

"Indicate and pull over to the curb," Gerome said.

Heart stuttering in my chest, I obeyed, managing not to scratch the hub caps.

"Put the hazard lights on when you stop where you're not meant to," the vampire explained, pushing a triangle button on the dashboard. "They're like a pass. People assume you're in trouble and can't move. This way, you'll always have a park."

Foot still jammed down on the brake, I took a deep breath. A calming breath. Because I was calm. Totally, totally calm. "Why did you do that?"

His phone was out again. I listened to a recording of my shriek and the screech of tyres.

He'd staged a video for Kyros.

I was calm. I was— "*You fucker.*" Slamming both hands on the wheel, I grabbed for his phone. He placed a hand over my face and held the phone out of my reach.

I bit down on his finger as hard as I could. Judging by his face, my bite possessed the strength of a day-old puppy.

"You scared me!" I pulled back. "I thought I'd hit an old lady."

"Well, I didn't expect you to stomp on the accelerator. Turned out better than I could've hoped."

I turned to face the front, scanning the road as my heart reined in a notch. "You said you'd take this seriously."

Kyros's brother didn't glance up. "No, I didn't. You said you had a feeling I wouldn't. I'm proving you right."

"How old are you? No, wait. Don't answer that. Your mental age is evident."

He didn't take the bait. "For the record, you should know how to stop in a hurry. Every time I yell stop, indicate to the closest curb, slam on the brakes, and pull over as quickly as possible."

"You're not turning this into a game." I withered, turning off the hazard lights and pulling out after a few cars.

"Stop," he shouted.

Nope.

Gerome frowned at me. "I said stop."

"Get fucked."

He caught my eyes. His eyes blazed blue, and suddenly my mind wasn't my own. My body didn't belong to me.

"Stop," he whispered.

My body obeyed, indicating, braking, and pulling over on autopilot. I pressed the hazard lights on and sat back.

A full minute passed before the fuzzy warmth in my head—the feeling that I was a bystander in my body—dissipated.

My hands shook on my lap. A tremble stirred my words. "What was that?"

On his phone again, the vampire glanced up. "Hmm? Compulsion."

"No, it wasn't. I've been compelled before." I drew in a breath.

"Maybe you got lost in my eyes." He winked.

"Last time the compulsion had to be permanent."

He threw me a cool look. "We compel humans and young Vissimo with our eyes for anything temporary—humans already in our employ and the like. The weaker their emotional attachment to what we're compelling them to do, the better, but there's always a risk the human will recall being compelled, so we hardly ever do it to those not under blood compulsion."

I tried to take that all in. "Why did you do that to me? That was horrible."

The cloudiness of the temporary compulsion left me with the vaguest sense of déjà vu.

"I'm Vissimo. Don't expect me to do human things."

Like play on your fucking phone all the time?

Gerome fidgeted on the seat, sighing as he failed to find a comfortable position. "You don't strike me as super coordinated. Now you've done that once, you'll be able to do it again easily."

"You didn't compel me because I told you to get fucked? Not even one bit?"

His lips twitched. "We both won something. Now start driving. Take the next left and stay on the freeway. Speed limit there is 100 kilometres. Look out for the blue signs."

Only 100 kmph? I'd definitely blown apart that limit two days ago.

The Vissimo kept his phone tucked away and settled into the lesson, correcting the positioning of my hands and feet. He pointed out parts of the car and drew my attention to the behaviour of other cars on the road, instructing me on how best to adjust.

I was willing to bet everyone who knew him was constantly torn between the urge to throttle him and relief he could be serious upon occasion.

I focused on sticking to my lane and the speed limit, but as soon as our direction became clear—and the fact I was driving to start with—my thoughts catapulted to my parents.

Every person had milestones in their life. Some teens were obsessed with their prom, some with nabbing their first boyfriend or girlfriend. I'd looked forward to both of those milestones, like others. But inevitably, each time I reached a milestone, I'd wonder what my parents' reactions would have been.

Some milestones were easier to handle than others.

When the time came to learn to drive, I just couldn't. My grandmother didn't force the issue when I turned down our butler's offer. Because I hadn't needed a licence to get around, I just let the matter slide.

I readjusted my grip on the wheel, a heavy weight sinking in my stomach.

My parents should have taught me to drive. But they were gone, and a vampire was in their spot.

My chest tightened with grief that always reared its head when I least expected it. I kept silent as Gerome directed us toward a place I loved and hated.

Bluff City had its own theme park and it featured heavily in what memories I had of my parents. At first, my grandmother kept taking me there because I loved it—like any child. By thirteen, I was old enough to process I loved it because of my parents. *Then* I'd visited the theme park every weekend to punish myself because Mum and Dad were dead and gone. That felt like my fault for a long time. Grief was so messed up. In recent years, I visited the theme park when feeling particularly morose—or when I wanted to be close to the people I only knew for nine of my twenty-one years. *That* thought always brought me nearest tears—my eighteenth birthday was horrible. At eighteen, I'd lived without my parents for as long as I'd lived with them. With each year I aged, the time I knew them seemed to shrink and the space they'd possessed inside me shrunk with it.

Like I'd never known them.

Gerome pointed to a parking spot out the front of the theme park. It was where Fred usually dropped me.

"Why are we here?" I asked in a hollow voice, looking up at the Ferris wheel looming overhead.

He watched me closely. "I thought we could spend the afternoon together. Hold hands and stuff."

Like fuck. Getting a straight answer out of him was impossible.

Gerome shrugged a shoulder. "The entertainment industry is under my control. I thought it was a good route, no other reason."

Figured.

Kyros's brother was all about fun. Made sense for the entertainment industry to be his.

I stared at the wheel, throat squeezing. "I'm finished with the lesson for the day. Can you pass my bag, please?"

"What?" Gerome blurted. "How will you get back?"

I don't care.

He didn't pass the bag over, so I leaned over to snag it and opened my door.

Kyros's brother got out of the car, too, striding around the vehicle to my side. "Are you alright?"

"Yes. Fine." Codeword for *leave me alone*. My answer of choice on days like this.

He hovered, fidgeting. Looked like it wasn't only small cars that made him uncomfortable. "Are you going into the park?"

I nodded.

Gerome took my hand, tugging me to the entrance. I thought about drawing away but didn't have the energy to. The vampire whipped out his phone, and I turned my face away as he took a snap of us holding hands outside the theme park.

"Gold." He snickered.

The teen ticket attendant stuttered at the sight of him. "Mr Gerome."

He beamed at the teen. "Hello there! I'd like a year pass for this woman, please. On the house."

"O-Of course, Mr Gerome."

I swung my pack on, my desperation to be away from everyone climbing higher. First I'd hit the rollercoaster, then the teacup carousel and the bumper cars. The Ferris wheel would be my final, lengthy stop.

Gerome placed the pass in my hand.

"Thank you," I mumbled to him and the gaping teen. "And thanks for the lesson."

The vampire ducked to meet my gaze. "I just need to know what's wrong for when Kyros tries to kill me because you're upset."

Kyros shouldn't care that I was upset. That made it sound like my state of mind was his business. And that wasn't the case—by my choice. And his. Or by our situation—I didn't know anymore.

Gerome was one of those *cover my real emotion with jokes* kind of people. I could see he felt secretly terrible about my sudden mood change. Not enough to stop taking pictures, but enough to give me a pass, hold my hand, and not feel right about going.

Reaching out, I squeezed his forearm, swallowing a rising lump in my throat. "It's not your fault, Gerome. It's just that my parents should have taught me to drive but they're not here anymore."

Alone, I strode into Bluff City's theme park for a few hours of misery.

21

I wasn't surprised to see Kyros at the bottom of the Ferris wheel when I pushed up the barrier and disembarked. I didn't know how long he'd been there—or if he'd watched me staring into space as I battled the burning behind my eyes and the pressure in my chest. Hopefully he'd just arrived.

My Ferris-wheel moments were private from everyone.

"Bye, love," the conductor said. "Keep safe."

I lifted a hand in farewell. "Bye, Don."

Kyros had my bag already, and I didn't bother asking why he was here. I didn't want to know.

"What happened?" he asked, voice strained. "What did Gerome do?"

I started for the exit in serene calm after the last five hours. A trip to the theme park always started morose, but it was my processing place. Like a meditation. When my grief over my parents built up to crisis level, this was where I came so my brain could put the files back in the right cabinets again.

"Like he didn't tell you," I said quietly.

Kyros clenched his jaw. "He didn't actually."

My brows lifted. *No way.* Joker boy defied family code to keep a secret? Upset females must really get to him. Or, more likely, he was still fucking with his brother. "I'd rather keep it private."

I regretted spilling my guts to Gerome. He caught me at a bad moment and looked like a kicked puppy at the time—

"You told my brother," Kyros accused, jaw clenching.

—*Kyros*, on the other hand, looked like a kicked cat aka a hissing sonofabitch.

I ignored his comment. "I was going to catch the bus back. You didn't need to leave your family gathering to come here." *I wish you hadn't.*

The vampire exhaled. "Miss Tetley, I don't need to do anything when it comes to you."

And what that meant no one fucking knew.

He'd parked his black car directly outside the entrance. I walked to it and stopped, waiting for him to unlock the doors.

When he didn't, I glanced over my shoulder to find him pacing, eyes blazing.

"What are you doing?" I asked.

"Trying not to lose my mind," he snapped.

Oh... cool.

I scanned the area. It had to be late afternoon, in the lull between day trippers and the time when teens and couples came in the evening, but there was still a crowd of families. Kyros was drawing attention.

"Is there something I can do to help you regain control? People are staring at your peepers."

Kyros crossed to me in a burst that was too fast for human norms.

I hissed at him. "Be careful!"

Why was I saying that? I *wanted* people to find out. The more the merrier—protection in numbers and all. But perhaps not a theme park filled with families.

His face worked as he blocked me in against the car. "Miss Tetley, it would mean a great deal to me if you would tell me what Gerome did. Not knowing is aggravating my protective instincts."

I searched his gaze—at least he'd regained the presence of mind to hood his eyes. "You have protective instincts over me? Is that an alpha thing because I live in your tower?"

He hesitated. "Yes."

"Tell me the truth."

A long warning growl filled the air between us. I folded my arms and waited.

"Not completely," Kyros admitted, looking furious—whether at himself or me I had no clue. "I have struggled to normalise my reaction to you after the blood compulsion."

Nothing he hadn't hinted at already, and that I hadn't put together myself, but it felt strange to hear the words aloud. Forbidden somehow. "Right. I expected that to be gone by now. Because of the present company, I'll tell you. But I hope you'll discover the solution to your possessiveness with all due haste. You know your attention is unwelcome."

His mouth twisted into a snarl.

I dropped my gaze. The key remote thing was in his inside waistcoat pocket. I could see the slight bulge.

"When I miss my parents, I come here to feel," I rushed to say.

With that done, I slipped my hand beneath the top button of his waistcoat and fished out the keys. I clicked the only button on it and the car lights flashed.

I tugged on the door.

His hand slid over my shoulder and prevented me from opening it.

"Please don't be mean to me today, Kyros." The filing process left me calm but exhausted. In some ways, I was *more* fragile in the hours after, though I always felt lighter on the whole.

"I don't intend to be mean. Why are you always so defensive?"

"*That's* mean, you jerk," I snapped.

He snapped back, "I was *going* to be nice."

We both realised how ridiculous the conversation was at the same time. My shoulders shook as I laughed, turning to face him. He chuckled in a deep rumble, rubbing the back of his head.

I stared at his triceps and rubbed my chin in case drool had escaped my mouth hole.

"I'll try again." Kyros pushed off the car so I was free from his cage. "Thank you for telling me," he said. "I have to be careful with all my workers. The competition likes to get involved. Sometimes behaviour like yours is a sign someone is being blackmailed or threatened."

"They do that stuff? I thought they were just like your clan."

His eyes flashed.

I held up a hand, sighing. "I didn't mean to offend. Look, can we go? I'm hungry." And embarrassed that I'd assumed his protectiveness was confined to me. Lingering effects of blood compulsion aside, he'd nearly lost the plot because his clan may be under threat.

Kyros opened my door, and I chucked my bag in, ducking to get inside.

He slid into the car a moment later. "What do you want to eat?"

"Just take me back to the tower. I'll grab something from there."

"You dragged me away from my family weekend. The least you can do is let me feed you."

"I didn't drag you away from anything. Gerome did—as you saw from the video and pictures he sent."

Kyros's grip on the wheel looked painful—for the wheel. "I'll hunt him down after."

Hunt being a literal or metaphorical use of the verb? "He was fine, really. Aside from the mind compulsion part. I didn't like that."

A roar overwhelmed my senses.

I clapped my hands over my ears, a scream choking in my throat. The beats of my heart blurred into one, dizziness assaulting me. Bile surged up my throat, and I shifted a hand to cover my lips, gagging.

Black dots filled my vision, and I slumped in the car seat, my belt the only thing holding me upright.

The roaring was coming from Kyros.

"Ky-ros," I slurred.

The terrible, guttural sound cut off and cursing took its place. The car came to a screeching stop, but the vampire didn't touch me. Instead, the car door opened and shut.

Silence fell.

With each wheezing breath, the cold vice around my body and mind loosened. Awareness of my thoughts and my surroundings returned. With shaking hands, I wiped at the sweat on my brow and leaned forward to put my head between my knees.

I'd just seen Kyros lose control.

Incorrect.

I *heard* Kyros lose control and could only feel relief I hadn't had the full experience. The last of my dizziness ebbed.

Where was he now?

I lifted my head and slumped against the leather seat, trying not to notice that my sweat covered it.

We were on the freeway.

Crap, what if he'd crashed while having a roaring meltdown? I searched for him. Squinting, I spotted him a few hundred metres away.

This man, this *creature*, required several hundred metres between him and humans when he really let his freak flag fly. Was this the real him? If so, wasn't it hard to cover that kind of power?

My presence in the tower must be a constant drain on him.

"Kyros, I'm better now," I said. My stomach churned in revolt of the statement.

The vampire didn't immediately listen, though he'd turned when I spoke. I gave up watching him after a few minutes and closed my eyes, waging war with my stomach.

The car door opened.

I didn't look at him as he settled into the driver seat. Cars whipped by and we sat in silence.

"Are you okay?" he said in the same tone I used around a skittish horse.

By this point, I had no illusions about the differences between us and could only be surprised I was alive. "Just nauseous. Otherwise fine."

"You need to eat," he said, revving the engine. He pulled out in a gap in the traffic.

My appetite was gone, but Kyros's tone was way off. If I had to guess, I'd pick shame as the predominant emotion—though understanding the feelings of a vampire his age seemed like a stupid thing to do.

Yet he'd shown up at the Ferris wheel to see if I was okay. Whether because of the weirdness between us or to ensure his clan wasn't under threat... that gesture had wormed its way into my heart.

"I shouldn't have said anything about Gerome," I said, keeping my eyes on the dashboard.

"You absolutely should have. Understand that when a Vissimo uses blood compulsion on another, it ties them together in a sense. It's an impersonal and weak tie, but a tie, nevertheless. It's considered bad manners to compel a being under another Vissimo's compulsion."

"How bad?"

He gripped the wheel. "My brother went too far. A tendency of his."

I'd intended to drop Gerome in the shit as payback, but not this much. "He did it so my body would know how to do an emergency stop."

Kyros snorted. "With my youngest brother, the third answer is the truth."

Good to know. Bastard. "He gave me a one-year pass to the theme park."

"Miss Tetley, don't defend him. He will answer for his actions—as he intended and has probably had time to already regret."

I stared out the window. "Did I just see you at full power?"

He slowed for a corner. "Full power? Without muting at all? No. I just roared."

Oh my god. There was *more*? "I couldn't handle more than that."

"Most humans can't handle even that much. Most cannot bear to be within a metre of me, or close to Vissimo in general, and certainly not in the company of more than one. You are resilient." He sounded surprised to be voicing the words.

I was surprised to hear them. They soothed the raw, tattered pieces of my soul after a hard day.

"Come into the world stubborn, leave it stubborn." My grandmother said that should be our family motto.

Grandmother. If Laurel wasn't on Basi duty tomorrow, I'd take a taxi out to see her. I worried at my bottom lip. Would Kyros track my movements though?

I dropped my gaze to my hands.

"You're sad. Why?" he asked without looking at me, parking in front of a black building.

I ignored his question. "This isn't your tower."

"No," he agreed, hopping out of the car. "We'll get takeaway here. I'm hungry too."

I watched him rounding the car, wondering if I should make a big deal of this.

Kyros held the door wide as I stepped out, grabbing my pack.

"You can leave the pack. My shout," he said.

I put my pack on in answer to *that*. The only shouting we did was the vocal kind.

The vampire pressed his lips together, shutting the door. "Miss Tetley, you are the most infuriating person that I have ever met. And that *includes* Gerome."

Burn. Having met Gerome, I was nearly offended. "That's just because we're attracted to each other but haven't had sex. If we had, you'd think my behaviour was adorable."

"No kidding," he muttered.

His mind stopped back at the sex part, if I had to guess.

I stood in the dark laneway and scanned the black three-story building. What *was* this place? It looked expensive...

Maybe I shouldn't be stubborn on the money front. *Or.* "I don't like this food, I want to go somewhere else."

"What kind of food is it?" Kyros quirked a brow.

Dang.

I shrugged. "The place has no signage and no handles on the outside. It's in a dark laneway and in Black. Therefore it's expensive. I can't afford it and I'm not letting you pay for my food. But don't hesitate to eat here yourself. I'll find something and walk back to the tower."

I turned in a circle.

Shoot.

"Which direction is the tower again?" I hadn't received my commission yet. And I didn't want to waste it on delicious food. Scratch that, I did. But I wouldn't.

"It's not expensive," Kyros said at last.

I threw him a wry look. "Try again."

"It would make me feel better for scaring you if you'd stop resisting and eat."

I crossed my arms. "This is a power thing for you, isn't it? You're pissed because I don't want to eat with you."

He glanced away. "A deal then."

"I'm all ears."

"I'll answer any questions you have about Vissimo while we're at the table. In return you will eat anything you want off the menu and not pay me back."

I thought about it.

My stomach still hadn't settled, so I wouldn't be eating much. Really, it was a win-win for me. Except I'd be catering to Kyros's pride issues.

"Counteroffer," I told him. "You'll answer my questions on Vissimo and I can ask you five questions in the future, at any time, and you must answer honestly."

His lips twitched. "Three questions. As long as answering does not harm my clan in any way."

I held out my hand, and amusement flickered in his green eyes as he shook it.

The doors were opened by two waitresses dressed in traditional Pha nung outfits. I eyed their embroidered sarongs and fitted long-sleeved blouses.

Not expensive, my butthole.

Judging by their outfits, the food was Thai. My favourite.

Dropping Kyros's warm hand, I peered at my white tank, white shorts, and white sneakers combo.

"You look beautiful," Kyros said.

Yeah, well he had a thing for white. "I'm worried I'll make the waitresses feel insecure," I answered, striding into the building. "You're on. Let's do this."

"*That* wasn't so hard," he muttered behind me.

I made the mistake of feeling triumph over his begrudging tone as I climbed a winding set of wooden stairs.

Then I realised exactly what he was referring to with *that*.

My eyes widened.

Wait, he didn't think this was a fucking date, did he?

22

Kyros and I sat opposite each other, facing off like enemy knights. We were the only people on this level. Either the place was crap or Kyros had kicked everyone out to accommodate us.

Either way, I assumed with his hearing he could tell if anyone was eavesdropping.

"Do you watch *Truth Ranges*?" I asked. This awkwardness reminded me of season three, episode eight, when Darleen didn't like what Lynda cooked for Christmas lunch and made the mistake of saying so at the beginning of the meal.

He frowned, looking confused. "No. What's that?"

We were incompatible. I'd said so from the start. "A show."

"A musical?"

"That would be freakin' *epic*. But no. It's a TV show."

He lifted a shoulder. "My free time is limited. I don't like to use what time I do have watching television. My second eldest sister forces me to watch *X-Men* movies with her, however, and I spend a week watching television every six months to stay current with human mannerisms and slang."

That was... mind-boggling. "You're missing out."

"I do like the play on words in the title," the vampire said. "I assume *Truth Ranges* is both the setting and the premise of the show?"

Usually, I'd gush over the double meaning with whomever brought it up. With Kyros, it just pissed me off. "Yes. But down to business. Question time."

We'd already ordered and, rather than looking resigned to answer my questions, Kyros appeared caught between wariness and intrigue.

"Vampires exist. What about other supernatural creatures?" I asked with bated breath.

He dipped his head. "Yes, all manner of creatures. There are only Vissimo in this city. We are extremely territorial."

You don't say.

"Which creatures?"

Kyros leaned forward. The table was a couple table—meaning that it was small enough for the occupants to lean and execute a spaghetti bolognaise kiss in the middle like Lady and the Tramp.

This tramp wouldn't go there though.

"Werewolves," he said.

"Jacob," I whispered, thinking of *Twilight*. People *actually* turned into wolves.

I shivered.

He threw me a confused look. "Fae, demons, witches, and mages, to name a few. Their proper names are different, but that's how humans identify them in literature."

No way.

Discovering vampires existed had sent me off the deep end. Now I knew the world wasn't the world I'd known, finding out about the other races was nearly exciting. I pestered him on everything to do with the different classes of supernatural races until he paused me to allow the waitresses to present the entrees.

My stomach had chilled out, and I pounced on the food. *Yum.* I loaded up my *Mianq Kham*, sprinkling diced shallots, slivers of coconut, kaffir lime, and two strips of chili into a lettuce leaf. I drizzled on the palm sugar and sour tamarind dressing. Wrapping the package up, I wasted no time shoving the whole thing into my mouth. It was called *one bite* for a reason—even if the person who named it had a bigger than average mouth.

I set myself to the task of chewing. My lips didn't quite close around the food.

Kyros hadn't moved to touch his bao sliders—if he didn't eat them, I would. Food jealousy was a bitch.

"I wondered if you'd fight me about eating too," he admitted. He rested an elbow on the armrest, jaw propped on his hand.

I continued chewing, cramming the bits that fell out back between my lips. Amazing food was the part of my old life I missed the most—aside from Grandmother.

I swallowed and made up the second lettuce parcel. "I like food. Good food, good health. I don't like that the current system keeps people without much money poor from health issues due to bad nutrition."

He dipped his head. "The world has become a business. Those who rule it see poor health as another opportunity for revenue."

Wrapping my second parcel, I remained mute. Only because I agreed and didn't wish to.

"I'm surprised to hear you enjoy food," he said before things became awkward again. "You don't eat enough."

"Recent events robbed me of my appetite."

He picked up a slider. "I see."

I watched the vampire chew on the human food, unsure what I'd expected.

"How can Vissimo be killed?" I enquired.

Kyros choked, and I smirked.

Win.

He glared when he saw the curve of my lips.

"That is where humans are remarkably accurate," he replied after sipping at his beer. "Beheading. And any injury to the heart that our healing ability cannot cope with. If we are restrained, fire can kill us over the course of several hours—depending on the power of the burning Vissimo."

"That doesn't sound pleasant."

He selected another bao slider after careful study. "It isn't. So if you decide to kill me, I'd prefer a stake to the heart."

"I'm not going to kill you," I answered. "Not that I could. But I don't want to kill anyone."

"That's surprising." Kyros rested back, putting down the second slider. "You hate me."

I rested my lettuce parcel on the plate. Did I hate Kyros? If I'd left the tower directly after the thrall, I might still hate him. Since then, we'd interacted too much. I'd seen facets to him that a heartless monster wouldn't possess. If anything, the fury I had left was because he'd stolen away my loathing before I was ready to give it up.

"I hate that you haven't once apologised to me for what you did that night. And during the thrall. Amongst other things."

"Amongst other things?"

"Take it or leave it." I shoved the second lettuce parcel in my mouth.

"I'm to gather that an apology, now you've informed me of the reason for your hate, wouldn't be accepted?" His green eyes burned.

What was he annoyed about?

"Correct. I have no idea why you would want to."

Suddenly, the craziness of this whole interaction hit me. "Christ, Kyros. What are we doing here? Why are we having dinner—that *isn't* takeout, by the way. And why did you pick me up from the theme park? On that note, why is your brother trying to get to you through *me*? You're a fucking vampire trying to take over Bluff City. What the fuck do you want with me?"

Lucky the place was empty; I'd gone from a whisper to a shout.

Groaning, I dropped my head in my hands. "This sucks." I hiccupped on my snicker. *Sucks.*

"Has it occurred to you to give in to your attraction for me?" Kyros asked, tapping a finger on the table.

I was startled into a laugh.

"What's funny?"

That was just such an *I'm older than a century* thing to say.

I met his meadow-green gaze. "*You* just want to give in?"

I'd be lying if I pretended my body wasn't way overdue for some sweaty, intense nooky.

"If it was up to me, you would have been in my bed for the entire thrall."

I snorted. "Seventy-two hours, huh? What about your game? You just admitted you don't have much free time."

Kyros didn't shift his attention from me. "In our culture, certain occasions warrant time off. Hold your next question, the waitresses are coming back."

Vampires got time off to have sex.

I settled my napkin on my lap again.

"It doesn't add up," I said after our plates were exchanged for the main and the two women disappeared once more.

Mmm, Khao Soi.

"What doesn't?" Kyros asked.

"You're gorgeous. It can't be hard for you to find partners. Don't you have a harem?"

He frowned. "Who told you about that? And no. I don't care for harems."

My blonde braid slithered over my shoulder, and I tilted my head. His gaze followed its swing. I searched his face, rooting for the reason behind that confession. What man *didn't* want a harem? Or woman for that matter. "Because of the uncertainty surrounding your birth?"

Kyros glanced up from his *Tom Yum*. "Correct. Well done."

"Gee, thanks, boss." I settled into my curry, slurping back a mouthful of soup and crunchy noodles.

He settled into his shrimp *Tom Yum*. It smelled really good.

Dammit.

"Am I allowed to leave the tower whenever I want?" I asked before I forgot.

"As long as you're safe. I'd prefer that you not go out at night without a guard."

I was allowed out during the day without a guard when I wasn't driving? Good to know.

"Is that something you ask of all your employees?" I said after swallowing another mouthful.

"Most of my other employees can protect themselves."

I thought of his fangs and shuddered. "Yeah, I bet. Is Laurel really powerful?"

He didn't blink at the subject change. "It's considered rude to divulge that information about another Vissimo. You'll need to ask her yourself."

That wasn't our deal, but I let it slide. "Being able to *mute* means someone is more powerful, yes?"

"It does." He pulled the tail off a shrimp.

Aside from when Kyros drank from me, I'd never seen him or any vampire drink blood. "Where does your blood source come from? You can't have a blood compulsion over enough humans to sustain the whole population, can you? Everyone would know."

"When it comes to blood, the clans have treaties. Most of our workers alternate feeding days at blood banks."

At the blood banks.

I thought back to when I'd donated for the grocery voucher. "Oh my god. The tubes go into the wall. Are you telling me there was a Vissimo sitting on the other side drinking my blood?"

Kyros stilled, lowering his spoon. "You've donated blood?"

I pulled a face at the memory. "Last week."

His fingers curled around the spoon, and I watched as the metal crumpled. He crushed it into a ball and rested it on the table.

Shit.

"So the possessiveness." I licked my lips. "I don't know if it's a Vissimo thing, an alpha thing, a blood-compulsion thing, or a Kyros really wants in my shorts thing. Maybe a mixture. And I need to know."

His eyes blazed.

"I'll give you a moment to rein in your control." I returned to my curry and didn't look up again until I'd polished off every bit of the spicy tofu and chicken drumstick goodness.

Kyros was watching my mouth when I did.

"Spill," I said, wiping my lips with the napkin.

"I don't know what it is," he said, glancing away.

I leaned over the table. "Bullshit! You just don't want to tell me. *I'm* the one you're sniffing around, Kyros. I deserve to know."

"I am telling you the truth, Miss Tetley. And I'm not *sniffing* around you. I'm unsure what's going on. Vissimo don't usually feel attracted to humans. I can only say that I want the urge to go away as much as you do."

I blew out a breath, passing over my used spoon so he could resume eating since he'd destroyed his. "That's some reassurance at least."

A growl slipped between his teeth.

Eyes narrowed, I jerked the spoon back. "You're not going to crush this one, too, are you?"

"It's always possible around you."

Yeah, yeah. I was annoying. Whatever.

I passed the cutlery over. "It's got my germs on it."

"We're past that now, Miss Tetley," he purred.

Mmm. That sound did things to me.

I tossed my braid back. "Why don't vampires and humans mix?"

"Our species cannot have children together, and children are the priority of most Vissimo. Added to that, you've experienced what it is to be in my presence when I lose control. Such fear can kill humans. To be with a human, whether sexually or more, is akin to a dog constantly cornering a rabbit. We can never be sure when the human's heart will stop."

Shit. Tell it like it is. I'd been a monkey and a mouse, why not a rabbit too? "I'm a rabbit then?"

"You're not. What you are is a surprise. A beautiful, hurt, and complex surprise."

I wasn't prepared to hear a compliment from his lips. Uncertainty flickered within me and I turned my face away.

"And that," he hushed, tracing my movement, "that's how I know you want me. I knew it today when Gerome sent the last picture. And now, when you're unsure how my words make you feel though your body has decided."

I forced myself to face him once more. "Kyros, I'm well aware how my body feels. And I'm well aware that I don't want it to feel that way. What are the options moving forward?"

He leaned forward in a blur, and I slammed back in my chair.

"Option one. I can bend you over this table right now."

My breath hitched. "I didn't mean those kinds of options."

"It'd make both of us feel better. Half of the time, I think the suspense of not knowing how your naked body would feel against mine is what draws me so strongly. Plus, if the sex is terrible, our problems will be solved."

Despite myself, I laughed. "Don't sound so hopeful. Rabbits aren't known for their lack of enthusiasm."

His lips spread into a slow grin.

"But seriously. We're at the truth table, you need to answer my question."

"I said I'd answer questions on *Vissimo*."

Nice try. "You are a Vissimo. Therefore, questions about yourself are also allowed. You should have better defined the parameters if you couldn't handle them."

Fuck, we were nearly nose to nose. When did that happen?

Clearing my throat, I picked up my water glass and retreated. *All the way back.*

"Sleeping together *is* an option, whether you want to hear it or not. After that, the best idea would be to remain separated. If this attraction is the lingering effects of the thrall, time should help me recover."

I was okay with Plan B. "Is it normal for the effects of the thrall to linger?"

His lips pressed together. "No. But not unheard of."

Phew, that made me feel somewhat better. "There's a third option?"

"I drink from you again and see if it's an obsession with your blood. If so, I will deal with that as a separate issue."

"You think it's my blood?"

He swallowed. "Possibly. Or just that I drank from your neck. Due to our need to remain hidden, we don't often drink from the source."

Rabbit. Mouse, Monkey. Source.

"It is possible that's drawing out my... possessive tendencies—as you called them."

I mulled all that over. "Let's try Plan B."

"Hard to do in a tower."

"Hard to do when you track everything I do," I shot back. "From texts to whereabouts. *You're* the one with the obsession issue. You need to rein yourself in. Not me."

He eyed me. "I'm the one with greater power and therefore the more powerful reaction. I am not the only one with the issue. Your words say one thing and your body another, Miss Tetley. I can smell your want as easily as if it were perfume. I can hear your heart and see the rise and fall of your breasts, and your fucking pulse is like a siren's call. All I can think about is what it would be like to put my head between your legs, pleasure you until you shatter around me, and sink my fangs into your femoral artery."

His head between my legs?

Eyes wide, I stared at him, my thighs clamping together.

Kyros pushed back from the table, sending the chair scattering along the wooden floor. "We need to go unless you want an option A and C combination?"

I grabbed my pack and shuffled off the seat.

The staff was nowhere in sight, and Kyros stalked out ahead of me, seemingly unbothered about paying.

His unsatisfied urges were only partly to blame for his temper, I knew. The rest was because his control was lapsing again. He really didn't cope well when that happened. Was that why Kyros simultaneously wanted and didn't want to be around me? Did the cravings or urges he experienced around me make him feel unbalanced?

The car lights flashed, but I lingered inside the entrance of the restaurant.

"Should I walk?" I asked him, eyeing the tight confines of the car.

Because he was right about everything.

I'd thought it was a Vissimo thing—some kind of power to attract. But I'd spent the day with Gerome and felt nothing. Whatever Kyros was feeling, I'd caught it too. It wasn't his temper that scared me. Not really. It was my reaction to him. A reaction I didn't want to have. Even after acknowledging I didn't hate him, I couldn't go there. Sex with Kyros was too much after what he'd put me through, and he was a fucking *vampire*. A powerful one. One night with him wouldn't be *just one night* if his current possessive behaviour was any indication.

Kyros blurred to me, and I stumbled back into the building.

"You're not walking," he rumbled.

I leaned against the wall, placing my hand on his chest. "I was asking, Kyros. No need to get toothy."

"Would you like to see my teeth, Miss Tetley?" He lowered his head, and I watched in fascination as his fangs descended.

Fuck me, they were hella sharp.

His eyes blazed into mine. *His smell. His warmth.* He blocked everything out, not just from his sheer size. His nearness overwhelmed my senses.

In a daze, I reached up and ran my finger down the closest fang, careful to avoid the gleaming tip.

Kyros groaned, and the sound pulled at me. I stepped closer.

"I need you to get away," he said, his entire body shaking.

I stared into his green eyes and placed my hands on his shoulders, rising on tiptoes. His head was already tilted down toward me.

No hesitation filled me as I traced the line my finger had just taken with my tongue. His shaking intensified. I pulled back, instinctively knowing repeating the ministrations on the other fang would push him over the edge.

"Basilia," he breathed.

We collided.

Our limbs tangled in our haste. He sorted the mess of our bodies out, his hands moving with blurring speed. My legs were around his hips.

He ground into me, and I saw the same wonder fill his gaze before my head thudded back against the wall behind me.

"More," I pleaded.

Kyros snarled and nipped at my collarbone.

I yelped and gasped as he wound his hips against my core again.

"White drives me fucking insane," he murmured, staring at the swells of my chest above the tank top.

Pressing my body against the wall with his hips, he slipped a hand under my ass as the other freed one of my breasts.

He latched onto my nipple with his mouth, and I choked on a wordless shout. *Jesus*, there was a line attached from my nipple to my core. The last of my forbidding thoughts fled and I circled my hips against his erection, suspended.

His satisfied purr rattled the confines of the entrance, and our pace slowed now we'd both realised this was only going one way. He shifted his attention to my other breast, and the ache in my lower stomach gained a sharp edge.

"I need you inside, Kyros," I panted at him.

His head snapped up and my eyes watered at the brightness of his green gaze.

"If I were you, brother, I'd take her up on the offer."

I screamed, and Kyros roared.

My haze of lust muted the fear his roar usually inspired. Or at least the sound didn't affect me as it had in the car.

Kyros pushed me behind his body, crowding me against the wall. Wordless snarls erupted from his mouth.

Who was it? One of his siblings? I tried to peek out.

"What are you all doing here?" he growled, trying to press me farther into the wall.

All his siblings? I whacked his back.

My gaze fell on my breasts. *Oops.* Not that his siblings hadn't seen them anyway, but since the top wasn't torn this time...

I tugged my bra and tank back into position.

"*Brother*," another breathed.

One of his sisters. *Great.* I tried to edge out, but Kyros blocked me.

I slapped at his shoulder. "If you keep slamming me against this wall, I'm going to stake you."

The air chilled.

"Did that human just threaten our crown prince?" a woman asked.

Kyros threw me an annoyed glance over his shoulder, which I returned full force.

He shifted forward, and I sidled out to stand next to him. "Yes, that was a fucking threat."

Damn it all. Seven of them were here. At least Gerome had the sense to make scarce.

"You have some explaining to do, Kyros," his sister said, shifting her eyes between us. The pantsuit one. Apparently, the outfit was a running trend with her.

"Safina. Not now."

"Let the man get rid of his boner," Rory said. His glinting eyes shifted to me, and I found somewhere else to look. I'd hoped to never see *that* one again. He hadn't recalled who I was, but pushing my luck was a bad idea.

"It's nothing," Kyros said curtly.

Auburn turned huge blue eyes on him. "It's not nothing, Ky. Why won't you tell us?"

The hard edge around his eyes faded. *Yup*, she was the youngest.

"I will, Francesca. I promise." He was wrapped around her little finger.

I snorted. "*It* has a name. But I agree, there's nothing between us."

A warning growl began in Kyros's chest.

One by one, the siblings grinned. In weird unison, they focused on me with muted gazes. Something was going on. There was a silent conversation happening. Because if his siblings were cats, *he* was the canary.

They knew something I didn't. And if they knew it, Kyros certainly did or he wouldn't be uncomfortable.

Kyros hadn't told me everything. For *one fucking second*, I thought we might be figuring this shitstorm out together.

I took a large step away from him toward their barrier. "We should have just gone with Plan D from the start, Kyros."

That drew his gaze from Safina and Francesca to me. "There wasn't a plan D."

"*Lies and omission*, Kyros. A great idea—your best, really. It's a certain solution to our little problem. There's no surer way to turn us against each other."

I stormed to the line of his siblings who blocked the entrance. Pantsuit winked at me and turned sideways so I could pass.

I turned once out in the lane. "Is someone going to drive me to the tower? Or should I walk?"

They slid their eyes toward their eldest brother, their *crown prince.*

Whatever.

"Walking it is," I declared, braid whipping around as I turned on my heel.

23

I sighed at Laurel over the top of the car—the silver trash car was nowhere to be seen today. I was back in the white one. The scratches I'd caused were gone, and I could only suppose I'd been trusted with the flashy vehicle again for the sake of appearances.

I stood outside the three-bedroom, two-bathroom property of Mr and the future Mrs Polton in Green.

"They could be watching us," I told the vampire. "Wait down the end of the street or out of sight. I don't care. But it'll be weird if you're in the car waiting like my caretaker."

Laurel clasped her hands behind her back. "I'm sorry, Miss Tetley. I have my orders."

She had her chains.

"Do you have the number of someone in the tower?" I asked, rubbing my temples. I'd been awake half of Saturday and Sunday night, replaying Kyros's groan when I licked his fang. Thank god, his siblings interrupted us. Their bad record after Level 66 was officially wiped clean. Pantsuit even gave me a lift back to the tower in the end. I was considering asking for a transfer to the industry she covered—whatever that was. I'd put my money on Finance.

The Indebted stared over the top of the car at me. "Yes, I do."

I rounded the car and held out my hand.

With a shrug, she passed her sleek device over after dialling a number. Not as easy to hold as Beast, if truth be told. It probably didn't have brick snake either. Phones had gone backward.

I held the device to my ear.

"Laurel."

Crap. "Angelica," I said coolly.

"Miss Tetley?"

"The same," I answered. "There's an issue. Laurel has orders to remain with me, but she's going to weird out my clients if she does. Can you expand her orders so she can wait at the end of the street?"

Silence met my query. "I'll have to clear that. Hold, please."

I listened as she placed the phone down and spoke to someone else in the room. I assumed she was clearing it with Kyros—my babysitter.

The speaker snapped as Angelica picked up the phone again. "*Five houses away. No more.*"

That seemed extreme. "Laurel was only appointed to me because I don't know how to drive... right, Angelica?"

She paused. "Word has reached our ears that Clan Fyrlia is aware we have a human in our employ."

"So?"

"We have never had a human in our employ, Miss Tetley. It's unexplored territory for us, and Kyros decided to take the safe route."

If growing up in a drama-fuelled rich world had taught me anything, it's that both contenders in a war always believed they were right. The clan I worked for weren't as squeaky clean as they liked to harp on about. The other clan probably sprouted the same propaganda against them.

"Sure. I'll pass that on to Laurel."

"Thank you. And so you know, King Julius rolled a three last night."

A three. "Green?"

"Green."

I didn't know the various probabilities of the dice combinations, but from my own experience with board games, three didn't crop up much. Yet here I was. What was the bet that all the staff with appointments in the most likely suburbs were scrambling to adjust their days?

I snorted and hung up, turning to Laurel. "Catch all that?"

She was already moving down the street. "Got it."

"Okay. I usually take a couple of hours unless they slam the door in my face." *Or I fall asleep.* I could only hope the owners of 1061 Bugles Street weren't prone to curtain peeping, like Mrs Gaughton, and had missed the ten-minute argument between me and Laurel.

Grabbing the file off the roof of the car, I opened the gate and admired the white stone path to the door. *Pretty.* Lifting the golden knocker, I rapped three times.

The door wasn't opened straightaway. Wrinkle between my brows, I listened to the crashing and muffled laughter within. *Oh my god.* I grinned. They were totally banging.

"I'll come back later," I called out, backing away from the white door.

Fiancés.

The door was yanked open. The flushed face of a young woman filled the frame, her body out of sight. Wrapped in a sheet, I was willing to bet.

"We'll be *just* a moment, Carla," she said. "Hold on a tick."

The door closed.

Uhm. Who was Carla?

I hovered outside, studying the immaculate garden. They had several thriving lavender bushes—poor Mrs Gaughton.

The door was wrenched fully open this time.

"I apologise! We didn't expect you for another hour."

I opened my mouth. "I think there's been a mistake. My name isn't Carla."

"But you're from the realtors, yes?" Her eyes roamed over my royal blue dress with the sweetheart neckline. "Yes, I can see you are."

"I am," I replied, smiling. Was there a Carla at Live Right? I had no idea.

"Come on in. Henry's just getting... Well, he'll be with us shortly."

I smiled at her. "Of course. I've heard being engaged is a lot of fun."

She glanced at me, but her shock quickly melted to amusement. "It is. But please pretend you have no clue what we were doing. Henry was raised in Black."

"Say no more," I murmured. Riches and secrets went hand in hand. There was a way of teasing someone with money about the same subject, and it wasn't by blurting it outright as I had with the future Mrs Polton.

She led me to a small conservatory filled to bursting with colourful flowers aside from the small glass table and wrought iron chairs positioned in the centre.

"This is really cute," I told her.

She glanced around the space fondly. "Thank you. Henry made it for me. He's the gardener. Not me."

They were an adorable couple. A legit couple. I held out my hand. "Where are my manners. I'm Basilia from Live Right Realty."

Her face dropped.

Mine followed.

She recovered and took my hand, face working. "I'm Bess. But I'm sorry. We were expecting someone from Foremost."

Foremost. Never heard of them. I grimaced. "I apologise, Bess. I'm new to Live Right and I assumed there was someone on the staff called Carla. I'll leave you to your appointment. So sorry to inconvenience you."

A lean man, the opposite of Bess's curvy and short frame, bent his head to enter the conservatory.

"Carla? I was just on a phone call."

He held out a hand, and I shook it automatically. Bess threw me an amused look at his *phone call* excuse.

"Of course," I murmured. "It's no trouble. But my name is Basilia. There has been a mix-up."

Bess glanced at Henry. "Basilia is from Live Right."

His face darkened.

Eek.

"Just started there," I admitted. "Let me get out of your hair so you can get ready for your actual appointment."

My face burned. Henry was putting out some serious dislike. He either hated being pestered or had other beef with *Live Right*.

"No," Bess said as I turned away.

"Bess." Henry accompanied her name with a pointed look.

She met it head-on. "She seems nice. We're selling already. We may as well see what she thinks the property will go for."

Henry abandoned his attempts to silently convey his reluctance to her. He flushed, throwing me an irritated look.

"You've clearly had a poor experience with Live Right in the past," I said. "I apologise on their behalf, and I'm happy to take your feedback to the company."

His brows lifted and he glanced at Bess before returning to me. "I wasn't here when the last person from Live Right came. But they scared Bess."

"And you were understandably upset," I replied.

She sighed. "They didn't *do* anything as such. I can't really say why I felt so uncomfortable."

Because you have good instincts. "We keep records of site visits. I'll look into the matter and follow it up. You should never feel uncomfortable in your own home."

Henry contemplated me and shot another look at his fiancée. "We may as well hear what you have to say."

I was so fucking good at this.

Bess gestured to the table. I took a seat, watching as Henry pulled out the chair for his fiancée.

So freakin' cute.

I placed the file on the table. "You said that you're thinking of selling?"

They nodded.

"Upscaling for a future family?" I asked, glancing between them.

Henry frowned, and Bess took his hand.

"Actually, Basilia. We're downsizing to pay for IVF treatment."

I was terrible at this. Talk about pride before a fall. "That was an assumption. I'm sure those kinds of assumptions get really old."

His brow cleared at that. "It's okay. We only received the news a few months ago, so it's new for us too."

Did I say I was sorry? That seemed like a shitty response to a heart-breaking issue. "I really hope IVF works out. So many people have children who don't seem to give a shit. It doesn't seem fair when the good ones can't have them."

Bess's eyes misted and she swallowed hard when Henry wrapped an arm around her shoulders.

"Thank you," she whispered.

I studied them, my chest clenching with their pain. "So you need as much money as possible?" Odd, with Henry coming from Black. But I'd left money too. I shouldn't assume everyone was a greedy *sonofabitch*.

"Well, yes. I guess so," Bess said. "Our main thing is we want a short settlement period. The sooner we have the money, the sooner we can get started. We've been trying for eighteen months and it's become this huge thing. Starting IVF as soon as possible would be a huge relief. But we know there's a process with selling properties—open homes and such."

Henry squeezed her shoulders. "We'd like to get an idea of what price similar houses are selling for in Green."

He still didn't trust me. That was fine. Vissimo frightened his wife and he was still pissed. That just made him a good partner.

"Live Right keeps up to date valuation records of each area," I told the couple, drawing out the report and placing it before them. "This is the current valuation of your property." I pointed to the numbers at the bottom.

"Seven hundred and seventy thousand." Bess's eyes widened. "We hadn't expected that much with the value of houses dropping."

I nodded grimly. "You haven't had a great experience with Live Right so far, but I will tell you the decline in property value is forecasted to continue."

Of course, now I knew why that *was*. The clans owned so much of the city that they controlled supply and demand. Not only did they make it far cheaper to rent than buy, but they relentlessly approached houses still privately owned. They'd progressively plugged demand and were now picking off remaining houses for cheaper as owners panicked and sold. Two years ago, this couple would have got at least one hundred thousand more for the same property.

"Live Right are working to ensure the house market doesn't crash," I grumbled.

Henry frowned. "What do you mean?"

"Oh shoot, I'm getting ahead of myself." I scrounged up the line Katerina used on a solo mother last week. "I take from your comment that you've noticed that houses in Green aren't really selling."

"We have," Bess said uneasily. "Everyone's talking about it."

I nodded. "Live Right is the largest realtor in the city, and they'd like to stop the market imploding for the sake of house owners such as yourself—"

"They're a business," Henry scoffed.

I smiled. "—and because the house market crashing doesn't bode well for a real estate company."

He smiled sheepishly. "That makes more sense."

Bess tapped the sheet. "So if we sold to Live Right, we wouldn't need to do open homes or any of that?'

"Nope," I said. "And Live Right offers a twenty-four-hour settlement."

Henry leaned back.

I'd gone for the kill too soon.

I hurried to add. "They do that because they research properties extensively before offering these deals. They don't offer this kind of thing to everyone, just select homes in target areas, and only to homes that they believe will make a difference to the market condition."

There. That wasn't so bad for talking out my ass.

"What's the initial offer then?" Henry asked, studying the valuation. Bess looked at me eagerly, but Henry seemed regretful.

They'd shown their desperation for money already. It weakened their position in a negotiation.

That was *if* I cared about how much money Kyros had.

"Let's see," I said, humming. "They give me three contracts, and I'm supposed to offer the valuation price of course, but I think the world needs more couples like yourself."

"Why are you telling us this?" Henry asked, his gaze flying to mine.

I snorted. "I'm a terrible realtor. I wouldn't be surprised if I'm fired soon." *And eaten for lunch.*

He cracked a smile, and Bess laughed.

I slid the top contract in front of them. "Live Right won't offer you more than this. I'd be surprised if anyone else does. *However*," I stressed, "this is our same-day contract. You will have a week to move out, but settlement will be by 11:00 p.m. tonight."

Their mouths bobbed open at the same time. "Eight hundred thousand!" Bess exclaimed.

Henry rubbed his jaw. "It's far more than we expected. I just don't understand why settlement has to be today."

I nodded, mind working rapidly. "It's unusual. You don't know me, so I won't ask you to put trust in me, but I can ask a client of mine from last week if he'd act as a reference. He signed his house over to Live Right via a same-day signing too."

"That would be good," Henry said, glancing at Bess.

They locked in a silent exchange.

"How about I leave you with this contract?" I said, rising from my chair. "It's valid until the end of my shift—5:00 p.m. You can already tell that I'm a terrible realtor, so I have no qualms in telling you to see what Foremost has to offer first."

"There's no way you'll last as a realtor." Henry chuckled.

I grinned at them. "Nope. So I may as well give you as much money for IVF as possible before they fire my ass."

The couple laughed.

"If I hear from you, great. If not, I wish you my sincere best for treatment. I hope you're blessed with octuplets."

Henry looked ecstatic at that. Bess not so much.

I smiled at them and made for the door.

"Wait, how do we get in touch with you?" Bess called, hurrying after me. "And we need that reference too."

Oh yeah. Drat, I only had Beast. He'd be sleeping by now. "Of course. I'll head out to my car and call my client from last week. And I'll get my number for you. New phone and all."

Nuts, I didn't even have the car keys. "Laurel," I hissed when I reached the vehicle.

"Over here," she called softly.

I rounded the car to find the vampire crouched beside the driver door. Glancing up, I waved at Henry and Bess, who watched.

"I need your phone."

"I already called Angelica for the number of your client."

"Thanks, but I need to fake getting in the car to get the phone first. They're watching."

Laurel shuffled left as she pressed the button on the keys.

I slipped into the car and faked riffling through my pack while palming the phone from her. Then I got out again.

This was ridiculous.

The cell number was already on the screen, so I pressed Dial and waited as the phone rang.

"This is Vern."

My lips twitched at his chipper voice. "Vern, it's Basilia—from last Thursday."

"The agent who took a nap on my couch Basilia?"

How many Basilias were there in Bluff City? Old men made the worst jokes sometimes. "That's the one. I wanted to call and ensure everything ran smoothly after the signing."

I listened as he gushed about his new RV and the stress of packing. The excitement from the sale of his house hadn't ebbed one bit, and my smile softened as he detailed his travel plans.

"I'm so happy for you, Mr Yersaw. I wonder if I could ask you for a favour though? I have two clients—a young couple. They're eager for a quick sale but want to speak to someone who'd gone through the one-day contract process. Is that something you'd be comfortable doing?"

Less than a minute later, I passed the phone to Bess and Henry and retreated back to the car and crouching vampire.

I folded my arms, staring in the opposite direction so they wouldn't feel pressured. "You heard that whole thing inside, huh?"

Laurel smirked. "Sure did."

Crap. I'd been busted throwing away Kyros's money. "And how detailed is your report?"

"Kyros only asks questions on occasion. When this happens, I must tell the truth." Her eyes slid to me. "Not necessarily to the letter."

My lips twitched. "Good to hear."

"...Thank you, by the way. I heard your conversation with Gerome. I got paid double."

I was burning to know how much she got paid to take me on driving lessons. I refrained. *Just.* "No worries. Gotta get you out of those chains sooner rather than later."

"The woman is about to walk down the driveway, and a car is pulling up. I'll wait down the street," Laurel said calmly.

I waited a few seconds, then rounded the car to take the phone from Bess. "Get everything you need?"

She nodded. "You fell asleep on his couch during a *Truth Ranges* omnibus?" Laughter burst from her lips.

"I was hungover," I confessed.

Her laughter swelled.

"Let me jot my number down for you." I opened the passenger door and wrote it down on the file, tearing the corner off. "Sorry, super professional. But here it is. Call me with any questions. I have another visit today, but I'll get back as soon as possible."

A car had pulled up during our conversation, and I glanced at the man exiting the vehicle. Almond-shaped, bright hazel eyes snapped to mine, and my heart began to pound.

Fuck.

Vissimo.

One from the other clan—or at least he looked like Clan Fyrlia's king.

"Basilia?" Bess asked.

I laughed lightly. "What was that?"

"I said, we'll be in touch. Thank you for the information." She glanced at the man and back to me.

"You're most welcome," I replied, whispering, "Have fun with Carla."

Her lips trembled, and I turned for the car.

Bess greeted the Vissimo who'd toned his eyes right down since glaring at me. If he was muting like that, then he had to be powerful—not ideal.

I opened the car door.

"Excuse me, Bess. I forgot the file. I'll meet you at the top."

Shit.

I yanked the door wide. One foot was inside when the vampire shoved the car door into me. My body was forced to twist, but I yelped as the bottom of the car door smacked into my shins, crushing against my chest.

"What the hell," I gasped through the sting, shoving at the door.

Yeah, Basi. Engage in a battle of strength with a fucking vampire, you moron.

"Get off me or I'll call the police," I snapped.

The vampire sneered. "Drop the act, human. You know about us. You're not nearly scared enough."

True. Dammit. His eyes blazed, and I quickly dropped my eyes to his garish tie.

"*Hmm,*" he said. "Resilient. Kyros has picked well."

Nuh-uh. I wasn't being labelled Kyros's anything. That was a sure pass to being hurt by every one of his enemies. "He didn't pick shit."

The vampire gripped my chin. "That's not what I have heard. But it's of no consequence. What *is* of consequence, *Basilia Tetley*, is that this house belongs to me. Come between Foremost and this property, and you will learn what fear really is."

I gasped as his grip tightened. Tears of pain sprang to my eyes, and his lips curled.

"I could kill you in less than a second," he whispered in my ear. "Remember that."

He was going to break my jaw.

"I'll remember," I hissed.

The vampire let go and straightened his suit as I sagged over the door.

As soon as he disappeared into the house, Laurel was in front of me, a finger pressed to her lips.

She opened the door and caught me as my hip gave way. Lifting me, she opened the back door and placed me along the long seat. My mind was just coming to grips with what happened as she guided the vehicle from the curb.

When we were on the freeway out of Green, she finally spoke, "I didn't come to your aid because of my orders. I am not to interfere if doing so causes more harm. If Clan Fyrlia discovers you have a guard, they may decide Kyros values you and up their efforts to hurt you."

I propped myself up and studied my shin. A huge lump had risen, and the unbroken skin was darkening. "That's gonna be an ugly bruise."

"I'm sorry," Laurel repeated, eyes flickering.

"You have your orders," I said. "No biggie." *Big biggie.* I hadn't expected to walk away with my legs and jaw unbroken. My heart still pounded. Not from my reaction to the *Vissimo*—because the flare of his eyes was a drop in a lake compared to Kyros's roar—but to his physical strength. That man *could* kill me in less than a second. And the memory of his smirk and glinting hazel eyes told me he'd enjoy it too.

I rubbed my jaw. *Fuck's sake.* More bruises. "Will Bess and Henry be safe?"

"Yes. It's against the rules of *Ingenium* to coerce signatories in any way. They're safe."

I suppose a mind compulsion would leave Henry and Bess aware vampires existed, and a blood compulsion would result in the thrall. "Good, they deserve better than that."

Laurel sighed. "Just so you know. I'll have to report this to Kyros."

Ugh. "You have to?"

She dipped her head.

"Can you delay it until the end of the day?"

"I cannot."

"Does it have to be *Kyros* you report to?"

Her eyes shifted to mine. "Yes, Miss Tetley."

I lay back down again, staring at the car ceiling. "Fucking great."

24

I sat behind my desk, researching clients for the next day. A doctor had examined my jaw, shin, and hip. But surprisingly, Kyros didn't come down from his office on Level 65 to see me.

Maybe something I'd said last night got through to him. Or maybe his siblings' reactions had shamed him about his dalliance with the *human*. Whatever it was, I was happy not to deal with the roaring alpha Vissimo for a day.

I stood and hobbled around the room. My hip was fucking killing me. When the vampire doctor was here—Clan Sundulus's personal doctor—the pain wasn't that bad.

"Basil?"

I froze and limped around in a circle. "Tom?"

It was Tommy. *Fuck!*

"What are you doing here?" I asked, covering my surprise with a wide smile. "It's 4:00 p.m. You're usually at work. Is everything okay?"

"Public holiday. And shouldn't I be asking *why* you're at work?"

It was a public holiday? I guessed that's why Bess and Henry were at home on a Monday. "No rest for the wicked."

I tried to stand naturally, unsure how long she'd hovered in the doorway.

"Why are you limping?" she asked, deflating my small hope.

"I fell down the stairs," I answered. The game was up, so I hobbled to the desk and perched on the corner.

Her eyes fell to my shin. "And was that how your shin got a massive black fucking bruise too?" Red blotches stained her cheeks.

She walked toward me.

I lifted a shoulder. "Yep. Hit the corner of the railing. Hurt like a bitch. Still does. I need some drugs."

Tommy searched my gaze, and I kept it steady. Wait, I'd never do that normally.

"You want to say something? Spit it out," I told her. "You're looking at me like you're angry about something."

Who let her in here when I was hurt? *Clearly immortality didn't always come with a high IQ.*

"You fell down the stairs," she repeated, stepping closer.

I nodded. "A few hours ago."

Tommy hummed, reaching around to place her bag on the desk. I nearly flinched. She was fucking scary when she got protective.

"And tell me, Basi," she whispered, looking into my eyes, "how did you get the fingermark bruises either side of your jaw?"

Ah, shit.

"It's not what you think."

Her eyes flared. "That bastard is abusing you." Her colour heightened.

Every bad thing I could think of happening to Tommy ran through my mind in the space of a sharp inhale. To have her go through what I went through. For her to be compelled. For her to feel as isolated and afraid as I did every day now. The simple thought that she could be frightened to death in their company. All of that hit me in a solid, icy wall.

She opened her mouth, and I held up a hand. "I need you to leave."

Tommy jerked back, staring at me with a rounded gaze. "What did you just say?"

My voice was cool. "I love you. But I'm working, Tom. I can't do this at work, so I need you to leave."

"*My god.* What are they doing to you? How are they controlling *you* of all people? You're *limping*, Basi."

I didn't budge. "You're wrong. And I need you to leave."

Her voice rose, and my panic surged with it. How many vampires were listening to her? Dread curled around my heart.

"I'm calling the police," she spat.

I arched my brows. "To tell them what? And to what end when I set the matter straight?"

She pressed her lips together, lifting her chin. "I'll call your grandmother."

Air lodged in my throat. "Tommy! If you do that I will never, ever forgive you."

She halted, phone already in hand.

"This isn't what you think," I stressed. She couldn't bring my grandmother into this.

My friend straightened, murder etched on her face. "Then you need to tell me what to think. Not that bullshit you spun."

"I told you the other day—"

"And I'm telling you now that I don't buy that line anymore. If I was standing in front of you in this state, you wouldn't rest until the person was in a grave."

True.

Vampires exist, I tried to say. Only a gurgle sounded. Writing it down would have the same effect.

I hopped off the desk and limped to my seat. "I can't give you what you're asking for, Tommy. There's no problem. I'm not sure what you want me to say. But I'm 100 percent serious when I say that if you overstep and bring my family into this, we're through."

"I want you to tell me you're leaving this place and coming with me," she shouted, whirling on me. "What the fuck is he doing to you? Why won't you talk to me?"

Because I can't.

Her hands shook as she strode around the desk to grip my

shoulders. "No more, Basil. Tell me now. If you value our friendship, tell me. Or I'll walk out that door."

It was the first time I'd considered that I might lose her over this. We were so strong. Our friendship had lasted through every single hurdle along the way. But I'd never heard her speak in that tone.

I'd never seen that look in her eyes.

I had to tell her everything, to leave, to get out. Yet that didn't mean a thing with the chains Kyros had looped around my mind.

I'd been at *Live Right* for nearly two weeks and looked like death warmed up. There would be more bruises and more threats in my future. Tommy may forgive me this time. She may take back what she'd said after a few days. But she'd never stand by as I strung her along with lies over months or years.

"Basil? We'll sort it out together. But I'm dead serious, lovely. I need to know what's happening right now."

I met her frantic chestnut gaze. "Or you'll walk out that door?"

"I swear I will."

Shoving down the urge to pull her into my arms, I hardened myself to her hurt. I whispered, "You know how I go with ultimatums, Tom."

It was as though I'd slapped her. She reeled back, her arms falling away from my shoulders.

Her throat worked as tears rushed into her eyes, and I mentally focused on the pain in my hip. I deserved every bit of it.

"That's all I get after sixteen years of friendship?" Her voice broke.

I tore my gaze away, facing the computer screen. When I could trust my voice, I said, "There's nothing more to say. We both know where we stand. I guess I'll see you around."

A knock sounded.

I glanced up in irritation. If it was Kyros, I'd wring his neck.

Laurel stood there, phone in hand. "Those clients from earlier are on the line. Should I tell them you're busy?" Her eyes slid to my friend, who'd frozen on the spot. "Oh, hey."

Tommy reached for her bag and turned from me. She walked to Laurel. "Don't speak to me as if you know me. You're part of this too."

She brushed past the Indebted, and I closed my eyes, hunching as though I'd been punched in the stomach.

My best friend was gone.

And I couldn't feel a thing because she'd meant too much to me. My body couldn't feel so much pain and loss on top of everything else, so it just didn't.

"Thank you, Laurel," I said quietly.

Her eyes were full of sadness and nearly undid me. The fear of becoming undone made me cling to my cold, empty calm.

"They're really on the phone?" I asked.

"They are. I can tell them you'll be free in an hour."

An hour wouldn't help me. Not after what I just did to Tommy. "Pass it over, please."

She surveyed me and crossed the room to obey.

A fake conversation sounded about the nicest place to be right now. "This is Basilia," I spoke down the line.

"Basilia!" Bess's relieved voice poured down the phone. "I'm so glad I caught you."

I glanced at the time on the computer screen. *4:45 p.m.* "You sure did."

"Listen, I know your shift is nearly over. Henry and I didn't mean to ring you this late, but we wanted to take the contract to a conveyance lawyer and check it was all fine. I'm not sure if I should tell you that, but obviously everything was in order because I'm calling you! If it's not too late, Henry and I would love to accept your offer."

A reason to leave the tower and scream? *Absolutely.* "Bess, of course you needed to make sure everything was up to scratch. It's no trouble for me to whip down there to get the papers lined up for you and Henry. I can be there in twenty?"

"You can? Where are you right now?"

"*Uh*, Grey?"

"Peak-hour traffic," she said. "It will take at least an hour to get here. Oh, that makes me feel terrible! I hate to drag you out on a Monday night."

I smiled. “It’s not an issue, I promise. There are future babies on the line.”

“Well, how about I cook dinner in return for braving the Bluff City car park to come out here?”

“That would be lovely, Bess. I’ll see you soon.”

I hung up and flipped the phone in my hand. “What’s the Bluff City car park?”

Laurel had perched on the edge of my desk. “It’s what humans call the roads in the Grey during peak-hour traffic. Everyone is bumper-to-bumper, so it resembles a car park.”

Huh.

Laurel stared at the keys in her grip. “Do you want to talk about it?”

“Nope,” I sang, rising to my feet. I clutched my hip, sucking in a breath. “But I do want some fucking painkillers. Ouch.”

The Indebted blurred to my side and supported my forearm. “Come on then. Bess didn’t include the time it will take you to get to the car.”

“She didn’t, did she?” I chuckled.

We both pretended not to hear it for the pitiful warble of a chuckle it was.

I looked up at the knock. It was a welcome distraction from my dark thoughts.

Tommy hadn’t gotten in touch.

That was the whole point of what I’d done though, and I had to deal with the bed I’d made. Or whatever that stupid saying was. I’d only made one bed in my life and Clint stole it after. They should make a saying about *that.*

“Miss Tetley,” Angelica said. “I’ve received your notes and wanted to talk with you directly about them.”

The notes asking why I hadn’t received my commission from selling two houses? “Where’s the money?”

"Before I get to that, I wanted to clear the air between us. I know you feel I betrayed you with what happened on Level 66. If it's not too painful with your hip, could you please follow me?"

My hip was on the mend after the last two days, so I limped after Kyros's aunt into a small concrete cupboard. Was that an old hot water cylinder?

She shut the door.

"Why are we in here?"

Angelica rapped the walls. "One metre of concrete surrounds us and a healthy wrapping of steel. If we speak quietly, our conversation will remain private."

Was that a good or bad thing?

"Angelica, are you interfering in Kyros's love life by dressing me in certain colours and by forcing me into his company during the thrall?"

She blinked.

That's right, dark horse. I'm on to you.

"Yes," the vampire admitted.

I leaned back.

Okay, I hadn't expected that. "Why? Kyros and I don't like each other."

Angelica shot me a derisive look. "I love my nephew. From the moment he opened his beautiful green eyes, I'd do anything for him —not that he needs my help. But from the moment he drew breath, he has been part of this battle. In his adult life, despite the best work of the queen and myself, work had overtaken his existence. I would change that."

I stared at her, trying not to laugh. "And you both hope I can do that? Me. The human."

"My sister is unaware of my intentions in this matter. But yes, I do. I've never seen Kyros so angry as when he's in your company."

I squinted. "And the fact we make each other murderous with rage makes you think we're perfect for each other?"

Angelica smiled, staying silent.

Changing gears, I said, “Do you realise how humiliated I was that night on Level 66?”

She nodded. “I saw it in your eyes. Though why I can’t fathom. Your body is a masterpiece.”

I frowned, shaking my head. “What? No. That wasn’t my point. That’s not why I was humiliated.”

“Humans place great value on physical privacy.”

I pinched the bridge of my nose. There was literally no point having this conversation with a Vissimo.

“I want to convey my sincere apologies on that front,” she said, standing still, hands behind her back. Her blue eyes lit up the tight confines of the closet.

I just couldn’t be bothered fighting with her. My emotional quota was being used up by everything Tommy at the moment. “I’ve realised in the last week that I held you to a higher standard than the other Vissimo in this tower. That was my mistake.”

Her gaze flickered.

“I have since lowered my standards when it comes to you,” I said. “So I’m willing to put the matter behind us in the knowledge that I’m trapped in this fucking place for the foreseeable future.”

She lowered her eyes. “I am sorry to have disappointed your faith in me. Know that only the deepest love for my nephew spurred me to do so.”

She was barking up the wrong tree there.

I waved a hand. “The commissions.”

“Live Right owes you over thirteen thousand dollars.”

After just one week in the normal world, my mind boggled at the sum. Money was armour in this world. With none, I was at Kyros’s utter mercy. With thousands of dollars, a little less.

I shot her a look. “It should be more than that.”

“The top commission bracket is reserved for those who secure properties at the lowest valuation price.”

In other words, I was shooting myself in the foot by securing homes at the top offer. I didn’t give a shit. Thirteen thousand could go a long way. "Why don't I have the money?" I pressed. "What's the latest excuse you'll make up to trap me here?"

Her tiny wince confirmed my nagging suspicion. Pretty sure that's why Angelica hadn't paid me in advance that one time. She knew I'd have to return to work the following week. Looking back, the excuses she spun were bogus.

"We operate legally, Miss Tetley. We require a bank account number to process large sums."

I sighed. "I don't have a bank account or tax number. What's another solution?" I'd used the lease agreement Kyros gave me and my driver's licence to order a passport. When that came, I could apply for a tax number. It would be weeks away.

"There isn't one. Without both, we cannot pay you the commission."

I leaned against the cool concrete, playing out various scenarios in my mind. One where I bluffed and told her I'd have an account tomorrow. Another where I threatened to go to a lawyer.

In every scenario, I lost. "I see. Is that all?"

She searched my face.

I took it as a yes and opened the closet door, feeling the air-con wash over me.

"Miss Tetley, I'd like for us to be friends," Angelica said quietly.

She went there.

"I had one friend," I told her, my spine so rigid it might snap. "Now she's gone. No one will replace her. I have no idea why you're entertaining the idea of friendship between us, but I will tell you games is a bad fucking start. I don't play games with anyone. *No one.*"

"Noted."

By my record, she'd apologised once before. "I won't hold my breath, Angelica. Now, please excuse me. I've got work to do."

25

"Go away," I yelled.

"It's Rory."

I muted *Sailor Moon*.

Rory. What the hell was Kyros's brother doing here? Scrap that, I could guess. But would he go away if I didn't make another peep? Sailor Moon was about to find out who Tuxedo Mask really was.

Rory's muffled voice reached me through the door. "I can hear your breathing. You're in the back corner of the room."

I rolled over as quietly as possible.

"You just moved to the right."

Fucker.

"What do you want?" Why *him* in particular? I needed to hide from the vampire for more reasons than one.

The man who'd unknowingly humiliated me in my teens growled. "What I don't want is to break Kyros's tower. He gets shitty."

"That's an incentive, right?"

His louder growl convinced me to haul ass. I glanced at my white tank and white underwear combo.

Eh. He should have called first.

I swung the door wide and peered into the bright blue eyes that once made me swoon. Now they made me feel nauseous with remembered mortification—even if that remembered mortification was dressed in a tux that hugged every line of his athletic body. He must have been a sprinter in his last life. *Hot damn.*

His eyes swept down my frame, lingering on my bare thighs.

Shit, I was swooning.

I grunted. "What?"

He held up a dress bag. "It's Friday. I need a date."

"Hell no." I slammed the door shut.

Nearly.

Rory held the door ajar. "It's a social function. It won't mean anything. You'd be doing me a favour."

"This is to torture Kyros."

The bastard didn't deny it.

"I always take a human date. People find it easier to talk to me when a human is in my company even when I'm muting completely."

"Are you telling me that you dazzle them?" I called, leaning against the door with my entire body weight.

The door didn't budge.

"I believe our first meeting left *you* speechless."

Oh how right you are. Just not about where we first met. "Things between Kyros and I are finally settling down. I'm not screwing with that."

Rory snickered on the other side of the door. "You think he's settling down?"

He wasn't? No, I didn't care.

"Since Saturday night, everything has been better. With regards to me and him." I couldn't speak for the rest of my life.

"You should've seen him when Laurel called about that Fyrlia scum attacking you."

"I don't want to know!"

He pressed on the door, and I stumbled backward into the room.

Kyros's brother stepped into the room. "Come, and I'll shut up."

Spinning on my good leg, I limped to the bed. "Nope."

"Come with me, or I'll drain you dry."

My heart skipped a beat. "Nope."

"That scared you though. What will it take?"

Hmm. Now that I could work with.

Grabbing Beast, I typed out my request and tilted the screen toward him.

I need a bank account opened, and a tax number, but I lost my ID. Can you do it?

I peeked up and caught his grin.

My stomach flipped as he brushed back sandy blond hair. He really was handsome. *Shampoo commercial on steroids* handsome. Seventeen-year-old me had great taste—if not great pick-up lines.

"I control the finance industry in Bluff City. Yes, I can arrange for that to happen."

Dang, there went my guess about Pantsuit aka Safina controlling finance. "Can you do it if Kyros goes against you? I don't want him to be able to reverse stuff after the fact."

"By the time he finds out, you mean?" His eyes sharpened. "There won't be an issue. The finance sector is mine and mine alone."

"I thought Sundulus operated legally." I crossed my arms.

He pursed his lips. "We do. Alas, not all of our contacts have the same upstanding code."

And that kept them squeaky clean? *Yeah, right*—but I wasn't about to discourage him.

"Can I take that as a yes?" he murmured, smoothing his tie.

"I don't want Kyros to find out about this date."

"Hard no," Rory said, hand going to his tie. "Is there a mirror in here?"

I held out my hand for the garment bag. "In the bathroom. How long do I have?"

"An hour. Angelica said she'll do you up."

Already back to her matchmaking ways, was she? A pissed-off Kyros was unlikely to keep his distance. "In a body bag?"

Rory's eyes flashed.

A light knock sounded from the open doorway, and I grimaced.

"Not quite, Miss Tetley," Angelica said drily.

Sighing, I threw the garment bag on the bed and unzipped it. I stared at the sparkling, spangled black dress within. Full length. "What kind of social event are we talking about?"

Crap. I might know people at this thing.

"I've changed my mind," I said. "Don't like the dress."

Rory stepped forward, snarling. "I picked it. And I have exquisite taste."

And ego to spare. I shook my head, wrinkling my nose. "Nah, don't like it."

He pulled up short, eyes glimmering. "What made you change your mind so suddenly, Basilia?"

"It's Basi."

Kyros's brother studied me. "Don't forget what you stand to gain. A few hours and you-know-what is all yours."

Thirteen thousand dollars. And all future commissions. Plus, figuring out a way to get paid the money would be a small fuck you to Angelica. Without that money, I had just over eight hundred dollars to my name. I wanted out of this game and away from here. Ironically, to do that, I needed the very thing I left at the estate. Power from financial clout.

"Three hours maximum." I glowered. "No more." A few bathroom breaks and I'd knock that down to two.

He snapped his fingers. "Put on the dress, Basil. I'll return in an hour. We need to be out of here before Kyros gets back from dinner."

That explained his openness. They were fucking cowards, the lot of them. "Don't call me Basil."

The comment floated to where he'd disappeared.

Jerk.

Angelica took his place, two huge black bags in her hands. "Shower first?"

"Yeah," I said on a long exhale.

This was definitely an occasion for *shave, cleanse, and hydrate.*

Damn, but I loved looking good. The full-length spangled dress hugged me in the right places, accentuating my breasts and the curve of my ass, leaving the golden skin of my back on display.

Rory *might* have exquisite taste.

The six-inch heels weren't ideal with my sore hip, so I'd taken an extra painkiller. Unnecessary as it turned out. Rory supported my entire right side with a slight pressure under my forearm. Probably looked like nothing to everyone else.

"You didn't mention a red fucking carpet or that the media would be here," I hissed at him. If I didn't know for a fact that estate security would never let these pictures see the light of day, I'd be *truly* livid. This could have otherwise busted my cover with Kyros and his tower of fangers. So far, the lack of information about me was holding up. If the Vissimo had run background checks, they wouldn't have found anything. But I had to ensure that wouldn't change.

He kissed the back of my hand and cameras flashed.

"Didn't I?" he murmured.

I beamed a smile at him. "I wonder what a stir it would cause if I ditched *Rory Senrite*, Bluff City's most eligible bachelor, in the middle of the red carpet."

He stared at me through hooded blue eyes. "Try it."

Swallowing, I angled my face away. Cameras flashed. "Knew your ego couldn't handle it."

Even if that's close to what he did to me over four years ago.

"Am I to understand that you've followed me in the tabloids over the years? Is this why I dazzled you so in my brother's tower?"

By now, I'd seen Rory check himself in mirrors enough times to know he dazzled himself most of all.

"No," I replied.

The only thing I was dazzled by was my own hypocrisy. I'd left this shit behind. No, I hadn't even attended this shit *when* I was at the estate.

Ugh.

"Can we go inside, or would you like to preen some more?" I asked him. "I could go ahead so you have space for some solo shots."

"The kitten has claws," he retorted, standing behind me. He circled his hands around my waist. To humans, it might look like he whispered in my ear. I'm sure any vampires here would notice his teeth were positioned over my pulse.

Rory only wanted *one* vampire to notice.

Which made it extra satisfying that no pictures of me would survive this encounter.

I snorted despite myself. "You are such a *brat*. Why does Kyros put up with you? I would have strangled you and Gerome a century ago."

He ran his nose up my neck, inhaling. "Our youth and antics remind him there is joy in life."

That was... really sad. "How old are you?"

"That's a rude question," he chided, a smile plastered on his face.

My brows climbed as he guided my arm through his once more. "No, it isn't."

He studiously ignored me as we entered the building and the flashing cameras were left behind.

My jaw dropped. "You don't like aging?"

He was totally, *totally* vain. As vain as humans at least. I felt like an immortal should know better. "Talk about dodging a bullet."

The curled length of my hair tickled my lower back as I gave full throat to my chuckle. Angelica had worked the top half into an elegant swirl that coiled neatly at the back of my head.

Rory pulled me against him as another camera flashed. *Man*, did he have a paparazzi radar?

"What do you mean *dodging a bullet*?" he whispered in my ear.

Peering around, I eyed a gilded clock, the centrepiece of the lobby. I'd been in this building many times. One of my grandmother's best friends—Sir Olytheiu—had his main offices here. He was the founder and owner of Bluff City Bank and one of the richest people in the city. Internationally, the Le Spyre estate had him beat, but locally, he came out on top. *Thank fuck* I'd never come to these things. The only people I might know were my grandmother's select few friends. Hopefully none of them were attending tonight.

A thought caught me. "How is it that two clans can fight to own the city when so many others own a chunk? You'll have to battle rich humans at some point. And some of them are seriously fucking rich."

I'd said too much, but Rory didn't notice.

"They're a front. Various CEOs and Head of Estates are tied to one of the clans via blood compulsion. Through them, most of the city rich are in our employ and control, and they carry our holdings in name only. If two families own everything, humans get angry," he murmured, waving to a middle-aged couple I didn't recognise.

I contemplated that my grandmother was one of their puppets and our family wealth belonged to Sundulus or Fyrlia but disregarded it quickly. The Le Spyre estate was hundreds of years old. And when this place was a *village port*, the ancestors of the current-day elite owned the land. We'd been here longer than *Ingenium*.

"I suppose that makes sense. People would stop selling to you."

Rory slid me a look. "They would. They are."

If my list of trouble properties was anything to go by, the vampire was right. "What happens if a clan lands on the estates?"

He sighed. "Not much. The estates don't sell. And it's against the rules to coerce a human into signing. Anyone tied by blood compulsion falls under that umbrella, so although the city elite help us to do business in many other ways, we cannot secure their assets directly."

Interesting. It made me very glad the Le Spyre fortune was generated and invested internationally for the vast majority.

"I have another quibble."

He rolled his eyes heavenward. "By all means, ask away."

Don't mind if I do. "I feel like Vissimo should stay out of the media because you're as unchanging as Cher." Oh my god, was Cher a vampire? She didn't age, but I put that down to surgeries and whatnot.

Rory nodded at a young woman, who fluttered her eyelashes in response. I'd never been able to do that. Tried for a whole hour one time.

"We take turns," he replied. "Plus, we control the media within this city. There are enough royal siblings that we only need to take ten years every century. This is only my second turn."

Somehow I gathered it wasn't a chore for him.

Rory scanned the room again, and I did another sweep. I couldn't see anyone I knew in the main chamber. We'd turned up an hour late, so mostly everyone should have arrived. Maybe I could just relax for the next few hours.

Actually...

"Two hours and fifteen minutes to go," I said in glee.

"We just got here."

"The time frame was inclusive of travel."

He shot me an irritated look.

I sighed prettily. "You should negotiate better, Mr Senrite. Terms and conditions, my boy. Terms and conditions."

"You are intensely annoying." He straightened as a couple approached.

I smirked. "That's what your eldest brother says too."

"Not sure that's the word he's looking for," Rory murmured, gaze settling on my breasts as another camera flashed.

Laughter bubbled in my throat. He was trying so hard to piss off his sibling that I couldn't be angry about it. A waitress with a tray of champagne sauntered by. I snatched a flute.

"Free booze!" I sipped at the contents, my insides welcoming the honey explosion of bubbles like an old friend. Though I'd only had one person I'd put under that umbrella.

The sweet bubbles soured in my mouth.

"Mr Ringly," Rory greeted in a cold tone.

I glanced at him and deduced the conniving vampire had become an asshole vampire. He posed like a fucking king at my side, expression aloof.

The middle-aged couple gaped.

Rory cut me a look.

My turn?

Leaning into Rory's side, I fixed a smile in place. "Mr Ringly, a pleasure to meet you."

The man's eyes bounced to me so fast and with so much relief, I nearly snorted.

"I'm Bas, Rory's date." I'd never gone by Bas before. Hopefully that helped confuse any rumours.

"B-Bas," Mr Ringly repeated.

I peered at the woman on his arm. She gaped at Rory, reminding me entirely of my seventeen-year-old self. He was probably lapping it up.

"This is Mrs Ringly," the man said, drawing her forward.

She didn't seem in much of a hurry to shift her gaze from Rory. Not that I could judge—but if she knew he'd looked in the mirror ten times on the drive here, she may reconsider.

"Lovely to meet you both," I murmured, sipping at my champagne.

Mr Ringly licked his lips a few times. I slid him a glance, frowning when he did it again.

He licked them a third time.

No way.

Either Mr Ringly had one hell of a nervous habit or he was a Licky Lips! Just like my drugged-up homeless man. Was Mr Ringly high?

I hid a grin behind another sip of champers.

"Have you had a chance to look over my new proposal, Mr Senrite?" the man spoke to me.

I peered up to Rory. "Have you, baby?"

He choked and covered the slip with a cough. "This would be the loan proposal for subdivision of Wells Row? You sent another one?"

"Yes. My development application was finally approved."

That sounded about as interesting as watching paint dry. Rory was vain *and* dealt with boring stuff. Definitely dodged a bullet. I bit my lip to hold in the snicker, sipping again.

Arm in arm with the vampire, I scanned the crowd as he and Mr Ringly spoke. A few groups glanced my way. At little ol' *me*, the woman with the magical vagina that snagged Mr Ageing Complex beside me.

Typical rich snobs. They darted looks and murmured to their friends over their drinks, sharing arch smiles. Like that wasn't totally obvious.

In fact, it made the one person not doing the same stick out like a sore thumb.

One person was staring at me without any of the frills.

My jaw dropped.

Rhys!

Jeans and black tee boy brushed up nice in the smart black tux. What was he doing here? His attention lifted from my boobs to my eyes. He coloured and returned his attention to the woman he was next to. An older woman.

I had the hots for a one-hundred-and-forty-nine-year-old, so power to him. And her.

Last time we'd spoken, I'd promised to call him. I wanted to smooth things over. And honestly, the sight of Rhys in a tux was doing all kinds of pleasant, normal, and *human* things to my body; I wasn't losing my mind; I wasn't jumping on him in a restaurant building; I wasn't getting so lost in him that his eight siblings could sneak up as we clawed off each other's clothes without detection. With him, I was in control of myself—of the situation and where it would go.

I was attracted to Rhys and his normalcy. *Go figure.*

"Darling," I purred at Rory, knocking back the remaining contents of the flute. "I must go see a man about a dog."

What did that even mean? *Shit,* I always forgot that champagne didn't behave like wine. Better just have one more, but at least I couldn't feel my hip anymore.

His jaw clenched as he followed my line of sight to Rhys. "Hurry back, my love."

Mrs Ringly sighed, and I giggled. *Oops, champagne.*

I passed my flute to a woman who, in retrospect, might not have been a waitress.

Rhys saw me coming and turned back to his conversation with the older woman and two elderly men.

"Oh my god. Rhys, is that you?" I said to his rigid back, faking astonishment.

The group turned, and the older woman glanced at Rhys.

"Basi," he said, bowing slightly. Must come with the tux.

I approved.

"You know this woman, dear?" said the woman.

He met my gaze for the first time. "Yes, Aunty."

Oooh. Not a cougar. I could see the family resemblance. Kind of.

"Go have fun. I'm sure our chit-chat is boring him," she simpered at the two older men. They laughed and stepped closer.

She was good.

Looking like he'd prefer to sink through the floor, Rhys offered his arm, and I took it, snagging another flute of champagne with my free arm—because women were fucking multi-taskers.

"You didn't call," he said, sending me a lopsided smile.

My brows shot up. "You're full of surprises, Rhys."

I'd never expected to see him wearing and pulling off a tux. I mean, he had the body to wear it. But to look at home in the threads? Yes, definitely surprised. And then to take the bull by the horns by bringing up my non-call.

My interest in him deepened.

Rhys faced forward. "That means what?"

That this champagne was the shit. That's what it meant. "I didn't call. Only because your number smudged."

Rhys's eyes narrowed. "Smudged or was smudged?"

Whoa, Rhys could read possessive male? Maybe he could write me a guidebook or something—"How to Tame a Douchebag Named Kyros."

"*Was smudged*," I admitted. "But only after I ran into someone and coffee poured on my arm."

"You realise it sounds like you're letting me down easy," he said, dark eyes warming.

I swung my hair back, fanning my face. "I have no qualms with letting people down the hard way. So no. That's not what I'm doing."

He stepped closer as I fanned my face again. *Clever man.*

"Would you like to go outside for some air? Or is that going to step on your date's toes?" he asked.

"Rory is a friend."

"You have friends in high places," he said, drawing me to the nearest bifold doors.

I grumbled. "I'd rather friends in low places."

Grinning, he replied, "It sounds like you mean that too."

"Aren't you of the same mind? Your aunt rubs shoulders with Bluff City's richest and yet you're hand-delivering your résumé."

I closed my eyes as cool air rushed over me. "Ah, that feels so good."

Rhys's eyes were fixed on me when I opened them again.

He blinked slowly and pointed at a bench seat. "Can you sit in that dress?"

I squatted down before straightening again. "Yep. We're good. Stretchy stuff."

Laughing, he said, "Can't say that question has ever had that result. You must be a few drinks ahead of me. I need to catch up."

He asked that question a lot, did he? Better yet, did alcohol mix with pain medication? I had a feeling it was possible.

Holding up the flute, I winked. "Then you can stop evading my questions."

He snagged two flutes from a passing waitress, gulping one back. "Fuck, I hate champagne."

"Let me guess. You only drink beer."

"Shiraz man, actually."

"See? What did I say? Full of surprises. And you're still evading my question." Spotting a camera, I tossed him a huge smile, pushing back my hair. I ignored the camera flash.

Ha! Screw you, Rory.

Rhys leaned in, draping his arm over the back of the bench. *Oh yeah*, I was totally down with some him-and-me time tonight. That's just what I needed. All of me was in agreement on the issue. My body was in a serious state after the constant deprivation since meeting Kyros.

"I was born into money and left because I wanted to make something of myself," he said quickly.

I stared, taking a sip. "A DIYer, huh?"

"I guess. The money didn't feel real. I couldn't accept everything that came with it, like my friends did. I left right after school—been living off my own back for seven years."

We'd probably gone to the same school—there was only one the elite went to—but he was a few years older at least. Things could have been so different if we'd known each other.

I nodded. "I can understand that."

For vampire ears, I added, "Well, I can try my best. I'm not sure I'd do it myself. Free car. Someone doing my laundry. Sounds perfect."

Rhys rubbed his jaw. "My family has a lot more than that. Probably sounds weird to someone without an estate."

Finally, a fucking compliment. "You think I'm poor?"

He coloured. "Oh, I'm—"

I clinked my flute against his. "No apologies tonight. I'm poor as dirt. Cheers to that!"

When I lowered my drink, he was watching me.

"You know, I *think* that I find you fascinating." Rhys rubbed his jaw again. "I'm not sure people really say that anymore."

Uhm. Adorable.

And I knew for a fact Mr Rhys was more than adorable. Oddly, part of me could say the same about him. The fascinating part. He had secrets. If he'd left the rich game, he had unusual integrity and unpopular world opinions too. What more could I ask for?

"*Basilia, my love?*"

I rolled my eyes. "Yes, Rory darling?"

"Could I borrow you for a dance?" I caught the flinted edge to his eyes before he bowed.

"I was just about to kiss Rhys here though." I smiled as Rhys choked on his bubbles.

The Vissimo held out his hand, eyes hard.

Fine. "Hold my drink?" I asked my fellow human.

Rhys's answering grin was unexpectedly saucy.

Mmm.

"See you later," he told me.

That I would.

Rory tugged me away faster than I thought necessary.

"Might I remind you that you're meant to be here as my date. How do you think it looks that you're all over that boy," he spoke low and harsh in my ear.

"Okay, old man. Not everything is about image." I remembered who I was talking to. "Rhys and I could get married in two years for all you know."

"Darling, *darling,* that life is no longer an option for you." He tugged me to him, hand around my waist, partially supporting my weight.

My face must have reflected my hurt and shock at that statement because the edge left his high-boned features though he didn't apologise.

I placed one hand atop his shoulder, and rested the other in his offered hand, avoiding his gaze.

"You know about our kind now," he continued, directing us into the dancing couples. "That will remain a barrier between you and the rest of the human population for the rest of your life. You're not the kind to live a lie, Miss Tetley. You realise your path has altered for good whether you're willing to admit it or not."

That wasn't true. "People have told me what my life would be since I was a young girl. They were wrong."

"Were they?" he mused.

My gaze snapped to him, but the vampire was looking elsewhere.

"I can't let you go home with the boy," he said next, navigating us expertly between the couples. "Kyros—"

"I'm sick of hearing about Kyros," I hissed. Desperation tinged my words.

"He's my brother."

I snapped my head up to glare at him. "The brother you're baiting by taking me as a date to a social event? What kind of sibling does that?"

Not a speck of remorse showed on his face. "Our games are not your games."

Boy, did I know it.

"A deal then." I was going home with Rhys and no one was getting in my way.

Rory snorted. "No."

"What was the Wells Row deal for?"

"... A loan. He has a large plot of commercial agricultural land that he wishes to rezone into residential land and subdivide for mass sale. It's a good deal for us—with Lionel's shift to vertical agriculture, the city won't suffer from the loss of agricultural land. If this worked out, it could be huge for our clan."

"Could be," I said, pursing my lips.

His grip on me tightened before he groaned. "What do you know about him?"

I liked a man who knew when he was defeated. "My terms are that I'm not hindered in the slightest from taking Rhys back home to engage or not engage in adult activities. I'm allowed to stay out all night—with Laurel as protection, if necessary. But she waits outside and *hidden*."

"You realise I could compel you for the answer?"

I lowered my gaze just in case. "How did that work out for Gerome?"

Rory grimaced.

"Shoot, was it bad? Is he hurt?"

Kyros's sibling arched a brow. "He'll mend. Nothing Gerome didn't expect or mean to test. Though none of us expected Kyros to lose it to *that* degree. It surprised him too, I think. After that, he got a ridiculous notion in his head that avoiding you was the best answer."

"The best answer to what?" I dared to ask.

Rory brought his lips to my ear. "To his *insatiable lust* for you. To thinking of nothing else but you. You know, he's kept it all from our father. Well, no, *that* wouldn't be possible. But the extent of his reaction he has kept very quiet. Saturday night was the first time we, *his siblings*, learned he was anything other than in his usual, perfectly controlled self."

He told his siblings everything though.

From the conversation with Kyros, I knew he didn't want to be feeling whatever was going on between us. Whether because of shame or because he had a relationship with someone else. "This... situation has happened before, right? Where the urges of the thrall extended longer than three days?"

Rory grinned.

"That *fucker*," I spat. "I knew he was lying. It's not the lingering effects of the thrall that are making him act this way."

"He's not lying as such. *Some* people do suffer from similar symptoms after the first blood exchange."

His tone was off.

"What do they usually do to sort out the problem?" I studied every flicker of his expression.

His eyes danced with suppressed mirth. "Why, Miss Tetley. They exchange blood again and again. Again, again, and again." He counted to himself and added, "*and again*."

That sounded kind of like I'd die. I blew my hair off my face. "*Whatever*."

"Counteroffer. For all I know, the information you have on Mr Ringly is useless. As a show of good faith, I want something additional from you. You recognised me the first night on Level 66. I want to know where from. In return, I will grant your request, *and* supply condoms."

I screwed up my nose. "I'm sure we'll be right on that front."

Rory's face smoothed. "Have it your way. What's wrong with Mr Ringly's offer?"

"*Ah*," I said sagely. "Nothing with the offer." Surveying the crowd, my gaze snagged on Rhys's ass.

You've seen better.

I shoved the thought aside. My brain didn't know shit. Kyros had short-circuited my synapses somewhere along the line. I needed someone to shock me with those paddle things off *Truth Ranges*.

Rory shook me slightly, a growl slipping between his teeth.

"Vissimo have terrible tempers." I spotted a camera coming and bopped him on the nose. The flash startled him.

Gotcha.

His scowl deepened.

"I can see why you've done that all night." My shoulders shook. "That was really fun."

"*Basi*."

"Keep your hair on, Rory. Mr Ringly is a rug addict."

The vampire wrenched us to a halt. "What's a rug addict? Is this a young thing?"

I hiccupped. "Oh shit. Champers. I meant to say drug addict," I explained. "I don't know if he only took them tonight, but the guy kept licking his lips like crazy while talking to you. And I feel taking drugs to attend this event is a sign his usage isn't just *here and there*—or whatever the term is."

Kyros's brother fell silent—though resuming our dance. The song ended and merged into another. I glanced around for Rhys. If he'd disappeared after I'd gone to all this trouble to broker a deal, I'd be pissed.

"I couldn't smell anything in his blood," Rory muttered.

Oh.

"So I was wrong?" *Dang*, maybe I shouldn't lump everyone who licked their lips in the same basket.

"No, I think you're correct. His behaviour was strange, even for being in my presence. If I couldn't smell anything, it means he's using the purest kind of heroin."

The big H. "No way! That seems more serious than, like, ecstasy."

Rory's amusement had fled. "Yes. Very much so. Thank you, Miss Tetley. This changes everything."

He glanced down, and for the first time since he arrived at my room waving around the garment bag, I didn't feel like a human puppet to him.

I caught sight of another camera. Reaching up, I smooshed his cheeks together, smirking at the flash. "Look at me like that more often, Mr Senrite, and I might think you're not a vain douchebag." I let go of him. "Anyway, the night is young, and I've got—"

"Not so fast." He snagged an arm around my waist again. "You're forgetting something."

Peeking up, I sighed at his amused look. "Fine."

"Where have you seen me?"

This whopper would have to be a mix of truth and lies. "Four and a half years ago, you attended an opening ceremony at *Sky Glitz.*"

Rory shrugged.

"I was seventeen at the time and attending with a friend and her mother. I saw you and was taken with your looks. You asked me to dance, and I made some comment about finding you handsome. You walked off and left me in the middle of the dance floor. My *friend* told everyone at school, and they laughed about it for months."

The vampire stared at me. Dancing couples moved around us, glancing between us.

Rory's eyes lit and his mouth dropped. "I remember!"

"That was a dick move. I was seventeen."

"Exactly. Not exactly a great look for me. I thought you were much older, if memory serves. I must have discovered otherwise during our dance."

It wasn't quite an apology, but I'd take it, considering he wasn't the shining Adonis I'd built him to be in my teens.

Kyros's brother wheezed in laughter and let go of me to clutch his side.

I smiled at the onlookers while he had his moment. Rory clamped a hand on top of my shoulder for support.

"Glad you find my humiliation so funny," I said between clenched teeth.

"I didn't have to bring you here at all," he gasped. "I can hold that over Kyros forever."

Enough of fucking Kyros for one night!

"So that's why you were struck speechless," Rory said, sniffing hard and straightening.

"Yes, Rory. Utterly speechless. You're so good-looking."

Still chuckling, he slipped a hand into his jacket, drawing out a string of condoms and passing them into my hands.

The cameras flashed, and he howled, erupting into fresh laughter.

Flushing, I shoved the condoms back in his pocket without ceremony, beaming at the cameras. "*What are you doing?*"

His answer was to laugh harder.

The vampire walked off, weaving between the couples.

"Where are you going?" I called after him.

The surrounding couples peered at me. Half in shock, the rest in pity.

My jaw hung ajar. "That *shithead*."

He'd just left me alone in the middle of a dance floor. *Again.*

My knight in shining armour slid into the spot the vampire had just occupied.

"Are you free again?" Rhys asked.

I wrapped my hands around his neck. "Sure am, handsome. How about we get out of here?"

His eyes widened. "Really?"

My lips trembled. "Why is that so surprising?"

A wrinkle appeared between his brows. "I'd resigned myself to being strung along."

"That's terrible," I replied, snorting. "You can't tell me you'd be okay with that."

His eyes glinted. "There are worse things in life than being teased by a fascinating woman."

Rhys dipped his head to mine, and I met him halfway. His warm lips melded to mine. Soft and inviting. Testing, not demanding. He wasn't claiming me. Rhys was human, not Vissimo.

I pressed myself against him, deepening the kiss and enjoying his moan.

He slipped his tongue into my mouth, and I reciprocated, shivering as his fingertips trailed down my forearms.

I pulled back. "How about it then?"

He interlaced his fingers with mine. "My place or yours?"

"Yours," I said firmly. *Shit*, imagine taking him back to the tower.

Ducking, he lay a quick kiss at the base of my neck before tugging me through the crowd.

And like the twenty-one-year-old I was meant to be, I stumbled after him, gasping with laughter.

26

"How far?" I asked Rhys, hiccupping. These heels were getting to me —more accurately, my hip. I needed more champagne. Or meds. Or both—that worked pretty well.

I shrieked as he swung me into his arms.

"Just around the corner," he announced, grunting.

Poor guy. I wasn't exactly a pocket-size woman. Yet he clearly felt he was strong enough to carry me, so I'd give him a minute and make an excuse to hobble again. Or wave Laurel down for a ride. I'd glimpsed a black SUV a few times that I assumed belonged to my guard.

"So we're clear," he said, glancing at me, "I don't want to assume this night is heading where I think it's heading. If it is, we'll need to stop for condoms."

That. Fucker.

I patted Rhys, and he set me on the ground.

"*Rory, you piece of shit.*" I bellowed down the empty city street.

He searched the street. "Uh, what?"

I stomped off in the direction we'd been taking. "Rory offered me condoms and I gave them back." Now I knew what his shit-eating grin was about.

"Oh... I was asking my aunty for some. Did he hear?" Rhys shook his head immediately. "You were dancing with him. He can't have heard."

Oh, Kyros's brother heard alright. *What a dick.* I couldn't really be mad at him either because he'd offered condoms to me twice. "You asked your aunty for condoms?"

Embarrassing. For me, that was.

"She's cool."

I recalled the way she handled the two older guys with her. "She does seem pretty cool. So what are we going to—"

Rhys swore and jerked to a halt, grabbing me.

Searching for Kyros, I wasn't sure if I clutched the base of my throat in terror or relief when I caught sight of the three men in the shadows.

Rhys wrapped his arm around my shoulders and directed us in a large semi-circle around the three tall men.

His lips touched my ear. "I don't like the look of them. Get ready to run."

My heels were the strap-on kind. Not ideal.

That was the least of my worries. These guys were *really* tall and muscular. Maybe there were just three oversized humans on the street.

Or maybe that wasn't the case at all.

The middle man pushed off the wall and sauntered toward us. "Lovely evening, isn't it?"

Rhys tensed, pulling me behind him.

My heart sank at the almond shape to the man's hazel eyes. It was a Vissimo. Where was Laurel? I didn't want to glance left to where I'd last spotted the black SUV in case it gave her away.

She'd save me, right? This wasn't a middle-of-the-day real estate head-to-head.

"It is," I replied, ignoring the rapid beat of my heart. "And we have plans, so..."

The vampire was as gorgeous as all Vissimo, possessing tanned skin and golden locks that curled at the top of his neck. Danger poured off him in waves.

It happened so quick.

Crack. Rhys's grip was torn away as the Vissimo's hand slammed into his breast bone. The wet bang as his bone caved inward was like a car backfiring.

A scream tore from my lips.

I managed one step in his direction before two warm bodies slid either side of me. An arm clamped across my chest, another low across my hips. I struggled, kicking out my legs and clawing at the arm just below my throat.

A man almost identical to the one who'd attacked Rhys was before me. Or was it the same one?

He ground his hips into mine. "This is Kyros's little human."

I'd come too far to die. I wasn't saying anything that could get me into trouble. Lowering my gaze from his hazel orbs, I stared at his broad chest.

"Who knew he'd like a woman without a spine," said the man behind me.

Oh, I have a spine, asshole. I just wanted to keep said spine. I inhaled as quietly as possible.

"I'm not so sure," said the man before me. His bright hazel eyes roamed over me. They bored into my face before lowering to my breasts. "This one might just be smart. She's secured two houses already."

I sucked in another shallow breath.

God, where was Rhys? I couldn't see the third vampire. I couldn't hear anything through my reaction to the two Vissimo sandwiching me.

Should I mention Kyros to them? Tell them Rory was meeting us soon? Or assure them that Kyros would give them what they wanted?

I wanted to live, and I needed to help Rhys. His entire chest had caved in.

The vampires lowered their mouths and licked twin lines up the sides of my neck. My heart sputtered in cold terror, expecting the sharp pinch of fangs entering my neck at any second. The two Vissimo laughed as I thrashed to each side—the instinct to run uncontrollable in my panic.

Was this it?

It couldn't be.

I threw myself back—attempted to—as the vampire in front gripped the front of my dress. With a quick jerk, the beaded and spangled front of the dress tore down to my waist, exposing my bare chest.

Tyres screeched behind us, the sound vague and distant through the pounding in my ears.

"Stay away," I whispered, trying to avoid his hazel eyes.

Neither answered, and I fell backward on my ass as the vampire behind me stepped away. I scrambled on the hard pavement, but my body wasn't obeying and I went sprawling a second time.

The Vissimo who'd been behind me was identical to the other two. Triplets.

"Not bad," one said, crossing his muscular arms as he studied my breasts.

The other smirked. "For a human, you mean?"

Black masses blurred over my head. Desperate fear choked me, holding me immobile as the blurs clashed with the two Vissimo, forcing them back into a lane branching off the main street.

Was it help?

The vampire who'd hurt Rhys sprinted back from across the street, barrelling into the shadowed lane after the main fight.

"*Miss Tetley, we need to get out of here.*"

Mouth ajar at the barely comprehensible scene before me, I lifted my gaze.

"Laurel," I said hoarsely.

She bodily picked me up. "Did they touch you?"

I shifted to look at my bare chest. "R-Ripped my dress."

"And put their scent all over you." She broke off to swear long and hard.

Rhys.

"Rhys!" I shouted in her face. "Where is he?"

"One of my colleagues is taking him to the hospital."

She'd brought friends.

My hands shook. "Is he alive?"

An Indebted I didn't know opened the door of the black SUV. He was dressed from head to toe in black like Laurel.

"He was still alive when the car left, yes," Laurel answered, expression grim.

My breath hitched. *Still* alive?

"How bad is it?" I clutched at the front of her *Dark Angel* get up. He'd only been hurt because of me. Because I'd been so fucking stupid.

"Right now, my priority is getting you and my team to safety. We can't possibly know more on the status of your friend yet. When you're safe, I'll get more information."

Exhaling, I let go of her leather jacket.

"Lie in the back seat."

I didn't object. My head sparking and echoing.

I didn't move as Laurel arrange the scraps of my dress over my chest again. I focused on breathing in and out to control my sudden urge to throw up. Was it the meds, the champagne, or fear?

How had the night taken such a turn for the worse?

We'd been laughing and joking five minutes ago—two young humans having a good time.

The nausea faded. The trembling in my legs and hands ebbed. And my mind began to sharpen. Enough to realise the car was moving.

"Sir," Laurel said. "There has been an incident with Miss Tetley."

I covered my face with both hands. "Please don't, Laurel."

There was another vampire in the passenger seat, so when she ignored me completely, I didn't press the issue.

My eyes widened at the roar audible even through her phone speaker.

She flinched and yanked the phone away. She listened for a full minute.

"Yes, sir. Two minutes."

Was that the ETA to the tower? Getting attacked wasn't enough? Now I had to get attacked for getting attacked in the first place.

Gingerly, I sat, holding the pieces of my dress up. I blinked over the seat at two *more* Vissimo in the back seat. "Kyros is in a shitty mood, I take?"

Laurel cut me a flat look, but the male in the passenger seat grinned out the window.

"He's not pleased," my bodyguard said.

"Yeah, heard his roar. Shoot, Laurel. I'm sorry for dragging you into that."

Her lips pressed together. "It's my job."

But she was a slave. Would any of tonight's events come back on her? I really hoped not. "I had it handled. A few more seconds and they were going down."

Laurel choked on a laugh, and the male fully turned to look at her.

"What?" Laurel flung at him. "You try being professional in her company."

The male glanced back at me, appearing to consider that. He nodded and faced forward.

"Do we really have to go back to the tower?" I whispered as the tower in question came into view.

I'd managed the better part of a week without running into him. Things were finally starting to feel normal.

Normal, like going home with a handsome man I was into.

Normal, like being attacked by three members of the enemy clan.

Kyros's enemies.

I groaned and lowered my head into my hands, dropping the top of my dress. These people were immortal. They'd seen boobs before.

None of this was normal. *I'm not normal anymore.* I just played pretend for a few hours. And now Rhys was in hospital.

Tears stung my eyes. How could I ever get out of this?

Laurel's voice cut across my misery. "Are you okay, Miss Tetley?"

I laughed, drawing my forearm across my face. "Okay? Yep, sure. Just the champers I drank. And shouldn't I be asking you guys that?"

The man peered at Laurel again. She met his gaze and arched a brow.

I straightened. "Were any of you hurt? I forget you guys can be injured and—"

"It's fine, Miss Tetley. Stop babbling. We're all okay. It was seven against three."

Three terrifying Vissimo who'd been powerful enough to send me into a panic.

Laurel directed the SUV into the garage of *Kyros Sky,* and I peered ahead, swearing under my breath when I spotted a certain pacing Vissimo ahead.

She stopped the car, and I waited for her help to get out of the car, scrambling to hold up the front of my dress again.

I expected to be yanked away by Kyros straightaway.

Nope.

Rounding the front of the car like some kind of sheepish nine-year-old who'd taken the car out for a spin, I fidgeted next to Laurel.

Kyros kept his distance, scanning me. His eyes rested on my knees, on the tatters of my dress, and skimmed my face which, I imagined, was a mess.

He strode to the nearest car, a navy blue fancy thing. Shoving his hand through the windows, he picked up the car, shifted it overhead and hurled it at the cars on the far wall. I gasped and jumped closer to Laurel, who bumped her shoulder against mine. Kyros didn't roar.

The vampire didn't utter a single word as he picked up another car, and another.

Then he got to a certain white car.

"Not that one!" I shouted, tripping forward to stop him. As if I could even get there in time.

His back was to me.

"That's my car," I added, simultaneously remembering that wasn't true at all. The car belonged to him.

Damn.

Kyros wouldn't really want to be smashing up his garage though. He hated losing control of his temper or power or whatever the correct term was. That I'd get a scary lecture was inevitable, but I didn't want his employees seeing him like this. That would torture him more than anything.

Why I cared about this man's pride was a fucking mystery.

Kyros's hand was resting on the bonnet, shoulders heaving with his pants.

I edged closer, free hand outstretched. "Leave the nice car alone, Kyros."

A growl filled the garage.

Seriously? That was a joke. "For the record that was sarcasm. If it makes you feel better... *please*."

Was it safe to touch him? He wasn't mad enough to roar, but I couldn't recall seeing him throw cars around like hay bales before.

I rounded the car and reached out.

He spun, catching my hand. My eyes were already fixed on his chest, and I focused on the pounding in my chest as rage rolled off him.

"*Where. The fuck. Did you take her?*"

His question was aimed over my head. I could feel him scanning me again.

Crap, Laurel was about to be minus a head.

"Rory," I blurted.

Kyros froze.

"I went to a social function with Rory," I said, lifting my eyes as high as I dared. "I can tell you about it upstairs."

His heaving pants were smoothing out into normal breaths. Kyros was calming down.

I snuck a peek up and froze.

Not calm. Not calm.

He took hold of my other wrist. The dress fell away, but his eyes didn't follow its descent or look to what was revealed. "I need. Fuck, I need—"

Most of me didn't want to know what he needed. But I didn't want to see him made the fool. Colour me surprised after all that he'd done, but I didn't.

I stepped into his arms and rested my head against his chest. "Let's go upstairs, Kyros."

He stilled.

It wasn't his *don't tell me what to do* warning. It wasn't even a *I don't get hugs* confusion.

Kyros went predatorily still.

"Miss Tetley, back away now," Laurel called softly.

I turned to glance at the pale-faced vampire.

What was happening?

Kyros lowered his nose to my neck, features as hard as stone. He sniffed up the length of my neck. Up both sides.

Those fuckers had done the equivalent of a dog pissing on a plant if I interpreted his expression correctly.

His fangs descended.

Shit! "They didn't touch me, Kyros. I swear. Only tore my dress and made me smell like them."

The vampire lowered his mouth to my neck.

"They only did it to get to you, dumbass," I said, kicking him in the shin. With heels on, it had the force of a newborn Jackie Chan.

My diplomatic words stopped the teeth slicing into my neck.

"I'm so angry," he whispered against the side of my skull.

Yeah, yeah. I was in trouble. Were his fangs still out?

He gathered me against him, one of his hands cupping the base of my skull, his fingers tangling in the waves of my hair.

"Your hair smells like me," Kyros murmured.

Oh... great. *Good.* That was perfect. My dream in life was to smell like a fucking bouquet for him.

I jerked as he hoisted me up to cradle me in his arms.

Ouch, his pelvis wasn't so good for my sore hip right now. I gripped the front of his shirt as he started for the elevator.

Please not the stairs. I wasn't sure my hip could take it.

I peeked at Laurel over his shoulder, who—bless her behind—seemed genuinely ready to intervene and save me.

Car-throwing Kyros was a new one for me. This Kyros's behaviour seemed like desperation layered on possessiveness. I didn't feel unsafe with him right now.

"Have the night off," I sang to the four Indebted in front of the black SUV. "With double pay for your earlier deeds."

Kyros didn't stop, snarling over his shoulder, "I'll expect a report in one hour, including details of how my brother's orders somehow superseded my own tonight."

Pure malice filled his voice. Sounded like I'd spend that hour smoothing things over for Laurel. Which was the least I could do.

The elevator arrived, and we fell into silence as the doors closed.

I fidgeted in his arms, my hip throbbing like a bitch.

"Stay still," he snapped.

"My hip is sore," I admitted.

I squeaked as he spun me around so my other hip was pressed against him. Glaring, I tipped my head forward and flung my hair back off my face.

His gaze lowered to my chest. And remained.

"Kyros, you're welcome to look because I'm too tired to pull up the dress, but I'll karate chop you in your throat if you get handsy."

Ding!

He took off, kicking his way into his office a second later. This time, he had the sense not to place me in the torture chair. He didn't place me in anything. I exchanged a glance with the other vampires in the room. Angelica and three minions I didn't recognise.

Kyros spoke too rapidly for me to understand, and soon two of the screens mounted around the room flickered to life.

One showed an empty office room.

The other, a street I'd recently stood upon.

I patted Kyros's front for him to let me down. He disobliged. So I watched from his arms as Rhys and I came into view.

Ah, shit.

Hopefully there wasn't sound—

"*We'll need to stop for condoms,*" Rhys's voice crackled through the monitor.

I groaned, speaking loudly in an attempt to cover the rest of the conversation. "I'm only going to tell you about the attack because I was assaulted by *your* enemies. The rest of the night is my business and my business alone."

And someone could figure out how to stop the other clan from coming for me again.

Rory was wrong. This wouldn't be my life forever. Sure, it wasn't normal right now, but one day it would be. I could have a normal existence with a human man like Rhys. I just had to figure all *this* out.

Kyros ignored me. Everyone ignored me. They watched the CCTV—or their own personal city footage.

I winced as the two Vissimo sandwiched me, recalling the feeling of their presence. I turned my face away.

"Watch it, Basilia," Kyros ordered. "Watch it all and learn."

Learn what? That monsters existed? That I'd made a mistake? That ship sailed weeks ago.

I nevertheless obeyed the vibrating vampire holding me, gritting my teeth as an Indebted picked up Rhys and ran to a second car. Laurel collected me and once I was out of the way, the rest of the Indebted abandoned the fight.

The screen turned black.

"It's the Tonyi triplets," Angelica said. "Three of the royal children from Clan Fyrlia."

I was right. Triplets. That had to be some kind of miracle in the vampire world.

I shivered. Three psychos.

"Why is Rory not on the phone?" Kyros grated, squeezing me tighter.

"Human in your arms," I gasped, tapping him frantically.

A growl slipped between his teeth, but he loosened his hold. What were the odds he'd set me on the office chair? I assumed next to none. "Would you like to hear what happened?"

Green eyes bore into mine.

He was angry. With me. With himself. Probably with his brother. It might have been easier to list who he wasn't angry with.

"I went to the party with Rory and left with someone else," I said, not moving my gaze from his. "Rory and I made a deal. Laurel would follow, and I was to be left alone for the night. We were attacked—as you saw—on the way back to Rhys's. They called me your little human before ripping my dress and leaving their saliva on my neck."

I watched him swallow, and through everything I was feeling, a strain of pity found its way to me. A vampire as old as him, struggling to control this reaction.

I hurried on, my voice shaking. "How did they know I was there?"

"Why were you with Rory?" His voice vibrated.

I didn't stop to roll my eyes at that. More and more, I was realising that asking these kinds of questions secretly killed him. Which was good because most of them he had no fucking right to ask. "He needed a human for a date to a social event. People are more likely to relax in his presence if a human is there."

"What did he offer you? Did he threaten you?"

Damn, threatening was his second guess? That was kind of flattering. "Confidential."

"Kyros, Rory just answered. He'll be here presently."

Great. "So it wasn't Laurel's fault."

"They allowed you to move without my knowledge."

I set my jaw. "Their orders are to accompany me when I leave the tower. Not to take me to a Kyros-approved location list."

"Basilia, I'm warning you that now is not the time to push me," he replied calmly.

I snapped my mouth shut, heeding his words.

A different approach then.

I pushed back a few strands of his toffee hair. "Please promise me you won't punish them. It was my fault. I've learned my lesson."

He didn't budge in response to my touch. "What lesson is that?"

I lowered my hand to his chest, blinking a few times. "That I can't have a normal life anymore."

Yet.

At his continued staring, I angled my face away. "Can you put me down?"

"Kyros," Angelica piped up. "We have teams waiting to hear from you before they set plans in motion for tomorrow."

Oh crap! The dice roll. It was the middle of the night.

My eyes narrowed. "That timing is way too suspicious. They're fucking with you at a strategic time."

"Who's fucking?"

Rory's face swam into view on the screen.

I pulled up my dress.

"Too late," Rory said, grinning. "I saw them. That's twice now."

His brows slammed together. "What happened?"

Kyros strode to his office chair and placed me in it. I sighed, clasping my dress to me, and throwing my leg out. The pain in my hip subsided straightaway.

I spun in the chair, so Kyros couldn't see me and took the first semblance of a full breath I'd managed since seeing him.

"Basilia was attacked by Fyrlia," he said mildly. "The boy she was with is in critical condition."

I covered my mouth. He was?

Opening my eyes, I caught Rory's furtive peek my way.

Don't feel sorry for me yet, bucko. I dropped you in it.

"Did you make a deal with Basilia and take her to a social function tonight?"

Rory nodded, watching his brother closely.

I wanted to do the same. Kyros was way too chill and that was freakin' terrifying.

"Did you allow her to go home with a human male, knowing what her intentions were?"

Rory's gaze dropped. "We made another deal."

Kyros turned away.

"She bribed me with information."

That fucking swine! Though… I had. He'd dropped me in shit right back. I guessed we were even-stevens now.

Kyros kept his back to his brother. "You let me down, Rory."

He flushed. "I went too far, perhaps. I didn't know she'd be attacked. I made sure Laurel took extra guards."

"You knew she was attacked last week," Kyros roared, spinning to the screen.

I covered my ears, squeezing my eyes closed until the echoes in the office subsided.

"I didn't take my brother for an idiot," he finished, pacing again.

The boom of Kyros's agitated footsteps was the only sound, until Rory replied, "Brother, I admit fault. But I want you to know that I only treasure one thing in this world. Miss Tetley's information helped to protect our family tonight. We avoided what could have been a catastrophic deal because of her observation skills."

Catastrophic? Really? The deal was that big?

"I'm surprised to hear you value anything more than yourself," Kyros responded, slamming a finger down on the keyboard to my right.

The screen went black.

Eek. Kyros just hung up on his bro.

"Sir, your father has called twice. We need his approval before we can launch today's movements," Angelica murmured.

I didn't just make mistakes nowadays. Someone was in hospital, I'd come between two brothers, and interrupted the dealings of an entire clan.

I spun the chair around. "You can't let them play you like this, Kyros."

"You've seen the depths to which my enemies will go," he murmured, eyes glinting.

No, my *ignorance* of his enemies made me afraid of them. I was no more afraid of them than I was when I had no idea what Kyros and this clan would do to me. A Vissimo was a Vissimo in my eyes.

"What's it gonna take for you to get your shit together and work like normal?" I asked him. Those fuckers attacked *me* and yet my guilty conscience had to make sure everything was fixed.

Kyros glanced at the others.

I squinted at them. *Holy shit*, were they pressed against the back wall? Someone needed to invent a Geiger counter for Kyros's rage.

Readjusting my grip on the top of my dress, I scanned everyone. "Well?"

Kyros sighed, moving to the desk and flicking back a panel. His fingers blurred as he entered a combination that rivalled Mary Poppins' Supercalifragilisticexpialidocious. I wrenched to look left as the middle third of the stone wall parted in two, the sections swinging inward like—

"*Batman's hidden lair*," I breathed.

One of the vampires choked. He was one of the men from the first night when Kyros tortured me. When he paled, I didn't have to guess why.

I stood, wincing as my hip screamed. "Seriously, Kyros. A lair?"

My lips twitched. His didn't.

Maybe I'd make fun of him in the morning.

"What's up there?" I asked.

"That's where you'll wait," Kyros answered. He swung me up into his arms.

"I can walk, dammit."

"No, you can't. You're limping."

Semantics.

"Is it your dungeon?" I asked, shifting higher in his arms.

"It's a solution," Kyros replied, not looking at me.

Fuck. That wasn't reassuring whatsoever.

I met Angelica's gaze over his shoulder, eyes narrowing at the sight of her broad grin.

27

A hand stroked my cheek. "Basilia."

Mmm, rumbling. "Volcano," I murmured, not shifting.

The hand on my head stilled. "Volcano what?"

The person should never stop stroking or talking. "Throat lozenges."

"I sound like a volcano and I need throat lozenges?"

Duh.

I complained as the man moved away, but he returned and slipped his arms underneath my back and thighs, lifting me.

The slight jolt of his footsteps helped me to throw off delirium, and I squinted up at Kyros in the dark. Only his shadowed outline was visible, but *lawd* knew I'd studied his jawline enough to recognise it blindfolded. Which made about as much sense as me studying it in the first place.

"What you here?" I slurred.

"This is my room," he answered after a beat. "Why were you sleeping on the sofa chair when the bed is right there?"

His grip tightened.

Sofa chair wasn't a kind enough term for the cotton-candy happiness I fell asleep on. It was one of those big circle numbers that young couples wearing fluffy socks watched movies on—at least they did in the adverts.

"Comfy," I mumbled in reply.

"You did look comfortable," he said, depositing me on the bed. "Like a kitten."

I sank into the bed, sighing as I rolled onto my side and pulled a pillow in to hug. Maybe the bed wasn't so bad either. "Panther."

"No," Kyros said low, standing over me. "I meant a kitten."

Whatevs.

"Time?" I said around a yawn, my eyes fluttering shut.

"2:00 a.m." His voice moved away with his footsteps.

And he'd woken me? I hadn't expected to sleep until Kyros returned from Level 66, actually. Guess I was wiped after being attacked and all.

I opened my eyes a crack.

He'd taken my spot on the sofa.

"Is that the best spot to sleep?" I wouldn't put it past the guy to move me and claim it.

His teeth gleamed. "I sit for a while before sleeping."

I adjusted the pillow I was hugging and nuzzled into it—it smelt like him. This whole fucking place did. "You're back from work early." He didn't finish until 3:30 a.m.

"Yes."

Yes, what?

My heart sank. "Are things really messed up?"

He lifted a shoulder. "We got a late start today. Not ideal circumstances for our turn, but we've handled similar situations in the past. The whole clan will work overtime to ensure things come together."

Yep, things were screwed up. It wasn't my fault the other clan attacked Rhys and me, but it sure felt that way. I'd been on a *my life is still in my control* bender. People got hurt because of it. Rhys might not be alive because of my actions. I opened my mouth to ask about him but snapped my mouth shut. That subject would push Kyros's buttons, and I was too tired for that shit.

"What was the roll today?" I said instead, trying to keep my eyes open.

"Blue," he answered shortly. "I see you found my clothes drawer."

I lifted the pillow to glance down at the black tee I'd pilfered. "Going to sleep in a torn gown didn't appeal." And stealing his clothes to see what his reaction would be *did.*

"I should have offered you clothing. I was caught up by other things."

No kidding. "You hoped I'd still be half-naked if you didn't."

His teeth gleamed in the dark, and I propped up on my elbow, jaw dropping. "Oh my god! You did."

His grin grew. The only bit of him I could clearly see. Could he see in the dark? Certainly better than me at any rate.

I threw myself flat again, bouncing on the cloud bed. "Who thinks like that? Wait, don't answer that. Someone who has played a game their entire life."

His grin remained. "You weren't playing a game by going into my drawer and wearing my clothing?"

That was different. I was having a laugh at his expense. Not setting him up to be naked in my lair.

"No," I told him. "I don't play games."

"Everyone plays games, Basilia. We learn to manipulate from a young age. We just get better at hiding what we're doing."

I considered that. "Yet if we see that's how we're behaving, shouldn't we feel duty-bound to eliminate the fault?"

His grin faded. "That would depend on whether we accept it as life or define our base nature as a fault at all."

"If Vissimo listened to their base natures, would there be any of you left?"

His eyes gleamed, the meadow-green colour indistinguishable in the dark. "Only the powerful."

I swept hair off my face. "Well, maybe humans are more capable of greater growth in a short time because we don't live as long." I peeked through my lashes at him.

"Kitten is the wrong word for you," he acknowledged.

Glad he'd caught up.

"Vixen is more accurate."

That made me sound like a sexy, annoying person.

... I was okay with it.

He continued. "I'm glad you helped yourself in any case. I can't say a woman in my clothing has ever done it for me, but you're proving that wrong."

Uh. Did he just compliment me on a whole other level? To my memory, most of his prior compliments were backhanded—or said with pity.

My tongue stuck to the roof of my mouth. "Do you have water up here? I have the champagne dries."

"I'll get it." The huge shadow that was Kyros stood.

As he moved farther into his lair, my eyes narrowed.

Kyros just offered to get me water. Without a dig at me drinking too much. *Kyros.* Not a word about my slight hangover or the man I'd intended to go home with last night. I'd expected a lecture and more rules—and to have to talk him around about Rory and Laurel.

Yet he hadn't.

He'd grinned at least once and complimented me twice—if the vixen thing could be lumped in there.

I swung my legs over the side, grimacing at the pain in my hip, and reached over to flick on the lamp. Where was the switch?

"Bedside light on," Kyros said.

The hanging lamp flared to life.

I bit back a groan. Of course his lair was ultra-modern. He had super speed and couldn't be bothered to flick a damn switch.

Blinking rapidly against the burst of light, I accepted the glass of ice-cold water from him and two pills.

I glanced up at him.

"Pain medication. Your breath caught when you moved."

Yep, something big was coming.

"What do you think?" he asked, returning to his chair. He kicked off his *Freens*, still in his suit.

I threw him a surreptitious look as I gulped back half the glass. Swallowing, I said, "About?"

"My *lair*."

He'd deposited me unceremoniously several hours ago and I'd inspected his room immediately—I wasn't perfect. The snooping left me disappointed if truth be told.

"The words cold and empty come to mind," I answered.

Settling back in the couple-movie sofa again, he pondered my words. "I don't like clutter."

Sure, I got that. Marie Kondo got that too. But she also understood the need to spark joy with the possessions in your space. Where were the family pictures? Where were presents he'd received over the years? Cards. Ornaments. *Hell*, even paper and rubbish.

The space was minimalist. Contemporary. Beautiful.

Impersonal.

Bed. Bathroom. Drawers. Kitchenette. The warmest part of the room was the circle sofa which is why I'd gravitated there. Even Kyros did without realising why.

Don't feel sorry for the vampire, Basi.

Darn it all. I did.

I felt sorry for a one-hundred-and-forty-nine-year-old fucking vampire. Because the softest part of his apartment—in the same building where he worked—was a sofa he liked to sit on before bed.

"I see." I settled on, shoving down my honest opinion.

He tapped a finger on the side of the couch—which he filled. There wasn't any room for me. I'd be squeezed in either side or more likely elect to sit on the floor. *Squeezed in.* That's what was wrong with the tension between us.

If each year added to my life distanced me from the bond I'd shared with my parents, then the opposite was true with regards to Kyros. I'd lived for a fraction of his life and known him a tiny blip of that. How could what lay between us mean or amount to anything *ever*?

Over a century and a half of *living* lay between us.

"Out with it," I told him wearily, guzzling the rest of my water.

Kyros raised his head.

"You're buttering me up for something. Spit it out." I'd come up blank. Not surprising in this shitshow.

His lips twitched and he rested back, tapping his finger on the curved armrest again. "I came back an hour early because my seconds, several of my teams, and my siblings have raised concerns that our situation poses a moderate threat to the smooth running of *Ingenium*."

Our situation. The temptation to scoff was real.

"More specifically, my... lack of focus."

Phew. I imagine Kyros received that feedback with all the happiness of a grizzly bear recently woken from hibernation. "Right. Your response?"

He cast me a flat look.

"Thought as much," I said. "But you know what I meant. You must have listened to them. That's why you're here and not on Level 66." My hand inched up to my throat. "Holy fuck, are you going to kill me after all?"

Darkness flittered over his face. He stood in a blur, scowl firmly in place. "I'm not going to kill you, Basilia. Why would you say something like that?"

Uh, a lot of reasons.

I lifted a shoulder. "Wouldn't it solve your problems?"

He shoved both hands in his pockets and tilted his head back to stare at the ceiling. "No, Miss Tetley. It would not solve my problem."

I brightened. "Oh good."

"Something needs to be done. Distance has not worked. Ignoring you was fucking pointless."

From our conversation over dinner, I knew there was another option. "You want to drink from me again."

Kyros sighed. "No, I want to *exchange* blood with you again."

He was 200 percent out of his mind. Wasn't that just another blood compulsion? That's what got us into this mess!

I surged to my feet, crossing my arms. "No. Nope. Never again."

"There are cases like ours where—"

Balling my fists, I rounded on him. "Cases like *ours.* Tell me straight, Kyros. You owe me three honest answers from dinner the other night. I'm calling one of them in. Why the fuck is this happening to us and what are the implications?"

He'd evaded the same question so many times prior that I had zero expectation of receiving an answer.

The vampire put the round sofa between us, leaning forward on it. He cursed under his breath, lifting his gaze to mine. "It means, Miss Tetley—"

Shit, I was getting an explanation?

"—that for reasons unfathomable, my blood considers you a potential mate."

Mate, mate, mate.

The word bounced around his cold, empty lair.

Mate.

I gulped audibly. This seemed like bad territory to be in. I lumped the word mate in with irreversible matrimony. "Like dogs or something?"

Kyros didn't laugh. His face was as solemn as I'd seen it.

"If we're going with animal analogies," he replied, "then much more like ducks."

I didn't know what that meant. Did ducks do one-night stands? Maybe there was hope. "What does that mean?"

"It means I want to drink your blood and fuck you forever. Potentially. If two people's blood is compatible, the initial drive appears after the first blood exchange but can recede after the second and third exchanges. If the drive is still there after that, we're a true match."

The scraps of my hope evaporated.

I was human though! And— "How can it be that your clan knows so little about this? Or have you just strung me along pretending not to know what's going on? Mates can't be that rare. Can they?"

Kyros's shoulders relaxed. *Whoa*, he should *not* take my question as a sign I was okay with this conversation.

"We rarely mate," he said. "With our need for harems to boost reproduction rates, mating causes unnecessary complications."

If his behaviour was anything to go by, I could imagine. "So there's a good chance the mating drive will disappear if we share blood again?" I pressed.

He nodded.

I squeezed my eyes shut. "Kyros, I know I called in one of my three questions, but I still don't know if you're lying to me or not, and I really need to know if you're telling the truth."

If Kyros's yearning for me disappeared, half my problems could be solved—the more life-threatening half of my problems too. The other clan would lose interest once they heard Kyros had tired of me. Maybe we could leak rumours about another woman. More importantly, Kyros wouldn't track my movements so closely. He may even let me leave the tower to rent somewhere. Escape would be that much easier.

He closed the space between us and towered over me. "I believe this is the answer to our issue or I wouldn't be here."

That didn't cut it. "What happens if a second blood swap doesn't work?"

He fidgeted. "We'll be the same, just more intense."

I glared at him. "That's the secretive shit I'm talking about! How intense?"

"Around 10 percent more."

How the fuck could he know *that* but not know if this would get rid of the mating call? My chest rose as questions flooded my mind.

Eyes wide, I glanced up at Kyros.

"Basilia," he said, stepping closer. "It will be okay. This is the best course of action. I swear it."

That was just it though. I didn't know him. Him swearing anything meant jack shit.

"I only have your word for that," I whispered. "I have none of the facts. You're either purposefully obtuse with the exact details, or it doesn't occur to you what I am ignorant of. And I suspect the former."

"We need to do something." His jaw clenched. "The situation is too volatile. It's affecting the game."

The game. "What about my life, Kyros? What about *yours*? Is the game everything to you?" I asked, ripping my arms free of his grip.

"Yes."

"That's so fucking sad," I told him.

His eyes flashed and he crowded me. "You know nothing of why I play the game."

Angelica had filled me in on Level 66. "Your clan would become part Clan Fyrlia if your family loses."

He regarded me and said, "The working Vissimo in our clan, yes. But not the royal family."

I stared at him. "What happens to your family?"

"Execution." He turned away, shoulders and back rigid.

Execution.

Fuck. "All of you?"

He didn't turn back. "All of them. My sisters. My brothers. Everyone with a blood connection to my father will die. Only my mother and I will live—to join their clan also. If we win, the same will happen to Clan Fyrlia."

My throat worked.

That put a different spin on his addiction to the game. "I see."

"Do you?"

I didn't let his sarcastic tone rile me. "My parents died when I was nine, Kyros. So yes, this orphan understands loss—*traumatic* loss."

"How did they die?" Kyros faced me.

Craning to look at him hurt my neck, so I studied the bottom of his waistcoat.

I pursed my lips. "Crash."

I had a feeling mentioning it was in their private helicopter and over the Maldives could raise uncomfortable questions.

He opened his mouth, and I shot in, not eager to answer more personal questions or hear his apology for something he hadn't caused. My parents' deaths weren't anyone's fault. Shit things just happened.

"Is it fair to say that everything you do is for the game to protect your family?"

I would attempt to move the fucking sky if in the same position. Especially if I had to live on.

His answer startled me. "It is."

I'd known the game was everything to him, just not exactly why. "Then the answer is no. I won't agree to a second blood swap. I don't know what it will do to me. Or you. I *do* know that I'll have to survive the thrall again."

"There will be proper precautions in place this time. There won't be a repeat of what happened last time."

My muscles coiled with the unchecked nerves and energy coursing through my body. I stood again. "Why are you talking as though it's happening? It's not."

Kyros stepped closer, eliminating the space between us.

I stared at his waistcoat, pressed my hand against his stomach to stop him. "What are you doing?"

He didn't answer, pushing me gently. I bounced flat onto the bed. He blurred down on top of me, hovering above.

"Kyros—"

"Do you feel that, Basilia?" he murmured, drawing his nose up to my temple.

Did I *ever*. Pure heat coursed through me.

I breathed hard underneath him, hands poised to shove him away. Or to pull him closer.

His furious gaze met mine. "*Do you feel it?*"

The crackling between us was akin to anxiety. Desperation itched in my fingertips. In my toes. It wanted to get out. It wanted Kyros. I'd battled this since first sipping his blood.

"Yes." I choked.

His meadow gaze flared as his control slipped. "Can you live like this?"

"I want it to go away," I said, squeezing my eyes shut against his bright gaze. Against his nearness. A pointless endeavour.

"That's what I thought." The bed dipped down as Kyros moved off me to sit on the edge.

Opening my eyes, I studied his back. "I can't take 10 percent more of whatever this is between us. There are things you're withholding. If you were me, would you leap for the opportunity?"

Kyros stared straight ahead. "It's unlikely you're my true mate. I've told you humans are incompatible with us. They don't survive a long-term relationship and our kinds can't reproduce together."

Was that meant to *convince* me?

"There's a greater possibility this plan will succeed than fail is what I'm saying," he finished. "I'm in the game of probability, and that's enough for me to continue. But you're right. There is something more you deserve to know."

I tensed.

"Clan Fyrlia is aware of your existence now. I only put basic restrictions on your mind in the first compulsion. I'll need to place more during the second exchange in case they get a hold of you."

I sat, ears buzzing. "More? I haven't done anything wrong. You said you'd only do that if I fucked up. I haven't fucked up, Kyros. I've done everything you said."

My breath came in ragged bursts. This couldn't happen. I didn't want him controlling me like that. Or *anyone*. Not with their eyes. Not with blood.

It took a while to notice Kyros was watching me, his expression carved from stone.

"You still fear me so." The words were low. He broke off, and the only sound was my fear-filled breaths. "I've tried to rid you of fear. You hide it so well, I'd started to think... Yet disgust fills your eyes."

Could he blame me? Not that his words were entirely true. He wasn't a monster. I hadn't seen him that way for a week or more. But fear? Yes. In spades. "You expect me to rise above my base instincts? Weren't you arguing against that before?"

"Such a thing is impossible for any creature in the presence of its predator. I just know that when you look at me like that, I want to fucking kill someone."

He cared what I thought of him? Or was it the lack of control over his response that bothered him?

"This is new to me," Kyros admitted.

I had to understand one particular point because we weren't on the same wavelength. There were a lot of reasons for that, but there was something I needed to understand right now. "Kyros. Do you want this connection between us?"

He inhaled.

I bounced off the bed and padded around to study him. His head still came to the level of my chest. "Do you?"

"I'm not in my right mind," he replied. "Everything is telling me to drink from you and force my blood down your throat; to lock you up here, naked, for days on end. So yes, *I want this*. If I was lucid? No idea. I haven't been lucid for weeks."

Right. "That's about what I feel too," I said heavily. At his surprised look, I scoffed. "You know I'm attracted to you."

"I know you view that attraction with fear."

I released a pent-up breath, fists curling as I spoke words I'd rather keep inside. "It's overwhelming. I've never been so overwhelmed in my life. Ever." Disbelief tinged my words. "When I'm in your presence, I can't think of anything else. I hate that. Because it's not real. It's Vissimo voodoo."

Kyros's eyes glinted, his focus shifting to my breasts.

I scowled at him. "That wasn't encouragement."

The vampire reached up and loosened his tie.

My mouth dried. What was he doing?

His fingers went to the buttons on his sleeves next. Throwing his tie to the ground, he started on his top shirt buttons.

"Not that I disapprove, but should I put music on for you?" I asked drily.

He arched a brow. "It's time to sleep."

Uhm.

"Weren't we having a conversation."

"I asked a question. You said no."

He pulled his shirt overhead, not stopping to undo the lower buttons. *Holy hormones in my motherfucking ovaries.* Or whatever body temple the holiest of hormones lived in. Kyros removing his shirt was no mortal sight. It was a looping GIF I needed to deposit in my wank bank without delay.

"To be clear, I said no to the blood swap," I whispered as his hand moved to his pants.

He popped the top button, pausing. "You did. I'll think of something else."

Okay, but what about no-strings sex?

His hand moved away from the zipper. I looked at him in outrage that only swelled when I caught sight of his smirk.

I shoved his shoulder and flopped on the bed beside him, snapping, "That was really mean. I can't help it."

"I could help it."

"I know," I said huskily. *God*, could he help.

Large, warm hands slid up my thighs and I choked on thin air. Kyros's lips trailed in the wake of his palms, and I froze. Utterly.

Mother of Zeus.

"Smooth," he murmured against my golden skin. "And so fragile."

My heartbeat ratcheted. "Kyros?"

I squirmed on the bed as he reached for the bottom of my borrowed shirt. It had hiked high on my thighs. His tongue traced a line on my skin just beneath the hem.

My back arched and my legs bent, coiled with the surge of heat filling me. Kyros cupped my knees, helping me to lift them. He blurred into position between my legs and ground his erection into me.

I groaned at the rock-solid feel.

"My lust for you trumps anything I have felt before," he said, breathing hard. "One hundred and forty-nine years teaches a being to welcome the new, not run from it. I would show you the meaning of ecstasy, Basilia. *Believe me*, fear of being overwhelmed would be the last thing on your mind." His fangs descended. "Any more than you wish for it."

My body quivered in our current position. Maybe this should

happen. Maybe we should have sex before any blood swapping was looked into again.

Maybe this would cure everything.

Except that was fucking ludicrous. Kyros had slobbered on my thigh and given me the most erotic experience of my life. If we had sex, I'd be ruined for mortal men.

He leaned forward, grinding into my core again—before kissing me quickly.

"I need to shower," he announced.

Huh? "Why?"

Weren't we doing... each other?

"Because this will happen between us, Miss Tetley. Once you're rid of human doubts."

Human doubts. Really? What a cheap shot.

He lifted himself off, and I placed a foot in the middle of his chest to *help* him away.

Grinning, Kyros swiped up his discarded shirt, tie, and waistcoat, traipsing around a jutting segment of wall to where I'd found the bathroom earlier.

I catalogued the sight of his bare back, heat throbbing low within me.

The vampire had learned a few tricks over the decades and felt pretty proud of that from what I could tell. He was far too pleased with himself.

"My doubts are *normal*, not human," I said sulkily, the heat in my belly furious at the change in plans. "Stupid Vissimo jerk."

"I can hear you," he called before the shower started.

I jolted and sniffed as I crept under the bed covers. "Good. Then I don't have to wait to inform you that you're sleeping on the fucking couch."

28

I woke up groggy and warm.

An attempt to move my arms and legs proved futile and I panicked before recognising I'd wrapped myself in the bed cover.

Sometimes I formed midnight cocoons. Trussed up, I blew my hair out of my face and glanced behind.

Kyros had ignored my order to sleep on the couch and took up most of his oversized bed. He lay sprawled on his back, not a square inch of bed cover on him.

Oops.

But there were perks.

I swallowed at the sight of his grey cotton boxers and the bulge I could easily make out beneath them. Those muscular thighs of his were pretty nice as well. In fact, none of him wasn't nice.

Crap, where were my grown-up words? *None of him wasn't nice.* They'd gone down the drain with everything else.

With a grunt, I craned my head the other way, reading the white alarm clock. *12:00 p.m.*

That explained my grogginess. This room was so dark it had messed up my normal wake up time.

Perving on the Vissimo beside me was tempting, but I was done with sleep.

I had things to do.

Kyros stirred when I returned from the shower wrapped in a towel. Part of me was surprised to find vampires could sleep that soundly. Or maybe he'd lain in tortuous wakefulness for hours like me last night—though his shower was long enough to suspect he'd done something about his libido before returning to bed.

"What are you doing?" he grumbled.

I studied the remains of my ballgown. "Trying to decide if the walk to my room will look worse if I go wrapped in this towel or if I borrow more of your clothes." Both options seemed as bad as each other. Then again, I wasn't likely to encounter anyone on my walk of externally perceived shame.

"Where are you going?" he snapped.

Sheesh. Grumpy much. "I'm going to work," I said cheerfully, knowing that would annoy him most.

"It's Sunday."

"Like that stops any of you."

"We're Vissimo. You are human."

Yeah, and this human fucked up yesterday and felt the urge to do something to right the situation. The roll landed Clan Sundulus on Blue. I had a ton of Blue properties in my trouble folder. And I had to ring the hospital to check on Rhys without further delay. Which I dreaded in no small measure.

Kyros rubbed his eyes. "Basilia, it's your weekend."

"*Kyros*, don't think I haven't noticed you using my name. Stop it. I've told you only my grandmother calls me that."

"No, you said that only one person calls you that," he replied.

Fuck. I had. And I just mentioned my grandmother.

I riffled through the drawers under the television, pulling on a pair of trackpants under my towel. Turned away, I dropped the towel, my back bare. Rolling the waistband of the pants several times, I found a long-sleeved merino number and pulled it on, turning back to Kyros.

"It's Sunday," he repeated huskily. "Go do human things. See your friends and family."

I jerked violently at his words, and he stilled.

"No," I said casually as my heart took off—something he couldn't fail to notice. "I don't want to."

I had no family that I could visit without everyone finding out I was Basilia Le Spyre. Tommy hated me, and I had no other friends. *Dammit*, maybe guilt wasn't the only reason I felt like working. I could easily forget misery when busy.

Kyros swung his legs over. "You're not working today."

"I am," I snarled. "Why the fuck should that bother you? I work *for* you."

He studied me in the dark. "My life is my job, and I don't wish for it to become yours. You're upset about your friend and using work to avoid thinking about it."

The mention of Tommy was a knife in my heart.

Dragging in a ragged breath, I snatched up the tatters of my dress for no other reason than to have something in my arms. "I'm not talking about this with you."

He paused. "She still loves you."

Which meant he'd heard everything. *No surprise there.*

I strode for the door but slowed when I reached it. "I just thought it would take more than a couple of weeks of lies to destroy our friendship is all." I'd thought nothing could break us.

"The stronger the friendship, the quicker it dissolves. Weaker friendships are willing to put up with more. There is bittersweet solace in that."

Dissolve was all I heard. Like sugar in boiling water. That was me and Tommy. How did I let it get to this point?

I willed the burning behind my eyes away—away for good. I was sick of feeling so close to tears. It was almost as bad as actually letting the damn things fall.

Kyros's voice was soft. "Why don't you cry, Miss Tetley? You've gone through more than most will in a lifetime in the last few weeks."

The question was nearly my undoing.

I balled the gown in my hands tight, letting my nails dig into my palms through the material. "I'll take Laurel with me. More if she thinks it necessary. That okay?"

The vampire didn't move from his position perched on the side of the bed.

Seconds, each heavier than the last, stretched between us before he sighed. "Yes, that's fine. Fyrlia won't try anything. It's their roll tonight."

"Good," I whispered, wrenching open the door.

"She'll come back to you," he called just before I pulled the door closed.

So what if she did give me another shot? I was tied to these creatures, to this tower, for the rest of my pitiful fucking life.

I leaned my forehead against the wall in the stairwell, knowing full well he could hear me. I *hated* that my grief wasn't private.

Tommy wouldn't come back.

I'd pushed my best friend away, and there was a great reason for it. That's what I had to remember.

No matter how fucking hard it was.

I'd had no luck with anyone in Blue. I had thirty trouble houses in that suburb and the occupants of the six I'd visited were either out for the day, on vacation without their teens, or had gates and weren't answering their com.

Fucking rich people.

"I called the hospital while you were yelling into the com," Laurel said, casting a look at the male Vissimo from last night who I'd learned was named Fernando.

Hearing his name had only reminded me of *Fernando's Eighth Ab* and made me heartsick for Tommy.

I caught the Indebted's steady gaze in the rear-view mirror. "Is he still here?"

"Yes, but he isn't doing so well. The nurse I spoke to said he took a turn for the worse during the night."

Blood pounded in my ears. *Oh god*. I did that to him. I put him in the hospital. He might not make it.

The Vissimo real estate agent said that if I didn't back away from securing that house, he'd hurt people I cared about. I hunched forward. They could have hurt Tommy. Or my grandmother. *Her* chest could be caved in now.

"It's not your fault," Fernando said after sharing a look with Laurel.

She nodded. "He's right."

I didn't argue. I knew differently. My actions that night were entirely selfish. I'd acted like a rebelling twenty-one-year-old. Acting that way with what I knew—and who knew *of* me—bordered on insanity. I would've never behaved that way if it meant danger to Tommy or my grandmother.

Rhys might pay with his life because I'd shoved aside danger for one night of normalcy.

Ignoring the churning in my gut, I straightened. "I need to go to the hospital."

Silence met my words.

"... The hospital is on your blacklist," Laurel replied.

"It's what?"

"Kyros—"

Fury rocketed through me with a strength I'd never felt. I held up a hand. "Say no more. I'm going."

Laurel's cloak descended. "I'd be duty-bound to stop you. We both would."

"Then how much to take me there?" I snapped at her. "You're mercenaries, right?"

Their faces hardened and neither answered.

I scrubbed my face with both hands. "That was uncalled for and insensitive to your situation. I apologise sincerely."

Laurel unlocked.

Fernando didn't.

"Can I borrow a phone?" I added. "I'm going to yell at Kyros if that's any reparation for what I just said."

Fernando passed his phone over immediately.

You clearly don't like Kyros.

His phone wasn't all that much better than Beast.

"You got Snake on this thing?" I asked him. When he dipped his head, I asked, "High score?"

His dark-brown hair was cropped short. He was decked out in black leather like Laurel but seemed younger. Maybe more hopeful.

"Two thousand five hundred," he said, grinning.

My jaw dropped. "You're fucking with me?" Mine was two hundred and thirty.

Fernando lifted a shoulder. Like that high score was nothing. I was in the presence of a king.

"Mad respect," I told him. "Do you have Kyros's number?"

He took the phone back and pulled up the info. With a look at Laurel, he passed the phone back.

I snorted. Kyros was listed under D-bag. "Don't worry, I won't say a word. It'd bounce off his ego anyway."

"I overheard talk that you spent the night in his private quarters," the male Indebted blurted.

I eyed him, opening the door. "Yet you handed over your phone. So I won't justify your question with a reply. You know things aren't what they seem."

Laurel whacked him on the shoulder, and he yelped.

Taking the conversation with Kyros outside the car was stupid, really. Like they wouldn't hear everything anyway. But the distance made me feel better.

I checked the time—*5:00 p.m.*—Kyros would be awake.

Pressing the dial button, I gritted my teeth.

"What's wrong?" he snarled over background murmuring.

Did his phone even ring before he answered? If that was how he greeted the Indebted, no wonder they had him listed under D-bag.

"Kyros," I said sweetly.

The background murmurs cut off.

"... Basilia, one moment."

I placed my free hand on my hip. "No, not Basilia. It's *Miss Tetley*."

"Are you hurt?"

I wouldn't break the phone. Only because it wasn't mine. "Why have you banned Laurel and Fernando from taking me to the hospital?"

"Because Clan Fyrlia could be watching the area."

"Me visiting another male could only dispel their notions that there's something between us. And how could they attack me in a hospital during the day?"

He didn't make a peep.

"Of course, you *could* admit this has nothing to do with them watching me and everything to do with your fucking possessiveness."

A growl reached me through the phone. "My Indebted have their orders. I will not alter them."

Rhys was in ICU because of me. Did Kyros understand how fucking sick with worry and guilt I felt? I had to be there right now.

"I'll be going anyway." I pulled the phone away from my ear and held it to my mouth, shouting, "*Asshole*."

I threw the phone as hard as I could.

It bounced across the ground, and I clapped both hands over my mouth. "Oh shit! That's not Beast."

After a hasty glance at Fernando—who definitely hadn't missed my missile launch—I scuttled through a garden bed to retrieve his phone.

When I climbed into the car, Laurel had her phone glued to her ear.

She cut me a look in the rear-view mirror. "I believe she feels guilty about what happened to the human, sir. Yes. She is not herself. The male is unconscious and unlikely to live long."

My eyes widened, and Laurel shook her head at me, her eyes glittering.

I passed Fernando's phone over, mouthing "*Sorry*." Luckily, there wasn't any damage.

He snorted and pocketed the device.

Laurel spoke again. "Yes, sir. Of course. I'll call in more of my team to sweep the area and control the perimeter."

Because *that* wasn't a huge sign to Clan Fyrlia. I folded my arms and slumped in my seat.

"Yes, sir. Here she is."

Laurel stretched the phone back to me, and I sighed heavily before taking it.

"What?" I grumbled.

"Miss Tetley, what have I told you about my low tolerance for your mouth?"

I smirked. "Can't recall. Did you have something to say, Kyros?"

Several moments passed during which I imagined him pinching the bridge of his nose. Maybe taking some Advil.

"You entered the car and heard the pertinent part. I want you to know that this concession is not easy for me. I'm doing this because it's important to you."

I pondered that. "You still hope I'll say yes to the second blood thing."

Laurel and Fernando stiffened in their seats.

I guess that was still a secret. From the Indebted at least—or maybe Kyros's lair was soundproof.

"You're already aware that I think it's the best course of action. I don't wish to discuss our personal matters over the phone. Go to the hospital. See this human. I'll see you tonight."

What? Why did I have to see him tonight?

A click told me he'd hung up.

Wordlessly, I passed Laurel's phone back. "See? That wasn't so hard."

She shook her head, lips twitching. "You've got balls, Miss Tetley. Or vagina."

"Definitely vagina." I studied her profile. "Thanks for calling him."

She started the car and navigated us away from the house in Blue. "He called me."

Dammit.

Why couldn't he just be reasonable when I called him? Did he think I enjoyed losing my shit like that?

"Second blood exchange," Laurel said casually as we reached an intersection.

Kyros didn't want me to discuss personal matters. Laurel had to report to him, so any questions I asked her had to be with that in mind.

"Yeah," I said after a beat. "Ever heard of it before?"

"Heard of it? Yes. Doesn't happen very often these days." Her hands gripped the wheel tight.

I stared at them. Her eyes were glittering again. Was she trying to tell me something? I caught Fernando's subtle head shake her way. They knew something but couldn't risk telling me?

"In your experience, why do people undertake a second blood exchange?" I hedged.

Laurel pulled onto the freeway and didn't immediately answer. I tried to remain relaxed as her face worked.

"Our master knows why he's doing it," she said eventually.

I replayed her words. *Our master knows why he is doing it.* She usually called Kyros by his name when we were out of the tower. Was she purposefully reminding me of her position as an Indebted? If there was an unstated subtext to her words, that seemed like it...

Was Kyros enslaving me somehow?

"I hear you," I told her, watching her hands and eyes.

They loosened, and she blinked a few times.

"I know the blood swaps can be a mating thing too," I added.

Fernando jolted.

"It can," he blurted. "That really only happens in the upper middle classes nowadays—those who aren't rich enough to support a harem but hope to improve their family status sometimes combine wealth with another middle-class family through the mating ritual. Doing so comes at the risk of never having children, so it's still unusual."

Laurel hissed under her breath, and he snapped his mouth shut.

I wasn't sure what to make of his explanation. Kyros was plenty rich. He'd openly told me humans and Vissimo weren't compatible to reproduce. I even knew what I stood to lose if the mating drive didn't disappear after the second thrall—my libido would get 10 percent stronger.

The posture of the two Indebted in the SUV made it clear they wished to tell me something but couldn't.

I needed to know one thing.

"I hope this question doesn't put you in an awkward spot. But can you tell me if I'm in danger with this second blood exchange?"

Laurel shook her head. "Your *life* is not in danger."

I relaxed. Kyros was telling the truth there at least. If she was implying that my heart or mind might be in danger... Well, I was okay to risk those to possibly rid myself of a vampire stalker.

The ride to the hospital passed in silence as I stewed over what they'd said—and hadn't said. The truth was I had a huge decision to make. There were good reasons to consider the second blood compulsion. If Kyros lost interest, it would keep me—and more importantly, my loved ones—safer. However, there was the small issue of not being fully informed and the extra restrictions he'd put in place in my mind during the exchange.

... Then again, if I posed a security risk already, Kyros would compel me further whether I liked it or not.

Which made it sound a whole lot like I had zero choice in the matter.

"I'll take you in," Laurel said, pulling up.

Leaving Fernando to park, she led me through the hospital and spoke with a nurse, introducing me as Rhys's girlfriend.

We followed her through a set of swinging doors down a long ward.

"What were the police told about this?" I asked Laurel in undertones.

She didn't break stride. "Clan Fyrlia altered the street footage to cover their tracks. All that remained was you and Rhys walking down the street prior to the altercation. Kyros told the police you weren't willing to give a statement."

My stomach flipped. "I didn't know he did that."

"At the moment, this is just an assault charge against three unknown men."

At the moment.

The nurse directed us into a quiet and dark ward with a large nurses' station in the centre. Rooms lined the perimeter. She stopped outside a room in the far corner and turned to me.

"I'm sorry to say that your boyfriend took a turn in the night. He came in with a crush injury that shattered his sternum and dislocated seven ribs. There was damage to his lungs and heart. He woke briefly after surgery, but our specialist has placed him in an induced coma to keep his stats level."

My breath came fast and shallow. Not just a reaction to her words. It was this place. That Rhys could be in here when last night he'd been happy and laughing and calling me fascinating.

"I didn't tell you to upset you," the nurse said, eyeing me. "I tell you because Rhys is attached to a lot of machines right now. They're helping him to breathe and monitoring his stats. Sometimes seeing a loved one like this is a shock, but Rhys is still there, and he needs you to be strong. You must always be positive in his hearing."

"Okay," I said hoarsely.

She smiled grimly and led the way into the dark room.

Her warning couldn't have prepared me for the sight.

I stopped just inside the doorway, horror rooting me in place. "Oh god, *Rhys*."

The nurse cut me a stern look, and I clamped my lips shut, recalling her warning.

He looked so fragile.

So small.

His face was pale—nothing like his bronzed complexion yesterday. All manner of flashing and blinking machines were plugged into him. So many wires and stands that I had no idea where they started and ended or what they were for.

A vase of flowers sat on a corner table.

"His family was here?"

How could they even leave his side when Rhys was like this?

The nurse drew the covers high to cover his shoulders. "I

encouraged them to take care of themselves for a couple of hours. They'll be back soon." She threw me a curious look.

"New girlfriend," I explained. "I haven't met the family yet."

I stared at Rhys again and forced myself forward to the bed.

"I'll give you a few moments," the nurse said. "Please keep your voices low and calm."

Eyes closed, I listened to her leave. Laurel took a seat by the door, not uttering a word.

"Rhys," I whispered past the lump in my throat. "It's Basi."

I listened to the sluggish blip of his heartbeat on the monitor. *So slow.* His chest beneath the bedspread was misshapen. A chest wasn't meant to look like that.

The Tonyi triplets. They did this to him. *Vissimo* did this to him. Because of a stupid fucking game.

"You're going to get through this," I told Rhys fiercely. "You've got to make your own way, remember? You'll end up richer than your mum and dad, and you'll be proud of every cent of that money."

I wanted to beg him to come back. *Fuck.* I so desperately wanted to say sorry, but those were words to make myself feel better. They wouldn't help him recover.

I sniffed hard, squeezing his limp hand. "I'll be back tomorrow to see you. I'll bring some of that champagne and we can pick up where we left off. Well, maybe not exactly where we left off."

Smile brittle as glass, I leaned forward and kissed his gaunt cheek. "Until then, don't do anything I wouldn't do."

The nurse startled as we passed a station in the hall. "Done already?"

My chest rose and fell as I battled back my reaction. "Can't stay." The words were barely audible.

Laurel exited, moving to my side.

"I understand, dear," the nurse said, reaching out to take my hand. "It's hard. Something we never expect we'll have to do."

I nodded, thankful not to see condemnation in her eyes. "I'll be back tomorrow." I really didn't want to encounter his parents, but hopefully they'd leave at the same time each day.

The nurse's eyes darkened briefly before she recovered herself. "Of course, dear. We'll see you then."

My walk was just shy of a run as I hurried to escape the cloying hospital walls, my chest tightening to panic levels. Fernando joined us as I sped past him in reception. He beeped the car open before I reached it, and I dove headfirst into the back seat.

Hugging my knees up, I bent my forehead to my knees as my mind screamed.

"Back to the tower, Miss Tetley?" Laurel asked softly.

The tower?

No, I couldn't go back there. Not yet.

Voice muffled by my knees, I said, "Could you just drive for a while?"

"... Sure. Where to?"

To my grandmother. To Tommy.

"Just around. Maybe the estates. It's nice out there."

That was as close as I could get to my grandmother or she'd end up like Rhys. The vision of my grandmother's chest caving in place of Rhys flashed behind my eyelids, forcing bile to my lips.

Tucked in a ball on the seat behind Laurel, I stared out the tinted window as the houses in Black—the second richest suburb—stretched into the sprawling lawns and manicured gardens of the place I'd always called home.

Hedges, three-metre-high fences, and gates. This was what I'd always known. Hundreds of hectares owned by a handful of families—the financial and societal elite of Bluff City.

What a joke. We were the elite of jack shit.

Every one of us was a chess piece, whether compelled or not.

The Le Spyre estate was coming up, and I counted three seconds per inhale and exhale in a bid to regulate my heartbeat. Coming here was pushing the boundaries, so I couldn't show any sign of recognition; nothing could get back to Kyros.

The sight of the familiar matte-black wrought iron fence nearly undid that determination.

We drove along the fence for several minutes until the main

entrance gate came into view.

I could push open the car door. I could sprint to the com and shout for Fred to let me in. *God*, I could fall into my grandmother's arms and tell her all about Clint, and Rhys's condition.

I could let her see my anguish and pain and confusion.

She was just through those gates, five hundred metres down the tree-arched driveway. I could almost feel her strong arms around me.

My vision blurred as we left the main gate behind.

Hope.

Gone in a blink.

I didn't dare look back, focusing on my breath.

Minutes passed, and Laurel turned around. "It's getting dark. I'd prefer to be back at the tower for nightfall even though it's Fyrlia's turn."

My heart leaped.

We'd drive back past the estate? I assumed she'd continue all the way out the other side and circle back through Orange to Grey.

Could I handle going past again? It was a stupid question, really. I'd suffer much more for a glimpse of the only home I'd ever known.

Laurel swept back the way we'd come, and we were soon gliding back past the estate.

My eyes widened at the sleek black car exiting the gate. Fred was in the front seat.

My grandmother would be in the back.

"Stop the car!" I said.

Laurel screeched to a halt.

"*What is it?*" Fernando hissed, twisting in his seat to scan our surroundings.

Shit.

I broke off my stare at the car containing my only family member. She was so close. "Thought I was going to hurl. Seeing Rhys got to me more than I thought."

Oh my god. Fred was getting out of the car. The family butler always had a friendly smile on his face and it was no different now.

My heart nearly broke at the sight of him.

"Phew, that human is as cold as ice," Fernando whispered.

My brows crept up and I glanced at the butler again. *Nope*, couldn't see any speck of coldness. Just saw his smile.

The windows of our black SUV were tinted, so I huddled into a tight ball and pressed myself against the car door as Fred approached Laurel's window.

She lowered it.

"Having car trouble?" he asked.

His clipped tones washed over me like a warm memory.

"My companion felt sick," Laurel replied. "Thank you for your concern." Props to her, she somehow made that sound like a big *fuck you*.

"Oh, good," Fred replied, his warm smile growing. "In that case, Mrs Le Spyre kindly requests you get the fuck out of her way."

Laurel and Fernando gaped at him. I bit down hard on my lip, struggling not to laugh as the butler tipped an imaginary hat to the two *Vissimo* and returned to the car.

The back window rolled down and a pale arm stretched out, her middle finger extended.

Agatha Le Spyre was flipping the bird. At us.

My laughter got the best of me, erupting in a loud peal. Fred whipped his head around as Laurel sped us away.

I pressed my fingertips to the window, low enough to hide the gesture from the vampires with my body. I didn't know if the butler could see. But if he'd recognised my laugh, perhaps he'd tell Grandmother. She hadn't heard from me since my email several weeks ago, but at least now she'd know I was safe.

I'd come here hoping to catch a glimpse of the estate. I got more. My grandmother was going about her usual life. She was safe and charging through life unapologetically.

... Knowing that righted something within me.

She was my rock. My magic rock.

"To the tower, Miss Tetley?" Laurel said quietly.

I lowered my hand and released my knees, placing my feet on the floor like someone who wasn't at breaking point. "Yes. Let's go back."

29

The phone trilled.

I stared. It had never rung before. Shaking out of my stupor, I glanced at the alarm clock.

1:00 a.m.

I'd sat in silent misery for longer than I thought.

I picked up the black handset. "Yeah?"

"Miss Tetley." Laurel's voice filtered down the line. "I have something to discuss with you. Is it okay if I come up?"

Her tone was impersonal.

Wasn't as if she was tearing me away from anything important, even if the 1:00 a.m. call was unusual—even for vampires.

"Sure. But can I come to your room? These walls are getting to me."

"Uh," she blurted. "I sleep in the Indebted quarters."

"Oh. I'm not allowed down there?"

"You are. It's just... we don't usually have visitors."

I pulled a face at that. "If you're up for one, I'd really like to not go insane in here."

"Of course. Level LL4, room 54. You'll have to go to the basement and exit the lift. There's a separate elevator that brings you down to us."

"Okay, see you soon," I told her, hanging up the phone.

Throwing on a royal blue cardigan over my white-collared, two-piece summer outfit, I slipped into white loafers and grabbed my key.

Part of me expected Angelica or someone else to be waiting at the elevator to stop me, but I stepped off the second elevator—a far older model than the one I rode each day—without issue.

I eyed the concrete floors and exposed plumbing of the Indebted quarters. The doors to their rooms were like the ship doors on *Titanic*—heavy and metal. Many of the doors were open and the occupants fell silent as I passed by. Not hostile. Yet not welcoming in any way, shape, or form.

If I was an Indebted and this was my safety net, I'd feel pretty pissed to see non-Indebted down here.

I stopped outside number fifty-four and knocked, wincing as the sound boomed through the entire level.

With a deep groan, the door swung inward.

"Miss Tetley." Laurel greeted.

"Hey," I said, smiling. "Found you."

She opened the door wider. "Come in. Take a seat."

There was only one seat to take. *Jesus*, it was like a prison cell in here. I'd called Kyros's room cold and empty, but it still had creature comforts.

A metal-framed bed was shoved against the far wall. A tiny inbuilt wardrobe was the only storage space, so Laurel had shoved her possessions underneath the bed to keep the floor free. All that remained was a crate table and a rickety chair. Nothing on the walls. The blanket looked decades old. Then again, why would she spend a cent on herself when she was trying to buy her freedom?

I sat on the wooden seat.

Her grim expression didn't budge.

"What did you wish to discuss?" I asked, suddenly very certain I didn't wish to know.

She sat on the bed. "I asked the nurse to keep me informed on Rhys."

I shot to my feet. "*Don't say it.*"

"He passed away just before midnight. I'm so sorry, Miss Tetley."

"No," I whispered, staring at her. My knees buckled and I sat heavily. "*How?* He was okay when we saw him."

"He was in an induced coma."

But he'd been breathing via the tube in his throat. "What changed?"

"His heart stopped. The nurse said it stopped twice during surgery last night, remember? This time they were unable to revive him."

"*Oh my god,*" I choked out, pressing a tight fist against my lips to keep the cries inside. I squeezed my eyes shut, breath held as I internally screamed myself raw.

"He didn't feel a thing," she continued quietly. "There was no pain."

Shaking, I lifted my head to her. "How do you know?"

"Because I smelled the medications they were using. His heartbeat was so slow he would have slipped away. I promise you."

I believed her.

"The nurse knew he wouldn't make it, didn't she?" I said hollowly. Her eyes had darkened when I mentioned returning tomorrow. She'd known there wouldn't be a tomorrow for Rhys.

Laurel dipped her head. "I think so, yes."

My breathing quickened and I shot to my feet again, hand pressed to my chest. *Exactly where Rhys was struck.*

I dropped my hand in horror.

I killed him. I killed Rhys.

A human was gone because of my actions. And horribly, *selfishly*, a part of me could only feel relief it wasn't someone I truly loved. Rhys, I barely knew—and I was coming apart at the seams. If one of my two people was ever hurt like that, I couldn't answer for what I'd become.

"It wasn't your fault."

I turned to the Vissimo, not answering her. Disagreeing would make her feel like she had to reassure me. I didn't need reassurance because I was 100 percent to blame. I could only hope to accept everything that came with my mistake in time and take steps to protect those I loved.

"Thank you for telling me," I told her. "And for thinking to keep in contact with the nurse. I appreciate it more than you know."

She half bowed. "Of course, Miss Tetley."

Had she ever bowed before?

I ignored the formality. "I'll see you tomorrow for work."

Laurel followed me to the door. It took two steps to cross the prison cell that passed for an Indebted's room. "Where are you going now?"

Where was I going?

Pausing in the hall, I met her blue gaze. I did have more than one friend, I realised. Laurel wasn't like Tommy in that we didn't have the same history. But I'd known from the first meeting that we could be tight if I let her in.

I stepped close and hugged the vampire, bringing my lips to her ear. The Indebted on this level would probably hear, but we were so far down the tower, hopefully no one else would.

"I'm going to do the second swap."

I pulled back and caught the sorrow in her eyes before she masked it. I was only telling her now because she clearly didn't want me to undergo the second blood compulsion.

Part of me agreed with her.

The rest of me knew the second compulsion was happening whether I agreed to the scheme or not.

The fact remained that if things went to plan, Kyros's enemies would lose interest. My family wouldn't be used against me.

Over my dead body would Tommy or my grandmother end up like Rhys.

I waited until 3:30 a.m. when the call for the king's approval would be over. Once Kyros came down, I wanted his undivided attention.

Vissimo, I tried to say. The resulting gurgle didn't bother me. I tried again. Then attempted to sing it. Abandoning that, I turned to writing the word on the bare skin beneath my white skirt.

I tried the individual letters, backward, and then as an acrostic poem.

"Fangs," I stated, much to my surprise.

Vampires have fangs. Nope. *Fangs to drink blood.* Nothing. The locks on my mind weren't budging an inch.

"Blood." *Huh*. So I could say some words in isolation. In the context of Vissimo, not so much. Interesting.

My door burst open, slamming against the wall.

"That didn't take long," I said.

The fury on Kyros's face melted away as he took in my seated position on the bed. He entered the room and his body coiled as he ambled toward me.

His jaw clenched. "You were testing the constraints to bring me here."

I lifted a shoulder. "Don't have your number."

"Because your phone is archaic and always dead."

Dead.

My face must have changed because Kyros bore down on me.

"What is it?" he asked, green eyes scanning me.

I tore my eyes from his face. "Nothing. We should get started on that second blood exchange."

Kyros stilled, and I kept my eyes trained on his *Freens*.

"Miss Tetley, what has happened?"

Hardening my resolve, I tipped my head back to meet his gaze. I silently told him about visiting Rhys, about how he'd appeared... what his skin felt like. I described the visit past the estate, about Fred and my grandmother. I moved on to my trip down to the Indebted—about the awful news I heard there. Then about how afraid I was all the time—for myself and for the few people I had left to me. Staring at Kyros, I told him what it was to lose my parents and how deathly, deathly afraid I was that I may lose someone else.

I cleared my throat. "It's the right choice. You were right. We should swap blood without delay if you have the safety measures in place."

He said nothing.

Stiff from sitting so long, I stood, sidestepping him. "Do you need to make a call or anything?"

Kyros's eyes tracked me.

"Where would you like to do it?" I pressed, a bite entering my voice.

He crossed the room, and I realised how hard I was breathing. With one finger under my chin, he forced me to meet his piercing gaze.

I closed my eyes, his gentle hold preventing me from turning my face away.

"Someone has hurt you, my beauty," he said softly. "Tell me who it was."

No. I couldn't do softness right now. I wanted hard anger. I wanted a fight. "No one," I hissed. "You're wasting time. If we do it now, the thrall will be over this time in three days."

He pulled me to the bed again as I babbled, forcing me to sit.

Sitting next to me, he was silent for a time before asking, "Why?"

Irritation bloomed. "What are you waiting for? You wanted this."

"I do want this." Kyros rested his elbows on his knees. "But something has happened that I'm not aware of."

"Welcome to the club," I snapped. He blinked and I burst to my feet, whirling away. "That was rude. I'm just tense about this. I don't know if I'm making the right choice. There's no way to know for sure?"

He wasn't going to agree to this if he felt suspicious.

"No. But you're lying to me. Should I call Laurel or will you tell me?"

There was a lot Laurel could say. I didn't think she'd mention our drive past the estates or the cryptic conversation we had about the exchange, but I'd rather not put her in an awkward position.

"Rhys died tonight," I said flatly. "That's not why I'm doing this."

It was.

A shadow flittered across his face. "Come here, Basilia."

"*Don't call me that*," I screamed.

I was shoved against the wall in an instant, Kyros's blazing eyes trained on me. I was past worrying about irking his alpha. I shoved at him as hard as I could.

It felt good.

I did it again and again, desperate cries leaving my lips with each one.

When the anger faded from his eyes and his fangs receded, I spun to face the wall rather than see his pity.

My arms wrapped around my body, I ignored my harsh breaths. "That's not why I'm doing this. It is why I'm upset. Rhys's death is neither here nor there for what we need to do. I'm not going to keep justifying my decision to you. If you've changed your mind, this conversation is at an end."

His hands appeared on the wall either side of me, his body hovering close to my back. "Whatever's on your mind, you feel unable to confide in me. All I ask is that when—*if*—you can confide in me, you do."

Confide in him. Was he fucking kidding me? Hell would freeze over before that happened.

"Sure," I said, hanging onto the detached calm I felt in the wake of my outburst.

"... Then come." He pushed off the wall and took my hand, tugging me to the door.

His focus didn't err from me, but I kept my eyes downcast, unsure if he'd change his mind.

Kyros walked at my pace, and we rode up to Level 65. He entered his long-ass password on the panel, and I moved up the stairs to the lair ahead of him. I'd cottoned on that Kyros walking behind was an alpha thing. Placing my back to him put me at a disadvantage, I assumed.

Because otherwise, I'd have him beat.

Mere hours had passed since I was last in his lair.

I felt so different.

I beelined for the circle sofa, shuffling to the back. Hugging my knees to my chest, I piled the few cushions around me in a wall. Kyros raised his phone to his ear, striding past to the kitchen.

I stared at the blank TV screen until he returned. The vampire prince sat on the couch and I shifted my gaze to him.

His hands curled to fists. "I'm trying to remain calm, Miss Tetley. You aren't yourself and it's tearing at my control. How can I make you feel better?"

He couldn't.

Scratch that. "Do the blood exchange."

"You didn't meet with anyone today," he asked, eyes heavy on me. "Anyone outside of this clan."

I'd expected that to be his first suspicion downstairs. "No. I told you why I'm upset. Can you please drop it?"

His hand remained clenched, and I got the sense he wanted to destroy the entire room.

"My blood will break any compulsion on you, regardless," he murmured. "Unless it has been placed by King Michael or my father."

Why would his father compel me?

I stared at his white knuckles for a moment longer and just *gave up* the fight.

Kicking the cushions away, I crawled to the sofa edge and onto his lap. There, I curled into a ball, placed my head against the firm expanse of his chest.

His arms slowly came around me.

Cradling me, Kyros moved us deeper on the sofa. He stretched out his legs, clutching me against his body. I bunched the front of his shirt in both hands, stealing what comfort I could from being in his arms. He wasn't the person I needed, but he satisfied something within me.

Only the bed lamps illuminated his lair and we sat in silence in the soft light and quiet. I fully relaxed against him and listened to the purr rumbling in his chest. My eyelids grew heavy at the sound.

He dragged his thumb up and down my upper arm in languid lines, and I released my legs from the tight ball I'd formed, curling them behind me atop of Kyros's legs. My hand inched up to his shoulder, and I turned my face into his chest, inhaling deeply.

The purr came again, deeper this time.

Kyros pressed a kiss to my temple, and while part of me longed for the simple gesture, the rest of me shrivelled inside.

The door to his lair was flung open.

A shriek lodged in my throat and I wrenched upright. Kyros held me to him until I registered the row of his brothers.

"*Ooo,* romantic," Gerome said, waggling his eyebrows at our position.

I exhaled and tried to slide off Kyros's lap, tugging down my skirt at the same time. He clamped me in place.

I returned my gaze to the row of brothers. Rory was there, looking uncharacteristically subdued. The one with the shaved head was Lionel, who was in charge of the agriculture industry. Which left Neelan who, while not the tallest of the brothers, was certainly the most muscular. Unlike the others, his skin more olive than golden. The shape of his eyes showed the almond curve I expected from Clan Fyrlia.

His mother or father took a dip on the wild side at some point.

"She agreed then," Neelan said, stalking into the room as if he didn't quite know how to be in Kyros's lair.

"*She* did," I said with a bite.

He cast a veiled look at me and returned his attention to Kyros over my head. *Hmm*, had I just discovered my least favourite sibling?

"Plan?" Lionel walked to the sofa, and the others followed his lead, creating a circle around us.

I glanced up at Kyros despite myself.

"I'll put up a fight," he told them, green eyes on me. "I want her."

Rory snorted. "At least you're finally admitting it."

Kyros didn't acknowledge him, and Rory's face fell.

"Why are you playing the game?" I asked, touching Kyros's arm.

A wrinkle appeared between his brows as he glanced up at his brothers and back to me.

"Exactly." I tilted my head to Rory, brows arched.

Amusement flickered in the depths of his gaze. Not removing his focus from my face, Kyros extended his hand to his brother.

Rory cast me a look as he took it.

They shook hands.

Fuck me. I was sorting out Vissimo quarrels now.

One mess down. Time to fix another.

I removed my blue cardigan. The white two-piece outfit wasn't ideal for the occasion. The crop top was sleeveless with a collar that fastened tight around my neck. The tulip skirt was tight at the waist and extended to mid-thigh.

Lionel smirked at me. "You're keen."

I didn't have the energy to form a witty quip. His smile faded when I didn't answer.

"What happened to her?" he demanded.

The vampire beneath me stiffened.

"None of your business," I forced myself to reply before Kyros could. "I have a request."

The brothers turned to watch me.

"How many Indebted would it take to hold you down?" I asked Kyros.

His gaze was riveted on my neck. He was almost salivating. No matter what he said, part of this obsession with me was about blood. If he tasted like a strawberry mojito, I may look at him the same way.

His hands wrapped around my waist, large thumbs extending beneath the bottom the crop top to rest on the skin between the two sections of my outfit. I narrowed my eyes but didn't make an issue of it.

"Eight of the strongest females," he eventually said.

I shivered as his thumb stroked small circles on my stomach. "I want ten female Indebted outside my room for the next three days."

Gerome laughed. "She really, *really* doesn't want to sleep with you, brother. Must have spoken to your other partners."

"It's because I stole her heart at seventeen," Rory interjected.

"What?" Kyros said, hands clamping around my waist.

I glared at Rory. "I just got your ass forgiven." Knowing the bastard would put his own spin on things, I fessed up. "I met Rory at an opening when I was younger. I was taken with him and he ditched me on the dance floor. The end."

Rory grinned. "She wanted me."

"I did until I discovered how badly you're aging," I shot back, going for the kill.

The vampire reeled back like I'd slapped him.

Lionel saved the day. "I don't understand though. She likes your touch. Her heartbeat changes. Her scent changes."

Ugh, wish I didn't know that.

A growl filled the air, and I placed a hand on Kyros's chest.

"She's comfortable with you," Neelan added.

I blinked at that.

No, I wasn't. I—

... Was on his lap, in his lair. We'd been snuggling.

Yeah, okay. I was *more* comfortable with the vampire. *Whatever.*

"Can you bite the right place with this?" I gestured at the collar.

Kyros shifted his furious gaze from Rory to my neck. "Yes, but blood will get on it."

Did I like the dress?

I liked the dress.

Stretching up, I ignored the way Kyros's gaze dropped to my exposed belly as I flicked open the collar button and struggled with the zipper.

He reached around my back and tugged the zipper down. Inwardly sighing at the presence of his siblings *yet again,* I drew the crop top overhead, exposing a cute, strappy bralette underneath. The nude garment matched my underwear because I'd had time to prepare for the worst-case scenario this time. And also because Angelica hadn't provided me any underwear that normal women wore.

Kyros inhaled sharply.

I hoped he was enjoying the fucking show.

Folding my top, I rested it over the armrest.

"I've seen her boobs twice now," Gerome announced.

Rory smirked. "I'm on three."

I straddled Kyros while they were still quibbling over Basi boob sightings—because straddling their brother was sure to start another round of banter. Loud mouths.

The vampire underneath me vibrated at their comments. His fists curled again, and I reached for one at a time, directing them to my waist. Kyros spread his fingers wide, and I jolted as his thumbs brushed the underside of my breast.

"Stop talking," Kyros ordered suddenly.

All four of them obeyed.

I murmured, "You should use that trick *all* the time."

He shot me a smile, then studied the men surrounding us.

"I have sworn to Miss Tetley that she'll be safe during the thrall."

The four brothers listened now, not a grin in sight.

"Do you understand what I'm saying? There will be no games this time. No fuck-ups. Nothing to make her uncomfortable or embarrassed or afraid," Kyros said, looking at each of them in turn. "That is an order."

One by one, they bowed their heads.

Kyros turned my face to his, and I flushed, painfully aware of what happened last time we did this. I didn't want to give his brothers more fuel to tease me.

Darting forward, he pressed his lips to mine, leaving me stunned.

"Ignore them," he whispered. "I do."

My chest was pressed against his. I tipped my head to the left, staying in position as Kyros brushed my long hair away, collecting it in a handful on the other side.

I closed my eyes to block out his family.

His kiss at the base of my throat took me by surprise. I gasped and pressed my lips together when Gerome snickered.

Kyros trailed his nose from the tip of my shoulder and up several times, like a human savouring wine in a glass.

His fangs slid into me with a sharp pinch.

I screwed my face up as he drew his first gulp. The pain dissipated, only to be replaced by a familiar pressure in my head. A whine slipped between my teeth as the pressure mounted. Just like the first time.

Except now I was lucid enough to resist.

The pain in my head rocketed as I shoved at the pressure. Kyros growled and tightened his hold in my hair, grinding into me below.

A whole different sensation ripped through me, and my instinct to resist whatever he was doing in my head slipped.

The tightness in my skull eased.

He took two more long drinks from my neck before retracting his fangs. I winced, my fingers digging into his shoulders as he lapped at the wound. I became aware his hands rocked me back and forward along his erection. I lifted up on my knees, severing the contact, and ignoring the quiet laughter from his brothers.

Kyros purred, green eyes taking on the dreamy quality. In a blur, he reversed our positions, so he straddled *me*. Flat on my back, he forced me down with his wrist across my mouth.

Hot thick liquid trickled down my throat.

I coughed, but he didn't relent, and I was forced to swallow again. My watering eyes sought his as I swallowed again and again.

Last time, he only made me drink a little.

A burning extended from deep in my stomach. Reaching up, I clamped his wrist to my mouth, drawing hard as I watched him.

He jerked, groaning, and his free hand went to my breast, rolling my nipple through the bralette. I moaned, relishing the snarl erupting from his mouth as he heard my pleasure.

I stretched my fingertips to the bulge straining in his suit pants.

The fire within me had mounted steadily, but when Kyros pulled his wrist away, heat shattered everything else.

Everything.

So much.

Unchecked.

A whimper escaped my lips. My body arched upward with the force. Kyros's mouth was clamped around my nipple through the lace of my bralette. My legs were hooked around his hips. His arm circled my back.

Hands reached for him, yanking us apart, but I was up and leaping for him in an instant.

Arms clamped around my waist, and a savage roar ripped from Kyros as he swung at the men holding him.

I panted, kicking at my captor.

"*For fuck's sake,*" the muscular man holding me puffed. "We should let them get it out of their system."

"You heard him," the sandy blond answered. "He gave us an order."

"Neelan, you dick," another with a shaved head shouted. "Get her out of here."

I bit down on the forearm holding me to no avail.

"I'm going. I'm going. I'll call the Indebted females on the way and come back."

"Hurry," the fourth vampire urged, tackling Kyros to the ground as he set one of the others crashing into a wall.

"*Kyros,*" I called breathlessly.

His head snapped up, and my mouth fell ajar at his pure *beauty.*

The meadow-green eyes were lost in a blur of movement as I was tossed over a shoulder and sped away.

30

I poured more beer into my bowl of ice cream, beaming as the ale frothed.

"See how it does that?" I whispered to the ten Indebted I'd insisted come inside the room instead of lurking outside. They couldn't stand out there for the entire thrall.

The women exchanged looks.

"Hold out your bowls," I instructed.

The small bench beneath the mirror was piled with at least five flavours of ice cream. And beer.

The vampires hesitated a second too long.

"*Out*," I snapped.

What was wrong with them?

Laurel had the sense to hold her bowl out. The rest followed her lead.

I weaved down the line, belching as I tipped my favourite beer, *Wren*, into their bowls. "See? It's a beer float. An adult version of a Coke float. We just swap Coke for beer. The ice cream is still the same."

The leather-clad row of women tested the mix.

I finished mine in the time it took them to take a nibble. "Well?"

Their expressions smoothed.

Laurel was alone in grimacing.

"You don't like it?" I asked her sweetly.

She lifted a shoulder. "No."

"*None for you then.*" Storming to her, I snatched the bowl away and shovelled the rest in my mouth.

Laurel grinned, and I pointed a finger directly at her face.

"I like you," I declared, grinning too.

Tossing aside the bowl, I pulled her into a tight hug and stroked her back. "I'm so sorry you live in a prison cell." I blinked at the rest of the women. "All of you. It breaks my heart."

Laurel returned the hug. "Thank you, Miss Tetley."

My gaze riveted on the smallest of the gathered women.

"Excuse me. Am I *boring* you?" I hissed.

The vampire leaped, shoving her phone in her pocket. *Too late.*

I bore down on the hazel-eyed beauty.

"Hand it over, young lady." I extended my palm.

The woman peered at me. "I'm sixty."

Channelling my grandmother, I set the full force of the Le Spyre glare on her. Sighing, she reached into her leather jacket pocket and slapped the phone on my palm.

I stared at the open app.

"Pinterest," I murmured in surprise.

Interesting.

Retreating to my massive bed, I crawled into the middle and lay on my back, scrolling through the app.

"Stomach hurts," I informed Laurel.

"It's because you ate a litre of ice cream in an hour."

Someone was jealous of how much I could put away.

I scanned the various blogs on Pinterest. "Wow, this has so much stuff on it. I've never been on before."

"I like the travel entries," the owner of the phone offered.

Odds were that she'd never get to see anything outside than Bluff City. The Indebted lived in comparative squalor to their brethren—no wonder she longed for escape.

My eyes landed on a blog titled *35 Home Craft Projects*.

Hmm.

Clicking on the picture, I flicked through the web page. "*Shit*, you can do a fuckload with crates. Who knew?"

I thought back to how devoid of life Laurel's room had been. No pictures, no warmth—except for the threadbare blanket.

"You guys just need a little happiness," I choked out. Scrolling through the remaining projects, my gaze alighted on the very last one.

Perfect.

"I need to go out and get supplies."

I had a shiny new bank card and over thirteen thousand dollars.

The vampire pursed her lips. "You're not cleared to leave the tower during the thrall. I can send someone out for them. What do you need?"

I was going to infuse their prison cells with warmth, that's what. The Indebted wouldn't know themselves when I was done. "How many Indebted in this tower?"

"One hundred and twenty."

Phew, I'd be busy. Lucky I had two and a half days before Kyros's boner went away.

Smiling, I rattled off my list of items.

I hiccupped the words to "Catch a Shooting Star", near tears as I flung the new bedspread out over the mattress in the last room.

While waiting for the craft supplies, I'd decided each Indebted needed a new duvet. I called Angelica and snatched the master key from her before pillaging tower rooms at random to borrow blankets. Some of the rooms I'd thieved from appeared lived in, but that didn't matter. *They* had money, the Indebted didn't.

I hiccupped through the rest of the lullaby and tucked the edges of the blanket in around Fernando who'd I'd caught napping when I barged in.

His eyes were wide and fixed over my shoulder.

Glancing back, I studied Laurel's wide grin before returning to my tucking ministrations so the blankets were right up to his chin.

I knew blankets would make them happy.

Fernando's wide eyes shifted to me.

"There you are. Sleep tight," I told the man, blowing him a kiss.

He didn't respond, probably overwhelmed with receiving the meagre scrap of kindness.

My lower lip trembled at the thought.

"I didn't miss anyone, did I?" I turned to Laurel.

Pinterest woman answered. "That's everyone, Miss Tetley."

I beamed. *Good.*

Laurel's phone buzzed.

"Your supplies are here," she said after skimming the message.

I waved my crew of Indebted out of the way. "Why didn't you say so?"

I hustled for the first elevator, the last of my crew leaped in just before the doors slid shut. The women exchanged grins as we rode up.

Totally happy.

When I arrived back at my room, my door was open and bags littered the floor.

"There are one hundred and twenty?" I asked the young woman Laurel had sent to the craft store. She wasn't part of my ten but seemed kind of familiar.

The vampire straightened, eyes on my feet. "One hundred and twenty pinecones, Miss Tetley. A hot glue gun, hot glue, burlap ribbon, and twine."

Yes, yes, yes!

"I'm going to make you one too." I bopped her on the nose. "I'm going to make *everyone* a decor pinecone." My smile faded as I looked at her again. "Where do I know you from?"

Laurel cleared her throat. "Deana recently joined our ranks after draining her human boyfriend."

The night came hurtling back to me. The way her fangs had lengthened as I stood cowering and confused in my office.

Red tears slipped down Deana's cheeks.

Her shoulders shook, her sorrow and guilt filled the room.

"I saw what happened," I said grimly.

She covered her face. "I loved him and I killed him."

"Your control slipped." I agreed, patting her arm.

Deana straightened, not wiping her face. "I deserve my punishment."

I stared. "How much do you owe?"

She flinched. "One million. Kyros should've given me more."

Her guilt reminded me so much of my own. Perhaps Kyros saw her remorse would be punishment enough. A family was mourning because of Deana. Ryder *died*. That warranted punishment. I just couldn't be comfortable with the Vissimo's method.

To be made a *slave*...

Turning from her, I ripped open a sack, selecting a pinecone from within.

"I'll make you a pinecone first," I announced.

She'd feel better in no time.

I stuck the final diamante to the last pinecone. I'd remembered my destroyed gown from Rory and torn it to bits, adding a bit of extra glam to each hanging pinecone.

My body ached from two and a half days in a hunched position—and too many beer floats.

Fuck me, how much ice cream had I eaten? Why the hell was I making decorative pinecones? It had seemed like a normal thing to do thirty seconds ago. Now, not so much.

Empty beer bottles littered the mirror bench space. It looked like a racoon had ransacked my room.

"Have I been acting like a crazy person?" I asked aloud.

The Indebted no longer stood in an awkward row against the far wall. They sprawled on the floor and on the bed around me. One of them was even eating a beer float.

I grimaced. *Gross.*

Had the thrall made me do all this weird shit?

Laurel was sitting against the front door. "Yep."

"Don't feel like you need to spare my feelings."

Her lips curved.

The rest came back to me. Oh, *shit*, I'd ransacked rooms in the tower for blankets.

I flushed. "Please tell me you haven't handed the pinecones out yet. We need to burn them."

"All handed out," a woman quipped. I couldn't remember her name.

I flopped back on the bed. "That's really embarrassing. Can you guys tell everyone to chuck them out? I bet they look like shit."

Who in their right mind wanted a hanging pinecone?

"They won't chuck them out," Laurel said quietly.

I moaned, turning to look at her. "I seriously wouldn't be offended."

Laurel pressed her lips together.

I held up the pinecone in my hand. I'd glued a burlap bow at the base of the stalk and wrapped twine around the stalk itself, forming a loop to hang the cone upside-down. Three black diamantes caught in the light.

I held the embarrassment out, my eyes squeezed shut. "Who's this one for then?"

"An extra. We had a spare pinecone," another Indebted piped up. The sides of her head were shaved, the top a floppy arrangement of beach waves that she *totally* pulled off.

I chucked the pinecone on the bed. *Ouch*. My stomach was really sore.

Laurel's phone chirped. She pressed it to her ear as I massaged my stomach. Felt like I was having food octuplets.

"What's the time?" I asked the closest vampire.

She leaned around three of her comrades to peer at the alarm clock. "4:00 p.m."

Huh. Twelve hours of the thrall to go. "Time flies when you're making a dick of yourself."

Bright blue eyes appraised me. "We don't think of what you did that way. No one has ever made something for me. It's probably the same for most of us."

A lump rose in my throat, and I battled against it. Okay, maybe I wasn't as clear-minded right now as I thought—though more lucid than the last two and a half days that was for fucking sure. Karaoke was my limit when it came to making an object of myself. Turned out the thrall symptoms got stronger the second time.

That would've been nice to know.

"Miss Tetley," Laurel said.

Her tone was so strange, I nearly gave myself whiplash spinning to look at her.

She extended the phone out to me. "It's a client from Black. They got your number from Mr Polton."

Mr Polton. Henry? The future husband of Bess.

I took the phone, frowning.

"You're speaking with Basilia Tetley."

A thin voice crackled from the other end. "Miss Tetley, I hope you don't mind me calling you directly. I'm sure you're a busy woman."

I glanced around the room, eyes landing on the spare pinecone, empty tubs of ice cream, and strew of beer bottles. An Indebted choked back her laughter, and I threw her a grin.

"Not at all," I replied, though the woman sounded sorry not one bit. "I understand you're an acquaintance of Henry."

"Yes, his aunt through marriage."

"Lovely to meet you, Mrs....?"

She let out a short laugh. "Where are my manners? Mrs Maria Fenton."

I rolled my eyes at another of the Indebted, who snickered.

"Mrs Fenton, how can I help you today? I hope Henry and Bess are well?"

"Oh, yes. They started IVF yesterday."

"I'm so glad to hear that! My fingers are crossed for success."

I heard the smile in her voice. "We all are. But I rang you because my husband and I have decided to sell our property in Black, 102 Victoria Avenue. Henry told us about the decline in the market, but... well, he also told us you were able to *get them a very good price*."

Laurel snorted loudly.

Crap. I really hoped Kyros couldn't hear this conversation. Or anyone other than the Indebted.

I chose my words with care. "I'm certainly able to present you with an honest range. The market in Black is steadier than Green, but there's a downward trend across the board in Bluff City. In one year, your property won't be as affected as Henry and Bess's, but you will make less than you would by selling now. You'd have made even more last year, if I'm honest."

"Our neighbours were saying the same," Mrs Fenton mourned down the line. "My husband and I have worked too hard to let this asset devalue before our eyes. We sold all of our other properties to afford it, and we're both regretting the move right now, I tell you that."

That was pretty sad, actually. "It's never nice to feel that your empire's at risk. Did you have a timeline for sale?"

"I have no immediate ties here. My husband will be working abroad from mid-month. My children are grown and moved out. Last night, I looked into the market in Hamburg. Moving there would remove the constant commutes for my husband. While a change of culture would be a new challenge for me, I find myself strangely excited by the thought of living in Germany for a year."

"What colour was rolled tonight?" I mouthed at Laurel.

She shook her head once.

Not our turn. The roll wouldn't happen until midnight tonight.

Blast.

I could lay the groundwork.

Mrs Fenton was still speaking. "My husband flies out mid-next week. So we'd love to meet with you as soon as possible to discuss it. I'd like to fly out with him if I can."

Holy shit. This wasn't happening to me.

I darted my eyes around and settled on my plan of attack. "A year abroad in Germany sounds like a dream. And of course you want to fly out with him. Being apart from your loved ones is no easy feat. Here's what I propose. Live Right keeps up-to-date records of properties in Bluff City. If you give me half an hour, I can pull up any records we have of your address. Then I'll be able to give an informed rundown of what you and Mr Fenton can expect."

The relief in her voice was plain. "That would be much appreciated. I'm sorry to rush you like this. I'm sure it must be near the end of your workday."

I didn't even *know* what day it was, but this time when she said sorry, she meant it. "I'm happy to help any relation of Henry and Bess. You'll hear from me within the hour."

We exchanged goodbyes.

"I've got a reputation," I murmured after hanging up.

Eek. I hoped selling houses for maximum valuation didn't get back to Kyros.

None of the Indebted spoke a word, but each of them concealed a smile. *Yep*, I was a crappy employee.

"What's Angelica stored under on your phone?" I asked Laurel.

She arched a brow. "Angelica."

"Original," I teased.

Her number was right at the top.

"Miss Tetley?"

"I got a call from someone in Black who'd like to sell. What are the dice looking like doing tonight?"

"You received a call from Black?"

I made a face. "A person who *owns* a property in Black. They're more than a house, Angie."

"What's she got?" a deep voice asked in the background.

My stomach clenched at the gravelly sound. *Kyros.*

"Why did they call you?" Angelica enquired after a beat.

I crossed my fingers behind my back. "I secured their nephew's house last week—the Poltons."

"I remember."

I tempered my impatience. "The roll?"

"Yes, I have the stats pulled up in front of me."

Oops.

It was kind of hard to tell what was real and what was remaining PMS thrall stuff.

"Seven is the most likely roll," she said. "It's Kyros's favourite number."

"I'm unsure how that's pertinent to the discussion." She was relentless.

"The most likely roll would put us on Blue. But Black and Red are the second most probable rolls."

That meant shit, really. A three was rolled just last week, which was one of the lowest probabilities. Except what if the dice roll *did* put Clan Sundulus on Black? I was still looking for a way to make reparation for the turn bungled by Fyrlia attacking me. This was it.

"The owner is waiting for my call," I told Angelica, bouncing off the bed to pace between the listening women. "I'd like to meet them face-to-face tonight to deliver the information. A prelim. Stringing them along will be easy if Black isn't rolled tonight, but my gut says they won't sign same day like the others. All their savings are invested in the property. If I go tonight and Black is rolled an overnight *might* be possible."

"Miss Tetley, the thrall won't finish for another... eleven and a half hours. You can't leave the tower before then."

"I feel fine."

"I've received one hundred and twenty complaints of stolen bedding in the last three days. Would you know anything about that?"

I gasped. "A thief got into the tower?"

"We have footage of you wrapping Deana in a blanket from Level 59 and singing her a lullaby. When I gave you the master key, you assured me it was to select a room with better Feng Shui."

Christ. "Okay, I took the blankets. *That's* how I know my mental facilities are restored. I'm not doing this for me, Angelica. How many properties in Black are offered up on a platter like this?"

Silence.

"Exactly. My ten Indebted will come with me. I'll be back in the tower before Kyros has time to freak out."

The phone crackled.

"I do not *freak out*." Kyros's voice flooded down the line.

"Oh, hey, Kyros! How're you doing?"

A growl reverberated. "Miss Tetley, you will not leave this tower."

"You don't want me to secure a property in Black? Are you crazy?"

"Utterly," he said. "That will be nothing to my state if you leave my territory."

Oh, brother.

"One hour, Kyros. You can't control yourself for *one hour*? I thought you were meant to be powerful."

"I know what you're doing."

"Hmm?"

"That won't work on me, Basilia."

I frowned at my reflection. *Yuck*, hair was plastered to my cheeks. I tried to pull it off, but the strands had fused to my face via the ice cream medium. "What would a property in Black mean for the game?"

I didn't have any *trouble* properties from Black.

"Fyrlia owns the majority of that suburb. They're the preferred realtor there," Kyros admitted.

Interesting. "And why are you playing the game, Kyros?"

He didn't answer.

He didn't have to.

"One hour," I pressed. "I'll have ten Indebted with me. I'm happy to take more as long as they keep out of sight so my clients don't die of fright. I'll be in and out."

I heard his inhale.

"Kyros, I have a good feeling about this or I wouldn't push you during the thrall."

"You constantly push me, Basilia." He sounded resigned.

Clever boy was learning.

I turned away from the mirror. "What are your terms?"

"Will there be a male on the property?" The words sounded physically painful for him to utter.

"No." I lied. "The property is owned by lesbians. They like women."

Laurel covered her trembling lips.

There was no chance of Kyros buying that, but perhaps all he needed was a lie to cling to so he didn't break the toys in his cot.

I listened closely as Kyros listed the terms of our agreement, and a wide smile spread over my face.

The house in Black was mine.

31

Was the Madame President visiting? Was Beyoncé in town?

Nope, just me—with a four-car convoy. Talk about overkill. Twenty Indebted escorted me. More were sent ahead before I left the tower. Another group followed at a distance in a perimeter around me.

Half the Indebted had to be guarding me right now. But Kyros let me out—he'd *listened*. That meant something to me.

Laurel sped us down the freeway, and even though part of my mind registered that it was lingering thrall symptoms, my eyes were glued to my outfit. *Black leather.* Every bit of it. From the jacket and ass-hugging pants to my kickass boots.

Every trace of ice cream, beer, and glue had been removed from my body.

All in all, I felt pretty fucking sexy. Just like Jessica Alba.

Why didn't I wear this stuff more often?

"Are you nervous?" Laurel asked, glancing at me in the rear-view mirror.

"Not really. Doesn't make much of a difference to me if I secure the house or not—apart from the commission." Which wouldn't go amiss at all. The property was in *Black*. Even selling at the top valuation price, I'd come away with a butt-ton.

A thought occurred to me. "What happens to the Indebted working for the losing clan?"

"Nothing. Still Indebted. Still alive."

Huh.

That was good to hear. Kind of. Not the slave part.

"*Ingenium* allows us to pay off debt much faster." Laurel continued. "Without it, our sentences will last longer. The end of the game doesn't bode well for our kind."

I never thought about it that way. "What are the Indebted working for Clan Fyrlia like?"

"Like us," she replied after a beat. "Not as lucky. Their mortality rate is 25 percent higher."

Shit.

"But they take the risk to shorten their sentences?"

Laurel dipped her head.

"That's really crappy."

"It's our life." Her eyes told another story. As did the pregnant silence of the other Indebted in the car.

I licked my lips. "What is Kyros like as a... boss?"

"One of the better ones."

Part of me loosened—just a smidgen because Kyros still kept Indebted, and that wasn't okay with me.

The vampire pulled the car over not long after. "Your turn to drive, Miss Tetley. Make sure not to run over their plants when you pull in."

It happened *once*. I did well on the freeway but tended to lose focus in the suburbs and veer off course.

Three of the Indebted left our car, blurring away. Laurel would stay in the back with two others, out of sight behind the tinted glass.

Shoving the gear into drive, I bunny hopped down the street. What the hell was wrong with this car? The brake was way touchier.

"Left," Laurel hissed. "You're going to curb the tyres."

That's what I've been doing? "I'm good at that."

I yanked the wheel left and directed the car into the sweeping driveway of 102 Victoria Avenue.

Mrs and Mr Fenton swung open the front door.

"Where's the handbrake?" I said, trying not to move my lips.

Cursing under her breath, Laurel reached a hand forward and flicked a switch up.

"Not my fault they keep changing things around," I said defensively, grabbing the file. "See you gals soon."

I slid out of the SUV onto cobblestones, fixing a smile in place as I strode to the porch.

"Mr and Mrs Fenton? So nice to meet you. My name's Basilia Tetley. We spoke on the phone an hour ago."

Whoa, nice place.

Houses always looked better at night when their lights were switched on, but the gardens were well tended to. The place looked brand new—though that was unlikely. Most of the houses in Black had existed for nearly as long as the estates.

Mrs Fenton's eyes nearly popped from her skull as she took in my outfit. Couldn't blame her. Not everyone could pull off this get up.

"Sorry," I said breathlessly. "I was about to head out on my motorbike when you called."

Her expression cleared.

"You're much younger than we expected," Mr Fenton said sternly.

Ha!

He was a mosquito compared to Agatha Le Spyre. *She* told vampires to get the fuck out of her way.

I met him head-on. "Young and keen to carve a lucrative career for herself."

Mrs Fenton flicked him a frown. "How old were you when you were promoted to CEO, Walter?"

His ears tinged pink, but his lips twitched under his thick moustache. "Spouses always keep you humble, Miss Tetley. Are you married?"

Funny story, I'm actually in the throes of a sexual thrall with a vampire. There's blood exchanges and mindless passion.

I shoved down the sarcastic narration and smiled. "Not yet. My career takes up most of my time."

"As it should," he declared. "There's no rush."

Mrs Fenton peered heavenward and gestured me inside. "Stop grilling her, Walter. I do apologise, Basilia. Won't you come inside?"

I held up the file and both of their gazes tracked the movement. "I'd love to."

"Did they go for it?" Laurel asked as I peeled the SUV away from 102 Victoria Avenue.

I glanced back at the Fenton's in my rear-view. They were smiling at each other. A good sign. "I left the contract with them. Guess we'll wait and see what suburb we land on."

My gut proved true. There was never any way they were going to sign the same day. If Sundulus landed on Black tonight, we were in with a shot for a signing tomorrow. "I said I'd have to apply for the top valuation contract for their property. Just in case I have to drag it out."

"Where did you learn to talk like that?" an Indebted called Kelsea asked. "All their questions. You knew exactly what to say. Or do you enjoy it?"

Me? Enjoy *Ingenium*? "I don't like games," I told her seriously. "But people are people at the end of the day. I aim to treat them like that." I paused before adding, "Plus, my grandmother is a force to be reckoned with. Sometimes I feel like she was training me to be a hardass from the moment I exited the womb." I laughed despite the miserable twinge in my stomach.

"Pull over up here," Laurel instructed.

I ripped to the right, shouting as I accidentally mounted the curb. I slowed and flicked the handbrake button. "Sorry about—"

Glass shattered as a vehicle slammed into the passenger side.

My head snapped back as the airbag exploded. Stars filled my vision and I barely registered the side-door bag exploding after.

Movement. Rolling. Crunching. Whining.

I choked on a scream, feeling blindly for my head as the SUV settled with a lurch.

The seat belt cut into my breasts, supporting my weight.

The car was on its side?

Where was everyone? Were they okay? I couldn't hear anything!

I'd pulled right off the road. I was up on the curb. How did this happen?

Oh god, was everyone alright?

"Laurel," I croaked.

Through the cracks on the windscreen, I saw a man approaching the car. He shoved his hands through the cracked windscreen, puncturing two holes, and yanked. With a high-pitched whine, the glass came away from its fixings.

I studied the almond shape of his eyes. His olive complexion.

Vissimo. Not the kind I wanted to meet.

Where's Laurel?

The ringing in my ears from the bags exploding obliterated everything else. I feared looking around in case my fragile grip on consciousness failed.

"Go away," I mumbled.

He slashed through my seat belt, and I fell onto the driver door, on top of the deflated airbag. I screamed as glass shards speared into my body, my voice swelling into panic as the vampire seized my wrists and dragged me over the dashboard and what remained of the bonnet.

He hoisted me in his arms, and agony ripped another scream from my lips. Grunting, he yanked a jagged length of glass out of my outer thigh.

White filled my vision.

I retched, jolting violently. Pain blanketed my mind, obscuring my surrounding.

But gunfire. I could hear gunfire. There was fire. *Smoke. Sirens.*

I retched again as the *Vissimo* holding me broke into a run. Bile surged through my throat, and I didn't manage to choke it back this time. Acidic vomit poured from my mouth down my front and onto the vampire carrying me.

He didn't stop.

The Vissimo ran. *Blurred.* And I clung to the scraps of my consciousness, trying to catalogue the passing buildings to keep my bearings. The colours—Grey, Blue, Purple registered.

Yellow.

I'd missed some suburbs.

Was I fading in and out?

Red.

Cold water poured over me, and I jerked awake for what felt like the fifth time.

Spluttering, I sat and knocked my head on the top of a—

A...

... Dog cage?

The taste of stale bile soured my mouth. Water dripped from my bloodied hair. I blinked droplets from my eyes, looking for the source.

A man held an empty bucket in his hand. The Vissimo who'd taken me hostage.

He wasn't alone.

There were ten of them in the basement. Half were female.

Three of the men I couldn't fail to recognise. I stared at the triplets who murdered Rhys, clamping down on a fresh urge to vomit.

I shifted, and my shriek at the sharp agony in my side was more surprised than anything.

"Fucker," I hissed, hands trembling over the wound beneath my ribs.

Glass jutted from my body through my leather jacket which was covered in bile. Other glass shards littered the right side of my stomach and thigh—smaller pieces the size of my thumbnail. But the one right next to my belly button was the size of my palm at least.

I stared at it in horror, swaying on the spot.

"Well done, Callum," a triplet said to the man with the bucket. "Casualties?"

"Just Indebted, brother. A small band tracked me as far as Red. I altered the route to shake them."

Laurel and the girls had come after me. I *knew* it. I could only recall gunfire and smoke at the crash scene though. How the fuck did Fyrlia get through my personal convoy *and* the perimeter guards?

The shaking of my hands intensified as I contemplated the glass again. Should I yank it out? Would that sever something important?

"She's still in the thrall with Kyros. Perfect. There's no way he won't come. Is everything prepared?" another of the triplets asked.

"Yes, brother," Callum said, lowering his gaze.

I listened in mounting terror, nearly forgetting the piece of glass embedded in my side as I strained to hear. They intended to capture Kyros?

Fuck, that meant I was bait.

They'd hurt him. I had to get out of here.

"She's not much to look at, is she?" one of the women said, sneering. Or maybe her face was always like that.

Another, the smallest of the ten Vissimo, threw her an amused glance. "Jealous, Vera?"

"No," she snapped back.

"Then I'm not sure this job detailed remarking on the human's appearance." The short woman faced me.

I peered out at the female who'd come to my defence. She could be a potential ally.

She met my gaze and frowned, reaching into her pocket.

"What?" she snarled into the phone.

Sliding the phone away a moment later, she smiled. "He's left the tower alone. They've certainly exchanged blood twice?"

The ten Vissimo turned to me and inhaled in unison. My heart hammered. They could *smell* Kyros on me?

"Yes," she purred. "He will feel her location. He'll come directly here." Her eyes snapped to the triplets. "He should be mindless with the urge to protect her, but there are measures in place if this isn't the case?"

My mind tripped over the *feeling her location* part, but I didn't have time to contemplate it right now. I needed to get all the information I could and escape.

The middle triplet rolled his eyes. "What do you think, Gina?"

Telling the three apart was impossible.

She approached him, showing fang. "I *think* you know better than to disrespect me, little brother."

Whoa, little brother?

Was everyone in this basement related?

He schooled his features, and I darted looks between them. Okay, so she was in control, but also seemed the nicest. Which probably meant I shouldn't trust her one bit.

Listening to their conversation, I dropped my gaze to the glass embedded in my stomach. If I had to run, this thing could do more damage. Until I had to move, it could stay put.

Peeking through my lashes, I studied my prison.

The cage was large enough to sit back on my heels. The four corners were bolted down. There wasn't any door.

Shit.

If Kyros was coming now, there was no time to wait for a tidy plan. *Waiting*—though it catered to my fear—felt like a big, six-foot-deep mistake.

"I need a doctor," I slurred. It wasn't all an act. I was bizarrely grateful to be wearing leather. Who knew how much glass would have embedded in my body otherwise.

One of the triplets smirked. "Your heartbeat is strong."

Fucking vampire senses.

Escaping the basement while surrounded by ten vampires was unlikely for a human, but maybe I just had to *mess* with their plan to capture Kyros. Undo one part of their strategy so the rest imploded.

I scanned the basement. The floor was polished concrete, but otherwise followed the recipe of most underground storage spaces. Shelves lined the walls, odds and ends—buckets, boxes, tools, were strewn across the floor. A short set of wooden stairs led to a white door. *Exit.*

The walls were formed of heavy concrete blocks.

Only one exit.

I inhaled and stilled at the acrid smell.

Petrol.

Gripping my side, I leaned forward onto all fours and located the source. Two huge cans of the stuff sat around a cleared area directly in front of me.

Vissimo could be killed with fire. Kyros said the stronger the vampire, the longer they took to burn. Which meant he'd suffer unimaginably.

Swinging my hair forward, I studied the cleared space between the petrol cans. It was irregular with the rest of the flooring. I took a second look at the strewn items throughout the basement.

My eyes rounded.

They *weren't* strewn!

The items were a funnel to the cleared space. And that area was positioned directly in front of my cage. I had no idea what to expect from Kyros. He hadn't seemed mindless while I was in the tower. Though he'd said that his condition would worsen if I left his territory. If the female vampire here expected him to be mindless, I was inclined to listen. And that meant Kyros would run for me without hesitation.

That couldn't happen.

Decision made, I sat up, channelling my grandmother's strength. Gripping the glass shard in my stomach carefully, I yanked it out.

I tossed the glass aside, hunching over as I swallowed my scream. I pressed my shaking hands to the burning wound.

"*What the fuck is the crazy bitch doing?*"

My head spun, and I choked on a laugh—not having thought past the ripping out the shard part.

Time to act.

"You thought you had it all figured out." I panted. "Didn't you realise I've been a fucking prisoner in that tower? Watched around the clock. I'm not going back there."

I reached for the glass shard. It was slippery with my own blood.

Fumbling, I slowly lifted the shard to my throat.

"Stop her!" someone shouted.

Please stop me.

I moved the glass shard in a sweeping motion.

One triplet ripped the entire cage off its bolted foundations. Another ripped the shard from my hands while the third wrenched me upright.

My knees shook, but I couldn't have these vampires on suicide watch. Then they'd really truss me up.

I pursed my lips, pressing my hands against the pouring wound. "I can't believe you guys fell for that."

The Vissimo in the basement froze, and the grip on my arms slackened.

Glancing to where one of the triplets threw the cage, I whistled. "Looks like that dog house is ruined beyond repair."

Perhaps I shouldn't gloat too much.

Right now, I stood to the left of the panel. The trajectory from the door to me meant Kyros would miss the cleared space and petrol. *If* that was the trap.

Gina unlocked her tongue first. "Suddenly I see the appeal."

Without shifting her eyes from my face, she snapped her fingers to the male who snatched me.

"Callum," she said. "Sit her down. Watch her. She can't get anywhere without help."

... There was that.

"Vera, get a first aid kit. Her heart rate is erratic."

Crap.

Dropping my eyes, I watched the dark blood seeping from my stomach. It wasn't bright. Which meant it was venous blood, not arterial. That was the better of the two. *Thank you, Truth Ranges.*

The triplet let me go, shoving me toward the other Vissimo, who kicked a box into the place where the cage had been. Hands on my shoulders, Callum forced me to sit.

Dammit.

Back to the start. But I wasn't in a cage anymore. One point to me.

The muted *pop* of gunfire sounded above our heads. As one, everyone glanced to the ceiling.

Breath catching, I squinted at a thick square groove on the ceiling directly above the cleared space before me. A wide track was carved out of the otherwise smooth surface.

I looked down. Then up again.

That had to mean something.

Gina lowered the phone from her ear, every trace of amusement gone.

She glanced at me. "He's here."

32

The door was ripped from its hinges.

Kyros stood in the buckled opening, which just admitted his towering frame. No more than five minutes could have passed since the first gunshot.

Five minutes was enough time to feel I'd lost crucial blood.

The vampires spread themselves throughout the room—not in an obvious funnel to the cleared space before me—but dotted at random in a manner I assumed was meant to mask the trap. The petrol had been moved away from the area before me as soon as the gunfire began.

Kyros's shoulders heaved, and I got the sense the uncontrolled panting wasn't from fatigue. An animalistic, ripping growl traversed the distance between us, and I shivered.

Kyros wasn't home right now.

A leaden beat thrummed through the room for a moment as everyone stared at him with something akin to curiosity—as though wondering how the coming fight would go down.

"The space in front of me is the trap." I spoke the words as fast as my mounting wooziness allowed.

He'd surely smell the petrol, so that would alert him to the burning threat.

"Shut her up," a triplet snapped.

That's right, asswipe. The little human figured your trap out.

Callum slapped me from behind. My head lolled from the blow, throbbing pain filling the left side of my face.

He returned his hand to my shoulder, holding me fast atop the box.

Don't lose consciousness. Please.

I dragged in loud breaths, focusing on the furious snarls and crashing that had erupted around me.

Kyros had moved.

Attacked.

Opening my eyes, I fixed on my leather-clad stomach and thighs slick with my own blood before forcing my weary body to search for him.

Not hard.

I gasped as Kyros backhanded Gina. She was hurtled over my head, crashing against the concrete wall behind me.

He hadn't been joking.

I'd never seen his power.

Not even close.

I could barely look at the dark creature cannoning through the basement. His eyes were beacons of green. His skin illuminated with unearthliness of a golden moon. Predatory power bulged his entire body, making his black shirt and pants strain to contain him.

My body trembled with distant fear despite the bone-wearing fatigue fast spreading through me. The vampires closest to me were glued to the action before us, tensed and ready.

Ten against one—what fucking cowards.

And they were *still* afraid of him.

Fierce pride swept through me. I had little concept of his power in comparison to others, but Kyros was a *warrior.*

I had to be a warrior too.

I had to get away from the cleared space. Something bad was meant to happen there, I was certain of that.

Pressing the heel of my palm into my dripping wound, I slumped where I sat atop the crate, pretending to lose consciousness. Callum's grip shifted.

I threw my head back directly into his balls.

He howled, releasing me to cup his crown jewels.

I didn't waste time, throwing myself forward to stagger through the midst of the battle in a drunken run.

Kyros was aware of me. He didn't look my way but shifted to keep me in his peripherals.

I leaped for an open box, picking up the first object my blood-covered hands encountered.

Shit! It was a fucking drill!

"That was a mistake, bitch."

A hand spun me and I shrieked, swinging my hands to cover my face.

Something stopped my right arm.

Callum grunted and jerked, and we both dropped our gaze to the drill bit stuck between his ribs. *Oh my god.*

I'd stabbed him with the power drill.

My fingers were wrapped around the handgrip.

In a daze, I squeezed the trigger.

The whir of the drill was lost to the Vissimo's screams. His raw pain filled my ears—I'd never heard a man scream. Horror caught up, and I released the power drill.

The tool didn't fall, wedged between his ribs, but *Callum* began to fall.

Not a stagger, not a slow descent to the knees. Before my eyes, his skin turned grey and his eyes black. His fingers clawed, stiffening with the rest of his body.

Like a *wooden board*, the vampire fell back, slamming onto the concrete floor like a toppled wardrobe.

Transfixed, I lifted my eyes to Kyros's.

The fighting had stalled. Suspended in time by my actions.

Nine sets of furious Vissimo trained on me, and my knees gave way, my body caving to its terrified instincts.

I couldn't deal with that on top of everything else.

I groaned, black spots filling my vision.

Kyros laughed, a cold sound, and called out, "Your brother is dead."

The four vampires surrounding him launched at him. Fuck, I'd killed their *brother*. Someone would come for me.

I had to move.

The door out of here was metres away. Running for that would make sense.

Escaping.

Removing myself as Kyros's weakness in the battle.

But taking one step required strength I no longer had.

Fuck!

A sob caught in my throat. I couldn't make it.

My muscles were drained of energy. I offered no resistance when a vampire gripped my hair and dragged my head back, exposing my throat.

"Stop," a woman ordered.

I blinked upward at Gina.

The crashing and roaring in the basement didn't skip a beat.

A jagged edge was placed against my throat. "Immediately. She has one second to live."

Whoa!

As though switched off, the chaotic frenzy froze.

"That's better," she purred.

I swallowed awkwardly as I swayed in her grip.

"Hurt her, eldest child, and I'll kill everyone in this room," Kyros said conversationally. "And I'll leave you until last."

"You cannot defeat everyone in this room, *eldest child*," she retorted. "Even you are not that powerful."

"You have no notion of how powerful I am, Princess Gina."

She dragged me to the side, forcing me to scuttle on my knees or say goodbye to my scalp.

"You may be more powerful," Gina answered. "But I match you for speed. You can't stop me killing her *unless* you step two metres to your left."

"Something happens with the roof over the panel," I gurgled.

Gina chuckled, shaking me like a limp doll. "You chose a smart one, brother. I'll admit she's brave too. Would you like to keep your human?"

Brother?

Why was she calling him brother?

I retched violently, the situation undoing me at last.

"I'll step into your cage," Kyros mused. "In return, you'll allow her to walk away unharmed."

"Agreed."

"*Kyros, no,*" I whispered, despair tinging my voice. No one was burning to death for me. I couldn't take more guilt. Losing him would be a hundred times worse than losing Rhys.

"My Indebted are outside, Miss Tetley. They will aid you," Kyros said in a calm voice that made me *furious.*

Who'd help *him*? I choked on the bitterness surging within me, wishing I could see his face.

Was this just a ruse? Did he have a secret plan? He always had a plan, right?

The floor shook as metal slammed into concrete, but I knew for sure he'd stepped into the trap the instant Gina let go of my hair. She even laid me carefully on the ground when I began to topple in a dead heap.

Kyros watched between the column-like metal bars of a cage. The cage had descended from the ceiling.

"Go," he ordered, shifting his eyes from my face.

Yeah... about that. His deal depended on me being *able* to walk.

His eyes landed on me again. "Get up and go."

Oh, is that all? Why didn't I think of that?

"This alloy costs a pretty penny," Kyros said, drawing the attention of the smirking *triplets*. He ran his hands up the metal columns, his fingers not quite able to wrap around the thick bars.

A triplet sneered at him. "It is for the imposter, Julius."

"King Julius, my father," Kyros replied.

"Brainwashed," another triplet said. "You're *our* brother."

And they were about to kill the man they claimed as brother? Then again, though appearing furious at me killing their brother, they'd hardly sobbed over his corpse.

Dang.

This floor was feeling increasingly comfortable. Comfortable concrete was probably a cause for alarm. I took several full breaths and returned a hand to my wound—not that I had any blood left inside.

I kept my eyes on the vampires, curling my knees toward my stomach.

Gina cocked her head to the ceiling. "They've broken through the outer defences. They're about to reach the house. Girls, with me."

Who was *they*? Was it Laurel and the others?

I froze as a stream of vampires blurred past.

Four were left.

The males.

Better odds. For Kyros.

Who was in a vampire cage.

If I stopped moving, it was over. *This* was my last chance. I managed to get my elbow under my shoulder and focused on staying upright when I made it to my haunches.

Fuck. I was going to be sick.

"Petrol, boys," one of the psychotic trio called.

The fourth vampire—not one of the triplets—hesitated. "Gina isn't here."

"She doesn't need to be," the middle triplet snapped. "The plan is set."

I choked on horror as the other two picked up the cans and splashed the reeking liquid through the gaps of the cage.

Kyros gripped two of the thick metal columns, unmoving as they doused his body with petrol. He held my gaze, and while the triplets worked around the back of his cage, he mouthed, "*Turn away, Basilia.*"

No. Not from this.

I leaned onto my hands and knees and began to crawl to him, gasping as my body demanded I lay down and submit to unknowing bliss.

Someone snorted. "Look who it is. The human is coming to kill us, boys."

"She killed Callum," said the fourth male.

Silence met his words, and I continued my sluggish crawl to the cage. A simmering heat filled me. I was getting closer. The thrall was warming me again.

The heat mounted.

Kyros had to feel it too.

His quiet calm turned to a menacing snarl.

I glanced up, but shoes appeared before me, halting my crawl. I swayed back and forward on my hands and knees, staring at the combat boots.

"She isn't leaving here," the owner of the shoes stated.

Kyros's snarl filled the basement. "You'd break your eldest sibling's word?"

"Accidents happen," the male replied.

Another set of shoes, casual sneakers, joined his. "We set him on fire. She crawled to him and caught on fire too. *Oops*."

Laughter swept under Kyros's furious snapping.

The combat boots and casual sneakers parted ways for me.

What?

They expected me to keep moving after that? I wasn't a dumbass.

"*Crawl*. Or I'll cut your fucking throat before setting you alight."

That changed things.

I resumed my crawl, and the heat deep in my stomach swelled. *Crackling. Soaring.*

Kyros's growl, his call, reached inside me.

My eyelids hooded, and the swaying of my crawl felt languid instead of bone-wearied. I bit my lip and peered at Kyros, my gaze raking him. The fire in me was an inferno. For him too.

Kyros was trying to rip the cage apart.

The swing of my hips was designed to entice. The extra arch in my back meant to drive him to insanity.

For me.

I held him captive as he attacked the metal confines. Releasing my lip, I licked the small wound I'd created.

Kyros was crouched and waiting when I reached the cage. I placed my hands on two metal columns, gasping in pleasure as he reached through and yanked me upright.

Fire consumed me as his fingers roamed my skin.

I let out my own snarl as I grabbed for him only to encounter thin air.

"Kyros?" *Where did he—?*

My leather jacket was ripped apart and my black tank rolled up. The flat of a hot tongue moved over my stomach, lapping with gentle, careful strokes.

Peering down, I studied Kyros as he licked the gushing wound there.

Enough of the gentle shit! I needed him now.

My tugging hands were encased in his before I could blink. Abandoning that, I tried to squeeze into the cage, my breath coming in desperate, frantic gasps.

Why wasn't he kissing me? Why wasn't he touching me?

I didn't care about the damn wound.

"I don't want your tongue there," I snapped at him.

His lips curved against my bloodied skin, but he didn't stop lapping. I groaned as he plucked glass from my torso, rotating me so he could continue his licking ministrations over the smaller wounds. He drew closer and closer to my breasts, and I tried to help him along.

When he touched them, I'd come undone.

I wanted to come undone.

He brushed the underside for a mere instant before returning to my largest wound, licking it all over again.

My cheeks flushed, and I sagged against the thick bars. "Please, Kyros. I need you."

I'd cry if it convinced him to take me right there and then.

Kyros's eyes shifted over my shoulder. People were fighting. I'd dismissed them because I was between the danger and my vampire.

At last, Kyros ran his hands up over the uninjured plain of my stomach.

The clothing had to go.

We were of the same mind. He tore my tank from my body as I went to work on my boots and pants. I shucked the remains of the outfit as Kyros's hands blurred on his own clothing.

Our mouths met desperately between the bars. His arms snaked out of the cage either side of me, drawing me flush against the metal columns where he proceeded to palm my breasts with one hand.

I made an angry sound when he pulled away, whimpering as Kyros used his fangs to tear at his wrist.

Blood dripped from the wound and I snatched at his arm as he stretched it to me.

His purr of approval rumbled through the basement.

I clamped my mouth around his wrist and sucked hard, peeking up through my lashes.

He was mine.

Under my spell.

There was nothing he wouldn't do for me.

"Inside," I gasped between swallows of his blood.

His eyes. His beautiful green eyes held mine. I was his prisoner, and I couldn't feel one shred of regret over that.

His hands already through the bars, Kyros drew my leg up, supporting me under the knee. Still drinking, I used my other hand to free his erection before sliding my underwear to the side.

I'd been denied too long. He occupied my thoughts entirely.

"I almost feel bad to keep doing this to them," a voice said behind me.

Kyros growled over my head, dragging me around the side of the cage with not-so-gentle shoves through the bars. His fangs gnashed when foreign hands wrapped around me from behind.

Not the hands I wanted!

"Kyros!" I screamed as the person dragged me from the cage, need cramping like a fist in my stomach.

I was shoved against the far wall of the basement.

I stared mutinously into blue eyes as my heat slid to pain. As fever burned away to fatigue.

Mindlessness melted to confusion.

My furious screams faded to silence.

The person's face filled my vision just before the white dots connected.

"G-Gerome?"

Sighing, I fell forward into his arms.

33

I groaned, hand moving to my pounding head. It wasn't just demons tangoing in my temples this time, it was the entire apocalypse partying in my skull.

I tried to roll onto my side and was stopped.

Wrenching awake, I stared at the hands on my torso and traced them upward to the owner.

Pantsuit.

"Safina," I croaked. Pain ripped through my dry throat. "*Ouch.* Water."

Arching a perfect brown brow, Safina spoke over her shoulder. "Francesca."

An exaggerated sigh drew my attention to the retreating back of Kyros's youngest sister. The two other sisters stood at the foot of my bed.

Safina took the glass of water from Francesca, holding it to my lips. I swallowed a few blissful gulps, resting back on what felt like one million pillows.

I stared at the two mystery sisters.

Safina followed my gaze. "Miss Tetley, have you met Deirdre and Lalitta?"

My head was caught somewhere between an onslaught of terrifying memories from a basement filled with Vissimo and the introduction.

Mute for the time being, I shook my head.

"I'm Lalitta," the platinum blonde said, blue eyes huge. "How are you feeling?"

"Like a used tampon," I croaked, trying to sit a few times before giving up. "What's the verdict with my wounds?"

Francesca rolled her eyes. "Kyros healed the worst of it in the basement. You should feel fine."

"She lost too much blood. Not to mention the knocks to the head, you imbecile," Dierdre snapped.

Yikes. Thanks, but *yikes.*

I rested my eyes on Dierdre, noting her similarity to Neelan. Her eyes held the same almond curve. Her skin was olive. She didn't look like a member of Clan Fyrlia, but somewhere between the two.

Yep, Mum or Dad definitely took a dive into the enemy camp. Twice at least.

Lalitta cast the youngest sister a softly admonishing look. "Franny. Be kind."

Safina, Lalitta, Dierdre, Francesca.

Smart, nice, angry, petulant.

I thought of Kyros's brothers. Gerome was playful. Rory, vain. I wasn't sure about Lionel yet, but I had a feeling Neelan was rebellious.

Shaking my head, I pushed down the bedcovers and immediately yanked them back up, eyes flying to the present company.

"Your clothes were sullied. We removed them so Kyros's bed was not sullied also." Safina's smirk showed all teeth.

"Right." Kyros's siblings had it out for naked Basi.

I held up the covers with one hand and ran my fingertips over the bandages covering my torso.

"Was it bad?" I asked.

Lalitta's smile faded. "For Kyros to heal you instead of fuck you during the thrall, it would have to be."

Uhm. Profanity sat weird on her. Like a primary school teacher swearing.

"I wondered about that," I admitted, recalling how furious I was when he wouldn't touch me.

Safina inclined her head. "Your survival comes first. The wound was dire."

They could say that again.

I didn't feel so good.

I lowered the covers, registering Kyros's Level 65 lair for the first time. They'd brought me up to his room. Why?

My stomach churned, and I eased back onto the pillows, closing my eyes. "Tell me, please. What happened? And how long ago?"

Safina replied, "Two days—"

Francesca cut in. "Fyrlia Indebted swarmed your convoy. They'd planned it well. The freeway turn-off was the weakest point of your route. One of your guards managed to get between the truck and SUV or your injuries would have been much worse."

Someone got out of the SUV in that split second? *Fuck.* Were they okay? Was it Laurel?

"By the time our perimeter guard reached the scene, the youngest of the royal brothers was running with you," Francesca continued.

Callum was one of the *royals*? And the youngest sibling. *Shitty fucker*, killing him would come back to bite me in the ass.

Francesca toyed with her auburn hair, to all appearances just sharing some casual gossip with friends. "Our Indebted forced the Fyrlia scum back while your personal guards took off in pursuit. Callum managed to lay a false track that misled them. Meanwhile, Kyros exploded out of this tower like Hurricane Testosterone—"

My mouth fell open. "That's right. He can sense my location!"

The four sisters fell quiet.

I remember, you bastards.

Hurt swirled in me. That's why Kyros wanted to exchange blood again? Not because I was a distraction to playing the game. He just wanted to know where I was all the time.

I tried not to let panic take over. "He'll always be able to feel my location?"

"It saved your life," Deirdre stated in a bored tone.

My life wouldn't have been in danger if Clan Fyrlia didn't think I was Kyros's favourite blood bag! How the fuck could I leave now? Kyros would know where I was. He could find me.

I couldn't *ever* escape.

I'd resigned myself to living this life for now but always expected to run away one day.

Kyros had torn my freedom from me forever. He'd lied directly to my face.

"So anyway," Francesca drawled. "We all followed *Kyros*. Your Indebted caught the right track, and we all arrived a few minutes behind Kyros. We handled the outside force while he went in. And then we stormed the basement to pull you both apart because you're like fucking animals going at it all the time." Her angelic face twisted into a dark scowl.

"They were still in the thrall, Franny," Lalitta said.

My heart skipped a beat. "I drank his blood again."

Safina stood, picking up my glass and holding it to my lips.

I swallowed again.

"You're currently on day three of your third thrall," she said.

Dread punched me hard.

Lying flat again, I stared at the shiny white panels of the ceiling without really seeing them. Three blood exchanges.

We hadn't had time to see if the urges between us had dissipated after the second compulsion. I didn't agree to a *third* blood exchange—this changed the entire risk I'd been willing to make. If the second exchange could increase the tension between us by 10 percent, what did the third exchange do? And what other power did it give Kyros over me?

Except the third exchange wasn't my fault and it wasn't his either.

It happened, and now there was one more thing to deal with on top of my injuries and his fucking lie.

"What about the others who were in the basement with me?" I asked.

Deirdre sat on the bed where Safina had been. "The Fyrlia royals? They ran while their Indebted held us back. It's usually how things go when they pull shit like that."

"The ten of them lived?" I asked, astonished.

Deirdre grinned ferally. "Nine now."

My stomach roiled. "Yeah, I guess so." The sickening squelch of the drill bit digging into the Vissimo reared in my mind. I covered my mouth, breathing thinly. I felt nothing but regret over killing Callum.

I managed to keep whatever was left in my stomach inside. "What are the ramifications of that?"

"An impartial clan assessed the scuffle. The Fyrlia royals alleged that when the opposing Indebted forces *happened* to meet, you attacked their youngest brother without provocation. They later conceded that they'd been in error. The impartial clan ruled that although Fyrlia attacked you and later Kyros, you did kill one of the royals. There won't be any further repercussions—aside from that which Clan Fyrlia decides to deal out unofficially."

That's what I meant in the first place. "And they'll feel the need to, I'm guessing?"

All four sisters dipped their heads.

The triplets would be among those roaring for my head. I couldn't win. I just couldn't catch a motherfucking *break*.

I exhaled loudly. "Someone needs to tell me why they were going to kill Kyros, who they believe is really their brother. I thought Vissimo weren't allowed to kill each other. Isn't that why you guys are playing *Ingenium* in the first place? To prevent all-out war?"

Dierdre scowled at me. "Calm down. Your heart rate is rocketing."

Because telling someone to calm down *always* worked.

"They weren't ever going to kill him," Safina said.

My mouth dropped open. "Yes, they were. They—"

"Were going to set him alight because even a Hyanium cage couldn't have held him more than a few hours. They wished to eliminate Kyros from the turn that day because we were racing each other to broker a large land development opportunity."

Never going to kill him.

"No one thought to tell me that?" I whispered. Though why would they? I hadn't been back to Level 66 *purposefully*. I wanted nothing to do with their game aside from what I had to do for money and survival.

"The deal?" I asked despite myself.

Safina pursed her lips. "We lost it. Fyrlia landed on agriculture yesterday and signed."

Shouldn't she be more upset if the deal meant that much? The lives of her family members were on the line if they lost *Ingenium*.

"Was the developer Mr Ringly?" I tapped my lip.

The four sisters exchanged a quick look.

Dierdre glared. "You know him or something?"

I snorted. "Did Rory claim glory for figuring out Mr Ringly's drug habit? Wouldn't put it past him. But I assume that's why you're not devastated about losing the development deal."

Clan Fyrlia just got fucked and they didn't know it yet.

A slow smile spread over Safina's face. Lalitta beamed.

"The Indebted who were with me. Are they okay?" I sighed, sinking deeper into the pillows.

Lalitta answered, "The female who got between the SUV and truck will take time to heal. She's hooked up to a blood IV at the moment. Two were killed from another car. Three from the perimeter guard."

That she took the time to enquire about the Indebted spoke volumes about her.

"Five died?" My chest tightened. Five more lives on my head. I'd handed them pinecones three days ago and now their rooms lay vacant on Lower Level Four.

"Who cares?" Francesca quipped.

"I care," I snapped back. "And you should, too, you brat. They were there to save your brother's fucking skin."

She swung her legs off the armrest of Kyros's circle sofa. "To save *your* fucking skin."

"*Franny.*" Safina's voice cracked like a whip.

Francesca's guilt-tripping ploy didn't work. I already knew Clan Fyrlia attacked to distract Sundulus while they made the development deal.

But five Indebted were dead. Five *people*.

I pressed the heels of my palms into my eyes.

"Why does she do that?" Dierdre asked.

"Kyros said she doesn't cry," Lalitta whispered.

"Good, I hate it when they cry. Makes me feel angry."

The word she was looking for was *angrier*.

I lowered my arms. "I want a pay raise."

They turned to me. Safina alone looked amused.

"I'm not getting paid enough to deal with you fuckers."

What were they smiling about? I was deadly serious.

I gave up sidestepping the giant elephant in the room. "How is Kyros?"

Safina smirked. How old was she again?

"Did they get him with the fire?"

Her smirk widened. "Our crown prince is well, Miss Tetley. Comparatively speaking. The overlapping thralls and recent threat to your life have had an exponential effect on his urges and instincts. He's not entirely in control of himself."

My mouth dried. "How bad?"

Safina tilted her head to the door. "We had to fill his office downstairs with Indebted. He's tried to break in eleven times in the last two days."

While relieved he hadn't managed to break through, I was just glad he was okay. That was the main thing.

I slowly sat up. "I need to see the Indebted downstairs."

"Not happening."

My eyes narrowed to slits. "*Happening.* With or without you."

Light danced in her blue eyes. "You realise you have no way to back that up?"

"You realise I killed one of your kind two days ago."

Her eyes took on a strange quality. She studied me. "Yes. You did."

"So can you bring Laurel up, please?"

Francesca laughed. "These are Kyros's private rooms. They can't come up here. *We* hardly come up here."

Blowing out a breath, I resisted the urge to attack his youngest sister. "Then I'll go to them," I said between gritted teeth.

"Don't worry," Deidre said, shooting a look at Francesca. "She pisses all of us off. She's going through her thirties. It's a trying time."

"Stop saying that!" the youngest sister shrieked.

I pushed the covers back, setting my feet on the floor. Butt-naked, of course. I was losing count of my naked displays by now.

Too tired to care.

Standing, I waited a full minute for my wooziness to clear and traipsed to the drawers. Kyros's T-shirt drawer was empty, so I nicked some sweatpants, rolling them at the waist a few times. I'd spied a wardrobe around the jutting wall. Hobbling stiffly around the wall, I pulled out a white shirt and shrugged it on, rolling the sleeves to the elbow and fastening most of the buttons.

It'd have to do.

I returned to find the four sisters contemplating me in varying levels of consternation. Francesca with open hostility.

They didn't like me in their brother's space. *Whatever.*

"Lalitta," I said. "Could you help me with the stairs, please?"

She beamed and blurred to grip my elbow.

Kindness. I needed it in droves right now.

She picked me up halfway down when dizziness assaulted me and kicked open the door, setting me upright at the base of the stairs.

I scanned the gathered Indebted. The sisters weren't wrong about the cramming part.

Laurel squeezed between two of her comrades and I stumbled in her direction, falling into her arms.

"*Laurel.*" My voice was muffled by her shoulder.

Her back was ramrod straight, but she returned my embrace. "Miss Tetley. I'm very happy to see you upright."

The lump in my throat choked my voice beyond recognition. "You were worried about *me*? What about you guys? I'm so sorry you were dragged into that. Going out to Black was foolish. Five people lost their lives. I'm just so, *so* sorry."

My eyes misted, and I paused to steady my shallow breaths until the urge to cry passed.

The Indebted woman squeezed my shoulder. "That's not how we view what happened."

How could they not?

Hiccupping, I surveyed the other women in the office. Five of their friends were dead. A sadness hung over them like a blanket, yet I couldn't detect any anger on their faces. Not toward me at least.

"You should have been safe in our hands, and for that, we sincerely apologise," Laurel said quietly, bowing her head.

Their fault?

I blinked. "That's not what I think at all. I'm just grateful you were there."

Really grateful.

"Will there be a funeral?" I asked quietly.

Laurel's eyes shot to Kyros's sister over my shoulder. "There will."

I took her hand. "If it's appropriate for me to attend, please let me know the details when you have them."

"I'll be certain to, Miss Tetley."

"Excuse me," Lalitta piped up. "Do you mind if I come too? I would like to pay my respects."

The ranks of Indebted shuffled and fidgeted.

I glanced back, watching as the princess's cheeks stained pink.

Laurel fixed the vampires crammed into the room with a blank look that stilled them before smoothing her features. She bowed in Lalitta's direction. "Of course, Princess Lalitta. I'll pass the details on as soon as I have them."

It didn't take a genius to sense they didn't want the royal there. Personally, I thought Kyros's sister was the only sane one of her siblings.

I jerked as shouts erupted from outside the office.

"Formation," Laurel called, arching a brow my way.

"Looks like my brother felt you move," Lalitta said, clearing her throat.

I gasped as he roared, the door between us barely muffling the sound.

"Let's get you back upstairs," Lalitta said kindly, her eyes shifting to the door. "Quickly."

At least there was only one day left.

Laurel squeezed my shoulder again. "For what it's worth, Miss Tetley, we really are happy you're okay."

"Thank you." I tried to smile, but my lips barely twitched. "Thank you *all* for saving my life. I wouldn't be here without you, and that's a debt I can never repay."

The Indebted went deadly still.

Crap, I'd put my foot in it somehow.

My knees shook as exhaustion crashed down on my head. I could only see a few of my crew from my pinecone frenzy, but I dipped my head to them, hoping to convey that my words weren't meant as an insult.

Laurel bowed to me. Low.

Those Indebted not next to the door did the same.

I stared back at them, at a loss for words. What the hell was happening? Should I bow back?

"Alright, sweet human," Lalitta said, scooping me into her arms. "Time to tuck you in before Kyros destroys his tower. He gets out of sorts when that happens."

I clasped my hands around her neck, still occupied with the stooped positions of the Indebted.

"We wouldn't want that," I said softly, listening to his thunderous growling.

34

I'd asked Angelica to bring my clothes to the lair so I didn't have to wear Kyros's stuff. Borrowing his things when I didn't have to felt too much like unwanted couple territory.

Angelica had decided my request meant that she should bring up *all* my clothing and possessions.

"She never fucking stops," I told my white jumpsuit. It was the loosest option on both racks. My stomach was still tender. Honestly, after reviewing my options, the temptation to shrug on another of Kyros's shirts nearly overwhelmed my desire to establish distance between us.

Ugh.

I grabbed my toiletries and dragged my weary ass to his shower, my battered body feeling every injury *and* the loss of a crucial pint of blood or three. At least the third thrall would be over in a matter of hours. Safina said that with my body so injured, she'd be surprised if I displayed any thrall symptoms of my own. But I'd be able to return to my normal room when it was done.

Did I really want the thrall to be over though? Kyros would feel where I was for the rest of my life. The exact ins and outs of how the homing beacon worked were a mystery to me for now. But I'd get to the bottom of that when Kyros was lucid once more, and I could fucking murder him for being a piece-of-shit liar.

We'd shared blood.

We'd kissed and touched while under the thrall.

Yet he'd lied to my face. Not just once, but several times. Even when I'd demanded the truth using one of my questions from our dinner.

The consensus? His word meant nothing.

I felt betrayed. Really betrayed.

Which was crazy because I'd kept my distance.

... Didn't I?

Why did it hurt so much that he'd shafted me *this* time?

Shower done, I tossed my moisturiser onto the counter and stared into the mirror.

My face was thin. *Drawn. Gaunt.*

To be expected, I supposed. Even with the recent attack aside, being trapped in this tower was draining my life force.

But if I left, he now had the ammo to hunt me down.

I just couldn't contemplate the ramifications of that yet.

Ringing blared from the bedroom.

Snatching up the white jumpsuit, I wobbled back into the main room to find Beast.

I swiped him off the charger cable and gingerly perched on the bed.

"Hello?"

"Miss Tetley."

I eased down onto my back. "Angelica."

The Vissimo cleared her throat. "This comes at a bad time, but I just received your friend at the reception desk downstairs."

Friend?

"Tommy," Angelica supplied in the heavy silence.

I forced my lips to move. "Why? What's she doing here?"

"She wouldn't divulge that, I'm afraid. She's insistent about seeing you. *Very* insistent."

Nerves twisted my gut. I hardly dared to hope she'd forgiven me.

Regardless, could I handle seeing her familiar face? Three days ago, I nearly died. I just wasn't sure I could keep things together around her.

Dammit.

"I can't see her looking like this," I said.

The bandages on my torso might go unnoticed. *Not* the bruises on my face. I'd told Tommy not to call the police, but if I saw *her* in this state, I wouldn't hesitate to call—even at the risk of her hating me forever.

"She won't leave without seeing you. Meet me in Kyros's office, Miss Tetley. I'll bring the make-up bag."

The phone clicked as Angelica disconnected.

Glancing down, I eyed the bruises on my arms. Sighing, I stepped into the jumpsuit, and strode to the rack. selecting a long royal-blue cardigan that would cover my arms and all the way to my knees at the back.

I slipped into some loafers and yanked my wet hair into a tight ponytail.

A quick look in the bathroom mirror told me I'd utterly failed at putting myself together.

Tommy was going to freak out.

Angelica better be able to work pure magic with that make-up.

She was waiting downstairs.

Indebted still filled the room, and I nodded at Laurel, whose eyes shifted to the make-up bag.

"Tommy's here," I told her, crossing to sit in Kyros's office chair. "She'll kick off if she thinks I'm being beaten up by Kyros." On that note. "Is he okay with me going down to see her? He's not going to barge in, right?"

It was 7:00 p.m. Five hours of the third thrall remained.

"No, he's faring much better today."

I held still as Angelica's hands blurred over my face. She turned my head this way and that, and within what had to be a paltry two minutes, she leaned away, inspecting her work.

"There," she declared. "I could only do so much to mask the thinness of your face, but your complexion isn't as pale now."

Better than nothing. "I'm taking Laurel and a few other Vissimo down in case Kyros decides to make a guest appearance."

Angelica cut me a glance. "Indebted?"

I refused to use that word aloud any longer. "*Vissimo*, yes."

"Whatever you deem necessary, Miss Tetley." Angelica dipped her head again.

The head dipping thing... That better not be a *you've swapped juices with our crown prince three times* hunk of bullshitery.

Squaring my shoulders, I walked to the door, glancing at a few of the Indebted. They fell into line behind me and Laurel.

"Could you take the stairs down and just hold tight behind the door on Level 44 so Tommy doesn't know you're there?" I asked her. "I'll ride the elevator."

"Roger that," she said.

My stomach churned on the ride to the *Live Right* offices. My mind scrambled to scrape together a plan. Tommy was either here to make another ultimatum or here to apologise. My friend wasn't short on self-respect, so I'd assume the former.

My reason for forcing her away hadn't changed, however, even if I was barely keeping my head above water without her. A chunk of me was missing, but more than ever, I had to keep her out of this world. The Fyrlia royals would seek their revenge soon, and Tommy couldn't get caught in the crossfire.

Ding!

The doors slid open and I braced myself, lifting my head to scan reception.

"Tom," I greeted, holding onto my calm by the skin of my teeth.

She looked exhausted—much like I felt. Her oval face was leeched of colour, her hair hung limp around her face. Usually a picture of vintage style, she'd donned patchy leggings and a threadbare top to visit.

"Basil," she replied without smiling.

The nickname didn't feel right anymore—a requiem of past times when everything was okay.

"You've lost weight," she added, not leaving her position in front of the reception desk.

If weight loss was all Tommy saw when giving me a once over, I considered that a win.

Then I frowned. "So have you."

Exhaustion was a mild term for her state. My friend looked... devastated.

"What's happening?" I asked, searching her expression. "Is your father alright? Are you alright?"

I had zero right to ask her personal questions, but Basi the hypocrite could still sleep at night—Basi the worrier couldn't.

She crossed to where I lurked by the lift and took my hands in hers.

My heart leaped at the simple human touch. Had she decided to forgive me? If she'd swallowed that big of a humble pill, maybe I could salvage some of our relationship.

I took a breath. "Tom, I'm—"

"Your grandmother passed away last night," she said quietly.

My face slackened. My insides, my *soul*. Everything I *was* dropped onto the floor.

Blood pounded in my ears.

"W-What did you just say?"

"Your grandmother has moved on, Basil. She passed last night from a heart attack."

I stared at Tommy, inhales shallow and fast. "No, she's not."

I covered my ears, spinning away only to stare at the grey of the elevator doors. I whirled in a circle like a cornered animal.

Trapped.

Tommy spoke low and fast. "She rang for Fred, but the ambulance came too late to resuscitate her. He said she went quickly. He's been trying to get in touch with you, but—"

"No, she's not!" I screamed at her, my throat ripping.

My friend backed up, watching me warily.

I paced, clutching my face. I paced as though that would unwind the last two minutes of my life.

When it didn't, I sank into a crouch, cradling my stomach as I pressed my face to my knees.

Oh my god. This wasn't real.

Tommy rested a hand on my back. "She's gone, lovely. I'm so fucking sorry. I know she was all you had."

All I had? The words rang in my ears.

All I had.

My grandmother was all I had, and now she was gone.

Dead.

Cold.

Empty.

Tommy stroked my hair but stopped as I lifted my head.

"Was she in pain?" I asked hoarsely.

"No, lovely. Not in pain. Your grandmother told Fred that she loved you with everything she had. Agatha said that watching you grow into the strong young woman you are today was her life's honour."

A strong young woman? If only she could see me now.

"I wasn't with her." Part of my heart crumbled away with the confession.

Tommy didn't have a reassurance for *that*.

My chest tightened anew. Hand pressing against my chest as though that could keep the splitting agony inside, I said hollowly, "I need to call Fred."

There must be things to do. What was I meant to do?

"He's expecting your call. He needs to go over funeral details with you."

I flinched.

Funeral details.

In the ground.

Not my warm grandmother who could silence a room will a tongue-lashing remark or a quelling arch of the brow. That person didn't belong in the ground covered with dirt.

I stared at my hands. "I spoke to her one month ago."

I'd seen her car *four days* ago. Heard her words via Fred. Seen her hand as she flipped vampires off.

Tommy drew a letter from her cloth bag. "I wanted to come here and break the news myself."

I hugged my rail-thin body. "Thank you. I appreciate it. I've wanted to reach out to you..."

She picked up where I left off. "...To tell me how you got the bruise on your cheek? To tell me why you appear to have dropped five kilos you didn't have to lose?"

"No, not that," I replied, closing my eyes. "To tell you I'll always love you no matter what."

"I called the police, you know—after last time. I was transferred from department to department for an hour. They hung up. I tried twice more with the same result. The call went as expected right up until I mentioned *Kyros Sky*. The third time, I went in face-to-face. I wrote a statement. They read it and asked me to leave."

Fuck. She'd called the police? Thank fuck nothing came of it. I had no idea if the police had alerted Kyros, but I assumed so.

And Tommy hadn't been compelled.

Not yet anyway.

"After that, I went to your grandmother," she said quietly.

I sucked in a breath.

She squared her shoulders. "She told me that if I wasn't willing to grow with you, I best stay out of your way."

Um, what? My grandmother loved Tommy. That made zero sense. "I'm sure she didn't mean it that way..."

Lifting a shoulder, Tommy held out the envelope. "Perhaps. I'll see you at the funeral to support you there. If you need to talk about your grandmother, I'm just a call away. That's because of the past we shared. But if you can't tell me the truth about what's going on, I'll take that as confirmation we *are* growing in different directions. And I'll stay out of your way. I can't do a half friendship; not with you, Basil. You mean too much to me."

I accepted her words without feeling a thing, my heart unable to sink further into the ground today.

"What's this?" I said thickly, taking the letter from her.

"From Fred."

I hesitated. *From Fred?* That could be a lot of things. "What if it's a letter from my grandmother?"

What if these were her last words? What if they were condemning or disappointed?

Tommy held out her hand, and I passed the letter over without second thought.

She broke the seal and drew out a thick letter.

After scanning the contents, Tommy held the letter out for my inspection. "It's safe to read."

My eyes blurred over the first line, but comprehension took longer. When it caught up, my mouth dried to bone.

No.

"Congratulations are in order," said Tommy quietly.

I didn't want her congratulations. I didn't want this at all.

Last Will and Testament
Of
Mrs Agatha Le Spyre

Grandmother left everything to me. *Everything.*

... I'd just become one of the richest women in the world.

VAMPIRE DEBT

Basil's story continues in Vampire Debt!

WHILE YOU WAIT

COMPLETE SERIES

~ Dragon Shifter Romance ~

Start Book One Today

BOOKS BY KELLY ST. CLARE

<u>**Supernatural Battle**</u>

Vampire Towers (Paranormal urban romance)

Blood Trial

Vampire Debt

Death Game

The Darkest Drae (Dragon shifter romance)

with Raye Wagner

Blood Oath

Shadow Wings

Black Crown

The Tainted Accords (Royal fantasy romance):

Fantasy of Frost

Fantasy of Flight

Fantasy of Fire

Fantasy of Freedom

Novellas:

Sin

Olandon

Rhone

Shard

Pirates of Felicity (Pirate fantasy romance):

Immortal Plunder

Stolen Princess

Pillars of Six

Dynami's Wrath

Veritas

Eternal Gambit

Mortal Trinity

The After Trilogy (Dystopian romance):

The Retreat

The Return

The Reprisal

www.ingramcontent.com/pod-product-compliance
Lightning Source LLC
Chambersburg PA
CBHW020932310726
48980CB00007B/731/J

* 9 7 8 0 6 4 8 3 3 4 4 7 7 *